RISE OF THE FURIES

SHIFTERS OF CAERTON : BOOK 4

BY

H.B. LYNE

Published by Weaver of Words Press
UK

Originally Published in 2017
as Echoes of the Past: Reaping of Summer
Published as part of the Shifters of Caerton Series 2019

This edition published in 2020

2

Book Cover design by Olivia Pro Design
Interior Formatting by Evenstar Books Ltd.

ISBN 978-1-913673-06-2
(paperback)
ISBN 978-1-913673-07-9
(ebook)

hblyne.com

Are we a Perfect Match?

Rise of the Furies is dark urban fantasy. In these pages you won't find sparkly vampires or teenage heroines with perfect hair.

I write dark, gritty, emotionally compelling stories filled with flawed protagonists, anti-heroes and deliciously dark villains.

There will be plot twists that bring out your most colourful language and yes, I write in British English.

If any of these things bother you, turn back now.

If however, darkness is your poison, then read on and lose yourself in the shadows for a while.

ACKNOWLEDGEMENTS

I want to thank my editor, Zoe Markham, who has been a joy to work with. She always keeps me in line, without compromising my style.

Huge thanks to Julia Scott for making the books in this series stand out and look stunning inside as well as out.

The folks in the writing community who have inspired me, motivated me and generally kept me on track when life got very hard; thank you all so much.

Thanks, of course, to my loyal patrons who have stuck by me through thick and thin; Andy, Linzy, Richard, Monika and Emé.

An extra special thank you to my incredibly supportive family, who have been behind me every step of the way in writing this book, and the series. There have been tremendous sacrifices made and I want to express my sincere gratitude to them for that.

And finally, my readers. It's all for you x

*"Crowns are for the valiant - sceptres for the bold!
Thrones and powers for mighty men who dare to
take and hold!"*

—Cold Iron by Rudyard Kipling

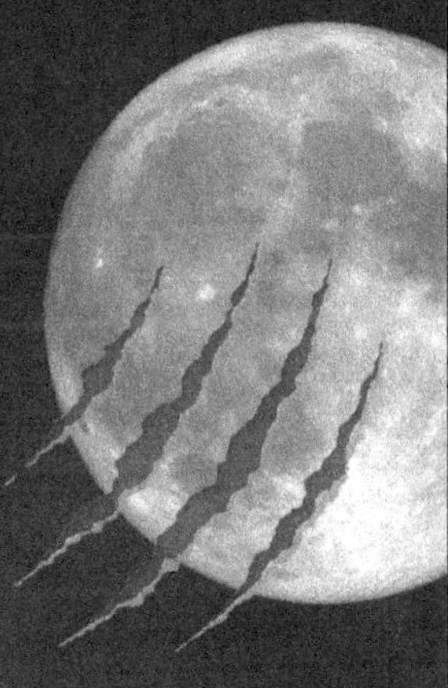

PROLOGUE

CLAWS-OF-LEAD

——· Early February ·——

'I NEED YOU TO DO A JOB FOR ME.'

'Okay. What is it?'

Claws tapped the end of his pen on his notepad, leaning casually back in his chair.

'A family heirloom has been stolen.'

'I see. And have you contacted the police?'

'Well, it's a matter of some delicacy.' The client sat with his legs neatly crossed. His pinstripe suit was crisp and pristine. His hands were folded gently in his lap, though Claws noticed the hint of anxiety in the way he idly spun his thick, gold ring.

'Is that so?'

'I'm afraid it is. There is the potential for city officials to decide that the artefact ought to belong to the city, rather than myself.' He ran a hand through his greying hair and down over his clean-shaven jaw. Claws cleared his throat and scratched the rough bristles of his own jaw. Most of his clients were not as well turned out as this one, and although he usually wasn't particularly concerned with appearances, he knew that it sometimes mattered to people like this when it came to choosing who to hire.

'I can handle it delicately, don't worry. I may need to avail myself of police contacts, however. But rest assured, I will protect your identity. Confidentiality is my top priority when investigating cases for my clients.'

'Thank you. My family will be most relieved if the mask can be retrieved.'

Claws nodded and gave him a reassuring smile.

'Tell me about it,' he said softly, leaning forward and holding his pen poised.

——·   Mid-February   ·——

'I can't tell you, mate. You know that.'

'There's always a choice, Harry. I'm sure we can find a solution that keeps my client happy and you safe.'

'It's the fucking Carlson family. There is no escaping them if they turn against you.' Harry shifted his feet and his rat-like eyes darted one way then the other on the dark and deserted street. 'I swear they're following me as it is. It took me an hour to shake my tail tonight to meet you.'

'Look, I'm sure we can get you into protective custody or something. Hell, I can get you a new identity and get you out of Caerton if it comes to it.'

'You don't get it,' Harry hissed, his eyes narrowed to

slits. 'If they want to, they will find me anywhere.'

'I do get it, honestly. Look, I know they arranged the theft. I just need the name of their fence. That's all you'd be giving me.'

Harry shifted his weight and glanced up and down the street. He chewed his bottom lip, which was already blistered and sore. Claws reached out and placed a reassuring hand on his shoulder.

'I can't. I'm sorry.' Harry shrugged away from Claws' grasp and ran away into the shadow of the railway bridge. A train rattled overhead, the lights from the windows flashing eerily on the darkened road below. The street light beside Claws flickered back to life. He sighed and turned to go.

The following day, Claws went to check his email and the news headlines to be greeted with a grainy picture of Harry's grim face.

"BODY FOUND IN RIVER".

Poor old Harry, Claws thought to himself, before slamming his fist down on top of the case file and sending the papers scattering across his desk and onto the floor.

'I'm sorry, I really am,' he said stiffly into his phone. 'But I've run into a dead end. Your mask is gone. There's nothing more I can do.'

'I see,' came the crisp, curt response from Claws' client.

'Orwell Carlson has the criminal underworld firmly in his grasp. No one will talk. The only lead I had was found drowned in the river the morning after he spoke to me. And he had refused to give me any information. The power this family has, well, it's frightening to be frank.'

'Of course. Well, thank you for trying.'

'You're welcome.' Claws hung up the phone and tossed it onto his desk. He stared at the wall and thought of the lost income from having to close the case without resolving it.

You know, a tiny voice inside murmured, *it might be interesting to find out which demon the Carlsons are in league with.*

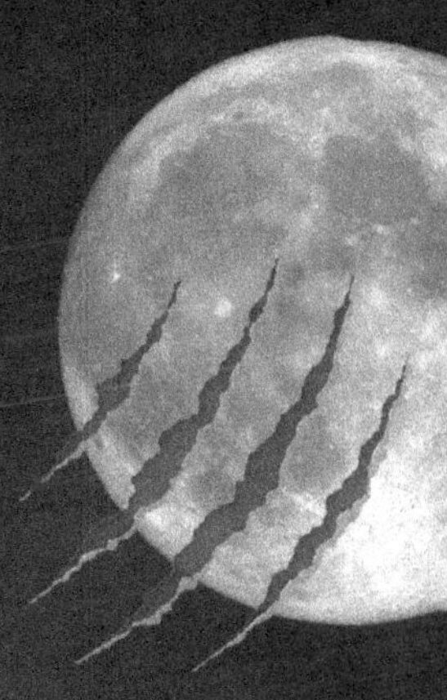

Chapter One

Stalker-of-Night's-Shadow

—.   3rd June   .—

She sprinted full pelt, not concerned with concealing herself. She vaulted a high, wooden fence and dropped onto the gravel with a light crunch. With barely a pause she was off again in hot pursuit. She leapt onto a wall and ran along it to pass some slow-moving pedestrians. When she reached the end she jumped across the gap to a huge stone ball that blocked the footpath into the park, bounced off it and into a forward roll on the wet grass and up onto her feet again without losing speed.

He was only a hundred feet ahead of her now; she could see his coat flapping behind him as he ran.

The cemetery! She kept up the chase, her feet pounding hard on the pavement. People stopped and stared as she whipped past them. She didn't care.

We see him, Weaver thought, her mental voice as

steady and calm as her typical spoken voice.

Stalker bounded over a metal fence and sprinted out into the road, dodging cars as they swerved to avoid her. Her hand landed on a car bonnet and she propelled herself across it on her backside and continued on her way. She had cut a huge corner that her prey had skirted around, unwilling to risk his life in the rush hour traffic. She was almost upon him now. He dashed through the tall, wrought iron gates and into the cemetery. Stalker was right behind him.

Her heart thumped wildly in her chest as she gained on him. She knew his scent now and confusion flooded her conscious mind. He kept to the path, following it as it curved left and down the slope towards the first row of grave stones. Stalker took a flying leap onto the fence that lined the footpath and dove through the air straight towards him. She collided with his shoulder, wrapping her arms around his chest and pinning his arms to his side as she barrelled him to the ground.

She raised a fist and punched him hard across the face.

Footsteps pounded on the path behind her and she felt the presence of her pack mates.

'Herald!' Stalker snarled. 'What the fuck do you think you're doing?' She released him and stood over him as he raised a trembling hand to his bleeding nose.

The rest of the Lightning Lords gathered around her. Fights-Eyes-Open strode forward and held out a hand to the intruder, helping him to his feet.

'Does Rust know about this?' Eyes said curtly. He adjusted his tie and brushed down his suit jacket.

'No,' Herald replied, still nursing his face. He refused

to meet Stalker's accusing eyes.

'Why on earth are you running through our territory uninvited?' the Alpha asked, a little more softly.

'It was an emergency. I couldn't wait around for permission. I'm sorry.'

Weaver went rigid beside Stalker. All eyes turned to her. Her pale skin almost glowed in the eerie cemetery light; her long, blond hair lay still down her back, no hint of a breeze.

'What is that?' Weaver whispered. Her eyes were glazed over as she stared into the darkening sky. Stalker felt it then, now that her hammering heart had begun to quieten. The veil between worlds was blowing in the metaphysical breeze. The cemetery was suddenly plunged into darkness. It wasn't the most well-lit part of St. Mark's anyway, but the few lamps that lit the path near the entrance had blinked out.

'It's not me,' Claws said defensively, before anyone could ask.

Herald looked over both shoulders quickly, his face twitching. He took off, running deeper into the graveyard.

'Hey!' Stalker yelled and set off after him. 'Don't make me hit you again!' The others were close behind her. Something felt very wrong. The air was totally still, yet the veil billowed as if caught in a gale. She felt dozens of eyes on her as she ran past dark headstones.

Herald stopped abruptly and wrenched a pouch from his coat pocket. He tugged out a crystal and held it over his head. Stalker skidded to a halt beside him and glared at him. The others came up behind them and gathered around.

'What is going on?' Eyes snapped.

'The dead,' Weaver said softly. 'The dead are here. Lots of them.'

'She's right,' Wind Talker said. He started fishing around in his bag, pulled out a large piece of crystal quartz and stood opposite Herald, raising it over his head. Wind Talker was broad and stocky, his sandy-coloured hair short and thick. He stood in contrast to skinny and scrawny Herald, yet they mirrored each other's actions perfectly.

Stalker watched them, her eyes narrowed and a sceptical scowl on her brow. Yet she could feel it all too clearly now. She caught glimpses of dead faces watching them, shadows moving among the gravestones. A shiver ran up her spine.

'Let the dead be banished. The Underworld is your home!' Herald called out. His voice echoed around them, bouncing back off a hundred gravestones.

'Be gone!' Wind Talker added firmly. 'This is not your world.'

Weaver closed her eyes and let out a low hum. Instinctively, Stalker joined in. Claws glanced warily at her before adding his voice. Eyes was the last to join the eerie chorus. Stalker felt the veil settle and the dead retreat. Wind Talker reached into his bag and scattered some herbs into the air. A breeze whipped up and scattered them across the little circle of shifters. Stalker smelled the familiar whiff of sage. The two ritualists stood facing each other, slowly mending the tear in the veil. Stalker felt it drawing closed slowly but surely.

'I don't understand what happened,' she said quietly when the job was done.

'It's happening all over the city,' Herald said, putting his crystal away. 'There was an incident in Old Town earlier and I had just finished doing this at the cemetery in Fenwick when I felt a tear splitting open here. There was no warning. I just had to get here as quickly as possible. I couldn't stop to call ahead or explain to you what was happening. You might not have known the ritual. I just had to act. I'm sorry for the border breach.'

He avoided meeting anyone's eyes and seemed genuinely humble.

'Alright,' Eyes said. 'Thank you. Your quick action could well have saved us from a serious incident.'

'What happened in Old Town?' Stalker asked. Ragged Edge immediately sprang into her thoughts.

'The same as here. The veil ripped open at the castle cemetery. One of my fae allies informed me.' Herald looked at Stalker, unblinking.

'Go,' Eyes said softly. 'Call him.'

Stalker turned away from the group and dialled Ragged Edge. She didn't expect him to answer. He was significantly slower on his feet than her and her young pack mates. He may have still been handling the situation. His phone rang for what felt like an age, but didn't connect to voicemail. Stalker tapped the back of her phone with her finger as she clutched it to her ear.

'Yes? What?' Ragged Edge snapped before she even realised that he had answered.

'The dead at the cemetery,' she panted. 'Is everything okay over there?'

'All in hand. I take it you've experienced the same phenomenon?'

'Yes. Here and in Fenwick.'

Ragged Edge grunted.

'I'll make a few calls, see who else has. Are you alright?' he added in a softer tone. Stalker smiled.

'Yeah, I'm fine. Thank you. Are you?'

'Of course I am,' he snapped and hung up the phone. Stalker laughed and returned to the group.

'What on earth is going on?' Weaver asked, leaning wearily against a large stone statue of an angel.

'I don't know,' Herald said, a look of grim determination on his face. 'But I will find out.'

The Lightning Lords escorted Herald back to the border at Redfield Park and watched him disappear into the darkness.

'We need help,' Weaver said softly.

'Sorry?' Eyes asked, raising an eyebrow.

'When Theodore, Rust and you carved up Fenwick between our packs you did what you could with it in a way that was fair to everyone involved with taking down the Witches. But it's resulted in us having a territory too big to defend. We're lucky that it was a friend who got in here tonight. What would have happened if it had been the Furies?'

Stalker sensed the tension and saw Eyes glaring at Weaver.

'It actually worked really well,' Claws said. 'The alarm system worked. We all got that message on our phones that there was a border breach and Stalker was on Herald's tail so fast. That chase was really impressive by the way.'

'Thanks,' she said with a grin.

'He's right,' Wind Talker chimed in. 'But Weaver has

a fair point. The territory is huge now. It was too big for us before, with all of St. Mark's, Redfield, Crossway and Northgate. Now that we have that piece of Fenwick too it's way too much for a pack of five. A pack of eight would struggle with it. I mean, The Hand of God are a pack of seven and they just have Fenstoke.' He stopped suddenly, his face went ashen.

'Six,' Stalker said with a croak. 'They're a pack of six now.'

'Yes, sorry.' The devastation was written across his broad face. It had been two weeks since the battle with the Green Man and Last-Breath-Echoes' death. At times it didn't feel real and even Stalker had moments of forgetting that her friend was gone. Each one punctuated her grief and made fresh the scar.

'What can we do?' Claws asked. His soft voice breaking the awkward silence. 'I mean, we can't just magic up new pack mates. This is us. Do we give away territory?'

Eyes and Wind Talker glared at him as if he had suggested they join the Spiral Hand. Stalker suppressed a snigger behind her hand.

'There's not really anyone to give it to anyway,' Weaver said. 'The Wrecking Crew could theoretically take on more of Redfield and the Glass Wolves could take Crossway, but they've both just been burdened with bits of Fenwick as well.'

'We are not giving away any territory!' Eyes snapped, a snarl in his voice. He set off walking away from the park and everyone fell into step behind him. 'We'll figure something out.'

Stalker's phone began to ring, piercing the dark night.

She hastily pulled it from her pocket and saw Scribe's name on the screen.

'Hello?'

'Are you having the same problems as us tonight?'

'Yeah. God, it really is the whole city, isn't it? Did you speak to Ragged Edge?'

'No, but something got driven out of Old Town and into South Stoke. At a guess that was his doing. Not his fault, obviously, I didn't mean it like that.' He spoke quickly and Stalker could hear in his breathing that he was running.

'Got driven out?' Stalker asked, coming to a halt. The others looked at her and stopped as well. 'You mean on this side? Not back into you know where?'

'That's right. It's still in the city. When I finished up at the cemetery here I felt it move on but not away, if that makes sense.'

'Yes I know what you mean. But that doesn't make sense. What time was that?'

'I don't know. About ten minutes ago I guess.'

Stalker looked around at the puzzled faces of her pack.

'That was a little after we finished up here. Where did it go? Are you tracking it?'

'What's going on?' Weaver asked.

'I am. Didn't you sense where it went from where you are?' Scribe asked, an edge of accusation to his voice.

'Across the veil,' Stalker snapped back. 'It went back across. Right?' She looked at Weaver and Wind Talker for confirmation.

'It seemed that way,' Weaver said, nodding. 'What is going on?' She asked again.

'I don't know,' Stalker whispered.

'We shouldn't be talking about this over the phone!' Scribe shouted. 'Where are you lot now?'

'Redfield,' Stalker replied.

'You have to meet me in the city centre. I'll call Ragged Edge as well. Get here as soon as you can. Not Crescent Park, the cemetery at the back of that old church near Burnside.'

'Okay. Shall we get Theodore?'

'That might be a good idea.' Scribe hung up and Stalker looked at her anxious pack.

'What the fuck is going on?' Weaver snapped.

'It's not just the dead,' Wind Talker replied, his voice low and ominous. 'The dead slipped back across the veil into the Underworld, that was what we felt. But something let them into this world in the first place. And it's still here.'

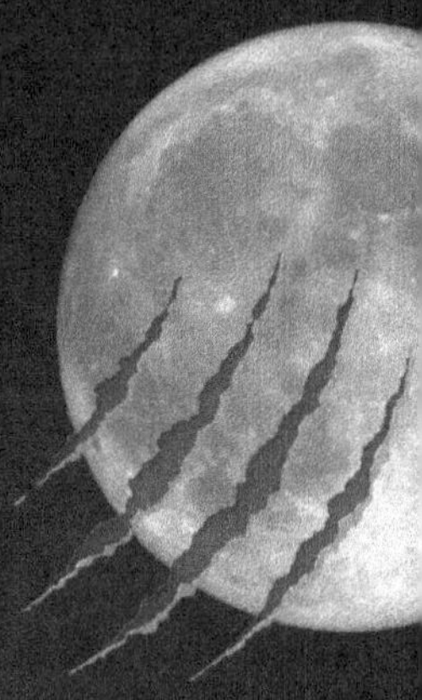

Chapter Two

The Lightning Lords pulled up in Eyes' car outside the church. It was a gloomy structure, long since abandoned. The rough stone was blackened from decades of heavy traffic polluting the street. The shifters climbed out of the car and ran quickly to the narrow alley between the church and a high breeze block wall that marked the boundary of the business property next door. At the back of the church was a surprising urban treasure: an old graveyard with a handful of dark and faded gravestones, overgrown with moss. Trees lined the little square and their branches hung low, obscuring the light-polluted sky. A tall, wrought iron fence surrounded the place, and ivy curled its way up each strut. The noise of the busy road was dulled by the church and the tall offices on either side.

In the centre of the graveyard stood Scribe, Ragged Edge and Theodore Harris, talking animatedly. They were just about the oddest grouping one might imagine. Scribe was in his full goth gear: long leather coat, huge boots, long black hair tied back and black eye liner around his tired eyes. Ragged Edge looked about eighty; he bore all the markings of a previously well-built man gone to seed, with a large belly and leaning heavily on a wooden staff. He wore a thick, brown coat that almost reached the floor and had long grey hair and beard. His leathery skin was tanned and lined and scars showed on various bits of visible skin. Theodore Harris, like Eyes, was dressed in a sharp suit, but he was significantly larger than anyone else there. He stood well over six feet tall and was built like a gorilla. Neat, square-rimmed spectacles perched on his broad nose.

Eyes led the pack over to them and Stalker felt a shudder run up her spine as they approached. The gap in the veil was allowing a draft of dark energy through. Movement at the back of the graveyard caught her eye and she saw a wisp of silvery hair disappearing from sight.

'We have to mend it now,' Theodore insisted.

'They aren't crossing though, look.' Scribe pointed towards the church and Stalker looked over her shoulder to see an elderly man, translucent and shimmering in the shadows. He stood watching them, a serene smile on his white lips.

'What are they doing?' Weaver asked, her voice soft and curious.

'We'll never know if we mend the veil now,' Scribe asserted. 'We need to communicate with them and find out what did this.' A murmur of assent went around the little group. Scribe took a few cautious steps towards the old man by the church, his palms out by his sides in a gesture of openness. The ghost tilted his head to one side and blinked slowly. His eyes shimmered in the low light.

The only other time Stalker had encountered the dead was on the beach, when her ancestor had crossed from the underworld to berate her. He had been translucent until the moment he crossed the veil fully and manifested in the world of the living. Then he became as solid and real as her, as her cheek could testify. She raised her hand to her cheek now, the memory of being struck fresh enough to rekindle the pain. Weaver caught her eye and gave her a soft smile. Stalker lowered her hand and shook away the memory.

The figure by the church took a few steps towards them. The deep lines on his face told a tale of a long and rich life. His clothing was vaguely Victorian: a high collar and smart waistcoat with a pocket watch on a chain strung across it. Stalker glanced around at the moulding gravestones, clearly each at least a century old. She wondered which one was his.

Theodore stood with his arms crossed, a frown etched onto his face. Scribe walked slowly towards the ghost, his eyes wide and mouth hanging slightly open in wonder. Stalker watched the scene unfold, an uncomfortable fluttering in her stomach from her proximity to such a bad tear in the veil.

'Hello,' Scribe said softly. 'Can you hear me?'

The ghost took another step forwards, out of the shadow of the church. He nodded slowly. His movements were slow and careful, almost slow motion. He smiled serenely. But Stalker could see a sharpness in his grey eyes that made the hairs on her arms stand up.

'Careful,' she whispered, hoping Scribe would hear her across the graveyard. Whether he did or not, he gave no sign. He continued moving slowly towards the ghost, his arms slightly raised. Stalker felt a creeping discomfort spreading up from the base of her spine, a tingle moving up her back and into her shoulders. She became aware of how tense she was. She glanced at Weaver, who looked just as uncomfortable.

Scribe had just lost one of his best friends, and he had been working close to death for years. Could he be behaving recklessly? Was he hoping to make contact with Last-Breath-Echoes? He was just a few feet from the ghost now. The ghost looked at him with his head tilted to one side, a curious smile on his thin lips.

The ghost's lips moved silently, his eyes narrowed slightly and his demeanour hardened.

'I can't hear you,' Scribe said, stepping closer and reaching out his hand.

'Don't,' Theodore warned, uncrossing his arms and lurching forward a few paces. Ragged Edge held out a hand to stop Theodore getting closer. They exchanged troubled glances. Stalker drank it all in, everything seemed to be happening in slow motion and her senses prickled with sensitivity. She focused on the ghost's gently moving lips.

Hungry, it seemed to say, silently. Its voice unable to cross the veil. It took one more slow step towards Scribe and a hand lifted weightlessly towards Scribe's outstretched fingers. *Hunger is coming.*

'Hunger is coming? *The* Hunger?' Stalker said slowly, her voice sounding a mile away. Fog curled at the edges of the graveyard, a closed-in feeling began to press in on her head. 'Did The Hunger do this?' She felt like her consciousness were just outside her body, taking in everything while she stood paralysed. Could anyone even hear her? Was she really speaking?

'Don't touch him,' Theodore snapped. Scribe stretched his fingers out, groping across the veil.

'No!' Stalker shouted. Her throat felt instantly sore, the shout tearing from her dulled body.

Too late. Scribe made contact with the ghost's fingers, there was a bright flare and he was flung backwards across the graveyard, slamming hard into a small headstone.

Theodore and Ragged Edge sprang into action, hurriedly lighting sage smudge sticks and chanting. Wind Talker was with them a moment later. Stalker still felt sluggish and hung there, not quite within herself. She watched the ritualists push back the ghosts and mend the veil. Weaver was at Scribe's side, making sure he was all right. Eyes and Claws stood by, watching with gaping mouths, as unable to help as Stalker.

The world slowly righted itself. The ghosts disappeared, the veil gradually knitted back together, and Stalker returned to her senses. She dashed over to where Scribe sat hunched over, Weaver rubbing his back.

'Are you okay?' Stalker asked, crouching down in front of him. He nodded meekly.

Theodore and Ragged Edge stomped over to them. Theodore's face was full of thunder, Ragged Edge just looked tired. Shadows dragged under his eyes and he rubbed a lined hand over his sagging cheeks.

'That was reckless and stupid,' Theodore spat. Scribe flinched and Stalker shot Theodore a warning glare over her shoulder.

'Hey,' she snapped. 'It's done now. The veil is mended. Drop it.'

Theodore glowered down at her and she felt a wave of regret and humility. He was one of the most powerful shifters in the city, politically and supernaturally, and she had dared to talk back to him. She swallowed a hard lump that formed in her throat, and looked away from his cold eyes.

'Come on,' Eyes said, breaking the uneasy silence. He held out a hand to Scribe and helped him from the floor. 'I'll give you a lift home.' Scribe winced as he straightened up, and a hand darted to his back.

'I'm fine,' he said hurriedly, before Stalker or Weaver could ask.

'I'll come with you,' Weaver said, placing a gentle hand on his shoulder.

'Guys, get home, check the territory, all of it.' Eyes gave meaningful looks to Stalker, Wind Talker and Claws. Then set off with Scribe and Weaver.

The remaining shifters exchanged troubled glances.

'Did anyone else get what the ghost was saying? Or hear me?' Stalker asked, looking around at the others.

They returned her gaze with mixed expressions of confusion and assent. Claws nodded and rubbed the back of his neck.

'The Hunger. Again.'

Wind Talker looked at the ground. Stalker stared resolutely at Ragged Edge, and away from her pack mate, whom she had tried to sacrifice to The Hunger.

'I didn't,' Ragged Edge said gruffly, clearing his throat.

'I didn't hear you say anything, Stalker. It was an intense moment. What's The Hunger?'

'A demon, we think,' Wind Talker said, a crack in his voice. 'We've been hearing things over the last couple of months. Something is rising and influencing things here.'

'The Alpha of the Witches was in league with it,' Theodore said. 'That's about all I know of it.'

'At the Danegeld we heard about cannibals in the city. Could that be related?' Stalker asked, looking expectantly at the elders.

'Possibly,' Theodore replied. 'If it was what raised the dead tonight, then it's not just your problem.' He looked pointedly at the remaining Lightning Lords. 'It's city wide, and we all need to be vigilant.'

'Is it gone?' Stalker asked, looking anxiously around the graveyard.

'No,' Theodore said. 'We kept the dead from crossing, and mended the veil, but I don't believe that whatever raised them was banished with them. I don't think it was here.'

Stalker felt a shudder go through her.

'I'm heading back home,' Ragged Edge said firmly. 'I'll check in with you tomorrow, Stalker.' He gave her shoulder a firm pat. 'Good night, everyone.' He stomped away, using his staff as a walking stick.

'Likewise. I suggest you don't loiter here,' Theodore said, a sharp warning in his voice.

'Loiter?' Claws mouthed silently as Theodore marched away. 'Does he think we're unruly teens or something?' he whispered. Stalker chuckled.

'Pretty much,' Wind Talker said softly, a small smile

on his lips.

The three of them set off, walking quietly down the narrow passage alongside the darkened church, and out onto the city street. Life went on, blissfully ignorant of what had just transpired in the dark and secluded churchyard. Traffic chugged past, pumping out fumes and noise. The street was brightly lit and seemed like a different world to the graveyard. Stalker let out a shaking breath.

'I'll take Crossway and Fenwick,' Wind Talker said firmly. 'Claws, you fly up to Northgate. Stalker, you take St. Mark's. Okay?'

She nodded, her mind far away. There was something she needed to do first. Claws disappeared back down the alley to shift form. Stalker looked up in time to see him soar away into the night sky, his owl wings beating. She smiled; he was finally overcoming his aversion to his ability to shift. Wind Talker cleared his throat and her attention snapped back to him. 'You flying or getting the bus with me?'

'I'll hit the sky, I want to check a few things out on the way.'

'Sure. See you back at the house later, then.' He shoved his hands into his pockets and set off towards the bus stop at the end of the street. Stalker watched until he was out of sight, then pulled out her phone. It was getting late, but wasn't yet too unsociable an hour. She hit Rhys's name on her contacts list and clutched her phone to her ear. It rang a few times, an agonising few seconds, before he answered.

'You okay? Did something happen?'

'I'm fine. I think so anyway. There was a— something strange, it's complicated. Can you meet me at the cafe?'

'Of course. I'll be ten minutes.'

'Okay, thank you. I'll see you there.' She ended the call and set off at a brisk walk in the opposite direction to Wind Talker. She reached the bustling city centre and headed for a small cafe opposite one of the shopping centres. It was a twenty-four-hour place that served decent coffee. She pulled the door open and stepped into the brightly-lit cafe. It was deserted but for the bored-looking waitress behind the counter, who looked up as she entered and gave a lazy attempt at a smile. Stalker ordered two coffees and sat down at a table at the back. A glance in the mirror that ran along the wall from the door to the back of the seating area caused a shudder to run through her. Her hair was just about long enough to tie back now, but much of it had come loose in the chase across the city that evening. The faded blue dye from the Danegeld had left her hair slightly grey. It was an odd sight. Stalker hurriedly re-tied her hair.

She stared at the menu while she waited, and picked up a sachet of sugar from the dish in the middle of the table. She turned it over and over in her fingers, gazing at it without seeing it.

The door opened and her attention was wrenched away from the little paper packet. She knew it was Rhys before her head had finished turning for the door, she felt him there. She was on her feet a moment later and they met in the middle of the cafe. He scooped her into his arms and sniffed her hair. She clutched his back and pressed her face to his chest.

'Are you all right?' he asked, his voice soft and urgent. She nodded and dragged herself away from his embrace.

They moved back to the table and the waitress brought them their coffees. She put them down on the table with a wary glance at the two shifters. Rhys was built like a champion fighter. Which is exactly what he was. He taught taekwondo now, but had a string of titles to his honour. His appearance, especially with intricate tattoos all over his arms, back and neck, could be intimidating, even though his natural shifter presence was suppressed by the secrecy demon riding him like a cloak. 'What happened?'

'Something tried to bring the dead across the veil,' Stalker whispered and sipped her coffee.

'Oh right.'

'Like, all of them. All over the city. There were tears in the veil at cemeteries all over Caerton. I think we sealed them all, but it's going to be a long night, checking and double checking. I can't stay long. I just wanted to check that you were all right.'

'I'm absolutely fine. But I knew something was going on. I felt how afraid you were. It's so strange, being connected like this. I still haven't got used to it.'

'I know. It's strange for me too. It's different from the bond with my pack. More intense.'

Rhys sipped his coffee and ran his finger around the rim of the mug.

'You haven't told your pack about me.' It wasn't a question, he knew the answer. Stalker swallowed a mouthful of her drink and shook her head. She glanced at the waitress, who was cleaning the coffee machine with earphones in, oblivious to their conversation.

'No, I haven't.'

'I've been thinking about this. I think you might have

to. At some point.' She looked up at him in alarm. Her heart pounded hard in her chest and he smiled, knowing exactly how she was feeling. 'It's not easy for me to say this, I've worked really hard to hide from your people. But like you said, this thing between us is intense. It's not the sort of thing that can be hidden for long. They are going to notice through your bond with them. They probably already know something. They'll see how distracted you are too. If you don't tell them and they find out some other way then it could all be blown out of proportion. It's better to be in control of when and how they find out.'

Stalker breathed a deep sigh and nodded slowly. He was right.

There was a slight ripple in the veil and she sat up straight, her senses suddenly sharp. 'What is it?' Rhys asked, looking around the cafe. The waitress was humming along to the song in her earphones.

Stalker felt a presence there with them. She looked all around, but saw nothing. Then movement in the long mirror along the wall caught her eye. Something on the ceiling. She looked up and leaped from her chair. Clinging to the ceiling was a grotesque monster of exposed muscle and sinew. It dripped, a huge globule of blood landing on the table in front of Rhys. He was on his feet too, staring up at it.

A phlegmy gurgle issued from its gaping maw of a mouth, filled with pointed teeth.

'Protect her,' Stalker hissed, nodding her head towards the oblivious waitress. 'I'll deal with this.' Stalker reached over her shoulder and wrapped her fingers slowly around the grip of one of her invisible Burmese swords.

It shimmered into physical form at her touch. She slid it from her back and held it out to her side, her eyes fixed on the demon. Rhys backed towards the counter, Stalker felt him watching her carefully. Her thoughts raced, trying to work out a way through this with no one getting killed and the waitress retaining her sanity.

At the exact moment that she decided what to do, Rhys darted for the bank of switches on the wall just behind the counter, next to the swing door through to the kitchen. With a flick of his arm, the cafe was plunged into darkness, leaving just a faint orange glow from the street outside. The waitress screamed and the demon let out a horrifying roar.

Stalker leaped up onto the table and drove her sword up into the middle of the demon with a sickening squelch. There was a terrible shriek from it and it slid down her sword, its grip on the ceiling lost.

A scuffle behind her suggested to Stalker that Rhys was bustling the girl out through the back door. She shrank away from the squirming demon impaled on her sword. She tugged it out of the ceiling, where the tip was lodged, and jumped back, withdrawing the blade from the demon. It writhed on the table, where it fell, hissing and spitting blood everywhere. She drew her other dha and plunged both blades together into the slug-like creature. She dragged the blades in opposite directions through its flesh, filleting it like a fish. Blood and gore oozed out of it and it sighed one last time before falling still and silent. The demon disintegrated, dripping off the sides of the table and splatting on the floor, before shimmering out of sight across the veil.

Stalker let out a long breath, a mildly hysterical laugh on the tail of the sigh. It was so much easier for her when they did that, no clean up to worry about. Movement in the shadows got her attention. She looked up, but there was no one there.

'Rhys?' she whispered into the dark.

'No, an old friend.' The voice was deep and echoed slightly. She knew at once who it belonged to. Her knees trembled and she let her head fall back. Her two dha fell to the floor with a clatter. The clink of metal armour sent a cold shiver down her spine. 'Very nice work.'

'Was it one of yours?' Her voice shook and she felt embarrassed at the evident fear in it.

'Oh no, nothing to do with me. It was an agent of The Hunger.'

'Oh god.' Stalker trembled all over as the Knight-of-Shadowed-Fear moved closer. 'It must have followed me here.'

'Yes. I expect so. I was drawn to the delicious fear in that poor young girl back there.' The Knight indicated towards the kitchen.

Stalker craned her neck towards the door, but she couldn't see or hear anything. What had Rhys had to do? Was the girl all right? 'I do love the way you react to me, Stalker.' The Knight was right behind her now. He radiated cold. The air around them dropped in temperature enough to cause Stalker's breath to cloud on it. She shivered, frozen and unable to move.

'I don't,' she hissed.

He chuckled, a throaty sound that reverberated inside his helmet.

'Did you find someone else to help you with your trinket?'

'No,' she replied. She had stopped carrying the talisman around with her. It was too dangerous while it was able to exert its powerful influence over her. It brought her Agrius beast inside to the surface, heightening her senses to a level she couldn't cope with, and making it more likely that she would lose control and turn into a slobbering beast.

'Why did you call on me to help?'

'A demon called Savaging Fury resides inside the tooth. It needs taming so that I can call on its power without being overwhelmed. Using the talisman will spread fear. I guess we thought you would appreciate that.' Her voice only trembled a little, but the fear was still paralysing.

'You miss the subtle nuances of fear. I am not interested in Savaging Fury, it is fear of the unseen that attracts me. The monsters under the bed, the feeling of someone following you. You understand what I'm talking about. Don't you, my dear?'

Stalker couldn't speak. She was stuck to the spot, needing every ounce of strength to hold back the Agrius that was clawing to get out. But she did understand him, she knew what it was like to feel eyes on the back of her head. She had felt it in Redfield Park on Bonfire night, just before she found out what she was. She had experienced forgotten memories that only left behind the fear they induced. 'No need to answer,' the Knight said softly. He towered behind her, casting his dark shadow over her. 'I can feel it inside you. You understand the darkness. You have felt and faced the fear.'

The Knight touched her back. She recoiled from his ice

cold touch, but couldn't escape him; she was rooted to the spot. His metal-clad finger ran down her spine, sending a violent shudder through her. Goosebumps jumped up all over her exposed skin.

'Please don't.' Her voice was soft, desperate, pleading. She needed him to stop. She needed to not go to pieces every time he was near her.

The Knight stepped back suddenly, and Stalker could breathe again. 'Will you help?' she asked, her voice low and husky, gasping for air.

'I will. But you must do something for me. I don't like your talisman much, but I do like you. One of my favourite types of fear is humanity's propensity to fear authority. Make them afraid of this police officer.' He clicked his metal-plated fingers together and a photograph spun from thin air and landed at Stalker's feet. She stooped slowly to pick it up. It was a newspaper clipping, with a photograph of a serious-looking police officer receiving honours for his service. The name in the caption read Sergeant Reynolds.

'And ruin his career?' Stalker asked, raising an indignant eyebrow.

'He's dirty,' the Knight replied silkily as he walked slowly around Stalker. 'He's killed people he shouldn't have. Dig, you'll find it. A very small number of people suspect and are rightly afraid of him, but I want more people to be afraid. Expose him. Make people even more mistrustful of Caerton's police, who, as we all know, look out for their own.'

'And if I fail?' She looked up from the picture in her hand into the Knight's empty helmet.

'I take your spine.'

Chapter Three

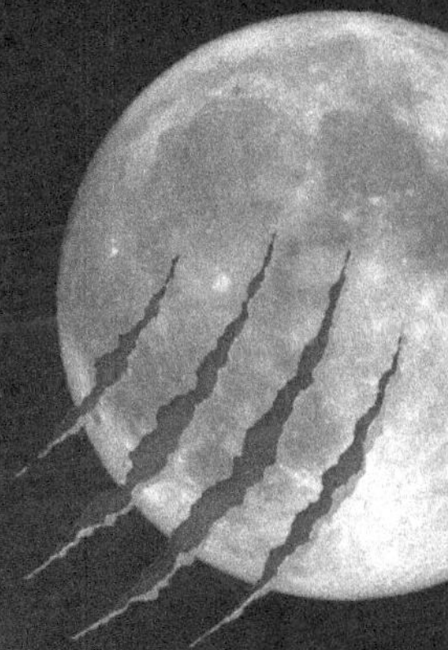

'Stalker? Are you okay?' Rhys's voice hissed from the fog. Stalker shook her head to try and clear it. She looked around, surprised to find herself in the cafe, the lights glaring brightly. Then she remembered the Knight. She looked down at the photo in her hand and over to the table where the demon had died. There was no trace of it. Rhys grabbed her shoulders and looked into her eyes.

'I'm fine,' she murmured.

'You were terrified. What happened?'

'A demon.'

'I know. Where is it?' Rhys looked around the cafe.

'I killed it. It's gone. The girl? Is the girl okay?'

'She will be.'

Stalker snapped out of her haze and glared at him.

'What does that mean?' She scooped her dha from the floor and roughly sheathed them. They disappeared from view again, blending into her body until she needed them again.

Rhys grabbed her hand and dragged her into the kitchen. The lights were mostly out in here, but some lamps over hot plates remained on over an island in the middle of the small, chrome kitchen. Behind the island, the young waitress sat slumped over, her eyes fixed and glazed. Rhys squatted in front of her and took her hand. Stalker watched warily.

'Hello?' Rhys said softly, rubbing her hand. 'Are you all right? I think you fainted.'

Stalker chewed the inside of her mouth and a deep frown knitted her eyebrows together. She didn't understand. The girl stirred and blinked a few times. 'Hi, it's okay. You're okay.' Rhys's voice was gentle and compelling. Stalker cocked her head and watched as the girl looked around with unfocused eyes.

'What happened?' she croaked.

'I'm not sure. We heard a clatter and came through after you to see if you were okay, seeing as you were here on your own. How do you feel?'

'My head hurts. But I think I'm okay.'

Rhys helped her to her feet.

'Is there someone we can call for you? Maybe get you a cab to take you home?'

'No, I think I'll be okay in a minute. That's so weird. I don't think I've ever fainted before.'

'Maybe you should call your boss?' Stalker said softly. 'We need to go, but I don't want to leave you here alone.'

The waitress nodded and allowed Rhys to lead her back to the front of the cafe and into a seat. Stalker looked around anxiously, making sure there were no signs of the fight. Rhys took care of the phone call, while Stalker checked out of the window at the front of the cafe. The city went on again, like at the church, unaware of what was happening in the hidden places. A few minutes later, Rhys was leading Stalker out into the cool night.

'What happened?' They both spoke at once. They shared a small laugh, before Stalker insisted Rhys speak first.

'I have a special ability. Part of my deal with my friend.' He tapped his shoulder. 'I can make little changes to people's memory, in order to protect myself.'

Stalker nodded; part of her suspected as much.

'Have you ever meddled with my memory?'

'No, of course not.'

'The time I recall finding out your secret was the first time?'

'Yes, absolutely.' Rhys held her firmly by the shoulders and looked into her eyes. She delved into them, reading his soul. He was telling the truth. She didn't quite have Claws' lie detecting ability, but she could see a person's innermost truth, their bare honesty, whatever it might be in that moment. Sometimes she found a fear, a weakness, a love, or a secret. Right now it was Rhys's honesty. 'I had to grab her and get her into the kitchen before she saw anything that would bring on the madness. She thought I was assaulting her. It wasn't nice. So I had to use my ability to protect her, as well as us.'

Stalker nodded.

'Of course.'

'What happened to you?'

'Oh, nothing. I... I killed the demon.' For some reason

she didn't want to tell him about the Knight-of-Shadowed-Fear. The way he made her feel was intoxicating, which was extremely confusing. She knew at once that Rhys knew she was holding something back, but he nodded and wrapped an arm around her shoulders. He wasn't going to press her. Their relationship was filled with secrets. She closed her eyes and forced back a tear that threatened to spill. 'I have to get back to St. Mark's. I've got work to do.'

'Okay. Call me in the morning, please, let me know you're all right.'

'Sure.' She nodded and stood up on her toes to kiss him on the lips. He held her firmly against his body as he kissed her passionately and her head swam with love for him. All confusing thoughts of the Knight vanished. Reluctantly, Stalker pulled away. 'I'll see you soon.'

'Yeah. Be safe. Love you.'

'Love you too.' She smiled and turned to go.

'Hey!' he called after her. She turned back, her pulse quickening. 'Remember what I said earlier? Think about it. Okay?'

'Yeah, I will.' Her smile faltered and she waved, before turning and setting off at a brisk walk.

When Stalker got back to St. Mark's, she took a quick run through the territory to fulfil her obligation. Nothing seemed to be amiss, so she headed back to Grove Street, eager to report on what had happened.

The rest of the pack were already back.

'Stalker?' Eyes called out from the kitchen. She went straight up the dark hallway to the back of the house. 'Are you okay?'

'There was a demon, an agent of The Hunger. It came

at me after I left the graveyard. I'm fine, I took it down easily. It could have been what let the ghosts across. But I don't think so, it was barely sentient. I think there was probably something else doing the technical stuff. Maybe this was its bodyguard or something.'

Wind Talker nodded slowly. The others looked a little surprised.

'That makes sense,' Wind Talker said.

'Scribe get home okay?' Stalker asked as she slid her coat off and slumped down into a chair at the small table.

'Fine,' Weaver replied as she bustled about. 'There's something else. What is it?' She glanced at Stalker, clearly not wanting a confrontation. Stalker sighed and rubbed her face. Every eye was on her.

'The Knight-of-Shadowed-Fear paid me a visit after I killed the Hunger demon.' She pulled the newspaper clipping from her pocket and pressed it out flat on the table. Claws took it and frowned. 'He wants me to expose this corrupt police officer. If I can make folk scared of the police, then he'll attune my fear talisman to me so I can use it safely. If I fail, he said he would remove my spine.'

'What?!' Eyes and Claws blurted at once. Wind Talker and Weaver didn't seem entirely surprised, but Weaver stopped washing up and leaned against the sink to look at Stalker. Eyes still had a plate and towel in his hands, but he had stopped drying and was glaring at her.

'How could you make such a deal?' he snapped.

'I don't know. I didn't really know I had until afterwards.' She felt foolish and didn't dare look at any of them.

'He's a tricky one. I thought something like this might

happen with him.' Wind Talker spoke softly, his voice laced with compassion, not ridicule or scorn. She looked up at him and gave him a thankful nod.

'How can we help?' Weaver asked.

'Erm, I don't know. I don't even know where to start. Claws?' She looked at him expectantly.

He looked over the brief article under the picture.

'I'll see what I can dig up.'

'Thanks.' Stalker stood up and bid the pack good night. She was exhausted from the evening's exertions. She trudged up the stairs, each step feeling heavier than the last. An old folk song crept into her mind and she idly began to hum as she continued past the bathroom and up to the attic. The little door at the top was locked and she quietly unlocked it and slipped inside, closing the door behind her. The tune hummed out of her lips as she moved across the dark attic to the corner, where a small hole into Hepethia was hidden in the eaves. She reached inside and took out a small, wooden box. 'Open,' she whispered, unaware of her actions. The box slid open. Inside was a growing collection of small items: playing cards, sweet wrappers, burned matches and so on. She squeezed her hand into her tight jeans pocket and tugged out a small sachet of sugar from the cafe. She tucked it into the box and slid the lid shut. She kissed the box and put it back in its hiding place, where it vanished from even her sight.

As she slowly made her way back down the stairs the song left her mind and she stopped her descent, one foot hanging in the air over the next step. 'What was I doing?' she mumbled to herself. Then headed thoughtlessly towards the bathroom to freshen up for sleep. She didn't see Claws standing on the landing, or the curious glance he cast up the stairs she had just come down.

35

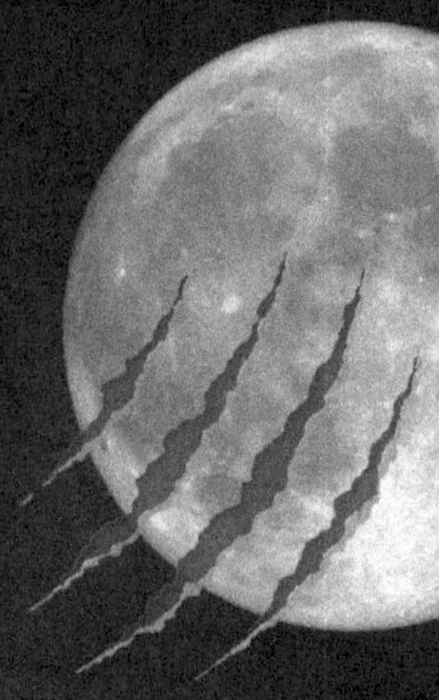

CHAPTER FOUR

FIGHTS-EYES-OPEN

TEMPLES THROBBING and a dull ache between his eyes that wouldn't abate. He pinched the skin between his eyebrows and squeezed his eyes shut. A red light blinked on the dashboard of his four-wheel drive and the eerie orange glow of the street lamps bathed the inside of the car in its sickening light. He looked out at the dark house. In his mind's eye it was still covered in thick vines that had gouged his skin. His wife and child were screaming inside and he couldn't reach them. The sign at the kerb declared the house "SOLD". Six months previously he might have got twice as much for it, but now it was tainted. The whole street's value had plummeted after what the public believed was a gang attack.

When someone is murdered in a house it leaves a mark. His stepfather's torn-out throat had stained the floor in the kitchen, his mother's screams had echoed around the room and been absorbed by the walls. Humans didn't really understand these things, some were superstitious about it, some would claim to feel a chill on entering the house. But Eyes knew, he understood the truth. Shifters dealt with the truth every day. A demon had been drawn here from hell by the events of that day and had taken up residence in the house's reflection in Hepethia. That was what sensitive humans could feel, but few had the truth really figured out.

The Knight-of-Shadowed-Fear was building an army for war and Eyes knew it was only a matter of time before the Lightning Lords would have to step in to protect humanity from the fallout. Now the Knight had his greasy gaze on his pack mate's spine. He believed in the literal interpretation of the threat, the demon was certainly capable of removing Stalker's spine.

He opened the car door and stepped out slowly, dragging his weary body onto the pavement. He could feel the waves of dread crashing over him as he trudged up the path to the front door. His key shook in his hand. *You really shouldn't have come here alone, you know.* He wasn't sure whose voice it was inside his head. These things were so confusing these days. His own inner voice, one of his pack mates communicating telepathically, or a demon. Who knew?

Eyes slid his key into the lock and slowly turned it. He stepped inside and across the veil at the same time. Soon he would lose access to this place. He had to tie the loose ends before the new owners took possession of the place. Last time he had been here it was dark and cold, the Knight in residence, haunting the house. At this late hour, he had been expecting a similar scene. He blinked as his eyes adjusted. Instead of a dark, abandoned house, the reflection in Hepethia was a bustling war room. It was dimly lit, after all, this was still the residence of a fear demon, however it was filled with smaller demons scurrying back and forth. Instead of the house, there was something resembling a military complex. But it was warped and wrong by human standards. This was the headquarters for a demonic war. There were walls and a roof, but they were constructed of dark quartz. Where the stairs had been in Eyes' house there was a roughly cut stairway up to a balcony that spanned the length of the war room. Eyes imagined the Knight standing up there, surveying his minions below. But right now he was absent. His little followers scuttled about, carrying documents and whispering in frantic voices. None of them seemed to pay the slightest bit of attention to Eyes.

He moved slowly into the space and the demons continued about their business, some slightly diverting their course to and fro in order to skirt around the shifter in their midst, but otherwise ignoring him.

There was a sudden rush of wind and the dimly glowing lights, which seemed to have no source, flickered. Every little imp and goblin in the place stopped still and fell silent. They all gazed upwards and Eyes found his head tilting up to follow their gaze. Up on the balcony a dark mist was forming. Cold settled over the room like a shadow moving over the sun. Out of the swirling fog stepped the Knight-of-Shadowed-Fear. Even through his plate mail armour, Eyes could feel the suspicion radiating.

'What do you want?' His voice boomed down, echoing off the quartz walls. The light flickered again then held steady. Eyes felt every little red eye of the swarm of demons around him swivel to settle on him. He swallowed hard and clenched his fists, staring fixedly up at the Knight.

'To talk.'

'Very well.' The Knight waved a plated hand and every black creature in the place darted for cover, disappearing into shadowy doorways and out of sight. Eyes watched them go, leaving papers scattered all over the floor and every roughly desk-shaped surface.

'What is all this?' Eyes asked in wonder as he looked around. His wandering gaze settled upon the Knight standing suddenly right beside him and he staggered backwards, his heart pounding hard in his chest.

'Preparations.'

'For war?'

'With the Baron-of-Blooded-Shards, yes.'

'You spoke with Stalker this evening. You threatened her.' Eyes tensed up, emboldened in the face of this formidable demon, and yet still overwhelmingly cautious. He used every ounce of confidence he could summon to stand tall before him. The Knight let out a low rumble that echoed inside his armour. Eyes had the impression, not for the first time, that there was nothing solid inside there at all, just darkness and pure evil.

'I did not threaten her. We struck a bargain.'

'With fatal consequences should she fail to do her part. She didn't know what she was agreeing to.'

'Are you disparaging the intelligence and wit of your comrade?' There was a smirk to the Knight's deep voice. Eyes stiffened and puffed up his chest.

'No, of course not. You tricked her, as I am sure you

are capable of doing to the most savvy of folk.'

'Have you come here to beg me to reconsider?' The Knight leaned over and Eyes felt his knees weaken slightly. He leaned back to move away from that imposing helmet.

'No, not to beg. I wanted some reassurance that you will give her every opportunity to fulfil the task and not impede her progress.'

The Knight sighed and stepped away, giving Eyes breathing room. The ice cold that seeped from the demon was beginning to get under his skin, causing goosebumps to break out under his suit.

'Perhaps you did not understand the deal we struck. I want young Stalker to succeed. I want the citizens of Caerton to fear the authorities. I want suspicion and anxiety to be rife here. It feeds me. While I do have a certain fondness for young, supple spines, I have no great desire to rip that of your pack mate's from her body. She simply needed a little motivation.'

'But your threat is real.' Eyes took a step back and composed himself, straightening his tie and smoothing his shirt. He ran a hand through his hair and instantly thought of Fortune and the way he used to do that.

'It is,' the Knight replied softly. 'You do remind me of your father.'

Eyes blinked at the demon, stunned into silence. The Knight cocked his head to one side and regarded Eyes through his visor. Eyes despised not being able to see the eyes of the being he was conversing with, it threw him off completely. The thing he loved so much about being in court was looking a witness or the accused in the eye and knowing what was going on inside their head. Had the

Knight read his mind when he thought of Fortune? Or had they coincidentally shared the thought?

'What do you know of the Blue Moon? You had bargains with them, didn't you?'

'I did. I knew them for a very long time. I could tell you stories that would make you shudder.'

'Stories about hidden underground prisons and torture by any chance? About killing home owners in order to gain access to their property?'

'The Blue Moon did some unspeakably dark things, young Alpha. All in the name of their cause.'

'They were defending this city. Perhaps they didn't always go about it in an ethical manner but—'

'But,' the Knight interrupted, 'they did indeed believe their actions were justified. As I am sure you do. When you turn this neighbourhood against one of their trusted police officers and make them afraid to report crimes, you may gain some insight.'

'I already have insight. I know what we've done and what still must be done.'

'I'm certain you don't. Not yet. Now get out of here and don't return. This isn't your place any more.'

A strong gust of wind lifted Eyes right off his feet and sent him flying backwards. His breath caught in his throat and his chest felt tight. He felt the veil shimmer around him and he landed with a hard thump on the floor of the hallway of his old house. The front door was standing open and he hurriedly exited through it. It slammed behind him and he heard the lock click.

That night, back at his mother's house, which he was staying at alone now that his human family had all left for safer locations, Eyes slept badly. He tossed and turned and was tormented by vivid dreams of the Blue Moon and the Knight-of-Shadowed-Fear. Stalker's spine featured prominently too, and more than once, Eyes woke with a start, gasping for breath and sweating profusely.

He gave up on sleep in the early hours of the morning and fixed himself some strong coffee. In the dining room he had set up a huge cork board, upon which he had pinned a map of Caerton and various notes about their ongoing campaign against the Furies. They didn't have long now to mount a defence against the war they knew was coming, whether they were ready or not.

As he sipped his coffee, Eyes stared at the board and tried to make sense of it all. The Lightning Lords' territory really was too big for them to handle. But he couldn't see any other option. Their neighbours to the north and south-east, The Wrecking Crew and Glass Wolves, were both stretched almost as thin. The three packs were the front line against the Furies. Without their cooperation and vigilance, the city limit could be breached at any time. He stared at the map, looking for something, anything, that he might have missed. His tired eyes began to glaze over as he started at the jumble of lines. He had noted the planned tunnels for Theodore's ambitious underground rail network onto the map and saw how they crossed to form a giant pentagram under the city. As he stared at the lines, he wondered dully if any of the hundreds of humans involved in the project had noticed. It was obvious to him now, because he knew about it, but until Theodore had guided him to it, he had been oblivious.

The line that ran from west to east through the north

of the city connected St. Catherine's to Fenwick, going straight through China Town, just south of St. Mark's. Eyes blinked the sleep from his eyes and stepped closer to the map. Every pack's territory was marked on it, all carefully colour coded. The city centre had been unclaimed for decades, everyone knew that. Everyone knew not to go there. He had once gotten a look at it in Hepethia from China Town and had no desire to get any closer. But China Town, that was the anomaly. Every area that was unclaimed was overrun by demons. With no shifters to control the population, things quickly spiralled out of control. St. Catherine's was the same. But China Town was immaculate. It was only a few blocks in the human city, but in Hepethia it stretched for miles of pristine crystal with no signs of life. Someone had to be in control of that. It had been a mystery for as long as he had been a shifter and no one seemed to know the answer. Whatever claimed that area was not one of them and had no desire to become known to them.

He marched to his room and dressed hurriedly in jeans and a t-shirt, shoved his feet into some boots, grabbed his keys and went for a drive.

The city was just starting to wake, the sky had turned to that dull grey that preceded dawn. Eyes drove quickly through the quiet streets. He passed a few joggers in their lurid Lycra running gear; and a grocer opening up for early morning trade. Lights came on in a handful of windows and slowly Caerton came to life. He pulled up at the kerb in the heart of China Town. Normally it was one of the most lively areas of the city, a shining diamond of trade and tourism, but here at the cusp of the day all was quiet. The street vendors had not yet arrived to sell their wares and the rush hour traffic that choked the narrow streets had not descended. There were ethnic clubs here, and herbalists in spades. Not to mention the dozens of restaurants and takeaways.

Eyes climbed out of his car and looked up and down the quiet street. Just out of sight, but within hearing range, was a construction site for one of the underground stations. The drilling carried on the cool air and across the street was a temporary road sign declaring there to be "Night works ahead until October". Work on the underground was in full swing across the city, thanks to Eyes and Theodore.

Eyes didn't have the tracking skills of Stalker, or the investigative ability of Claws, but right now he was determined to uncover some useful information. They had never caught the scent of a shifter here, nor any sort of territorial markings. But had they really been looking hard enough? If the area was claimed, they were going to great lengths to remain hidden. Perhaps there were subtle signs of their presence that didn't conform to typical shifter activity. He moved down the street slowly, looking for graffiti tags or anything else that might have been missed.

He got to the end of the street and turned left, intending to circle the block. After a few yards he caught sight of a creased playing card wedged into a crack in the wall near the ground. So far below eye level it could easily be missed. He almost dismissed it, but something told him not to. Stooping to look at it, he saw that it was a six of diamonds, though it was faded and weathered. At the next corner he saw another, a seven of diamonds. Instead of turning left again he went on and when he came to an alley he found an eight of diamonds wedged under the corner of a commercial dumpster. This couldn't be a coincidence. The cards were sequential.

There were cars rumbling along the street now, more movement behind windows and the occasional pedestrian passed him, glancing at him warily. He followed the trail to the end of the street, where the sequence came to a queen. Eyes turned back and passed his car, following the playing cards in the other direction. Life bustled around him as he traced the boundary. He turned right and kept his eyes peeled for another clue. Soon enough he found it, so obvious now that he knew the pattern. All along this street were cards from the suit of clubs, in sequence, tucked away just out of direct sight, seemingly discarded.

'These must be boundary markings,' he muttered to himself. A passing old woman looked at him warily. He tried to smile casually, but knew he needed to make his exit now, he was drawing attention. Besides, he had to meet Theodore.

The mystery of China Town and the playing cards would have to wait to be fully solved. The day was tedious in the extreme, negotiating the final planning permissions for the rail network. Eyes was glad to get to the end of another day of being addressed by bureaucrats as "Martin", a name he hardly recognised as his own any more.

When he stepped through the door of 32 Grove Street that evening, Eyes heard mumbling voices in the kitchen and strode down the hall to greet his pack. The four of them sat around the table, worried expressions on their faces. They looked up at him as he entered. Then Wind

Talker pushed something small across the table towards him, a grim expression on his broad face.

'Do you know what this means?' Wind Talker asked, his voice hard. 'It came through the door this afternoon.'

Eyes looked down at the ace of spades on the table. Scribbled over it in black ink was a phone number and "We need to talk".

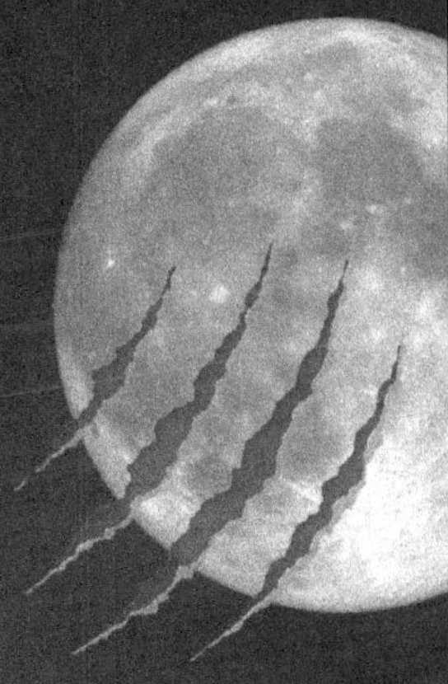

CHAPTER FIVE

'WHAT IS IT, EYES?' Weaver urged, worry creasing her face.

'I went to China Town this morning, looking for signs of who claims it. I found playing cards, lots of them. They mark the boundary, as far as I could tell. I must have been noticed.'

'Are they shifters?' Stalker asked, her arms crossed over her chest as she leaned back in her chair.

'I don't know. We've never smelled any there before, have we?' He looked pointedly at Stalker, knowing that she had by far the best nose, and that she was prone to solo exploration of the city.

'No,' she replied defiantly. 'I've never picked up any shifter scents there.' She looked most affronted.

'Hey, they've obviously been hiding themselves from everyone. The Blue Moon didn't know who was there either. They must have all sorts of tricks up their sleeves to conceal themselves. They might not even be shifters, they might be something else. Don't take it personally. Okay?'

Stalker lifted her chin and gave a slight nod.

'So,' Weaver said softly. 'Are we going to call them?'

'I suppose we have to,' Eyes replied, though he didn't relish the thought.

'It's only polite. You got caught snooping on their turf and have discovered their markings.' Claws nodded firmly as he spoke. Always the pragmatic voice of reason.

Eyes pulled out his phone and grabbed the card from the table. He tapped in the number and glanced around at the others for confirmation before hitting "dial". Reassuring nods around the table gave him the confirmation he wanted, and Eyes hit the button.

It only rang twice, before a crisp male voice answered.

'The Green Dragon. How can I help you?' Clinking, clattering and the buzz of lively conversation filled the background.

'Er...' Eyes faltered, unsure what to say. He glanced at the number, doubting he had dialled correctly. 'We need to talk?' He exaggerated the lift at the end of his question.

'Ah, yes. One moment please.' The phone clicked and hold music piped through the handset.

'Oh I've eaten there,' Weaver said, her eyes lighting up. 'Great food!'

'Who am I speaking to, please?' a new voice asked suddenly. The restaurant noises were absent this time, but the voice was as polite as the first.

'Martin Davison. I live in St. Mark's. My friends and I received a card with this number on. We are most anxious to meet the neighbours.' He looked around at the others, who were watching him avidly. Claws gave him the slightest nod of approval.

'Of course. It was you we noticed this morning, wasn't it?'

'It was. Could you tell me to whom I am speaking, please?'

'Harry Feng. I run the family business here. But my mother is the head of the family.'

Eyes nodded, understanding the mildly encrypted message perfectly.

'I see,' he said. 'And when would be a good time for us to meet?'

'Come to the restaurant tonight. We are keen to meet and resolve this swiftly.'

'Of course. We'll be there shortly.' The two men wrapped up the call and Eyes gave his pack a small smile. 'Looks like we're eating out tonight.'

There was a flurry of excitement as the Lightning Lords quickly prepared to leave. Eyes waited patiently, still in his shoes and jacket from walking in from work.

'I wonder what they are?' Weaver pondered as she slid her boots on.

'They may be something entirely new,' Wind Talker replied. 'I wish I knew more about Chinese mythology. Stalker, do you know anything from your kung fu?'

Stalker rounded on Wind Talker, her face aghast. Eyes held back a smirk.

'I don't do kung fu!' Stalker snapped. 'Oh my god. How long have we known each other? And you don't even know which martial arts I teach?'

Eyes took her firmly by the shoulders and steered her towards the door.

'I'm sorry,' Wind Talker called out sheepishly. 'It's judo, isn't it?' he muttered to Claws as they made their way down the hall behind Stalker and Eyes.

'And the sword thing, don't forget the sword thing. They're Burmese, I think,' Claws whispered in reply. A laugh burst from Eyes' mouth before he could stop it, but one glance at Stalker killed his grin. She glared at him with narrowed eyes and was the first out of the door, yanking it open with a little too much force, slamming it back against the wall.

'Tell me something about Weaver's PhD thesis,' Eyes said sternly as they climbed into the car. Stalker faltered and gaped at him. 'Point proven. Now get it together, all of you,' he added over his shoulder to the others as they squeezed into the back. 'United front for this meeting, please.'

The area around The Green Dragon was alive, in complete contrast to how Eyes had left China Town that morning. It was getting dark, but brightly coloured paper lanterns were strung across the street, zig-zagging their way and casting their light over the packed pavements below. Eyes parked in a cramped car park behind the restaurant and the five shifters made their way cautiously through the throng. Eyes was sure he could feel someone watching them and he scanned the crowd carefully as they went, occasionally glancing up to the many windows that overlooked the street. But each was as black as the next, with no sign of eyes upon them. But still that creeping feeling up his spine told him their arrival had been noted.

The restaurant was squeezed between an apothecary and a second-hand book shop. The facade was painted bright green and a huge window invited people in to a warm and lively place. A sign swung over the door, with a green dragon painted on it, the name of the restaurant was painted in red Chinese characters that Eyes couldn't read, but could guess at. When he opened the door, a little bell rang above it and a blast of warm air carried delicious scents of spices out into the street.

Every table was packed, yet the small space didn't feel cramped, it was open and inviting. A waitress hurried between tables, chatting animatedly with the regulars and making all feel welcome. As the five formidable shifters squeezed into the waiting space by the door, a short man in a neat suit and bright green waistcoat hurried towards them from the back of the dining area.

'Hello,' he greeted them brightly. As he approached, his smile faltered ever so slightly. He cleared his throat and adjusted his waistcoat. 'I have a private table for you, upstairs please.' He picked up menus and indicated for the Lightning Lords to follow him up a narrow staircase behind a screen. Eyes led the way, trying not to get too close to their escort on the way up. Eyes could tell that this man was not a shifter, his scent was human and everything about him indicated that he was a human lackey, who was intimidated by the five shifters in his midst.

Eyes stepped out into a private dining room with one long table, beautifully dressed with a silk table runner, candles and small wooden dragon ornaments down the centre. Paper lanterns hung overhead and stunning ink drawings hung in ornate frames on the walls. Their escort led them to the far end of the table and indicated for them to sit down. 'Your hosts will be with you shortly,' he said, handing Eyes a menu. Once he had passed menus to each shifter, he made a hasty exit back down the stairs.

'Is it safe to eat, do you think?' Stalker whispered.

'I don't think they would poison us in their own restaurant,' Claws replied. Although he looked around cautiously.

Eyes opened his menu, but stared at it blindly, waiting for something to happen. A moment later, a door at the opposite end of the room opened and his pack mates' heads all swivelled to look, as a man entered, followed by another six figures. Eyes stood to receive them, the others copied him and he felt the tension in the air lifting hairs on the back of his neck. They were shifters, Eyes felt the power radiating from them, and quite a sight they were.

Six men, two of whom were identical twins, all in sharp suits and shiny shoes; more than one were sporting ugly scars on their faces and several had visible tattoos on their hands and necks. At the rear of the line was a surprise: an old woman with dark grey hair tied back in a bun. She was wearing a green dress and her lean body showed a lifetime of hard work that had kept her fit and well. She strode purposefully, and yet her white eyes were completely blind. This was her domain, and she knew every inch of it. She confidently stopped an inch from the head of the table, as the men took seats around her. The Lightning Lords sat down, a subdued silence hanging heavily on the air.

'Good evening,' the woman said, not smiling. She pulled out her seat and slid gracefully into it. 'I am Mrs Feng. These are my sons and grandsons. We are The House of Cards. And you are?' She leaned forwards, propping her chin on her clasped hands, her elbows resting on the table either side of the white china plate in front of her.

Eyes fixed his gaze on her and waited for all of her names to come to him, but no more did. Mrs Feng it was. The men at the table were a mixed bunch. The twins were simply Harry and Jack, an older man, who bore a resemblance to the youngsters, went by Mike. The other three, however, had names that would be more at home among Caerton's other shifters: Winter's Mask, Deep-Shadow's-Fury and Three-Fold-Knives.

'I'm Fights-Eyes-Open. This is Stalker-of-Night's-Shadow, Wind Talker, Weaver-of-Sky's-Loom, and Claws-of-Lead. We are the Lightning Lords.'

'Welcome,' Mrs Feng said, her voice warming. 'Please, do take a look at the menu. The meal is our gift to you, as our guests.'

'Thank you, that's very kind.' Eyes gave an appreciative nod and glanced down at the menu. He immediately looked up again to see her as composed as ever, watching him sightlessly down the long table. 'I must apologise for the intrusion this morning. We have been curious about your territory for a long time and it has become somewhat pressing that we figure out the mystery. It was not my intention to cause offence.'

'Nor did you,' Mrs Feng replied, a soft smile playing at her lips. 'I understand. I was planning to reach out to you in the coming days in any case.' Her accent carried traces of her heritage, though only faintly. Eyes would hazard a guess that she had lived in Caerton her whole life, which seemed likely to have been extremely long so far.

'Oh?' Eyes felt his stomach lurch in surprise. On either side of him, his pack mates tensed up too.

This is interesting. Weaver projected the thought to him. He glanced at her and saw her looking firmly at her menu.

A waiter rushed in through the door and put jugs of water on the table, before taking out a pad and looking expectantly around for a sign that someone was ready to order. Mrs Feng ordered for her family first and Eyes had to wait to continue their discussion. He still didn't know what to order and could barely think about food. The waiter came to him last and he picked a main meal at random at the last moment. When the shifters were alone again, Mrs Feng smiled a wide and not exactly pleasant smile.

'E gui.'

'Excuse me?' Eyes blinked at her.

'E gui. Hungry Ghosts. They are early.'

Stalker cleared her throat and Eyes shot her a look of caution.

'I see,' Eyes said calmly.

'Our Hungry Ghost festival does not begin for a few months. We believe that in the seventh month of our calendar, the gates of hell are opened and the ghosts of our ancestors are free to roam the earth. If their families have not honoured them with enough sacrifices they may be dangerous. But we noticed that they began to walk among us early this year. This was most surprising to us.'

'I beg your pardon,' Claws said softly. 'But may I ask why this event would prompt you to make your existence known to us, and not anything else that has happened in the past?'

'We are not the same,' Mrs Feng said, her head tilting

towards Claws. 'We have existed here since China Town began to develop. We have seen the trouble in both worlds brought by the Greek ones, more trouble than you can imagine.'

I don't know about that, Stalker whispered into Eyes' head. He hid a smile behind his hand. The old woman may be blind, but her family weren't, and Eyes suspected she perceived more than one might assume.

'We have always shunned your kind, preferring to keep our own house in order.'

'Yes, we've seen. It's very impressive. How do you do it?' Wind Talker asked. 'Hepethia, we call it, the other world, your territory is pristine.'

'Thank you,' Mrs Feng replied.

The door burst open and the first food was brought out by two young, and sweaty wait staff. Again the conversation halted while humans were amongst them. Eyes couldn't help but marvel at their timing and at their host's composure. There was no hint of concern in her demeanour that they might be overheard and their secrets revealed. It was possible that the humans were privy to their employer's true nature, but he doubted it. These shifters were too careful to conceal themselves.

He looked at his food and his appetite suddenly appeared. The others were tucking in, and he wasted no time in picking up his chopsticks.

'I suppose it helps that there are so many of you and that you keep a tight territory close to home,' Eyes said, once they were alone once more. His sweet and sour pork was exquisite and he paused to enjoy it. Satisfied murmurs rippled around his pack. The House of Cards ate too, with gusto, and lively conversation broke out between the men.

'Indeed,' Mrs Feng's voice carried easily over the growing noise. She ate her soup slowly and with perfect ease. 'We have strict rules and routine and it works.'

'What was it in particular that concerned you about the Hungry Ghosts?' Weaver asked between mouthfuls of duck pancakes.

'As I mentioned,' Mrs Feng replied. 'We see the troubles your kind suffer. We don't normally see it spill into our territory or affect us. Many times the demons you fight are unrecognisable to us, there being nothing similar in our lore. But this time the ghosts walked among us all and we knew at once what they were. It is perhaps something we should work together to resolve.'

'We banished them,' Claws said, frowning up and down the table.

'For now,' Wind Talker said, patting the side of his mouth with a napkin. 'We haven't been able to find The Hunger itself and destroy or banish it.'

'What is The Hunger?' One of the men spoke, addressing the Lightning Lords for the first time. Eyes recognised his voice from the phone call and turned his gaze to Harry Feng. He had an immaculate haircut and fine moustache. He was more petite than most of the others, with only his twin of a similarly small build, but Eyes could tell he was quick and agile from the way he moved.

'A demon. It seems to have been working in Caerton for a while, building support. There are other demons who have been working for it, and even a pack of shifters, The Witches of Fenwick,' Wind Talker explained. 'It was The Hunger that raised the ghosts, although we do not understand why.'

Eyes felt the stiffness in Wind Talker's voice and ripples of regret flowing from Stalker. The rift between them was mending, slowly, but the emotions were still raw when their conflict was remembered.

'Where it came from will be important. You know this.' Mrs Feng's voice was soft and silence had fallen to hear it.

'What do you know of the troubles facing the city as a whole?' Eyes asked, his gaze fixed on Mrs Feng as he took a bite of his dinner.

'Enough to know that we want no part in it.' Harry Feng was the one to speak. Eyes glanced at him and saw a sharp look between him and his grandmother. The others shifted uncomfortably in their seats.

'Wars and troubles between the Greek ones are of no concern to us.' Mrs Feng was not smiling.

'You won't be immune, you know?' Eyes said carefully. 'When The Furies come they will sweep through the city taking everything they want.'

'They don't know about us.'

'You can't be sure of that,' Stalker said, her temper flaring in her raised voice.

'You didn't.' Harry Feng raised an eyebrow as he spoke.

'We knew someone was here, just not who. You can be sure their scouts will know as much as we did. They may even have found your territory markings by now too.' Eyes lay down his chopsticks and leaned back in his chair. 'The rest of us are working together, which as I am sure you know, is exceptionally rare. The threat is that great. We would be honoured if you would join with us to defend the city.' He looked around at the six warriors of The House of

Cards, longing them to agree.

'Perhaps,' Mrs Feng said, tilting her head as if surveying him. He wondered if she really were blind or if he had wrongly assumed. 'For now we must remain closely guarded. We will keep the ghosts at bay here, but you must put a stop to their crossing. You must find The Hunger.'

'We will guard your secret existence as best we can. You should know that other shifters have ways of learning secrets, however.' Eyes tried not to feel discouraged by their reticence. He had to believe they would recognise that it would be in their own best interests to help fight the Furies eventually.

'Indeed.' Mrs Feng smiled. 'But secrecy is our ally.'

Eyes felt something from Stalker; she squirmed ever so slightly in her seat and was wrestling to stop a thought from forming and being projected into the minds of all of her pack mates. He knew she kept secrets, he had accepted that, but something about this moment unsettled him. Had Stalker enlisted a secrecy demon to help her conceal something from the pack? What could be so serious?

The meeting seemed to wrap up suddenly. Their empty plates were being cleared and dessert wasn't offered. The larger of the Feng family stood to indicate the end of the meal and the Lightning Lords were hurriedly escorted from the premises.

As they clambered back into Eyes' four-by-four they all erupted into animated conversation at once.

'I can't believe it!'

'What was all that about?'

'What did we agree, exactly?'

'Was it just me or was that all a bit one way?'

'Eyes?'

He blinked, his hands were gripping the wheel tightly, but he hadn't yet started the engine.

'Hmm?'

'What are you thinking?' Stalker didn't really need to ask, he supposed, but she was being polite.

'I think this is just the beginning of our relationship with The House of Cards.'

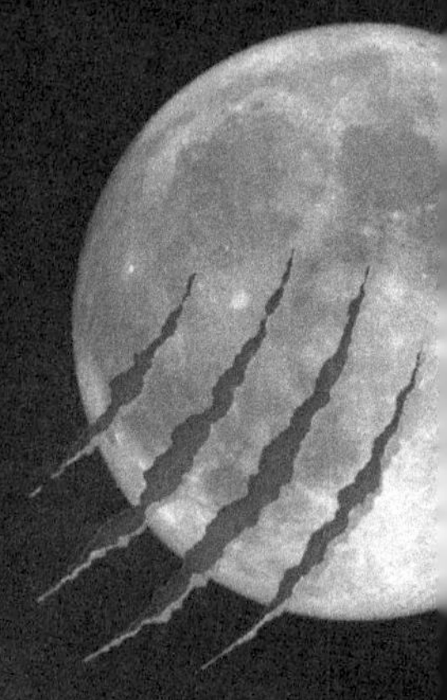

Chapter Six

Stalker-of-Night's-Shadow

'So, about my spine,' Stalker trilled as she poured herself a coffee the following morning. 'I'd quite like to ensure it's safe today. If that's all right?' she added, looking pointedly at Eyes.

'Of course. Claws, what have you found on this police officer, Reynolds?'

'I have a source who says he witnessed Reynolds killing a drug dealer a couple of months ago. He works on the drugs squad and is weapons trained. My source says he was in this warehouse in Northgate and heard raised voices. The dealer was denying something, shots were fired, Reynolds fled the scene. I confirmed this in the news archives, a dealer was shot on that date in that area, but police claimed it was drug-related gang violence and that they were pursuing leads. The case was quietly closed a week or so later, according to my guy on the force. No suspects were apprehended. It just went away.'

'I can look into why it didn't get anywhere,' Eyes said, his expression grave.

'So he killed a drug dealer? Is that it?' Stalker asked, unsure how this could help her.

'That's all, so far,' Claws said slowly.

'Ordinary people aren't really going to be concerned about that, though, are they? A lot of folk around here would see it as a public service.'

'We'll find the rest, don't worry,' Claws said, squeezing her shoulder. Stalker nodded, chewing the inside of her cheek, her mind racing.

By the end of the day, Eyes had discovered that there were around half a dozen cases involving Reynolds that had been shut down without thorough investigation and that nothing was getting to court.

'He's burying them,' Eyes said, a snarl on his tongue. Stalker could see that he took this personally. 'But we'll never prove it.'

'I wonder if he's got something going on with the underbelly of Caerton. That dealer who he shot, he was killed for a reason. Judging by what my source told me, maybe Reynolds thought he'd talked to somebody.' Claws was rubbing his temples. Stalker paced the kitchen, feeling impotent.

'Can we get it in the papers?' Stalker asked, stopping her pacing and looking expectantly at Claws.

'I don't know. I mean, we don't have much.'

Stalker growled and resumed pacing. She had to find a way to make ordinary people afraid of this dodgy police officer. All they knew so far was that he had killed one drug dealer, and maybe a handful of other shady characters, all off the books and without any known professional repercussions for him. He may have a judge in his pocket, he may be running some scheme, he may not even be the top dog, maybe the judge in question was. There was no way to prove it and no clear reason for law-abiding citizens to be concerned. This was all just a big distraction, anyway. It was about Stalker's desire for more strength, when she had plenty already. She knew this, yet she coveted the power promised by the demon in the necklace, Savaging Fury. The Witch that she had taken it from had punched a hole right through the concrete floors of several storeys of a tower block in an effort to escape. If Stalker had that kind of strength it could prove vital in winning the war against the Furies.

'I'm just going to have to stretch the truth,' she said, halting again and looking wildly around the room. She was committed to this now, whether she liked it or not. The Knight-of-Shadowed-Fear would rip her spine from her body if she failed. She grabbed a sheet of blank paper and the photo from the newspaper, placed the photo in the middle and scribbled "WARNING! WATCH OUT FOR THIS MAN!" across the top.

'Fliers?' Claws asked, raising an eyebrow.

'Well, what else can I do? My spine depends on this.'

Claws nodded in understanding.

'I know. Look, wait.' He caught hold of her hands and stopped her frenzied scribbling on the rough flier. 'Let's do this right.'

They went to his laptop and together found a better photo of Reynolds from Claws' brief surveillance of him, one where he looked vaguely menacing, with deep shadows under his eyes, rather than the newspaper clipping showing him receiving a medal. They quickly made a more slick poster with dire warnings of danger from this corrupt scumbag.

'Put gloves on,' Claws warned, as they waited for the posters to print.

'It's April,' Stalker said, cocking an eyebrow.

'I know, but he will get his hands on these soon enough and has access to fingerprint databases.'

'I'm not on file anywhere, as far as I know.'

'That doesn't matter. You've been involved in break-ins and all sorts since you changed. It's entirely possible your prints are in the system, even if they haven't identified you yet. Better safe than sorry.'

Stalker grudgingly agreed and found an old pair of gloves rolled up amongst her things in the bedroom. She also put on a hooded top and baggy jeans to hide her figure. With any luck, any witnesses would think she was a boy.

After nightfall, Stalker left Grove Street with fifty or so copies of the poster and a staple gun. She pinned a copy to every wooden surface she passed: telephone poles, bill boards and a few of those pillars that nightclub posters always adorned. She found her way to a block of flats near the police station, a particularly rough neighbourhood, and went inside. There was a notice board, where she stuck a copy. But the crowning jewel was the bank of mail boxes. With a grin, she roughly folded each flier and shoved one through each slot. She left empty handed and jogged back to Grove Street, taking a few short cuts along the way. She felt Pursuit-of-Midnight-Solitude running alongside her, a sense of approval from her demonic ally soothed her pounding heart.

As she neared home, Stalker tapped a quick message to Rhys.

> Hi. You OK? The other night was nuts, eh? Can I see you tonight? Just heading back to the barn, but I could meet you afterwards. Let me know xx

The elation of getting a significant step closer to being finished with the Knight was making her giddy. Rhys was right about needing to come clean to her pack, and she would, but she wanted to enjoy their secret just a little longer.

She entered the house and strode through to the kitchen. A wall of silence greeted her, and the stern faces of her pack mates.

'Everything okay?' She slowly tugged her hoody off over her head, ruffling her hair. In the moment it took to run a hand through it to straighten it out, Weaver had clicked the kitchen door closed and Wind Talker had moved to fill the back doorway to the garden.

'We need to talk to you.' Eyes was sitting at the table, his hands clasped tightly in front of him. Claws sat beside him, chewing his nails and refusing to look at her.

An uncomfortable lump had formed suddenly in Stalker's throat.

'Okay. What about?' They were worrying her, blocking her exits and confronting her like this. She had never known them act like this. Had they discovered her secret? How? Her eyes settled on Claws. He knew about Rhys, although last she was aware he believed Rhys to be human. Maybe they were concerned about her risking a human life with her entanglement with the Knight. Maybe she could turn this around and reassure them.

'Your secret, Stalker, we know about it, we know everything.' Eyes' voice was hard, accusing.

'Look,' Stalker said, taking a step towards him and raising her hands. 'It's not how it seems. I needed something for myself, I needed somewhere to retreat to when I felt overwhelmed. I wasn't hiding anything harmful, I promise. I know you probably assume the worst and I don't know how much you know about it. You say you know everything, but I guarantee you don't have all of the information. He's safe, I swear. He isn't on any side in this war, he's neutral, like Switzerland!' She nodded and pointed a finger in triumph, her eyes wide.

'Stalker—' Claws looked up at her anxiously. But she was angry with him for betraying her confidence, even if it had happened accidentally.

'No, really. Look, no one even knows about him. You all thought he was human for months. I know you must have smelled him on me. No other shifters in Caerton know about him and the Furies have no idea he escaped, they probably think he was killed along with his pack years ago. He has so many protections in place.'

'Stalker!' Eyes barked. He placed his hand on a box on the table that she hadn't noticed before. 'This isn't about your love life, although I want to come back to that in a minute.' He slid the box across the table and flicked it open. 'We want to talk to you about this.'

She was confused. She didn't recognise it at first, and leaned closer to see what it was. The box was stuffed full of little objects, everyday things like burnt matches and sweet wrappers.

'What is this?'

'It's yours,' Claws said softly. There was a look of deep regret in his eyes. Stalker's heart started to thump wildly in her chest. Sweat broke out on her palms and a queasy feeling rose in her throat.

'I've never seen it before...' She faltered, looking down at it again. Flashes of memory flickered through her mind's eye. A folk song that got stuck in her head whenever she set foot near the attic, picking up a packet of sugar at the cafe last time she met Rhys, a goblin assuring her she would never remember. 'What the...?'

The panic swelled up and she lurched for the kitchen sink and vomited violently into it. Weaver was beside her in an instant, rubbing her back. Two realities were crashing together, memories rapidly re-writing themselves. She screwed her eyes up tight against the swaying stainless steel sink and the stink of her vomit filled her nostrils.

She had nothing to trade for the secret box at the goblin market, nothing she was willing to part with. Nothing except the very memory of buying it. The goblin had suggested the trade with glee. She remembered his pointed face now, and him handing the box to her in exchange for the forming memory. She vomited again. She was never meant to remember this, but the box being found was undoing the magic.

'Goblins are tricky creatures,' Wind Talker said softly, a reassuring hand on Stalker's shoulder. She groaned and felt her knees buckle. Weaver and Wind Talker guided her to a chair and sat her down in it. She let her head rest on her hands on the table, not daring to look at the box again.

'We're not so much concerned with the box itself,' Eyes said softly. 'It's the hoarding. Why are you collecting this rubbish?'

'I don't know,' she croaked, her throat stinging. 'I don't really remember.'

Wind Talker cleared his throat and she lifted her heavy head to look at him. He shifted his feet uncomfortably and huffed.

'What is it?' Eyes demanded.

'Well, I have a theory. Some shifters have been known to develop peculiar habits when they experience serious clashes between their human and shifter moral codes. Last-Breath-Echoes used to scratch door frames, I don't know if any of you ever noticed? She left little tally marks here and other places as she came and went. It was unconsciously done.'

Stalker had noticed. She glanced towards the hallway, knowing the marks were still on the living room door frame.

'Are you suggesting this happened to Stalker?' Weaver asked. She was sitting beside Stalker, stroking her back. It was comforting. Stalker took a shuddering breath.

'Yes.' Wind Talker nodded. 'When we encountered Jorogumo.'

A new wave of nausea flooded Stalker's senses; a cold sensation filled her throat.

'Oh no.' She lurched from the chair and just made it to the sink in time. The demonic spider's eerie clicking and crackling voice came back to her, along with Stalker's unhesitating finger pointing at her pack mate when asked to leave a sacrifice for The Hunger. She groaned and spat the lingering sick from her lips. Tears streaked down her face.

'I fear that decision may have caused real psychological damage.' His voice was heavy with regret, he didn't want to be bearing this news. Stalker knew he was right, it made perfect sense. She wondered if he had experienced any consequences for his mental health from executing Hidden Voice and taking the Alphaship from Eyes. He didn't seem to have suffered, but maybe his ability to justify his actions to himself protected him from anything like what she was experiencing.

'We'll help you get past this,' Weaver said, back to stroking Stalker's back. Claws appeared beside her with a glass of water. She took it and stood up, leaning heavily against the kitchen worktop. Claws gave the sink a quick clean and caught Stalker's eye. He gave her a look that told her he hadn't said a word about Rhys, he hadn't betrayed her at all. She had managed to do that all by herself. She closed her eyes wearily and glugged down the water.

'Stalker,' Wind Talker said softly, getting her attention completely for the first time. She looked at him, regret heavy on her shoulders. 'I completely understand why you did what you did, and I forgive you.'

A silent tear ran down her cheek and she nodded. She hadn't especially wanted his forgiveness, nor did she consciously regret the choice she had made. But this bizarre habit of hoarding small objects told a different story of her subconscious.

Eyes, however, cleared his throat. He was glaring at her and she felt herself wilt again.

'As for your not-so-secret affair. So he isn't human

and is actually a shifter who has gone to great lengths to conceal his existence from every shifter in the city, except you? Is that right?'

'It sounds awful when you say it like that,' she mumbled, looking down into the empty glass in her hand.

'But it's a fairly accurate summary? Correct?'

She nodded.

Before she could say anything, her phone buzzed with an incoming message. Stalker rolled her eyes to the ceiling, knowing it would be Rhys replying to her message. Then she realised her phone wasn't in her jeans, it was in the pocket on the front of her hoody, which was crumpled on the floor by Eyes' feet. He stooped to retrieve it before she could do anything.

'Oh Stalker,' Weaver whimpered.

'He is most likely Spiral Hand.' Wind Talker's expression was grim.

'No!' she yelled, lurching forwards for her phone. But Claws caught her arm and held her back. Eyes unlocked her phone and read the message, shaking his head.

'You can't see him again,' he said sternly.

'He's not Spiral Hand!' The shriek tore from her aching throat and cracked.

'We could take advantage of this,' Wind Talker suggested. 'Stalker could lead him into a trap.'

'I will not!' She wrenched her arm free of Claws' grip and scowled at him.

'I thought he was human,' he said defensively. 'If I'd known he was a secret shifter I'd have advised you to stop seeing him immediately. You lied to us all for months.'

'Technically I didn't lie! I didn't mention him at all,'

she added sheepishly.

'That doesn't make this any better,' Weaver said, the hurt evident in her voice.

'If Stalker won't cooperate to bring him in, and she obviously has impaired judgement at the moment, we have to prevent her seeing him.' Eyes stood and dropped her phone to the floor. He stomped on it hard, smashing it to pieces.

Stalker charged at him, a scream ripping from her lungs. Wind Talker and Claws were on her in an instant, pinning her arms to her sides and lifting her from her feet. She kicked wildly, desperate to get free and longing for the strength of Savaging Fury to release her. The talisman lay in the box of madness on the table, out of her reach. Even if she could have got her hands on it, it still wasn't attuned to her and would more likely lead to bloodshed than escape.

Her screams faded out, all energy leached from her body, and she went limp in her pack mates' arms.

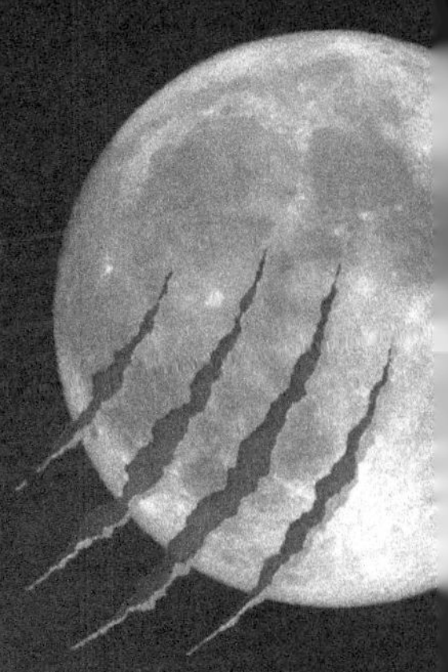

Chapter Seven

Numbness made her feet drag on the stairs as Stalker was marched up to the bedroom on instructions to rest. She was barely even aware of who was escorting her. Her shattered phone under Eyes' foot was all she could see. She lay down on her side on the squeaky bed with loose bed springs, her eyes glazed over, and the door closed behind somebody leaving the room. Tears rolled over her nose and down her cheek, pooling on the flattened pillow beneath her.

She had to see Rhys again. He would be worried sick if he didn't hear from her. He wasn't Spiral Hand. Why didn't her pack trust her judgement? The box of scraps might have more to do with that than anything else. Her eyes fluttered closed and she left the wet streaks on her face, drifting into oblivion without wiping them away.

Low voices nearby disturbed her some time later. The room was dark. A faint orange glow from the street lights filtered through the thin curtains.

'No, I absolutely believe her. There is no way she believed there was anything sinister about him.' It was Claws, defending her. A small smile crept onto her dry lips. She rolled onto her back and rubbed her eyes. They were thick with crusted sleep and her face felt grimy from her dried tears.

'Yes, I think you're probably right.' Weaver, barely audible on the other side of the door. 'But love can do funny things to a person's judgement.'

'So can hate,' Claws replied darkly. 'We've spent so long despising the Furies and Spiral Hand, mistrusting anything different, that maybe it's stopping us giving an innocent person the benefit of the doubt. If he is Spiral Hand, why would he seduce Stalker? What is he gaining?'

'She's special,' Weaver replied swiftly. 'You know that. She's different. Maybe the Spiral Hand would be interested in that, wanting to corrupt her, maybe?'

Stalker sat up, her head spinning slightly, and swung her feet to the floor. She was still fully dressed, including her shoes. Her feet thudded lightly on the bare floorboards. There was movement outside the door, Weaver and Claws getting to their feet, by the sounds of it. Stalker heaved a sigh and went to the door, opening it slowly. The hallway was darker than the room, no light from outside to lift the gloom.

'Hi,' Weaver said softly and far too brightly. 'How are you feeling?'

'Like I need a drink and to wash my face. Excuse me.' She nudged between them and crossed the hall to the bathroom, which flooded with light when she pulled the cord. She shielded her aching eyes and blinked furiously. She shut the door and locked it. Stubborn resistance to their agenda flared up inside her chest. Claws had been defending her, but they were guarding her. She knew what was coming in the days ahead. They would stick to her like glue, not letting her go anywhere alone. They would want to stop her collecting any more junk and absolutely prevent her from making contact with Rhys.

She stepped up to the sink and ran the hot water, waiting for it to warm up. Slowly it fogged up the mirror as she stood staring at her grim reflection. Eventually she dipped her head and began scooping up the water and splashing it onto her face. The hot water stung, in the best possible way, freshening her skin and making it tingle. When she was done, she ran the cold and scooped it straight into her mouth, drenching the parched feeling away. The taste of stale vomit ebbed away and she began to feel something like human again.

Claws and Weaver were still outside the door, waiting for her. She only had minutes. She wiped the mirror clean and turned off the light. Her eyes adjusted quickly to the dark and she stared at her shadowy reflection. Her eyes focused on the darkest shadows in the mirror, she willed to see movement. After a few seconds, there was a slight shimmer across the mirror and the shadows seemed to stretch a little deeper. Pursuit-of-Midnight-Solitude was there with her, she had answered Stalker's silent call. She could only hope that her pack hadn't caught it through their telepathic bond.

'I need to get a message to Rhys,' she whispered, as softly as possible so as to escape the notice of her guardian pack mates at the door. 'I need him to know that our secret has been discovered and my phone is gone. Can you get the message to him? Please?'

She had never tried communicating with the elusive demon. Their relationship was a coquettish chase through the city in the dead of night. The secrecy demon that had cloaked Rhys from shifters, demons and fae for so many years was sure to know by now that there had been a breach. She hoped that this was enough to allow a message to get to Rhys this way. If any demon or fae in Stalker's life knew about Rhys, it would be this one.

The shadows in the mirror flexed and then shimmered back to normal. Was that an agreement? Stalker took a deep breath and opened the door. Weaver and Claws stood anxiously in the hall, looking at Stalker expectantly as she emerged from the bathroom.

'It's creepy,' Stalker mumbled. 'You guys hanging around me.'

'It's for your own good,' Claws said gently. Stalker merely grunted before heading back to the bedroom. She remembered how the five of them used to curl up together in the living room when they first found the house. It seemed an age ago. So much had happened since then, they had been through so much. In one way they were closer than ever now, but they had also grown up. They weren't cubs any more, they were capable and responsible shifters, commanding their territory and bringing the city together to fight a war. For a brief moment, Stalker allowed herself the thought that she might not survive until her first anniversary of changing.

She knew at once that Weaver had caught the thought.

Weaver's eyes were shining in an instant and she grabbed Stalker and pulled her into a crippling embrace. Claws patted her shoulder awkwardly. Tears spilled from Stalker's eyes and she allowed herself to be wrapped up in the love her pack mates felt for her. Much as she resented their actions, in all honesty she understood them.

The three of them spent the rest of the night sleeping in the same room, although when she woke in the morning, Stalker suspected the others had taken turns watching over her to make sure she didn't slip out, based on their frequent yawns and barely concealed glances at one another.

As the pack assembled for a frosty breakfast, Stalker felt resentment prickling at every awkward silence and the forced politeness with her pack mates. Times like this put a strain on the pack bond. She remembered how Eyes had felt when Wind Talker stole the leadership away from him on the beach, the way she felt about the execution of Hidden Voice. This time it wasn't her and Eyes against Wind Talker, it felt like her against all of the others. She knew they wouldn't understand about Rhys, that they would suspect him and not trust her judgement. But she never imagined being held prisoner by her own pack. As she allowed her thoughts to dwell, unashamedly, on Rhys, the aching in her chest at the prospect of not seeing him again caused a tear to fall down her cheek. She knew the others would see, and that they would feel everything she felt through the telepathic connection between them all. But she didn't care. He wasn't her secret any more. They knew, even if they didn't believe her about him.

She had been so consumed with anger and grief over

Rhys, that she had barely registered the discovery of her hidden box. Its revelation had come as a complete surprise to her, but she hadn't had the mental space to process it yet.

She crunched on her cereal slowly and allowed her gaze to rise slightly from the bowl to take in her stoic pack mates busying themselves with their own breakfast around her. If she wanted to, she could give them the slip simply by shifting into a moth and fluttering out through the door, but she thought better of it. It would do no good to run now and could irrevocably break the pack. She took a steadying breath and glanced up again. Wind Talker stopped what he was doing and leaned against the kitchen counter, folded his arms over his chest and looked at her expectantly. He had read her thoughts and was waiting for her to voice them.

'So,' she said, her voice croaking. All eyes fell to her. 'This hoarding thing. I had no idea I was doing it.'

'We know,' Wind Talker said, nodding sagely.

'And it started, probably, around the time that I... that we... that you...'

'That's right.' Wind Talker didn't so much as flinch. The pack rarely brought up what had happened with Jorogumo, and it was always awkward when the topic arose.

'How do I stop doing it? If I don't know that I am?'

'Well, I think it coming out into the open now will probably be enough. Whatever spell that goblin put on your memory of the box is broken too, so if you do collect anything it should be more obvious to all of us.'

'What if I just find somewhere else to hide it?' Stalker

asked, worry and hurt gnawing at her insides.

'We'll keep a close eye on you,' Eyes said softly. There was no malice there, just concern for her well-being.

The rattle of the letter slot opening and something being stuffed through it drew all of their attention. They hardly ever received any post, as they mostly lived quite detached lives from the human world around them. Wind Talker frowned and strode down the hall towards the door.

'Stalker!'

She jumped at the call of her name and lurched up from her chair and down the hall to Wind Talker.

'What is it?'

He thrust a flyer into her hands and she saw that it was a poor photocopy of her own warning about Reynolds, the dirty police officer. She looked up into his face, her eyes wide. Without seeking permission or even a second thought, Stalker flung open the door and looked both ways. To the right, about three doors down the terrace, was a young man wearing a heavy satchel, his hand holding a thick wad of the leaflets. She charged down the street towards him.

'Hey! Excuse me!' she shouted. He looked up at her; his whole body went rigid, fear in his eyes. She thought for a second that he was going to bolt, but as he cast a wary glance up the street, he seemed to decide against it. She caught up to him quickly, vaguely aware of the pounding feet of Wind Talker just behind her. 'Where did you get this?' She held up the flyer.

'Someone has been putting them up around St. Mark's. A bunch of us saw them and decided to spread them further. Everyone needs to know about this.' His voice shook with passion and a hint of fear. Stalker and Wind Talker exchanged knowing looks.

'Right,' Stalker said, nodding. 'Yeah. Shit. Bloody pigs, eh?'

'Too right!'

'Well, thanks, for the public service. Be careful though, yeah? Don't get caught.' Stalker stared him right in the eye, searching inside him for his primary truth. Down through a dark tunnel, memories whipping past until she got right to the core of him, this boy, probably no older than her, but so much more innocent. A shrivelled and dark husk of fear was hunkered down inside him, hiding from the corrupt authorities that only looked after themselves. Just enough defiance to be out here, spreading the word, but not enough to overcome the fear. Perfect, just what the Knight wanted.

'Yeah, thanks,' he replied, looking at her warily. He stuffed the letterbox in front of him and went on his way down the street.

'That ought to secure my spine, don't you think?' she said quietly to Wind Talker as they walked back to number thirty-two.

'I hope so,' he replied.

Back inside, they filled in the others. A cold, hard knot twisted in her guts as she thought about what she had done. The memory of her first attempt to do a deal with the sinister demon, when she let the Beast take hold of her at her place of work, and trashed the building, left a sick feeling in her stomach.

Ron had found a church hall to hold some classes in while the dojo was repaired, but Stalker wasn't teaching.

She couldn't face it. She didn't know if she would ever be able to go back to it, not least because of her pack commitments taking so much of her time. Now that the pack were monitoring her every move, not to mention preparing for war, she also knew that she wouldn't be free to pursue her career right now anyway.

The day passed slowly, grinding through the motions of patrolling and preparing. Claws stayed with Stalker almost every minute, her watchful guardian. Whether the magic was broken, or the mental malady repaired, Stalker felt no compulsion to collect anything. No one needed to intercept her doing so subconsciously either. But perhaps with Rhys constantly on her mind, that other burning issue had fizzled out, for now.

As the days were getting longer, Stalker had to wait what felt like an eternity for night to fall. Somehow she yearned for the dark even more than usual. She needed the glaring sunshine to abate, for velvet blackness to swallow her grief. Perhaps her determination and defiance would kick in once she was surrounded by her familiar shadows. As the late afternoon stretched into early evening, the sky turned dusky orange and the shadows lengthened. Stalker could feel the energy bubbling up inside her. At the moment the sun dipped below the horizon and spilled red light across the sky, Stalker was washing up with Claws. The rest of the pack was out of the house. The kitchen was always darker than the rest of the house, due to the high wall around the north-facing back yard. Yet Stalker knew the instant the sun had set. The light barely changed, but she knew the moment had come.

As if on cue, the shadows in the room deepened and

stretched. Stalker's hands paused, covered in bubbles. A creeping sensation ran up her spine and the room grew five degrees cooler. Claws sensed it too. He fell still beside her, a tea towel limp in his hand, every muscle tense. Stalker heard the clink of armour and knew he was in the room. Slowly, she turned around. The Knight-of-Shadowed-Fear was standing in the middle of the kitchen, the black slit in his helm boring into Stalker.

Claws let out a small yelp, as his knees buckled and he slumped to the floor. Stalker lurched towards him, but was unable to move much, an invisible force rooted her to the spot. Her back shivered and the hairs on her bare arms stood on end.

'Are you happy?' she managed to croak. She narrowed her eyes to slits and shot the Knight her most venomous look.

'I am immensely satisfied, thank you.' There was something so dark and chilling about his tone of voice. The confused feeling that always overcame Stalker in his presence was working its way through her once again. His deep voice sent shivers through her, simultaneously repulsing and stimulating her.

'Good!' she spat.

'Your spine is safe, my dear.'

'Thank you,' Stalker said, more meekly.

'I believe I owe you this.' The Knight waved a hand. Stalker's talisman appeared in his armoured hand, tiny and insignificant against the dark metal. A single canine tooth on a black cord. It had been in Stalker's life since she had killed the young Witch that it had belonged to, so many months ago. She had felt its power, but never been able to harness it safely. The Knight raised it to his helmet. The visor slowly raised and Stalker watched, paralysed and transfixed, longing to see inside. There was nothing but inky blackness that seemed to stretch on far beyond the confines of the helmet. A rushing wind rose out of the empty armour, filling the kitchen with its eerie roar, like a gale down a chimney. Stalker's hair blew back and she blinked hard against the sudden rush of wind. The Knight's visor clinked shut, abruptly halting the wind. The talisman in his hand swung back and forth, jerking slightly with a mind of its own. After a few seconds it hung still, just turning slowly on its cord, drenched in shadow from the Knight, who blocked out all natural light from the small window onto the yard. He held it out towards her, and Stalker found she could again move. She reached out and took it.

The talisman hummed slightly as Stalker ran a finger over it. Claws shifted his weight on the floor beside Stalker, and she suddenly remembered that he was there. She dropped to her knees and put a hand on his shoulder.

'I'm all right.' He brushed her hand away and stared up at the Knight. Stalker rose to her feet again and stared down the demon.

'I take it that concludes our business?' There was no break in her voice, only strength.

The Knight merely nodded. He shimmered back across the veil, restoring the glowing orange light of dusk to the room.

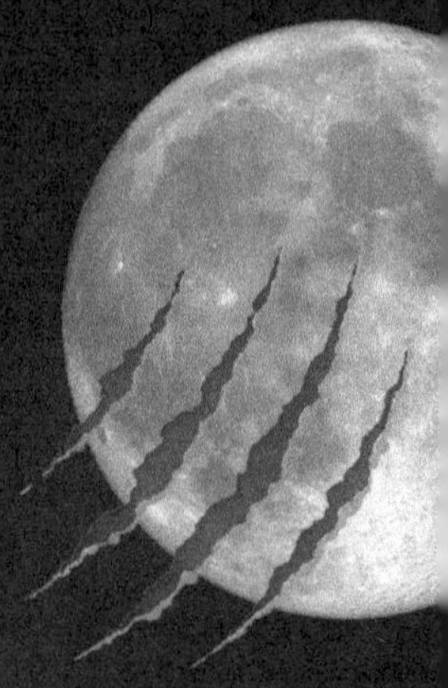

Chapter Eight

Stalker helped Claws to his feet. He looked pale and clammy.

'Will he ever stop doing that?'

'Probably not. But I don't think we will be having much more to do with him from now on.' Stalker flashed him a grin and grabbed his hand. 'Come on!' She charged across the veil, dragging Claws with her. The kitchen in Hepethia was a darker version of its human world counterpart. The kitchen table had been replaced with a meat block during their residency in the house. Stalker tried not to dwell on it and ran through the house and out into the street.

'What are we doing?' Claws hissed at her, following close at her heel.

'Testing my new toy. Where shall we go? Where can I really get a sense of what it can do?'

'What does it do again?'

'Well, I'm not totally sure, but the Witch I took it off

made a hole through the middle of a block of flats.'

'Right,' Claws said, giving her that withering look he always managed to pull off whenever she said something outlandish.

'It heightens everything; the Agrius gets stronger, basically. Heightened senses and greater strength. I want to hit something really hard. I need to, you know me. With everything that's happened in the last twenty-four hours. I'll feel better for it. Come on, let's find a demon!' She was bouncing on the balls of her feet, grinning like a lunatic. Claws stifled a laugh, rolled his eyes, then promptly shifted form, taking flight. Stalker grinned even more broadly then took off after him, shifting into owl form and soaring up over Hepethia. They flew together across the tangled, red brick maze of their neighbourhood.

They flew north towards the factories of Northgate and Stalker spotted something huge twisting its way between narrow terraces. *There!* She flew down towards it, Claws close behind.

They landed, shifting back into their human forms, just around the corner from the creature.

'Are you mad?' Claws snapped. Stalker peered around the corner and saw it clearly. It was the Baron-of-Blooded-Shards.

'Possibly.'

Claws grabbed her arm and yanked her back away from the corner.

'You cannot take that thing on, not on your own.'

'I'm not on my own.' She winked at him and spun away from him. A reckless desire for a fight had flared uncontrollably inside her and she didn't care. She had been ripped away from her human life, her shifter family slaughtered, fight after fight had taken its toll, and now her one source of calm and warmth, Rhys, had been taken from her. The fire inside flared passionately and she strode towards the powerful demonic construct, shifting into her Agrius form as she did so. This was no time to call on the lengthening twilight shadows, or the stealth of her fox moon. Just as Fortune had once stood in the path of a charging chaos demon on Red Bridge, Stalker strode out to meet the Baron.

On the edge of her subconscious, she knew Claws was there behind her, his gun drawn and aimed at the creature in her path. When she had worn the talisman before, it made her feel overwhelmed and ill. Now it was focused, attuned to her. The demon inside it knew her true name and was connected to her Agrius. She felt its power coursing through her veins. Her blood pumped more quickly, transmitting signals with crystal clarity. She could smell everything, hear everything, see everything. And when she drew both of her dha from her back they felt light and agile in her huge claws.

The Baron paused, and fixed his faceless gaze on her. She had been little more than an ant to him before, but now she was worthy of his notice. He could sense her power. Every scrap of metal and glass on his lorry-sized body glistened with blood. The metallic smell lingered in the back of Stalker's throat. A snarl rose up from her chest and she took a step towards the demon. It was fitting that she should encounter the enemy of the Knight-of-Shadowed-Fear now, when longing to test the new strength granted to her by him.

In the same instant, Stalker and the Baron charged at one another. A roar ripped up through her throat and she leapt into the air. The great, lumbering beast was too slow for her, and she landed on his back; the force of her landing was enough to halt him in his tracks and send his front end crashing down into the tarmac.

A shot rang out, but the bullet glanced off the Baron's armoured body, and Stalker heard Claws curse loudly. She raised her dha and drove them down into a narrow crack in the layers of metal and glass. The Baron roared and bucked hard, throwing Stalker to the ground. She rolled away from him as he twisted in pain. In an instant, she was back on her feet and going in for another strike. She was faster than ever before, the blood pumping to her muscles even more quickly than she was used to. With both swords in one hand, she leapt up again, grabbing hold of a protruding strut of metal with her free hand. She swung herself up onto his back once more and ran along it as he turned in circles, trying desperately to locate her. She found another weak spot and again drove both swords into the gap.

The Baron lurched sideways and crashed into a building, showering them both with dust and broken bricks. He groaned and lumbered across the street, crashing into the building on the other side and Stalker lost her footing. She slid down his back and narrowly avoided being trodden on by one of his huge feet.

She sheathed her dha and ran quickly towards his front end. If she could strike now while he was reeling and confused, then she could deal the final blow. She ran right past him, back towards Claws, who stood watching, helpless. With a skid, Stalker turned and ran back towards the Baron, gathering as much speed as she could. She raised her fists, leapt into the air and collided with the front of him. He didn't have a face, as such, but there was a roughly head-shaped bulge that had smoother plates of metal all over it. Her fists struck those plates and drove huge dents into them. A ripple ran right back through his body and glass shattered all over him, peppering the ground with broken shards. Every chunk of metal on his body seemed to bend and groan. It sounded like a vast building collapsing.

The Baron dropped to the ground, causing it to shake. Stalker landed nimbly beside him and stood tall and proud. There was a shimmer as every inch of the construct seemed to turn from solid, to liquid, to gas. And then he was gone. Stalker shifted back into her human form and turned to see Claws running over to her, confusion flooding his face.

'What just happened?' he asked.

'I was hoping you would tell me. Did I kill it? They don't normally do that.'

'We need Wind Talker. Come on, let's get back.'

The two of them moved quickly and quietly through the narrow, twisting streets. The sky was rapidly turning from orange, to purple. Soon it would be dark and Hepethia would be teeming with dangerous life. They knew these streets so well that it was impossible for them to get lost, even though they bore little resemblance to the neatly ordered rows of houses in the human world. Soon, they were back at 32 Grove Street and into the safety of their home. They crossed the veil and found Eyes and

Wind Talker back home.

'What's going on?' Eyes asked, his creased brow full of worry. Stalker was still buzzing with adrenaline and it took her a moment to realise that the strong feelings she and Claws had experienced over the last hour would have been picked up by the rest of the pack.

'The Knight paid us a visit,' Claws explained.

'And I wanted to test my talisman!' Stalker interrupted, bouncing as the glee mounted again. 'I took down the Baron! Can you believe it?'

'You did what?' Wind Talker asked, his voice leaping up an octave.

'I hit him really hard and he sort of shattered and then disappeared.' The bounce was gone from her step now and she wilted at the hard glares of her pack mates.

'I don't think she killed him,' Claws said softly, rubbing his stubble-covered jaw. 'It was strange. Not unlike when we kill a demon on this side and its remains cross the veil, except we were already in Hepethia and it was more like he evaporated.'

'A being that powerful can't be killed by smacking him in the face.' Wind Talker shook his head. 'Even with your undoubtedly great strength,' he added quickly, looking anxiously at Stalker's fixed gaze. 'No, it would take a combination of physical strength and ritual to banish him back to the demon realm. There is an awful lot that we can end permanently, but some forces are just that, a force, and you can't just get rid of it. It's like how humans understand physics, right? Nothing just begins or ends, it's all a matter of conversion from one form to another. Energy into matter, and back again. It's how we know the

King-of-Glass-and-Steel is alive. He couldn't just cease to be, he's too powerful.'

'Okay, so where did the Baron go?' Stalker asked, crossing her arms over her chest, her ego deflating a little. It had felt good to throw her strength into the fight, the elation was like a tonic. But that feeling was wearing off, especially with night falling outside the window. The shadows were twitching and calling her out to play and she knew she wouldn't be allowed to go alone.

'Perhaps he did cross over into another realm? Voluntarily?' Eyes offered an explanation.

'Perhaps. That would be unusual though.' Wind Talker chewed the inside of his mouth, lost in thought.

A shadow moved in the hall, an invitation to Stalker, drawing her towards the door and the freedom of the night.

'Is Weaver patrolling?' Stalker asked, her eyes flickering between the dark hallway and the faces of her pack mates.

'Yes,' Eyes replied, his thoughts not really engaged on Stalker.

'Shall I go out and find her? I could join her.'

'On your own?' Eyes' attention snapped firmly onto Stalker and she stopped, one foot in the hall already.

'Yes. Look, I'm twitchy from that fight. I need to run it off. None of you can keep up with me anyway. I'll be in Weaver's company within five minutes, maybe ten if she's right out in Fenwick. I won't go anywhere else or do anything else, just run to her.'

Claws gave an almost imperceptible nod, which Stalker saw and knew Eyes had too.

'Okay,' Eyes said. Stalker bounced and grinned. She mouthed "Thank you" to Claws and spun towards the door. 'But I want you both back in an hour. We're meeting Scribe.'

'No problem!' Stalker called over her shoulder, one hand already on the door handle. She flung the door wide and stepped out into the warm evening air. She was sprinting down the street in seconds, dodging pedestrians with ease. Around the corner, across the street, past the rows of bus stops on the bustling main street. The city was alive, more alive than she had ever known it. Her talisman felt warm against her skin and was changing the way she perceived everything. She was slower on the main road, due to the throng of people and cars; she could only pass at so much speed without causing an injury to some innocent human. She needed to get onto the back streets, away from the noise and stench of the people and cars.

Down one street, over a wall, up a taller building and onto the rooftops, and she was away. Sprinting across the territory. All thought of tracking Weaver gone. She was alone with the night air and the beautiful moonlight. Beside her, the veil rippled and a shadow passed through it. Stalker felt no alarm, only the familiar presence of Pursuit-of-Midnight-Solitude. She was called to the hunt more strongly than ever before and her patron allowed her to keep pace this time, not slipping ahead and spurring her on as usual.

'He knows,' the demon whispered, barely audible over the sound of the air whipping past Stalker's ears.

'Thank you,' she called back.

'He says he loves you and will see you as soon as

possible. Stay safe. Stay strong.'

Stalker slowed down and let the demon rush ahead. It was all going to work out, she suddenly felt confident of that. She ran on to the end of the terrace and jumped down onto a wall and then to the ground. She picked up Weaver's scent not far from there and raced to find her pack mate in Redfield.

Later that evening, the pack assembled by the bridge where the Scroll Archive was hidden. Scribe was waiting for them, anxiously looking up and down the river bank.

'You weren't followed?' he asked, still glancing around.

'No. What's wrong?' Eyes asked.

Scribe indicated for them to follow him under the bridge. Stalker checked that they weren't being watched, the coast was clear, as best she could tell, and they all dropped down over the wall and onto the clay bank. Scribe led them all into the narrow passage. The six of them barely fit inside.

'As I'm the last Scroll Keeper in Caerton, I make the rules now. This place was kept a closely guarded secret for decades. Echoes and I didn't even know where it was before you helped me find it after Flames-First-Guardian was killed.'

'We remember,' Stalker said softly.

'Well, that was for good reason. As far as I know, the only living shifters who know of its location are right here. Besides Father Ash, who I suppose we shouldn't forget about.' Scribe was speaking so quickly his words blended together.

'What did you find?' Eyes asked, his voice steady and patient.

'I've been researching the Furies,' Scribe replied. 'We know so little about them. The records here are good, but I have to view them with a historian's eye. A lot of them are, well, not necessarily reliable. Our job is to be impartial and keep accurate records, but like all passionate mortals, we can allow our bias to influence how we record events.'

Once again, Stalker felt herself drawn towards the small cubby on the wall that was stuffed with scrolls about the Blue Moon. The one for the Lightning Lords had been empty last time she had been here, but now two neat scrolls sat in their box. She wondered what was written on them, and who had written them.

'And?' Eyes pressed.

'Okay, so there are some references to the Furies, especially going back to the revolution. There are very few shifters alive now who were around when the last King of Caerton claimed the throne. Very few, like, maybe one.'

'Ragged Edge?' Stalker asked. But she knew the answer.

'Yes. And Father Ash.'

'What happened? How did it come to be that the Furies abandoned the city?' Weaver spoke up, her voice far away as she gazed at all of the writing on the walls.

'There was an uprising. For hundreds of years the two sects lived side by side in Caerton. The Furies were in charge, the Chosen of Artemis were subjugated, deemed inferior. During World War Two, a number of our kind joined the army to fight. It was a way of helping to protect humanity. But as many as possible stayed behind to defend Caerton. The Furies had to get their hands dirty, even though their goal has always been to conquer humanity.

There just weren't enough shifters to guard the veil. It gets difficult to sort through the propaganda. You know how history is written by the victors? Well, it seems the Furies decided to try and press their agenda while humanity was at war. They tried to bring humanity under their control more overtly, rather than the subtle manipulation that they had always engaged in before. Caerton was bombed in the blitz, we lost the docks. Lots of people died.'

Stalker felt a lump rise in her throat as she remembered Fortune telling the story of his first change one night in the betting shop kitchen. She didn't need to look at the faces of her pack mates, they remembered too, except Claws, who wasn't with them yet that night. Fortune had changed during the bombing and slaughtered the people in the factory where he worked. Their deaths would have been blamed on the bombing.

'Well, the Chosen of Artemis realised what the Furies were doing, using the bombing to mask their culling of the human population. It seems someone defected and revealed the Furies' plan to slaughter the humans and bring the survivors under their control. There was a revolution. We fought the Furies and executed the king. The survivors were exiled. Our predecessors believed the Furies would never survive out in the wild. But they did what they have always done, found a way to thrive. They spread out, encircling the city. We've pretty much been under siege for the last forty years. Not that our elders tell us this.'

'So we've all been going about, believing our side won and banished the Furies, when really we're trapped in the city?' Claws asked. Straight to the point, as ever.

'Pretty much. I mean, not entirely. We did kill the king and banish the Furies. We did really think we'd won. It was only much later that it became known how many Furies there were out there.'

'Where have they been getting their population from?' Wind Talker asked. He was thumbing through the scrolls on the pack shelves.

'A lot of in-breeding, I'd guess,' Scribe said, shrugging.

'The packs in the city have kept careful genealogies, so that new shifters can be traced and recruited quickly in a dense urban population. It has been necessary for us to spread out, because of our ethos and the effect we have on humans.' Weaver was speaking so matter-of-factly that it caught Stalker slightly off guard. She had been raised by Furies on the edge of the city. This subject couldn't be easy for her, but she remained dispassionate. 'But in the country the Furies have been able to avoid humanity while still living in big groups. They wouldn't breed with humans, because of their beliefs, which has kept their blood much more focused. Aside from the narrow gene pool thing. So you can pretty much guarantee that every child born will change.'

'They indoctrinate their young,' Stalker said. Her voice cracked a little, but she cleared her throat and went on. 'They're raising an army of zealots. But they aren't united, there is fighting between sects.'

'How do you know that?' Scribe asked, a deep frown furrowing his brow.

'She has a source,' Wind Talker interjected.

Stalker felt a flutter of appreciation for him keeping her secret.

'I see.'

'My source's entire pack was wiped out by another. He was on his own in the forest for his first change.' She lifted her chin and stared defiantly at Eyes, who avoided her gaze. 'I am certain of his honesty, I saw his inner truth.'

'That's really useful to know,' Scribe said, his face lighting up. He grabbed for parchment and ink and began scribbling in his tiny handwriting. 'Do you know any specific details? Names? Places?'

'No, and I can't ask right now.' She glowered at Eyes, who had the good sense to look down at his feet. 'Just that they lived in the forest, about fifty miles east of here, and that they were of the sect of Alecto. There are three.'

'That's right,' Weaver said softly. 'Alecto, Tisiphone and Megaira. If the heir has been able to unite them, we could be facing a formidable force. Hundreds of shifters.'

'How many shifters are there in Caerton?' Claws asked, tension in his voice.

'About sixty-five,' Scribe replied.

'Right, well, we know when they're coming,' Eyes said, puffing up his chest. 'We just need to be ready.'

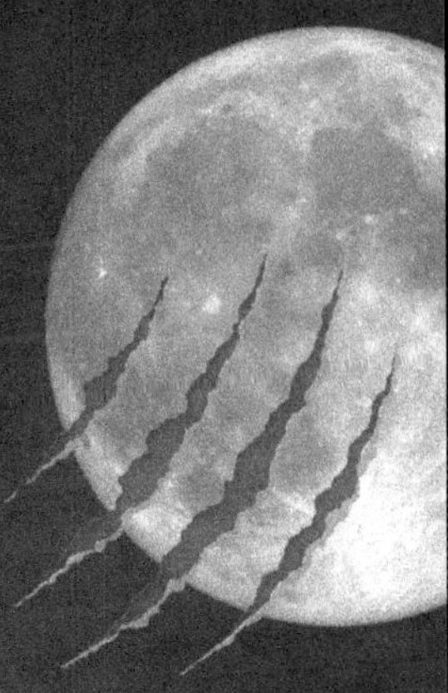

Chapter Nine

'We need him, Eyes. We just do. He has valuable information and may even be willing to fight on our side.' The pack marched briskly back towards Grove Street, after parting ways with Scribe.

'I don't see it that way, I'm sorry. It's too much of a risk. He knows too much about us already.'

'You don't know that. You have no idea. You weren't there for every one of our conversations. He hardly knows anything about us. Because guess what, I was unsure too! I kept him separate from you guys and you separate from him. Don't cross the streams! He knows our names. That's about it. He doesn't even know what forms you all take, or who our allies are. The only way he could even know our territory boundary is if he went sniffing around, which I have absolutely no reason to suspect he ever did.'

Eyes stopped abruptly and turned to face her. Stalker plonked her hands on her hips and glared at him. The rest of the pack came to a halt around them.

'It would be one thing if he were just a former Fury. But we know we are dealing with the Spiral Hand and have no way to rule out the possibility that he is one of them.' Stalker opened her mouth to object, but Eyes continued. 'I trust you, I really do. I trust that you believe he isn't. But the tricky thing about them is that they can conceal themselves expertly. That is what makes them so insidious. They can be hidden amongst our kind without a trace. After all these years, still no one really knows if Father Ash can be trusted or not.'

'Yeah, well, he's been banished, hasn't he? No one has spoken to him in ten years, except us. No one has taken the time to find out. They just exiled him on the spot.' Stalker huffed and crossed her arms over her chest.

'It's my understanding that there was actually a lengthy investigation,' Wind Talker said. Stalker shot him an angry glance.

'We weren't there. It's irrelevant. It could still be him, it could be just him. We don't know.' Stalker tried not to let her voice shake, but failed miserably.

'Exactly,' Claws said, gently placing a hand on her shoulder. She didn't immediately shrug it away. His calming presence caused her to draw a steadying breath. 'We simply don't know. For that very reason, we have to keep our counsel. We have to be cautious. I think you have a valid point, Stalker, I really do. I think Rhys could be extremely valuable. But we need to proceed carefully.'

'What are you suggesting?' Eyes said, frowning.

'I think I, at least, should meet Rhys, and ask him some direct questions. I can tell if he's lying.'

'If it were that simple, we would never have had a problem with Spiral Hand.' Eyes shook his head and set off walking again. The others scurried after him. 'Don't you think other half-moons have tried that? Don't you think that would be the very first thing any pack would do if they had a suspected Spiral Hand in custody? Why would the Blue Moon go to such lengths to lock away Hidden Voice, or the council exile Father Ash, if a yes-no question in the presence of a half-moon would do the trick?'

'Your ability is basically a shifter lie detector,' Wind Talker said, shrugging apologetically. 'It can be fooled.' Claws huffed, obviously rankled at the dismissal of his ability.

As the pack swiftly crossed St. Mark's in the dead of night, the streets still and quiet, Stalker felt an unpleasantly familiar creeping sensation up her spine. She came to a halt, the pack continuing a few steps before realising she had stopped.

'What's wrong?' Weaver asked, the first to Stalker's side.

'The Knight, he's here.' Everyone looked around, forming an outward-facing huddle. 'No, not here, here, on the other side of the veil, I think.' Stalker huffed impatiently. Beside her, Wind Talker grasped his talisman and looked across the veil, his eyes clouding over.

'She's right, and he's not alone. They're marching, all of them, his army is on the move!'

'We're keeping out of it,' Eyes insisted.

'We can't,' Stalker said, her cheeks drooping as reality dawned on her. 'Not after what I did to the Baron earlier. We're already involved.'

'Dammit,' Eyes hissed. 'We were supposed to be staying neutral.'

'The Knight may not know Stalker was involved,' Claws suggested, his tone feigning optimism.

'I think it's a safe bet he does, given our connection. I'm sorry, Eyes. I wasn't thinking earlier.'

'What's done is done. We'd better cross over.' Eyes led them off the main road and into a dark and deserted alley. They crossed the veil into Hepethia and moved cautiously back to the main road. Stalker heard them before she saw them, a vast army of stomping boots. The Lightning Lords were just coming upon them at the tail end of their column, and bringing up the rear, atop a jet black steed, was the Knight himself.

Without a word of a command from him, seemingly connected as one, the column halted. Every type of fear demon was represented: scuttling, spider-like creatures; twisted goblins; shadowy wisps; all clad in armour and carrying swords and shields. Stalker could guess at the demons with rank, they were bigger, stronger and although totally inhuman, they carried a familiar air of authority that sergeants and lieutenants did in films she had watched.

The Knight turned his head slowly towards the Lightning Lords and a heavy sigh rattled from inside his helmet.

'There you are. I wondered if you would come. Do you wish to join the column?'

'No,' Eyes said, firmly, raising his hands. 'We told you we wished to remain neutral. That is still the case.'

'Ahh, yes.' The Knight's voice hissed, snake-like

and satisfied. 'But my dear Stalker put an end to that notion today. The Baron's forces are in disarray with his disappearance. We must press our advantage.'

'I didn't mean to!' Stalker snapped. 'It was my talisman, after you attuned it to me it sort of, dragged me out to— Oh. It was you, wasn't it? You did something to it.'

'I don't know what you could possibly be talking about. I did nothing. It was you, it was your nature. I believe I understand that trinket better than you do. Are you sure you should be wearing it?'

Stalker folded her arms and glowered at him defiantly, but kept her mouth shut. She refused to be goaded into saying something she might regret. Her hot head had gotten her into enough trouble already.

'We won't join your battle,' Eyes insisted. 'What's done is done. You do what you have to do, but we are only here to protect our territory. Once the battle is over, you leave and never come back. We won't let our people suffer in fear any longer.'

'Strong little Alpha, boy, playing at tin soldiers. You desire to command an army of your own, you seek to unite your kind against a common foe. You pretend at everything. You pretend at defying me, just as you pretend at leading your people. You are a cub, not yet a year changed, and you think you can stand up to me, or any of my kind? You think you can defeat a legion of Furies knocking at your door? You think you can uncover a cult that has existed in the shadows for centuries? I know your heart, little boy; I know your deepest fears, I can smell them all over you. You fear failure, you fear rejection, you fear your friends and allies. All dressed up in Daddy's big shoes, but not enough flesh to fill them. You are a coward, Fights-Eyes-Open.'

Stalker dropped her gaze to the floor and covered her face with her hands. She felt Eyes swell beside her, fury flaring up inside him. She knew this was about to turn terribly ugly.

But Eyes was still able to surprise her. He laughed.

The Knight had leaned closer and closer during his tirade, seeming to stretch down from atop his steed, like a shadow approaching sunset, but now he flinched and retracted, shrinking back to his normal size.

'I won't fight your army. Your quarrel is not with us. Move along.'

The Knight pulled his horse around in a circle and when they stopped, the horse was frothing at the mouth and pawed at the ground. The army was twitching, growing restless. The officers looked to their General for a signal. Stalker tensed, ready for this situation to explode.

'I won't be going anywhere. My enemy is right here. Among your pitiful number.'

The army turned, as one, to face the Lightning Lords. A great sea of demons stretching away down the narrow terraced street. The Knight turned his eyeless gaze on Claws and pointed a metal-plated finger. 'In your weapon.'

'What?!' Claws flinched, his eyes wide and mouth agog. His hand went reflexively to his concealed gun, but he didn't draw it. 'What are you on about?'

'The Baron-of-Blooded-Shards is hiding in your weapon.'

'What? I...Eh?' Claws stumbled over words and sounds, seemingly unable to form a coherent string of them. He searched the faces of his pack mates, who were all as shocked as him.

'Oh!' Stalker pointed at him, realisation dawning. 'You shot at him. Remember? Before I hit him. I bet my swords are too simple for him, so he latched onto your gun when he disappeared and hid inside it.'

'But he's huge,' Claws objected, as he carefully withdrew his gun and held it out, gingerly, as if afraid it might suddenly go off.

'Size doesn't matter,' the Knight said with a smirk in his voice. A few nearby grunts cackled.

'He is a construct of machinery and murder,' Wind Talker said, staring avidly at the gun. 'It makes sense.'

'Fire it,' the Knight instructed. 'That way.' He pointed down the street, away from his army.

Claws glanced at Eyes for confirmation. The Alpha nodded solemnly.

'Brace yourselves,' Claws said, as he grasped the gun and pointed it towards a building fifty yards away. He fired a single shot, which echoed eerily. The shell dropped to the floor with a barely audible *clink*, and out of the barrel burst the Baron, in all his bloody glory. He erupted back to his full-sized self with a horrifying roar.

Eyes grabbed Stalker and Claws and dragged them hurriedly back towards the alley, Wind Talker and Weaver rushing with them. The five of them hunkered down as the Knight's army charged towards the Baron.

'Are we seriously not going to fight?' Stalker hissed, watching as the two forces clashed with roars from both sides and the clanking of metal on metal.

'Seriously. You can't honestly want to get caught up in

the middle of that?' Eyes nodded towards the fray. Stalker shrugged meekly, no apology or explanation necessary.

'He was in my gun. I can't believe it. How did I not know? How did I not feel it?'

'He wasn't in there for long. Maybe over days you would have started to feel more murderous?' Wind Talker said. 'He did want to stay hidden, remember.'

'True.' Claws still looked disappointed in himself, but Stalker suspected time would heal that. She could barely keep her eyes from the fight. From the rooftops around them, scuttling constructs came; the Baron's scattered forces coming to his aid.

The battle was frenzied, all pretence of organised, military precision abandoned in favour of a gruesome brawl. Stalker momentarily realised that that was true of all conflict, when you got right down to it. Demons scrambled over one another, the Knight's forces rushing wave after wave upon the Baron and his minions. They ripped and clawed each other apart, spilling black blood onto the tarmac. The Knight didn't move, he sat on his huge, black horse, watching the battle. Just for a moment, he didn't seem like a terrifying demon; he seemed like a medieval king, watching a battle dispassionately from afar.

His army made short work of the Baron's disorganised troops, vastly outnumbering them. Stalker was certain that she saw several of the Baron's underlings switch sides mid-battle, ultimately protecting their own interests above those of their master. Soon, the tank-like murder demon stood alone in a sea of jabbering little monsters.

The Knight's horse moved forward and the sea parted for him, a hush fell upon the crowd. The Baron was hunched, half on the ground, and groaning. Stalker watched, her breath caught in her throat. Her hand was curled around her new talisman and she could feel the pulse in her hand, racing furiously. A soft tingle ran up and down her spine as she waited to see what the Knight would do.

Without a word, the Knight raised his huge broadsword and drove it down, point first, into the neck of the defeated Baron. His minions erupted into gleeful cackling and the Baron fell to the ground with a thunderous clatter.

'You didn't think he would give the Baron a chance to surrender, did you?' Wind Talker asked, sensing Stalker's shock. She glanced at him, before returning her gaze to the celebrating demons in the street.

'No, not really.'

The Lightning Lords emerged, carefully, from the alley and stood on the edges of the throng of manic demons. The Knight, atop his huge, black steed, stood over his kill, surveying his minions, who had now grown in number with the defections of the last of the Baron's followers. Stalker watched as a ripple passed through the air from the Baron, into the Knight; the transference of energy. The Knight swelled and darkened, seeming to swallow the night that was folded around him. He had grown more powerful, both in himself, and in the legions under his command. Stalker chewed the inside of her mouth as she worried that he would not honour his vow to leave their territory once the fight was over. He may see this as his territory now. He had come back to this world thanks to the Witches' attack on Eyes' family and Stalker could imagine him not being eager to leave it now.

'My friends, our shapeshifter hosts have been exceedingly patient. But the time has come for us to return to our own realm. Svartalfheim calls to us. We shall return victorious and claim the power that is rightfully ours.' The Knight didn't need to raise his voice to be heard by the masses, his voice seemed to be projected directly into the minds of everyone present in the same threatening rumble that Stalker was now so accustomed to. She released a shaking breath and finally released her talisman from her sweating palm.

With a wave of his arm, the Knight opened a rift over the Baron's body, channelling some of the energy of the kill into what would take a shifter enormous effort. The throbbing crowd of excited demons tumbled towards the swirling rift. Stalker felt darkness leaking out through it and urged the demons to cross over quickly. The Knight remained on his horse, standing back to let his minions scurry through first. His head turned towards Stalker and her pack and he gave the slightest nod. Stalker felt sure that if he had a face, he would be smiling.

As the last trickle of demons flowed through the rift, the Knight's horse took a step towards the Lightning Lords. 'Thank you for your hospitality. This visit has been most.... productive. By the way, you might want to attend to the Bronze Lord sooner rather than later.' Without waiting for a response, the Knight turned his horse and cantered away through the rift. It spun shut and sealed tight behind him, leaving just a flicker of street lamps and thin mist in his wake.

Stalker looked into the shocked faces of her pack mates. One question hung on all of their lips.

'Who the hell is the Bronze Lord?'

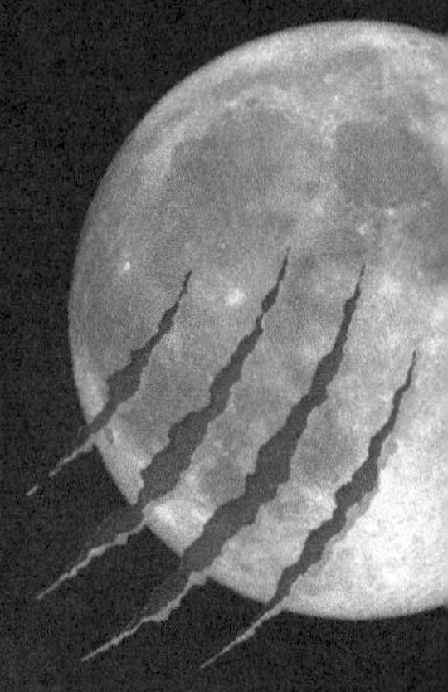

CHAPTER TEN

WEAVER-OF-SKY'S-LOOM

'RESEARCH MODE, THEN?' Weaver asked, as the Lightning Lords traipsed in through the door of 32 Grove Street.

'Absolutely,' Eyes replied. 'I want answers by the morning, please.'

Weaver nodded and exchanged nervous glances with Wind Talker. As the pack dispersed to their various duties, Weaver and Wind Talker went up to the attic and began looking through what notes they had.

'There isn't anything here.' Wind Talker sighed after just a few minutes. He leaned back against the bureau behind him, his hands behind his head.

Weaver watched the dust swirling gently in the light above. Her eyes felt heavy. It had been a long day.

'I wonder what the Witches did with all of the notes they took from here. We really should have tried to get them back.'

'I looked. After the Green Man. I searched the territory,

but didn't find anything.'

Weaver blinked at Wind Talker in surprise.

'Why didn't you ask for help?'

'It was something I needed to do for myself.' He shrugged and let his hands drop to his sides.

'Maybe they destroyed them.'

'I'd give more than my childhood memories to know where the Alpha went.'

Weaver let a small, sad smile play on her lips as she watched her pack brother. He had a defeated air about him that she was not accustomed to seeing. He had sacrificed so much for the pack. Most of the others would never understand it. The two of them had been the only ones to grow up with their shifter kin, fully aware of what the future may hold for them. Her parents had sought to shield her and her sister from the Furies, but they hadn't hidden everything. Weaver had always known the truth and was prepared for the change. But she had been away from her family for two years when it happened, living in Caerton against their wishes. Her parents had never left the Furies, no one ever did, but they had turned their backs on the ideology that was so poisonous and had spared Weaver any of the indoctrination. Her sister had not been so fortunate. The memory of her broken sister made her chest ache.

Wind Talker had sacrificed his childhood memories for the knowledge of how to defeat the Green Man. Weaver had sacrificed her sister. She tried to reconcile killing her by telling herself that Maria had been evil. But she knew that wasn't true. She had been brainwashed to believe the toxic lies of the Furies. Perhaps she could have been saved, the brainwashing undone. Humans did that with people who joined cults, so she knew it was possible. Perhaps she should have tried harder to save her sister.

But that chance was gone and Weaver knew she had to be pragmatic and put it behind her. This was her life and the risks were immense. She had always known that.

If only she could help Stalker to see that.

With a sigh, Weaver repacked the box that she had idly rifled through. Their notes these days were reduced to what she and Wind Talker could remember and had managed to copy from memory, with Claws' help.

Wind Talker shifted his weight and nudged the bureau. Its feet scraped dully on the wooden floor. There was a light *clink* and a small glass vial rolled out from underneath it, right into Wind Talker's leg. Weaver watched, her curiosity piqued, as Wind Talker picked it up and held it in the light. It was filled with a thick, dark liquid.

'Is that blood?'

'Looks like it.' Wind Talker's voice was far away as he gazed at the little sample.

'Whose is it?'

'How should I know?'

Weaver crawled quickly across the floor and pressed her face to the warm wood, peering under the bureau. 'What are you doing?' Wind Talker asked acidly.

'It fell from under here. I'm looking to see if there is anything else.'

Wind Talker put down the vial and moved away from the bureau. Together they shuffled it forwards a little then leaned it back against the wall. Weaver felt all around the base. There was a narrow ridge along the back, which must have been where the vial was hidden, but there was nothing else there.

They restored the little cupboard to its place and sat together to examine the vial more closely.

'Can we test it?' Weaver asked. 'Is there anything we can do to work out whose it is?'

'Perhaps.' Wind Talker had that far away tone to his voice again. 'I'm not sure if there is a ritual, there may be. But we may need your science.'

'Science is only any good with something to compare it to.'

'Hmm.'

'Flames must have hidden it though, right?'

'Yes, I think so.'

'Do you ever think that we just didn't know them at all?'

'Constantly. But that doesn't mean anything bad. We were all still so new when they died. We hadn't had the chance to get to know them yet. I still grieve for them, they were family.'

Weaver nodded. She understood. Speaks-With-Stone had been there when she changed for the first time and had been like a sister to her in the short time they were pack mates. The connection pack mates shared was beyond biological family, beyond blood.

'Oh!' She grabbed the vial from Wind Talker's hand and held it up to the light.

'What? What is it?'

'Remember that ritual just after Stalker joined the Blue Moon? Flames took all of our blood. Could this be it?'

'Shit. Yes, it could. But it could equally be anyone's. We

can't know for sure.' He took it back and stood up, holding it closer to the naked bulb hanging from the ceiling. 'If it is, I mean, of course he would hide it.'

He was running ahead of Weaver in his chain of thought, blurting out nonsensical phrases that probably wove together in his own thoughts but left Weaver hanging on for a full explanation.

'It would be potent, wouldn't it?' she asked, already knowing the answer.

'Very. Eight shifters' blood, a large pack, united by the bond. Fortune and Shadow's Step were very old. Their blood alone could be incredibly powerful.'

'What would Flames keep it for?' A nervous knot had formed in her stomach.

'A future ritual, probably.' He glanced at her warily, but there was a glint in his eye.

'What are you thinking?' she asked out loud, out of politeness. She had already heard his thought in her own mind through their telepathic bond.

'It might come in useful. It might help in summoning the King-of-Glass-and-Steel.'

Weaver nodded solemnly.

'We need to keep it safe then.'

'Absolutely.'

'But right now we need to find out who the Bronze Lord is.'

Wind Talker picked up his satchel, which was never far from his side, and tucked the vial away into a small inside pocket.

'We won't find anything here. We would know if we'd ever come across the term before. Could we try the Scroll

Archive?'

'Not without Scribe, it wouldn't be right.' Weaver shook her head.

'I'm a little tired of this. It's on our territory.'

'I know, but none of us is a Scroll Keeper.'

'You could change that.'

'Not in the three hours we have before dawn.'

'Maybe you could meditate on it?'

Weaver rubbed her eyes and nodded. It had worked before, bringing on a vision by meditating. It might work again. But the aching in her muscles told her she was too exhausted to focus.

'I have to sleep first. Eyes will have to wait.'

Wind Talker nodded sympathetically. They left the attic together and made their way downstairs. The front door opened as Weaver reached the foot of the stairs, and Stalker entered. She locked eyes with Weaver and stood frozen in the doorway.

'Er, hi. I thought everyone was asleep. I was patrolling.'

'On your own?' Weaver asked, raising an eyebrow. Wind Talker clucked his tongue and squeezed past Weaver without a word, disappearing into the living room.

'Check my pockets, I'm clean.' She slammed the door behind her and stood facing Weaver in the dark hall.

'I'm not concerned about that,' Weaver snapped. 'The hoarding will resolve itself. I'm more concerned about who you're communicating with.'

'Weaver, you are not my mother, thank Artemis!'

'No, but I am your sister and I care about you. I want to make sure you're making healthy choices.'

'They are my choices to make. I am my own person.'

Weaver sighed. She shook her head and looked down at the floor. There were only a few years between them, but at times she felt weary with the different stages they were at. Being a shifter was a privilege not to be wasted.

'You cling to your human past, Stalker. You have to be able to let it go. Being a shifter is not a solo sport, it's a team one.'

'Yes, and every member of a team brings their own unique strengths to it. That's why Artemis makes us all different, some of us more different than others. The whole goal of this life is to balance things. We protect humanity and have to live amongst them; we have to be able to blend in. You've seen the way humans react to us, especially the older, more powerful shifters. It's a problem. We have to try to retain our humanity so we can still live among them and not give ourselves away.'

'You aren't human, though. You are a shifter. It is fundamentally different. I'm not saying don't try to blend in, but we do that by mimicking humans, not by thinking we are like them.'

'You're too detached, Weaver. You can be so cold.' Stalker shook her head and pushed past Weaver, following Wind Talker to the living room.

Weaver watched her go, the sting of her words as fresh as a slap across the face. She waited a moment for the tears that threatened to spill to ebb away. With a deep breath, she slunk into the living room and surveyed the odd collection of animals curled up on the human furniture. From the lack of snores, and the chaotic thoughts dancing around the room, Weaver knew that no one was asleep. She shifted into her silky cat form and curled up under the window.

It took a while, but sleep finally claimed her.

She was drifting, swaying through the crowd. The red faces were greedy and anxious. The chequered floor beneath her feet shone with blood. Somewhere ahead was the grinding of machinery and when she rose above the throbbing mass of people, she saw the bones. A vast machine with cogs and conveyor belts churned away, clanking and banging as it ground bones to dust. At the other end of the hall was a throne. Upon it sat a finely dressed nobleman made of bronze. He sat as still as a statue. His face was covered by a wooden mask with narrow slits for eyes. At his feet, a dozen humans crouched around a dead body, devouring its innards with their bare hands. Blood soaked their hands and faces and stained their clothes. Their piercing eyes were fixed on the Bronze Lord.

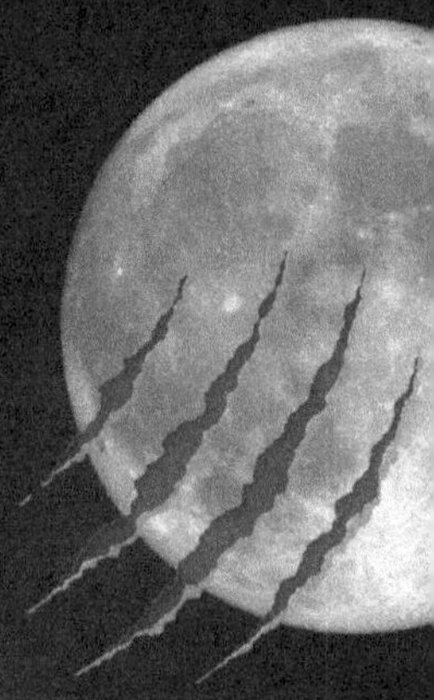

Chapter Eleven

Stalker-of-Night's-Shadow

Bile rose in her throat and Stalker was wrenched from sleep. She sat up, panting and coughing. She had shifted from her fox form back into her human self. Around the room, her pack mates were shifting and looking around in alarm.

Claws was the first to Weaver's side.

'It's okay, we're here. It was a vision. We saw.'

Weaver was shaking. Sweat shone on her pale skin.

'Why can't she send me visions of puppies and kittens?' She managed a strangled laugh. Stalker moved slowly to Weaver's side, pushing aside their argument.

'Any thoughts on what it meant?' Claws asked softly, rubbing Weaver's back. Weaver let out a guttural laugh. 'Sorry, silly question.'

'No, it's okay. I think it's clear that the cannibal cult and the Hunger are connected to this Bronze Lord somehow.'

'Well, in a way that's a good thing.' Everyone stared at

Stalker as if she had gone mad. 'No, listen, if the Bronze Lord was totally unconnected then it would be yet another demon to figure out, track down and get rid of, another distraction. But it's all connected. It's part of the same fight. It's another piece of the puzzle and we were really short on those, so this helps.'

'Stalker's right,' Wind Talker said gruffly, his voice thick with sleep. 'It's not yet another thing to tackle, it's a target. We've had so much on our plates, with the Witches and Furies and Spiral Hand, we've hardly had a chance to get a handle on our territory. The Knight-of-Shadowed-Fear may have left, but he was hardly our only resident demon, and now we have to deal with the rest.'

'The cannibals and the Hunger have been a problem across the city,' Claws added. 'We should share this new information and find out what other packs know.'

'I'll contact Ragged Edge,' Stalker said. It was daylight, but still early. Eyes wasn't with them, he had taken the last patrol and wasn't back yet. 'Odin's Warriors warned us about the cannibals at the Danegeld. He may know something that could help.'

The pack got up and busied themselves getting ready for the day. The lack of a phone prevented Stalker from calling Ragged Edge and she couldn't remember his number to use someone else's. So she had to revert to a traditional method. She cut her thumb and rubbed the blood against the wooden window frame of the bedroom. She opened the window and watched the blue sky. Sure enough, a raven appeared, winging its way to her. She hastily scribbled a note.

My phone got damaged. Hopefully I'll get a new one

soon. Need to know about Hunger and cannibals. We have news: the Bronze Lord is on our territory and is somehow connected. Do you know anything that could help? Thanks, Stalker

The raven landed on the sill and Stalker quickly rolled up the scrap of paper. 'I need this to get to Ragged Edge of The Watch. Can you take it to him please?'

The bird bobbed its head in assent, grasped the scroll in its beak and took flight.

With an anxious glance over her shoulder, Stalker decided to summon another ally. She sucked the blood from her thumb and closed the window. She moved quietly into the bathroom and locked the door, plunging herself into darkness. There was no window in the poky room and it constantly smelled damp. With nothing but a sliver of light around the door, Stalker stared into the mirror. 'Rhys?' she whispered anxiously. The shadows twitched around her and in the reflection she saw a dark figure peel itself away from the wall behind her. It was a secrecy demon. 'I need to know if he's okay,' she whispered, staring hard at the wisp of a reflection. 'Tell him we have to investigate something today, but that I will talk to him later. He can meet me in the mirror.'

The demon let out a low hiss and vanished. Knowing someone might come looking for her if she was gone too long, Stalker vacated the bathroom quickly and jogged down to the kitchen. Claws was swinging his jacket on, a piece of toast hanging out of his mouth.

'Off to do my mojo,' he said, chewing his toast. Stalker nodded in reply and watched him leave. Weaver sat at the table, sketching furiously. The images from her vision being brought to life by the dark lead in her pencil.

'How are you feeling?' Stalker asked, pouring a coffee. Weaver shrugged in reply and continued drawing. 'It was a particularly gruelling vision. They aren't all that bad.'

'No, but they all hurt my head and make me feel shaky.'

'That sucks.'

'Scribe is meeting me at the Scroll Archive,' Wind Talker declared, striding into the room. 'Weaver, do you want to come?'

'Yes,' Weaver said, jumping to her feet.

'What about me? You leaving me here alone?'

'Eyes is on his way back. I hope we can trust you to be alone here for a few minutes.' There was a snarky edge to his voice. Stalker shrugged it off and saw them out through the front door. She stood alone for a moment in the dark hallway, breathing in the silence. It was a relief to be alone, if only for a few minutes. When her secrets had been uncovered her world seemed to shatter, shaking to the core everything she had worked so hard for. The pack had been ticking along smoothly without arguments. Old rifts largely healed. But now she felt alone and separate from them forever. It seemed impossible to come back from this, but they would have to find a way to work together in order to prevail against the Furies, and everything else on their plate.

A thud on the door interrupted her reverie. Eyes would have his key and would just enter. There was a second thud, heavy and dull. Wood on wood. Stalker stepped forward and opened it, knowing who would greet her.

Ragged Edge stood there, leaning heavily on his wooden staff, his cheeks flushed.

'Did you run here?' Stalker asked, holding the door wide to admit him. His breathing was laboured and he replied with a grunt. 'You have to be careful, at your age.' She smirked as he rounded on her, glowering.

'Shush, missy.'

'Come and have a glass of water.' She squeezed past him in the narrow hall and led him to the kitchen. 'There was no need to come, you could have sent a raven.' She poured him some water and passed it to him. He held a finger to silence her as he slowly chugged down the entire glass. She waited patiently, watching her old mentor affectionately. He slammed the glass down on the table and pointed to a chair with a grunt. She flinched slightly, but took a seat, as ordered.

'You, young lady, are in a heap of trouble.'

Stalker sighed and rolled her eyes, channelling the petulant teenager within.

'I see.'

'Did you think word wouldn't spread about this? I am normally loath to interfere in the love lives of young shifters. What you get up to is largely your own business. But stepping out with a Fury?!' His face was as red as a cartoon Father Christmas. He huffed and shook his long leather coat, then began pacing the small kitchen.

'There is really no need to lecture me. Do you think I haven't heard all of this from my pack?'

'Has it sunk in? Has it really?'

'He isn't even a Fury. He was raised by an outlying pack in the wild. They were killed before he even changed. He's been on his own since.'

'It's not possible.' Ragged Edge stopped pacing and

shook his head firmly. 'No cub could survive on their own for long.'

'Well he did.'

'Have you considered the possibility that he has lied to you?'

'Yes! Of course I have. But he is telling the truth about all of it, I am certain of it.'

'Love blinds the best of us. You can't possibly know.'

'I know! I do. He is not a threat. He has never hurt anyone. He's been living as a human for ten years. No one even knew he was there!'

'How does that make it any better? Girl, don't be a fool. You are smarter than this. One of the brightest cubs I have ever known. We don't normally accept anyone as young as you into Odin's Warriors, you know? We could tell you were special, even before I knew of your uniqueness. There was something we could all sense. What do you want to go and throw it all away for? Some young man who has turned your head away from your duties and sense.'

'Come and meet him. If you have such good judgement, you come and meet him and see for yourself. Talk to him. Hear his story. See if you think he's lying.'

'How was he hidden, eh? How?'

Stalker shifted uncomfortably in her seat and cleared her throat.

'A demon.'

'A demon?'

'A secrecy demon was cloaking him, still is, I assume. I don't know. Maybe the bond is broken now that more shifters know.'

'And he says he had no contact with shifters at all until

you?'

'Yes.'

'But demons he's been dealing with? If he lost his pack and has never had their guidance, how would he know how to communicate with them?'

'He's been hidden from demons and fae too. Just the one secrecy demon who he invoked almost by accident, just by taking steps to conceal himself from our world. That hid him from everything else. He was raised among his own kind, he knew their ways. But he didn't accept their ideology. Once he was living among humanity he realised he had been lied to.'

'I see. But I still don't see how it's possible for a youngster to survive alone. Even in the human world. He must have had help. He could be corrupted.'

'He is not Spiral Hand!' Stalker snapped, getting to her feet and sending her chair scraping back across the floor.

The front door opened and Eyes entered. Ragged Edge and Stalker stood glaring at one another as he entered the kitchen.

'Am I interrupting something?' he asked coolly.

'I think we're done here. Mostly. You need to get control of this girl.'

'We have it in hand, I assure you. Did you have any news on the cannibals?'

'Hmph. Yes and no. Without anyone in the city morgue our information is sketchy. We're not necessarily up to date on human losses. But it makes sense that they are connected to the Hunger, and I was beginning to suspect as much myself. From the information I have pieced together, it seems that the Hunger has been operating in Caerton for longer than we thought. I suspect it arrived when St. Catherine's returned from wherever it disappeared to. The two may even be connected.'

'I see.'

'Did the Blue Moon ever talk to either of you about the city's Bone Anchors?'

Stalker sat back down and crossed her arms over her chest, shaking her head. Shadow's Step had hardly had time to teach her anything.

'Wind Talker and Weaver may know about them.' Eyes rubbed his unshaven chin and ran his hands through his hair, resembling Fortune more than ever.

'The city is essentially underpinned by them. At various critical points across the city there are these pillars. They hold Midgard in its place, between the other realms. There used to be one in St Catherine's, but it wasn't there when the area returned. It was shattered. We patched it, but couldn't restore the pillar. Without the Bone Anchors, the realms would come crashing together. There would be no veil. Shifter philosophers have speculated that there was once a Bone Anchor at Crescent Park, and that is why the place now has that odd quality.'

'But nothing gets through there,' Stalker said, her curiosity piqued. 'There is no veil, but everything stays in its own realm anyway.'

'Indeed. That is the part we cannot fathom. Speculation is that were all the Anchors to fall, the realms would spill into one another. If the Hunger did cross over at St Catherine's when the Anchor came down there then it is possible that it could be trying to bring down the others and let more of its kind through. The Bronze Lord may be helping.'

'This all sounds like something the Spiral Hand would be doing.' Eyes narrowed his eyes but didn't look Stalker's way. She felt his thoughts crushing down on her though. He was thinking of Rhys.

'It does rather.' Ragged Edge shifted his weight and tapped his staff on the floor.

'Did no one ever find out what happened to St Catherine's or who was behind it?' Eyes asked.

'No.'

Stalker exchanged nervous glances with her Alpha. It was on their doorstep. The Blue Moon had been dealing with the demonic overflow. It was possible they had investigated and knew something. Something that may have been noted in the records that the Witches had stolen from the attic. But The Watches' territory bordered St Catherine's too. If they didn't know anything, maybe the Blue Moon hadn't either.

'In Weaver's vision, there was that huge pillar in the middle of the room. Could that have been a Bone Anchor? And what about that machine that was grinding up bones? That could have represented the destruction of the Bone Anchors.' Stalker finally gave voice to her thoughts and looked up into the faces of Eyes and Ragged Edge.

'I wonder if it means they are assembled at one of the Anchors? There is presumably a ritual to take it down?' Eyes looked to Ragged Edge for confirmation. The old man nodded and grunted in reply.

'Where are they?' Stalker asked, panic rising. 'Do you know all of their locations?'

'There is a map. We have a copy. I would imagine there

are a few copies. It's important information for all of our kind.'

'Artemis sent Weaver the vision, and the Knight warned us of the Bronze Lord. It must be on our territory. The first target must be in St. Mark's.'

'There are two,' Ragged Edge said. 'One by Red Bridge and the other by the telecoms tower. There's one in Fenwick too. In an area you now claim, I believe.'

'The Alpha of the Witches was under the thrall of the Hunger,' Stalker said softly, staring at the table as her mind raced through all of the information they had amassed. 'The column, her disappearance there. That must have been the Bone Anchor.'

'I would bet my right arm it targeted her because of the Bone Anchor on her territory,' Ragged Edge said gruffly.

'Could other Alphas be compromised?' Stalker asked tentatively.

'It's possible. We must all be vigilant.' Ragged Edge cast a wary glance at Eyes.

'It's bad enough we can't trust one another because of the Spiral Hand, now this. Even if the two are connected.' Eyes shook his head.

'We need to root it out. Find it and destroy it.' Ragged Edge looked pointedly at Stalker. She swallowed a hard lump in her throat and glowered at him defiantly. 'I'll take my leave. Keep in touch.' He stomped down the hall and Eyes followed him to the door.

Stalker felt panic rising in her chest. She had to protect Rhys, that was all that mattered now.

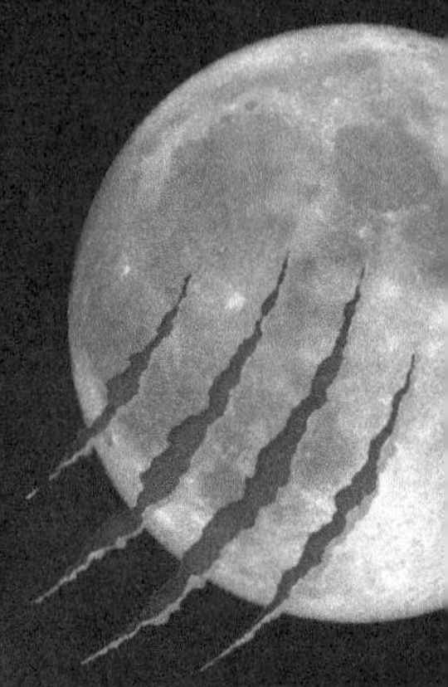

Chapter Twelve

Need to talk. Think I'm being followed. How many know about me now? Are you okay?

Stalker read the note over and over again, clutching it in her shaking hands, alone in the darkened bathroom. The secrecy demon in the mirror shimmered slightly, occasionally emitting a sigh.

'Can you let him see me? Is he there now? At his mirror?' Stalker whispered hurriedly.

The mirror shimmered in response and the reflection shifted. No longer was her own dingy bathroom reflected there in the shadows, a lighter, cleaner room emerged and Rhys's tired and worried face appeared.

'Stalker? Are you there? I can hardly see anything,' he whispered frantically.

'I'm here. I have to keep it dark for the demon to come and do the mirror thing. Are you all right? I feel awful about all of this. They want your blood. I can't believe this is happening. Even the shifters I trust most are freaking out about you.'

'Someone has been following me since yesterday, I think. I felt eyes on me on my way home from work and there was someone walking behind me. But I didn't see their face or get close enough to tell what they were. I could just be paranoid.'

'I don't think anyone knows enough about you to identify you. Is your friend still with you?'

'Yes, but I get the feeling he's not so helpful now that the secret is out there. How many know?'

'I thought it was just my pack, but Ragged Edge knows. I don't know how. Maybe one of my pack told him, or a fae ally or something. He gets visions, maybe that's how. I should have asked. He's my mentor. I'm devastated. I thought even if my pack turned on me I would have Odin's Warriors to go to, but now I'm not so sure.'

'I wish more than anything I could be with you now, to hold you and to know everything would be okay.'

'I know what you mean. They think you're Spiral Hand. It's not just the Romeo and Juliet-ness of this.'

'I'm not, you know I'm not.'

'I know.' Stalker heard movement in the house and held her breath. She racked her brains, trying to find a solution lurking there somewhere. They would never believe them, Rhys would never be free. Not until they caught the real Spiral Hand. He had the finger of accusation pointing squarely at him and there was no way to satisfy those who were out for blood. No one else knew what that was like, there was no one to turn to. The big white house on the hill popped into her mind. 'Of course! Father Ash. Can you get out of the city for a few days? Take time off work?'

'If I have to.'

'You have to. We have to keep you safe. There is a place you can go, someone who understands. But I have to warn you, he might really be Spiral Hand. He was exiled years ago under suspicion, but they could never prove either way if he was or not. He's powerful, he can protect you.'

'Unless he kills me.'

'Why would he? Either he is Spiral Hand, in which case he's playing the long game and killing you wouldn't be an advantage to him. Or he isn't, and he knows exactly what it's like to be accused.'

'If he is, he could kill me in an effort to clear his own name.'

'If you were dead there would be nothing but his word. He wouldn't do that.' A flicker of doubt intruded. She didn't know the full story around what had happened to Father Ash, but he had executed his own son for being Spiral Hand.

'I guess. Okay. Where is he?'

'You know that house out to the west? On the coast. Big white house. You can't miss it on the drive out of the city.'

'Yeah, I think so. Is he friendly?'

'Erm, yeah, sort of. I mean yes. Yes, he accepted us when we turned up there unannounced and was hospitable. But be careful, okay?'

'Of course. I'll be in touch as soon as I can. I love you, Ariana.'

'I love you too.'

The mirror returned to normal and Stalker rushed from the room. She knew it was likely that her pack mates had caught some of her strong feelings and thoughts through their bond, but she hoped they would take it for the upset she had experienced with Ragged Edge's visit.

Eyes was clanging about in the kitchen, restlessly, and as Stalker reached the hallway, Claws burst through the door.

'I know where they are!'

Eyes came rushing into the hall.

'Where?'

'There's this old church, it hasn't held a service in years. But I found a few police reports of suspicious activity over the last few months. Nothing was substantiated, but it's enough weird activity to suggest the cult is operating out of there.'

The door was flung wide again and Weaver and Wind Talker came in, chattering loudly. The hall was packed with the five of them now and without words, they all filed to the kitchen to spread out.

'What have you got?' Eyes demanded.

'We found a map.' Wind Talker held up a scrap of paper.

'You didn't take that from the Scroll Archive did you?' Stalker asked, shocked.

'No, it's a copy.' He passed it to her and she saw a hurriedly drawn line map of part of the city. Little stars dotted it: one by Red Bridge; one in the heart of Fenwick; and one by the telecoms tower, next to a cross symbolising a church. She pointed at it and showed it to Claws. He nodded firmly.

'Same one. That must be it.'

'Don't you just love it when everything comes together?' Eyes asked, grinning broadly. 'Let's not sit on this. Come on.'

He grabbed his keys and the pack followed him out to his car. Stalker pushed aside her fears for Rhys and thoughts of him risking everything by going to Father Ash for safe harbour. If she was wrong, about either of them, this could go very badly. Right now she had to focus on the task in hand. They were heading into a dangerous situation of their own.

The five of them piled into Eyes' four-wheel drive and set off for the church.

'Shouldn't we plan this? Do some reconnaissance?' Claws asked.

'No,' Weaver said firmly. 'No, I think my vision was a matter of urgency. We won't just barge in, we'll check it out first, but we need to do this now.'

'I agree,' Eyes said. He pressed his foot a little harder on the gas and Stalker gripped the handle of the door as he took a corner a little too quickly. Her heart skipped a beat and the fury talisman against her chest throbbed with anticipation of a fight.

It was the middle of the day and Caerton pulsed with life. The traffic prevented Eyes driving too recklessly. Stalker watched the bustling city pass by out of the window. People were strolling casually, unaware of the monsters in their midst. It struck Stalker anew how much her life had changed. She had once been one of those humans, going about ordinary life oblivious to shifters and demons, no clue about the evil that lurked beneath the skin of the world.

The car slowed to a halt opposite the church. It was a building that had clearly seen better days. A few small sections of the stained glass windows were missing and the front door was boarded up. The whole building felt grey and at odds with the beauty that surrounded it. The little grassy yard that fronted the church was unkempt and dull. But it was otherwise unremarkable. Just a relic of human history that most passed by without noticing.

Claws leaned forward to peer past Stalker at the building.

'We should take a closer look, discreetly.'

'Absolutely. You two check it out. Be careful.' Eyes indicated Stalker and Claws.

Stalker opened the car door and slid out onto the road, Claws right behind her. They exchanged nervous glances before crossing the quiet road and walking past the little church. It stood detached from the buildings on either side of it, with paths leading down both sides.

'If we get too close it could be obvious that we're checking the place out.' Stalker spoke softly, trying not to draw any attention to them. It wasn't a busy street, but traffic did pass them and there were people browsing in shop windows nearby.

'There's a side street up ahead. Perhaps it leads around the back? If the cannibals are using this place there must be a back door.'

Without a word, the two of them walked quickly to the side street and turned down it. It turned into a narrow residential street and at the end was another road crossing it, running back towards the church. The two shifters walked briskly until they reached the back of the church. There were cars parked on both sides of the road, many of them up on the pavement, making it too narrow to pass. On the opposite side of the road to the church were the backs of terraced houses with a high wall running the length of the street, giving the back yards privacy. Stalker and Claws approached slowly, down the middle of the road, between the parked cars.

'There are too many cars here to belong to the residents.'

'Agreed.' Claws nodded and indicated towards the church. Stalker craned her neck to see over the cars. To the side of the church was a narrow set of steps leading down to a back door at cellar level. There was a small window in the door and a light on inside. 'Let's take a look.'

Stalker looked carefully around for prying eyes. She couldn't see anyone, but couldn't take the chance that someone was looking out of a window nearby. She squeezed between two parked cars and moved quickly and silently over to the steps down to the back door of the church. Once hidden in the stairwell, she shifted into a small bird and fluttered up to the window. Perched on the narrow wooden sill, she could see in through the grubby glass. A cluttered and dusty basement lay beyond the door, lit by a bare bulb hanging from the ceiling. She could just make out another door on the other side of the room, it stood ajar and it looked like the room beyond was lit with candles, as the warm light flickered. Candles meant a ritual. She was certain of it. With great concentration, Stalker projected the image of the flickering light to the minds of her pack mates.

Within seconds, Claws was at her side. She jumped from the sill and flew up to circle the church. Soaring through the warm air, she spotted the rest of the pack jogging from the car to the back of the church. She circled back to meet them on the steps and shifted form once out of sight of the neighbouring houses.

'Are we going in?' Weaver asked anxiously.

'We have to. We have to stop them.' Eyes moved to the door and tried it. It was locked. 'I don't think we can do this quietly.'

'I can pick it,' Claws said hurriedly. Eyes made way and Claws got out his lock-pick set. Stalker tapped her foot, desperate to get inside. She felt sure they would be cutting it fine. She kept an eye on the cellar through the window. It was deserted, but there was definitely movement in the room beyond; she saw shadows crossing the candlelight.

There was an encouraging click and Claws turned the handle. The door opened with a slight creak. The Lightning Lords quietly moved inside. Stalker heard chanting in the room beyond. Whatever they were doing, it was happening now. The five of them moved swiftly through the basement, avoiding the stacked up wooden chairs, old pews, dusty boxes and other random junk that was piled up.

Wind Talker took the lead as they approached the door and used his talisman to look across the veil. His face went ashen and he took a deep breath. With a simple shake of his head, Stalker knew that they were too late to completely avert whatever was coming.

They may be murderous cannibals, but they are human, remember that. Whatever happens. Eyes' thoughts were crystal clear as they rushed through

Stalker's mind. The pack exchanged sombre looks. There was a good chance some, if not all of the people in the room were going to end up dead or mad and there was nothing the Lightning Lords could do about that now. Stalker closed her eyes and took a deep breath, hoping that Odin and Artemis would forgive her for what she had to do.

With a firm nod, Eyes stepped past Wind Talker and pushed the door wide. The room looked almost exactly like Weaver's vision. A black and white chequered floor stretched away. Pillars stood at intervals, holding up the low ceiling, with the empty church above. Opposite the door was a small dais, upon which was a tall-backed chair. In it, was a tall gentleman made of bronze, with a wooden mask over his face. Before him were about twenty people, all kneeling with their arms out in front of them in worship, humming an eerie chant.

At the sound of the shifters entering their sacred space, the cult members sat up and turned, those at the back noticing first and sending a wave of realisation forwards towards the Bronze Lord. He lurched to his feet and ripped the mask from his metallic face, which was filled with rage.

'The mask...' Claws murmured, a curious expression on his face.

'Burn it down,' Eyes hissed.

Weaver took a step into the room and focused on the nearest candle. She raised her hands and the flame trembled violently.

'No!' the Bronze Lord screamed. 'Get them!' His voice echoed throughout the room and the worshippers scrambled to their feet.

The Lightning Lords dashed forwards. Stalker braced

herself and as two of the crazy fools ran at her she again prayed for forgiveness. Drawing on the power of her fury talisman, Stalker clenched her fists and smashed them into the floor. The tiles rippled out from the impact and were ripped up in the shock wave. The two approaching cultists lost their footing and fell on their backs. She heard gunfire, but didn't have time to look to see what was happening, she knew it was Claws and knew he would be aiming to maim, not kill. She ran forwards and grabbed the two men by their clothes. She easily dragged them to the nearest pillar, although their feet thrashed and they clawed at her hands.

'Get out of here, you crazy idiots. Stop eating people!' She turned and charged into the fray that had erupted. On the floor at the feet of the enraged Bronze Lord, was a dead body, its guts exposed and the blood was welling up inside it, bubbling like a small fountain. Stalker felt the veil thinning and watched as the Bronze Lord knelt to examine the corpse.

'It's the Hunger!' Wind Talker cried, as one of the cannibals crumpled in a heap at his feet, his neck broken. Stalker watched as something rose up out of the body; a thick, bloody mess of flesh and bones.

'Take it down!' Eyes ordered, pausing in his dealing with several shrieking cultists. The humans were no match for any of the shifters, and the Lightning Lords were making short work of them. Several lay on the floor clutching flesh wounds, groaning. Others had fled. But Stalker knew if the Hunger finished crossing into their realm, it would be a truly formidable foe. She leapt forward, her wings talisman carrying her further than a normal leap, and she reached the Bronze Lord in a single bound. She drew a fist back and threw the punch of her life. Her fist struck his metal face and she felt bones shatter. He glared at her, unblinking and unflinching. Stalker cried out and reeled back, clutching her broken hand.

A shot rang out and the bullet hit the demon with a *clink* and a small spark, but fell to the floor without even leaving a dent. The smell of smoke filled Stalker's nostrils as she nursed her hand, Weaver had started a fire. Maybe they could melt the sucker. She took a steadying breath and drew a sword with her left hand. She spun it easily in an arc and grinned up at the demon before her. Darting forward again, her sword raised, she plunged it down into the bloody mess, slicing easily through the mangled flesh. It fell to the floor in two chunks and she stepped back to admire her work.

The Bronze Lord laughed and threw back his head. Stalker watched in horror as the mess reformed and again rose up, twisting in a sickening spiral of gore.

'Move!' Weaver called out. Stalker looked over her shoulder and saw Weaver advancing, her hands directing a swirling inferno. Stalker leaped aside and sheathed her dha. Wind Talker was right beside Weaver, using his ability to direct the breeze to keep the fire directed at the two demons. A jet of flames whooshed out from the column and blasted them both. The Bronze Lord recoiled and immediately began to look slick and glossy in the intense heat. The Hunger was engulfed in flames and quickly began to char.

The demon lurched forwards, spitting hot globs of blood towards Weaver and Wind Talker. When they hit the smashed tiles, there was an angry hiss and the blood seared through the floor like acid. Weaver leapt back and dropped the tower of flames. Wind Talker held fast, whipping up a wind to channel the remaining blaze towards the Bronze Lord, who was looking softer, weakening in the heat. He seemed rooted to the spot, unable to move. Stalker looked and saw that he had tried to lift a foot, but that the melting bronze had stuck to the floor. The foot was raised slightly, but like thick glue, had stretched and warped.

The Hunger was growing, despite the flames licking at the outer layers of flesh. With each laboured step forwards that it took, it seemed to swell. The few remaining cannibals that were hunched around the room looked horrified. One woman was sobbing close to Stalker's feet. Stalker looked down at the wretch, disgusted by her hypocrisy, but pitying her all the same.

She drew her dha again, with her left hand. Her right still ached, but she could feel the bones mending themselves already. She took a cautious step forward. The heat was extreme, making her skin prickle and sweat. But it was targeted past the Hunger and towards the Bronze Lord behind. Stalker took another step and swung at the demon. A lump of flesh was cut from the central mound, but even as it fell to the floor, the hole left behind sealed itself and a replacement bulge formed, like a massive scab.

With a lurch of revulsion, Stalker stepped back. It was no good, she wouldn't be able to rip it apart. Eyes seemed to realise this at the same time. He caught Stalker's eye across the room.

'Wind Talker!' Eyes shouted over the roar of the fire. 'We need to banish it!'

Weaver was back on her feet, controlling the flames that were steadily melting the Bronze Lord. His features were misshapen now, slowly dribbling down his form into a growing puddle at his feet. Wind Talker released the breeze and stepped back. He began rummaging through his satchel. The Hunger let out a horrific scream, spitting acidic blood onto the floor at Wind Talker's feet. He stumbled back and Stalker leaped into the demon's path. She drove her sword into the centre of the inhuman, pulsating column of flesh. She yanked her sword upwards with a furious roar. The Hunger split, folding out like the peel of a banana. But it only slowed for a moment. It reformed, growing even bigger.

'Each time we hit it, it only gets stronger!' Stalker shouted. 'Wind Talker! We need to get it back across the veil!'

'I know!' Wind Talker raised a knife and both hands over his head. He sliced into his palm with the knife and a streak of scarlet appeared. The blood trickled down his palm. The Hunger rasped and something tongue-like flicked out from a maw that opened in the front. Stalker kept pace with it as it trudged forward. She didn't know what she would do to stop it if it tried to strike any of her pack, but she was braced to do something. Wind Talker was now fumbling with a piece of chalk. He bent and hurriedly drew a line on the floor. He pressed his bleeding palm forward and a shimmering barrier appeared between him and The Hunger. 'Hades! Come forth and claim back this demon!'

'You can't invoke Hades!' Weaver shouted over her shoulder, as she pressed closer to the Bronze Lord, who was now a lumpy puddle of shining molten bronze.

'Watch me!' Wind Talker cried. Stalker watched, as powerless as Claws and Eyes. Brute strength and firearms meant nothing to these demons. 'Hades! Lord of the Underworld, take back this thing, this Hunger!'

There was a crack like a whip and Stalker lurched as the floor moved beneath their feet. A crack appeared just behind the barrier that Wind Talker had summoned. The floor jerked again and one of the huddled humans cried out. Claws and Eyes, on the opposite side of the room from Stalker, quickly started helping the survivors get out. Stalker was pinned down behind the barrier and The Hunger. Two terrified humans huddled behind her against a pillar. If the church came down on them, they would all be crushed. She had no intention of dying just yet. She grabbed the two men and pulled them to their feet. She hurled them with all of her strength across the room behind Wind Talker. Eyes ran forward to help them out of the room. The Hunger advanced towards the barrier and it fell, disintegrating in front of the demon like tissue paper in a fire.

Stalker roared and charged at it, summoning all of her strength. She shifted into her Agrius form and crashed into The Hunger. With enormous force of will, she pulled the demon across the veil into Hepethia, even though the blood that coated it burned her skin. A moment later, Wind Talker was at her side. She dropped the demon and it writhed away, shrieking and spitting acidic blood everywhere. Stalker shifted back into her human form and promptly vomited. The pain coursing through her body left her shuddering and her skin was alight with searing agony.

'It isn't from the Underworld, this is one of Surtr's demons,' Stalker gasped. Wind Talker nodded and raised a piece of dark quartz up between them and The Hunger.

'Surtr, master of Muspelheim, come forth and embrace The Hunger as one of your own.'

Stalker looked around. This part of Hepethia was nothing like the church basement. A vast, shining pillar of crystal quartz strutted up from the rough ground and stretched away into the infinite sky. A great long crack was visible down the middle of the pillar. There were rocky cliffs to the east, where the city limits would be. Beyond them was Fury territory.

The ground trembled and Stalker's attention darted to the writhing demon on the ground. It looked smaller now, diminished by its crossing of the veil, away from its food source; gluttony.

'Surtr! I beseech you, as one of Odin's Warriors, come and take this foul beast back into your arms!'

A great tremor knocked Stalker and Wind Talker to the ground. Stalker landed hard on her hands and knees. Her broken right hand throbbing with renewed pain. A crack opened in the ground beside The Hunger and with a final shake, the demon rolled into the crack and screamed as it fell back into the hell it had come from.

Stalker grinned and looked over at Wind Talker. His face was frozen in shock and horror. She followed his gaze to the vast pillar and the grin slipped from her face. The crack that had already been there when they arrived had split wide and as the two shifters knelt there staring at it, the entire thing lurched sideways. With a sickening crunch, the pillar split in two, with one side jutting out like a gigantic bone splintering.

There was the sound of rushing water cascading down an enormous waterfall and a dark shadow formed above the pillar. As the broken piece came crashing towards the ground, Stalker and Wind Talker leapt to their feet and retreated, sprinting away from the falling tower. The crash was deafening and the shock wave knocked the shifters to the ground. Stalker spun around in time to watch the veil fall.

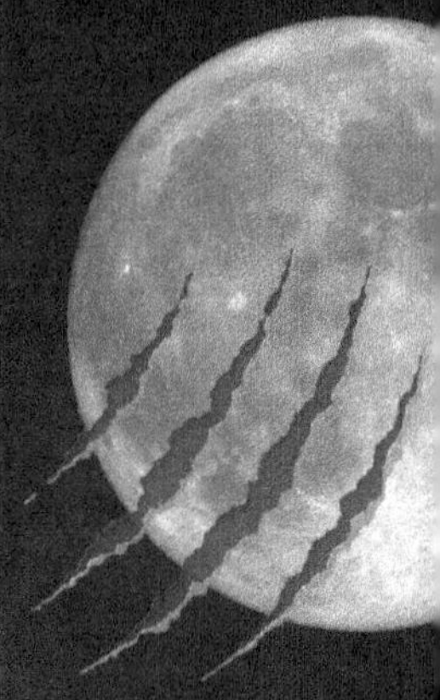

Chapter Thirteen

For a moment, Stalker could see across all of the realms, as if they all existed in this place at once. But they quickly sprang back into their proper places, for now.

'Shit.' Wind Talker got to his feet and gazed at the hole in reality.

'Can you fix it?' Stalker stood, transfixed. She could look up and see stars, or look down and see the Underworld, and Svartalfheim and Muspelheim and every other dark place, stacked on top of one another like a hellish layered cake. On the other side of the hole, where the Bone Anchor had stood, was the church basement, whole and relatively unharmed. Her pack mates stood there staring across the chasm at her and Wind Talker. The gap was about the width of a football field.

'Are you all right?' Eyes called.

'Fine. We're fine!' Stalker called back.

'Can you fix it?' Eyes shouted, echoing Stalker's

question, which Wind Talker had yet to answer. He shook his head slowly as he stared at the damage.

'Reality has been ripped. It's not too bad, this is just one anchor. If they all came down… it doesn't bear thinking about. But this is far beyond my skill to fix.'

'This might help,' Claws said, holding up the mask that the Bronze Lord had been wearing.

'What is it?' Wind Talker asked, squinting across the chasm.

'It's the mask I was commissioned to find, months ago. I let the case go in February after the trail went cold. Now here it is. It seems the Bronze Lord was using it to help channel the Hunger. If it has that sort of power, perhaps it can be used to heal the breech.'

'Maybe,' Wind Talker said, running his finger over his jaw.

Stalker and Wind Talker set off walking around the huge hole, trying not to get too close to the edge. Much like the hole that had been ripped in the veil when the betting shop had exploded, this one was like an elevator shaft, with access to every floor above and below. Things were bound to start crawling out of the pit soon. Sensing her thoughts, Wind Talker quickened his pace and soon they were sprinting towards their pack mates.

Claws tossed the mask to Wind Talker once he was close enough, and he raised it to his face.

'Careful,' Weaver and Stalker said together. They exchanged nervous smiles and watched as Wind Talker placed the mask over his face.

'Huh.'

'What is it?' Stalker asked.

'Nothing. I don't get anything from it.'

'May I?' Stalker held out a hand and Wind Talker passed it to her. She could feel something supernatural about it. In much the same way that she could often feel the condition of the veil, or when a fae or demon was nearby, she could sense there was something distinctly not-human about the mask. 'It has power.'

'Try it on,' Weaver urged.

Stalker lifted the mask towards her face. It vibrated slightly in her hands as she raised it and her breath shook with nerves. The wood was cool against her tender skin, still burned from tackling The Hunger. The mask was soothing and she pressed it firmly against her face. She could just see out through the narrow eye slits and looked around at her pack mates. She could see the human world and Hepethia laced together, in a similar way to Wind Talker's talisman. When she looked into the chasm, she saw each world in vivid detail. Demons were beginning to assemble at the hole and were fixing their sights on the shifters.

'We have to fix it, quickly. They're coming.'

'I believe I can help.' The voice was cool and crisp. Stalker spun to locate it. Standing a few feet away, dressed in velvet frock coat and an extremely tall top hat, was a pale young man.

'How?' Wind Talker asked, his voice scathing. 'Man-in-the-Hat?'

The man dipped his head ever so slightly and smiled. His lips curled up in an unpleasant manner.

'That mask acts as a conduit between worlds, it channels energy. I was drawn to it in much the same way

The Hunger was before me, and the Bronze Lord before that. You clearly have no idea what you're doing with it. No offence.'

'None taken,' Stalker said, shrugging, her voice muffled against the wood. 'I really don't.'

'Perhaps you can offer some advice?' Eyes suggested, crossing his arms over his chest. 'We certainly won't be allowing you to use it yourself.'

'I wouldn't dream of suggesting such a thing.' The man lifted his hat a little way off his head, revealing a bald head beneath it.

'So what do we do?' Stalker asked, growing impatient.

The Man-in-the-Hat cleared his throat and strode over to stand beside Stalker, looking out into the chasm.

'Is this your first repair-job?'

'No,' Wind Talker snapped. He reached into his satchel and took out a sage smudge stick and piece of crystal quartz. He passed the sage to Stalker and lit it. The smoke wafted up and Stalker dutifully waved it about, sending puffs of smoke out into the void.

'Now channel it,' the Man said softly. Stalker felt sure he must be a demon, but wasn't sure what kind yet. He was charming and helpful, apparently, but there was something unsettling about him. 'Imagine the smoke drifting into all realms from here.'

Stalker did as she was told and through the holes in the mask she could see the smoke drifting further away, as clearly as if it were still just in front of her, it was permeating every broken edge. Wind Talker was muttering a chant beside her, Weaver too. She could feel the veil mending itself, being drawn back together. 'You're not sewing a blanket,' the Man whispered. 'You're stitching a wound. Layer after layer of world after world, slowly being drawn closed over this injury. The skin will be the very last thing you stitch. Slowly does it.'

Stalker cringed slightly at his closeness and the imagery he was invoking, but it was working. She saw in her mind what they were doing and imagined the smoke as sutures, drawing the wounded flesh back together. The mask enabled her visualisation to become reality. The longer she stared out through the eye holes of the mask, the further away she seemed to drift, drawn away towards the other realms that she could peer into. Asgard was up there, her Valkyrie friend and spirit guide were waiting for her. There was a place laid at Odin's table in Valhalla and she would be able to go there. *Not now,* a voice inside her head cautioned. She couldn't be sure if it was an anxious pack mate, Rhys, or Fylgia. But she heeded the warning and forced her consciousness back into her head.

They worked for what felt like hours, slowly, patiently repairing the veil. The Bone Anchor itself was gone, but perhaps it would regrow in time. As long as the veil was repaired, nothing would be able to get between worlds without being summoned.

'With two Bone Anchors gone, the world is undoubtedly weaker,' the Man told them.

'Do you know what happened to the other one?' Stalker asked.

'I do. Chaos, utter chaos.'

The last stitch was in place and Wind Talker collapsed to the floor, exhausted. Stalker slumped down next to him and slowly removed the mask. It peeled away from her face as if held there by suction.

'Well?' she asked, looking up at the demonic helper.

'Naughty shifters out of their territory, messing about with forces they didn't understand.'

'Which shifters?' Eyes asked, his voice cold and hard. Stalker glared at the demon, knowing in her gut what words were about to tumble out.

'The Blue Moon, of course.' The-Man-in-the-Hat grinned his unnerving grin, lifted his hat courteously and disappeared.

The Lightning Lords glanced anxiously at one another. The church had disappeared as the veil had mended, they were fully in Hepethia with no gaping wound into the human world.

'We should cross over and check that all is well on the other side,' Wind Talker said, slowly getting to his feet.

'Wait a minute,' Stalker snapped. 'We need to talk about this, surely?'

'Now isn't the time. We don't know that we can trust The-Man-in-the-Hat.' Eyes held a hand out to help Stalker up. 'We need to check on the human world, see that the cannibals have disbanded and update the other packs.'

'They must have felt the Bone Anchor shatter, I'm sure of it.' Wind Talker was stuffing his ritual tools back into his bag. 'We need to reassure them that it has been dealt with.'

The five of them crossed the veil, though Stalker dragged her feet, frustrated at the lack of concern over what they had learnt.

Back in the human world, the floor of the church basement was ruined and there was a bloody corpse to deal with, not to mention the bizarre formation of molten bronze, which had now hardened again. The cult had disbanded. With any luck, now that the Hunger had been banished and the bronze Lord destroyed, whatever held the humans in thrall was now gone and they would return to their normal lives without hurting anyone else.

'I recognised some of the cannibals,' Claws said, his voice weary. 'They were members of the Carlson crime family.'

'What?' Eyes said, his gaze sharp and focused on Claws.

'That's who I found out was behind the theft of the mask. They killed my only lead. Now I know what it was about. They stole it for this ritual. They were serving the Hunger as well.'

The Alpha rubbed his eyes.

'Right,' he said, his voice strained. 'With any luck, that's the last we'll hear of them. We need to deal with this before any authorities come knocking.'

'We could burn it down,' Weaver suggested.

'Do it,' Eyes replied and he marched out through the back door. Wind Talker and Claws went after him and Stalker started to follow, but looked back as Weaver took out her lighter. She lit it and directed the flame with her hand, causing it to flare and turn into something resembling a flame thrower. She directed it at the remains of the Bronze Lord, then around the room at the wooden floor and furniture. Flames caught everywhere the fire touched and soon the basement was ablaze.

'Weaver,' Stalker said, panic rising in her chest. 'Let's go!'

Weaver clicked off the lighter and dashed towards the

door where Stalker was waiting. They ran out and up the stairs at the back of the church. Stalker didn't look back, but she could smell the smoke. They hadn't got much clear of the street when the fire engine siren reached her ears.

'I'm calling Theodore,' Eyes declared once they were back in the car. 'We need a full meeting of everyone, before the Council of Elders.'

Stalker barely heard him, her mind was still in the basement with the blood and fire. She was vaguely aware of the journey across the city but when they pulled up and filed out she was surprised to find herself at the back of the city museum, being greeted by Ragged Edge.

The Lightning Lords filed in through the back door of the museum. Stalker's heart was pounding in her chest. Ragged Edge led them down a narrow hall and down a steep flight of stairs. Stalker felt the veil ripple and they passed through it into Hepethia.

They emerged into blinding light and a vast courtroom with raised benches. Lined up behind a long table were four prominent Alphas. Theodore Harris sat in the centre. Either side of him were Red Scythe and Warden-of-Stones. Next to Warden was an empty seat and at the other end of the table sat Crimson.

Ragged Edge led the Lightning Lords to seats on the front row, then took his seat next to his Alpha, Warden.

'Two members of The Watch sit on that council,' Eyes whispered across Stalker to Weaver.

'I'd love to know the history of that.' Wind Talker leaned in to join the hushed conversation.

'I bet there's a record in the Scroll Archive,' Weaver said softly. 'I'll check it out later.'

'Has Scribe given you permission to go there alone?' Eyes asked, raising an eyebrow.

'He has.'

The chatting shifters around the hall fell quiet. All of the packs had sent at least one representative, though all but the Lightning Lords had left someone behind to protect Caerton. Stalker felt a stab of guilt that they hadn't thought to do that.

'Don't worry,' Eyes whispered, reading her thoughts. 'We all needed to be here for this.'

Stalker swallowed hard and nodded.

Theodore cleared his throat and silence fell.

'Thank you all for coming on such short notice. As I am sure most of you are aware, the city has lost another Bone Anchor today.' Muttering broke out again and Stalker felt hard stares on the back of her neck. 'The Lightning Lords wish to present a report to us all. Fights-Eyes-Open, you have the floor.' He held a hand out into the middle of the open space between the rows of benches.

Stalker was reminded horribly of their experience at the Hundred Court. But they were not on trial here today, they were simply updating their peers. She tried to shove the nerves she felt deep down inside. Her hands grew sweaty on the wooden mask still in her hands. Eyes stood and straightened his tie. He walked confidently into the centre of the floor and looked up at the rows of shifters gazing down. Stalker waited with baited breath to hear what he was going to say.

'My pack and I faced The Hunger today.' There was a gasp from the assembly and renewed muttering.

'All five of you are here before us,' Red Scythe said,

leaning forward and fixing Eyes with his steely gaze.

'We are. We were victorious. The Hunger, and its envoy, The Bronze Lord, have been vanquished.' The shifters erupted into lively discussion, some clapped and cheered. Stalker felt a grin light up her face. 'The Hunger had come to be here when the Bone Anchor in St. Catherine's fell.' Eyes' voice carried over the noisy chatter and everyone fell quiet again to listen. 'It had been manipulating demons and shifters alike for months. The Bronze Lord seems to have assembled a cannibal cult of humans to aid in doing the work of The Hunger. The cult has been disbanded, but we will keep a close watch on the members for any signs of continued activity. Unfortunately, the ritual to shatter the Bone Anchor and materialise The Hunger fully in this realm had already begun and we didn't manage to prevent damage being done. The Bone Anchor shattered. But we banished The Hunger back to its own realm and destroyed the Bronze Lord. We were able to repair the veil, though the Bone Anchor could not be salvaged. We were aided by The-Man-in-the-Hat, a demon of unknown origin. We hoped someone here would know of him and whether he can be trusted.' Stalker craned her neck to look at the crowd. Many of the shifters were talking animatedly to their neighbours.

The council of elders looked down at Eyes shrewdly. Warden leaned close to Ragged Edge and whispered something behind her hand. Stalker watched them closely and saw both of them glance her way.

Ragged Edge got to his feet and the shifters closest to him fell silent. A ripple of attention radiated out from him until all was quiet and still once more.

'I'm not sure anyone can help you identify the demon you mentioned, Eyes, my boy. But I have a question about how you were able to repair such a terrible tear in the veil. Did you have any other assistance?'

He looked pointedly at Stalker and she shrivelled under his gaze. Swallowing a hard lump, she got to her feet and joined Eyes in the centre, gripping the mask tightly in her sweating hands.

'What is that?' Warden asked, her voice carrying over the quiet muttering around the room. Ragged Edge gave her a wink and sat down. Stalker let out a breath and held up the mask.

'The Bronze Lord was wearing it when we disrupted the ritual. We were able to use it to repair the veil. It seems to aid the power of visualisation, I think. It doesn't work for everyone either.' She glanced sideways at Wind Talker, who shifted his weight and wouldn't meet her eye.

'Do you mind if I look at it?' Warden asked, holding out her hand. Stalker looked at Eyes, he nodded once, and Stalker took the mask over to Warden, passing it up to her. She turned it over in her hands and examined it closely.

'What is it?' Theodore asked, a note of impatience in his voice.

'You say this was being used in the ritual?' Warden asked, looking down her nose at Stalker.

'That's right.' She looked over at Claws and gave him an imploring look. He got to his feet and made his way out to join Eyes in the middle.

'If I may?' he asked, looking up at the council. Theodore nodded and made a lazy circular gesture with his hand to signal the hurrying along of proceedings. 'I was commissioned by a client in February to locate this mask. I'm a Private Investigator,' he clarified quickly, before anyone could interrupt to ask him what he meant. 'The Carlson family were involved in stealing the mask from its owners. My source was killed before he could give me any further information, so I was forced to drop the case. I had no idea it was an item significant to our kind, or demons. I thought it was a human artefact.'

'There are very few human artefacts that are of no significance to our kind,' Warden said coolly.

'I see.' Claws simply nodded meekly.

'The Carlsons are gangsters, aren't they?' Theodore asked, raising an eyebrow.

'That's right,' Claws replied. Other shifters around the court nodded and muttered. Evidently others had encountered them before. 'It would appear now, however, that they have their claws into our business. I don't know how involved they are. They may have been manipulated without their knowledge, but a few of them were at the ritual.'

'This mask is far more significant than you realise.' Warden held it up and got to her feet. She looked around to ensure she had everyone's full attention. 'This is one third of the Regalia.'

There was a collective gasp from several shifters, but far more blank stares. Stalker looked around anxiously. Weaver had clasped a hand to her mouth and Wind Talker covered his eyes with his hand, shaking his head.

'What are the Regalia?' Eyes asked.

'Three sacred relics of the city of Caerton,' Warden replied. 'The Crown, the Sceptre, and the Orb. This is the

Crown. They symbolise royalty. They once belonged to the Kings and Queens of ancient times.'

'The Furies, you mean?' Stalker asked, staring up at Warden.

'That's right. If the Heir gets wind of this item having been found, well, uniting the three would legitimise any claim to the throne that the Furies may have.'

Shouting broke out from the crowd. Stalker kept her eyes on the wooden mask in Warden's hand, desperate to get it back and run away with it, to hide it from every shifter in the room. There was every chance that the Spiral Hand agent was in their midst, or a Fury spy. Everyone had their suspicions about the loyalties of the Watch. She spared a glance toward Theodore, whose gaze was also fixed on the mask.

'We'll look after it!' Eyes shouted over the din. 'We can protect it. We found it, and we will find the others!'

The room gradually quietened down as more shifters took in what he had said. Warden looked down at him with narrowed eyes.

'This really is more my remit.' She held the mask a little closer to her chest.

'No,' Theodore said firmly. 'The Lightning Lords must look after it. It was found on their territory. They have a valid claim to its stewardship. Give it back to Stalker, please Warden.' There was a noticeable edge to his voice, a firmness of command that no one could miss. Warden slowly leaned over the bench and passed it down to Stalker. She took it and strode over to her Alpha, clutching it tightly in both hands. She could breathe a little more easily now that she had hold of it again.

'We will find the others, I swear it, and prevent the Furies from getting their hands on any of them.' Eyes was impressive, his chest swelling up and his voice firm with resolve. Stalker believed him utterly and smiled with pride.

'Very well. If any of us can be of assistance, don't hesitate to ask.' Theodore gave a final nod of his head, before banging a small gavel to dismiss the council.

Wind Talker and Weaver scurried over as the shifters on the benches around them got to their feet and began making their way out.

'What did you commit us to that for?' Wind Talker asked, breathlessly. 'The Regalia have been missing for decades. We'll never find the other pieces.'

'Not here,' Eyes said quietly. 'Come on, let's go.'

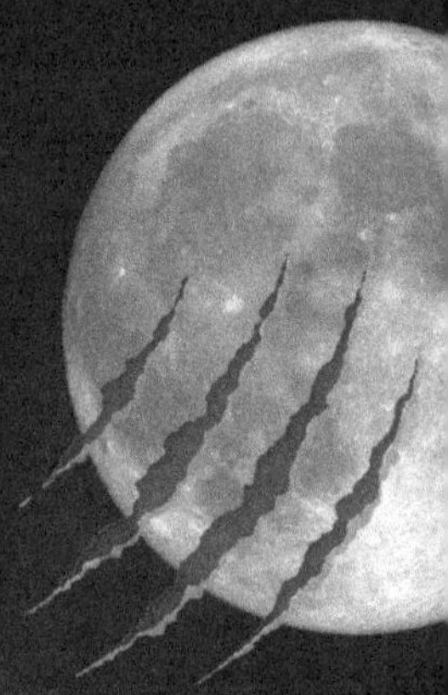

Chapter Fourteen

, back out the way they had come; up the narrow staircase, across the veil and into the back of the museum. A stream of shifters moved with them, many trying to strike up conversation with them, but Eyes fobbed them off and kept the Lightning Lords moving. Stalker tucked the mask inside her jacket and held onto it tightly.

They exited the museum through the back door and the crowd slowly dispersed, though many were hanging back to talk amongst themselves about the events.

'I'll head to the Scroll Archive to find out what I can about the Regalia, and the Council.' Weaver looked flushed and spoke quickly under her breath.

'Yes, good plan. Take Claws with you. Whatever you know about the mask and its theft could be invaluable.'

'It's not much, but I'll see if there's anything I missed during my investigation, now that I know more about what it is.'

Stalker looked around at the lingering shifters. Many of them kept shooting glances over at the Lightning Lords. She caught sight of Rust and Fury nearby, talking quietly and making no effort to conceal the fact that they were looking her way. Weaver and Claws set off at a brisk walk towards the river, to follow it north to the Scroll Archive. Having access to that amazing resource had changed everything for the pack. She thought of her parents' names in the birth registry, and that shelf on the wall stuffed with scrolls about the Blue Moon. What did the Scroll Keepers know about her family's history that she could now learn? Her gaze settled on Rust again, and her thoughts drifted to her mother.

She strode over to him and he squared his shoulders as she approached. He nodded courteously. Fury scowled and stalked away.

'Interesting developments,' Rust said softly, a small smile playing on his thin lips.

'Yeah. I wanted to ask you something. I recently found out who my mother was. I was adopted at birth and raised by humans, but both of my parents were shifters here in Caerton. My mother was Symphony.'

Rust's freckled face grew crimson suddenly and he looked away.

'I take it you knew her?'

'I did. I assume you already know she was Wrecking Crew. That's why you're talking to me about this?'

'Yes. And my father was Blue Moon. Please, tell me anything you know about them and how they died. I've got it into my head that it was a Romeo and Juliet scenario.'

Rust snorted with laughter and covered his mouth, quickly straightening his face at her obvious indignation.

'No, not really. There wasn't a great deal of enmity between our packs at the time. Vague mistrust, as is common in this city, but not like when you first turned.'

'If she hadn't given me away, if she hadn't died, I'd be Wrecking Crew now.'

'Most likely.' He looked at her with a new, soft expression. 'She was a remarkable shifter.'

'Was she?' A sudden yearning blazed inside Stalker. An intense curiosity and longing that she had never felt about her birth parents before. She was talking to someone who knew them for the first time in her life and it brought something to life inside her that she did not expect. 'I need to know everything.'

'I dare say there will be a chance to sit down and discuss your mother at length at some point, but I have to get back to Runmead now. All I can tell you about her death, since you asked about that first, is that we never found out who killed her, but my Alpha at the time believed that The Blue Moon were responsible. That's why our packs were... the way they were. It started there.'

'What? Why would they kill her?' Stalker felt the bottom of her stomach drop out from under her.

'I have no idea. I was only young at the time, barely changed, I didn't understand the politics. I still don't much care for all that.' He waved a hand towards the museum. 'But I knew your father too. They were very much in love and intended to live their lives together. I guess it's possible they were going to run away, leave the city and their pack obligations behind them. Some packs don't take kindly to deserters.'

'That might explain them killing my dad, but surely my mum was your pack's business. It doesn't make sense. And The Blue Moon weren't killers anyway. They were fiercely protective of us. They wouldn't kill one of their own, or anyone close to us.' She desperately wanted to believe what she was saying and Rust must have sensed it in her quivering voice.

'I can't really say I agree. But I really don't know what happened, I'm just relaying what my pack believed at the time.'

'Is there anyone else still around who might know more?' She looked around at the stragglers who still hadn't left. Eyes and Wind Talker were watching her warily, but giving her space.

'I don't know. Neither of them were Berserkers, but Ragged Edge and Red Scythe tend to know everyone. Theodore was around, and Crimson. Most of the city's Alphas really. But I don't think any of them really knew your parents personally. Sorry.' Rust looked genuinely regretful. There was something else going on behind his eyes. He had been entirely unsurprised when she told him who her parents were. It went beyond knowing them, he knew already who she was. Had he recognised her scent? Did she look or smell like her mother? Now was not the time to ask these questions. She nodded in appreciation.

'Thanks. See you later.' She turned away from Rust. Her thoughts were churning. She knew she wouldn't be able to keep this from her pack. Sure enough, when she reached Eyes and Wind Talker they gave her pained looks.

'Are you all right?' Eyes asked.

'It's a lot to take in. I need more information on my parents and what happened to them. It might help to explain why I'm different and why I can use this mask and Wind Talker can't.' She glanced at him and he simply nodded sagely, in that way he had of not taking a personal blow.

'Whatever you need from us, we want to help.' Eyes patted her on the shoulder.

'Rust told me that his pack thought at the time that The Blue Moon killed my mother. Why would they do that?'

Wind Talker took a deep breath and hugged his arms over his chest, bracingly.

'Perhaps they suspected she was Spiral Hand?'

Stalker felt the colour drain from her face. She hadn't wanted him to say it, but knew someone would. Maybe he was right. She didn't want to think about it.

'That would explain it. Shifters don't normally kill one another for any other reason.' Eyes looked at her with sad eyes.

'And my father?'

'Probably him too, yes. The Blue Moon may have had proof. It might be in the Scroll Archive,' Wind Talker said softly, glancing warily around.

Stalker shook out her arms, which suddenly felt tense. She let out a frustrated sigh.

'I need to train. I need to work this out physically. Is it okay if I see if Ragged Edge can spare an hour to train me now?'

'Yes, that's fine.' Eyes caught her arm before she could walk away. 'Stalker, give me the mask, please.' She blushed and took it out from inside her jacket. She passed it to him and he tucked it away. She moved away, through the clusters of lingering shifters, searching for her mentor. She found Ragged Edge deep in conversation with Warden. They stopped talking as Stalker approached.

'Quite a meeting,' Ragged Edge said gruffly, a smile playing on his lips.

'Will your pack be able to keep the mask safe? It belongs to the city, you know. Not you.' Warden narrowed her eyes as she stared at Stalker.

'Yes, we can keep it safe, and I dare say we can all agree on what should be done with it once the Furies are dealt with.' Stalker lifted her chin. Warden grunted and strode away. Stalker watched her for a moment as she began urging the remaining shifters to move along back to their own territories. She turned to Ragged Edge, who stood watching her patiently. 'I was hoping you were free to train me for an hour or so.'

'Yes, we can do that. Come with me.'

They walked swiftly into the city, not speaking. He was surprisingly brisk for such an old shifter who used a walking stick. Stalker found herself scurrying to keep up. She remembered what Shadow's Step had told her about Ragged Edge, that he could still be formidable in a fight and that he didn't really need the staff for walking. She smiled at the memory. He led her to the old fire station where Odin's Warriors had once met. Ragged Edge produced a huge set of keys from inside his long coat and rummaged through it for the right one.

Once inside the dark, cavernous space, Stalker felt everything she needed to say bubble up from inside.

'I found out more about my parents and they might

have been Spiral Hand and I need to know why they sent me away and if they knew I was different and there aren't many shifters left who knew them but you're one of them.'

Ragged Edge blinked at her, then smiled his amused half smile, barely visible through his bushy facial hair.

'I see. I didn't know their human names, but I may recognise their shifter names. What were they?'

'Symphony and Heart's Blood.' Stalker watched him, waiting for his reaction. He nodded slowly.

'That makes sense. I didn't know them well. But I knew of them. Wrecking Crew and Blue Moon, yes?'

'Yes. Rust says their deaths are the cause of the rift between the two packs.'

'I see. Well I don't know anything about that. Are we training or talking?'

'Can't we do both?'

'Of course. But let's get down to business, shall we?' He picked up a pool cue from one of the tables that lined the room and tossed it to her. She caught it easily and spun it in her hands. Ragged Edge shook off his heavy coat and grasped his staff in both hands. They circled each other, Stalker watched the way he moved and looked for any signs of tells or weaknesses. But he was giving nothing away. She didn't want to strike first, she felt sure she would end up hurting him with her increased strength and youthful agility.

'If the Blue Moon executed them for being Spiral Hand, would there be a record of that? Would the Council have been involved?'

Ragged Edge rolled his shoulders and tilted his head side to side, loosening his neck. Without warning, his staff flashed through the air and cracked down hard on the pool cue. Stalker flinched and pushed it back. She took a few steps in the circle then lunged and struck out. He easily blocked her move with his staff and stepped aside. She stumbled forward and picked herself up, glowering at him. He was much quicker than she expected.

'Not necessarily. I would remember if there had been a trial or anything. But until fairly recent history, we had a Hunt, who were responsible for taking down Spiral Hand as they saw fit. There was very little oversight, to be honest.'

'What happened? Why did the Hunt stop?'

'Father Ash.'

Ragged Edge struck again. Stalker blocked and ducked around him, almost getting a strike in at his back. But he was again too quick and spun around to block her.

'What about him?'

'He was head of the Hunt when he was exiled. Without him it all just disbanded and hasn't reformed since. It's been up to individual packs to deal with whatever comes up.'

They exchanged another few blocked moves, still circling the station.

'But that was nearly a decade after my parents died.'

'It was. But if the Blue Moon had proof of Spiral Hand activity they probably acted on it without involving the Hunt.'

Ragged Edge went in for a low blow. Stalker leaped up as the staff flew towards her legs, jumping right over it.

'Were any of the Blue Moon members of the Hunt?'

'Fortune was, before he became Alpha. I think he gave

up the Hunt because of his pack duties.'

'Right.'

Stalker went in for a strike and just clipped Ragged Edge around the shoulder as he moved to dodge the cue.

'Close,' he said with a smile. 'You're dropping your right shoulder. I can tell what you're going to do.'

Stalker straightened up and shimmied her shoulders. They were so tense, no wonder a tell was slipping in. She jumped up and down to loosen her body, then resumed circling her training partner.

'Who else was in the Hunt at the time? Maybe they had suspicions about my parents.'

'I was. I didn't.'

Stalker paused for a split second, just long enough to give Ragged Edge an opening. He landed a blow to her upper arm. She gasped and recoiled, the pain throbbing up into her shoulder.

'Apologies.'

'No need,' she said, her jaw clenched. She shook out her arm and grasped the cue more tightly in both hands. 'How do I get a hit in?'

Ragged Edge let out a throaty chuckle.

'Practice.'

'This isn't my weapon of choice.'

'I know.'

'And I broke my hand earlier.' She shook out her right hand. It still throbbed, but the bones had more or less mended.

'Excuses.' Ragged Edge tutted.

'Could we resume the Hunt? You and I? Could you train me to do it?'

'I'm not sure the current mood of the city is for such action. But possibly.' They circled each other again. 'You know, even if your parents were Spiral Hand, it was a long time ago and there is nothing you can do about it now. Your fate is not sealed. It's not as if you have to follow in their footsteps.'

'I know.' Stalker sighed. 'I just want to know the truth. It's all to do with honouring my ancestors, you know? Like we're supposed to in Odin's Warriors. How can I honour them if I don't know anything about them? Or if they were evil?'

'True. But you can honour those who came earlier, and you can honour your parents for the life they gave you. But you know,' he stopped and put the end of his staff to the ground, leaning on it, 'your name, the one they gave you, carries meaning. Not quite the meaning you found on the internet.' He smiled.

'What do you mean?' Stalker dropped her guard and stood facing him.

'Ariana comes from the Celtic moon goddess, Arianrhod. She represented the web of time and fate and the silver wheel of the year. Yates means gate keeper.'

Stalker blinked at him, taking in his words.

'You just said my fate wasn't sealed. Did my parents feel differently?'

'I don't know. Perhaps. But they could be wrong. Or they could have been good people and meant for you to protect the world.'

'Oh.'

'Your mother, if I remember rightly, was a seer. I find it hard to believe she would give you a name like that coincidentally. I think she may have had a vision of your future.'

164

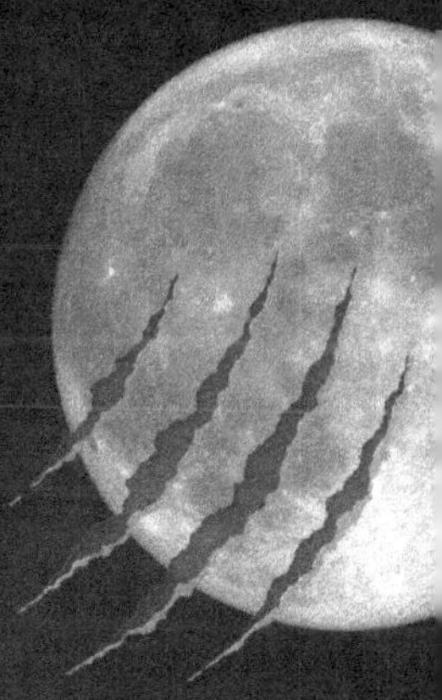

Chapter Fifteen

Weaver-of-Sky's-Loom

She was flying. Soaring over a vast forest. But something was wrong. The trees below were concrete, a vast forest as far as she could see but every leaf and branch was finely chiselled concrete.

She glanced down one sleek, black wing, then the other. She was a crow. She swooped lower, her gaze focusing in on one real tree amongst the urban tangle. Even this tree was wrong. As she flew closer she could see that where there ought to be branches and leaves, there were roots instead. The branches were buried in the ground. The tree was upside down. She came to land on the concrete branch of a nearby tree and bobbed her head as she looked at the peculiar sight.

Below the mess of muddy roots, on the ground against the trunk was a wooden throne. Sitting upon it was a masked figure. The mask, the Crown of the Regalia. In one hand, the figure held an ornate golden orb, encrusted with jewels. In the other hand was a sceptre. It was made from gold and crystal, with a small gold and bejewelled crown at one end, and a bulb of crystal at the other. As Weaver watched, the two shining items shimmered out of sight.

A rasp came from behind the mask and one word was buried inside the breath... "Immunsul".

Weaver opened her eyes. She was sitting, cross legged, in the middle of the garden at Grove Street, in Hepethia. Night had fallen and the clear sky was dotted with stars.

'What did you see?' Wind Talker urged her.

'I don't know how to describe it. Artemis is being suitably cryptic, again.'

She rubbed an ink-stained hand across her forehead. Claws was beside her in an instant with her note book and pencils. Weaver took them gratefully and began sketching furiously. The images remained vivid, even now. She allowed them to swim through the surface of her mind as she drew, knowing that she couldn't cling too tightly to any one detail, or it would start to slip away.

The landscape came first, as it had in the vision. The shapes of the bizarre trees, their heights and shapes might provide a clue. They presumably mirrored the city of Caerton, its buildings and structures. It was a map to Immunsul. Somehow she intuitively knew that it was the name of the place, the upside down tree, not the person. The person was just there to model the Regalia and she couldn't allow herself to get distracted by the figure.

Once the forest had taken shape on the page, she turned her attention to the Regalia themselves. As she made marks on the paper, gradually building a picture of the figure in the throne and the items, she began to feel certain that the Regalia in real life would look different.

The mask was wooden, simple, symbolic of a crown, not literally one. The Orb and Sceptre would surely be the same. Beautiful, ornate and evidently valuable items like these would be noticed by all who saw them. They would be hard to hide. Why couldn't Artemis have shown her what to look for in the real world? That would have been infinitely more helpful.

'There must be a record of this,' Wind Talker said, his voice edged with frustration. 'Warden knew all about the Regalia.'

'Yes, I'm sure there must be. But this place, this tree, this is important. I need to find it. See if you can find this on the map.' She passed him a sketch of the city-scape. 'I'm going to ask Scribe to meet me at the Scroll Archive.'

'Good idea.' He took the sketch and they crossed the veil. He trudged up the stairs towards the attic, where the map was kept. Weaver set off for the river, calling Scribe on the way.

'I need you to meet me. We have a clue.'

'Of course. Look, I know it's on your territory, and we talked about terms when we found it, but you know, it's only meant to be certain people who go there.'

'I know. And I want you to train me. I want to do what you do.'

'Okay, sure. I can do that. I'll be there as soon as I can.' Weaver could hear the smile in his voice and couldn't help smiling to herself. She practically skipped to the Scroll Archive.

Scribe met her under the bridge soon after she arrived, an eager grin on his face. She hadn't seen him smile like that before, certainly not in a while, not since before Last-Breath-Echoes died. Under all his goth make up, he had a handsome face. Weaver hadn't really appreciated that before.

He unlocked the door and led her inside. The torches flickered to life on the walls as they entered.

'Have you ever heard of Immunsul?' she asked, as he led the way down the tunnel and into the small room stacked with scrolls.

'No,' he replied, frowning. 'What is it?'

'A place, I think. An upside down tree. I had a vision of it and the Regalia.'

'An upside down tree?' he repeated, looking at her sceptically. 'Could it have been a metaphor?'

'No,' she said, more firmly than she felt. 'No, I'm certain it's literal, this time. Just a gut feeling.'

'Okay, well, we can look for it. I know there is stuff in here about the Regalia. I saw it once before somewhere.' He went to the rows of boxes labelled with each pack name. He started pulling scrolls out of the section marked "The Watch" and passed them to her. The topmost scrolls were newer, the parchment still close to white and crisp in her hands. As Scribe pulled out older ones, Weaver noticed the yellowed parchment lent and how soft they felt. 'It was one of these,' Scribe muttered, grasping a handful of ancient scrolls. 'You can put the rest back.' Weaver did as instructed, then followed Scribe to the desk. It was an ancient mahogany desk, littered with quills, ink and scraps of parchment.

He began uncurling a scroll and passed another to her. She carefully unhooked the delicate tassel that held it curled up and gently began to unroll the ancient parchment. It felt like no one had opened it in decades, probably longer. There was dust on the edges.

'I don't think you've read this one,' she said softly, almost afraid of the heavy silence of the place.

Scribe looked up and looked at the parchment in her hands.

'You might be right. Check it anyway, it's from around the same time as this one. First lesson of this role, anything you read in here about another pack is strictly confidential. You can't even let on to that pack that you've read it, unless it's a matter of life or death. These records are treated with the utmost sanctity. We are entrusted with the deepest, darkest secrets and not everything in here is good. Not all the packs even know this place exists.'

'Okay. I promise to respect the sanctity of the Scroll Archive. Is it only Scroll Keepers who ever write these records then? Never anyone else?'

'That's correct. We might sometimes interview other shifters about their experiences in order to make the records, or get accounts from fae or demons that we trust to be honest. There's a lot of bias in here though. You have to accept that right away. Most of these records are incomplete, sketchy or hearsay. Or downright propaganda. You have to know how to interpret what you find.'

'I see.' Weaver looked down at the scroll in her hands and very carefully uncurled it further, flattening it on the desk. The faded parchment was covered in neat rows of tiny handwriting. The ink had faded with time and was difficult to make out. She squinted in the torchlight to make out the date at the top. A gasp escaped her lips and she looked up at Scribe, who was poring over his own scroll. 'This is over four hundred years old.'

'That's right,' he said, not looking up. 'The Watch have been around for a very long time. Some say since the founding of Caerton itself. But there's no evidence of that.' He smiled at her as her eyes reflexively glanced towards the cave drawings on the walls. Someone had to have made those earliest marks. 'It seems like there weren't distinct packs until around a thousand years ago, when our numbers swelled. Before that, the Chosen of Artemis were one army, sworn to the Chosen of Nyx, the Furies.'

'I see.'

She looked back down at the cramped, slanted writing on the parchment. Finally, with a groan, she realised that it was written in runes, not English.

'I can't read much of this, I'm afraid. It's too faded and I'm not confident enough with the runes to decipher them.'

'That's okay. Take a look through some of the newer ones. No point looking at anything written in the last seventy years or so, though, the Regalia have been completely missing for at least that long.'

Weaver nodded and put aside the ancient scroll. She went in search of something a bit more recent.

'Exactly when did the revolution happen?'

'At the end of World War II. Our people rose up against the Furies and executed the King. We banished the Furies from the city and ordered them never to return. We tried to exile The Watch too, for fear of their loyalty to the King. They were his personal guard.'

'Is anyone still alive who remembers that?'

'Ragged Edge was there. Probably Red Scythe too. I know a couple of the Storm Riders were around, including the old Alpha. She died a few years ago though.' The air grew heavy with mention of this pack, who had been wiped out mysteriously a few months previously.

'What happened with The Watch then?'

'The first council of elders was set up and they debated it. It was decided that The Watch should stay. I think in part because our numbers had taken a hit in the conflict, and the elders were afraid of retaliation by the Furies. The Watch convinced them that they were loyal to the Chosen of Artemis.'

'And now two members of The Watch sit on the council.' Weaver raised an eyebrow.

'Yes, that is unusual. But Warden and Ragged Edge are two of the most experienced shifters in Caerton. Warden was elected after Father Ash was exiled. Ragged Edge was already on the council then. Did you know that Fortune used to be one of the elders?'

'No.' Weaver looked at him again. He was still hunched over his scroll.

'He still hasn't been replaced.'

'Oh? Is that unusual?'

'A little. But there isn't really anyone qualified. I think the elders are waiting to see if a candidate emerges amidst all this.'

'Is it just on age?'

'No, they look at deeds, responsibilities, leadership, judgement. All that stuff. Crimson was the youngest shifter ever elected to the council. She was only about fifteen years changed at the time.'

Weaver scoffed at the idea of that being young. None of her pack were even one year changed.

'How old are you?' she asked, on an impulse.

'How rude,' Scribe said with a smirk. 'I changed five years ago.'

'How old were you when it happened?'

'Sixteen.'

'I see.' She was a little older than him, in human terms. But those five years of shifter life that he had over her meant the world of difference, she understood that. He may as well be ten years older than her.

'I'd heard of the Regalia before, when Warden told us all at the meeting. Something from my childhood.' She hesitated, but decided she could trust him. 'I was raised by Furies, you know?'

'No, I didn't.' He looked up at her, his eyes wide.

'My parents had parted from their parents on bad terms though, and my sister and I were raised away from shifter life. But we heard things, we got glimpses. I was taught a song about the Regalia. But I'd forgotten it until I heard the word again.'

'What was the song?'

Weaver closed her eyes and tried to recall the words and melody. Snatches of it came back to her and she hummed them.

'I can't remember all of it. But there was a verse that went something like...

I heard it on the wind,
The story passing down,
Adrift among the willow trees,

The Sceptre, Orb and Crown.'

'Was the tree in your vision a willow?' Scribe asked softly. She blinked at him, emerging from her reverie.

'I don't know. It was upside down. The branches were buried underground. I couldn't tell from the roots what kind of tree it was. What happened to the Regalia? How were they lost?'

'That's what I want to find out.'

The two of them got down to work, poring over old scrolls. They prioritised those about The Watch, on the assumption that if any pack knew anything about the Regalia, it would be that one. Warden certainly knew, and Weaver accepted that they would have to talk to her about them in any case, as prickly and obstructive as she could be.

But aside from a couple of passing references in older scrolls, they found nothing that they didn't already know. They moved on to other packs' records. Weaver was examining one belonging to the Strom Riders some decades previously. Someone in the last few years had restored it, lovingly going over the writing with fresh ink, so it was easier to read than many of the others. It was startlingly detailed and written in the first person.

'I think the Scroll Keeper who wrote this was a Storm Rider.'

'Yes, there was a Storm Rider who was one of us. I remember Flames-First-Guardian talking about her. She disappeared a little before the pack went all odd. She kept excellent records about her pack. Not much about anyone else though.' A sad smile crept onto his face.

Weaver went back to the text.

The sky was blazing, purple and orange. It reminded me of fire. Then I saw them, the Regalia, glistening in the setting sun. The jewels set into the Crown were dazzling. The Orb was perfect crystal and the Sceptre shone gold. I knew them. They were like old friends. I had made them. I was ancient and uncompromising as I beheld them. I was one with the beings of Nidavellir, the constructs that built so much of our land. When the vision ended I knew the truth, I knew that the King was corrupt and that there was only one way this torment would end. I knew what must be done and I knew the Regalia would be the key. I entrusted no one with this secret. It was I, and I alone, who would be able to conceal the relics. And none but me would find them again.

'Who wrote this?' Weaver asked, searching the parchment for a signature. 'What was her name?'

'No one knows,' Scribe said, taking the parchment from Weaver to read it himself. 'She sacrificed her identity. No one remembers her real name, but she came to be known as Lost.'

'Is that who you mentioned before? The one who originally wrote this? Who kept great records? How old was she?'

'Yes. She probably restored it too, but there's no record of that. She was fairly old when she vanished. I never knew her, it was before my time, but I guess she would have been about a hundred.'

'How old is Theodore? And the other elders, for that matter?'

'About eighty I think. Red Scythe and Ragged Edge are older. I'm not sure about Warden. Why?'

'I'm just trying to piece together a timeline. It would be helpful to know who knew who and who might have told who what. If Lost knew where the Regalia were hidden, she says here she wouldn't tell anyone, but maybe she did. Or maybe someone found out. Maybe her disappearance is linked. And maybe she's still alive.'

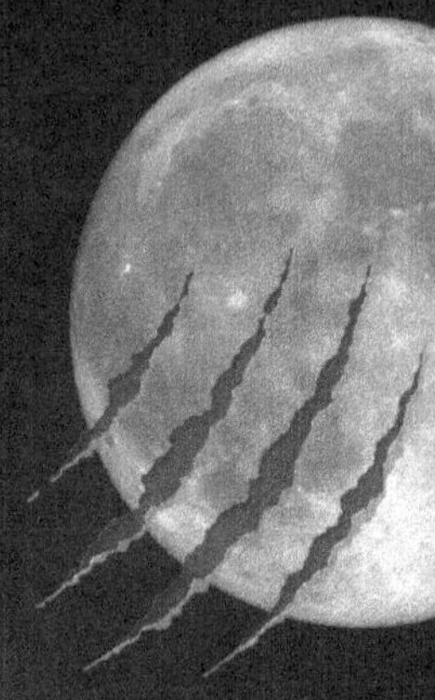

CHAPTER SIXTEEN

STALKER-OF-NIGHT'S-SHADOW

STALKER RETURNED TO GROVE STREET straight from training with Ragged Edge, although she was tempted to run and find Rhys. But her pack had trusted her to train unaccompanied and she didn't feel like betraying that trust was the best thing to do under the circumstances. Her heart ached for Rhys though, she knew she couldn't be without him for long. She would have to convince the pack of his goodness. Somehow.

The house was quiet and dark. Stalker felt the exhaustion of the day's events heavily on her aching muscles and collapsed onto the sofa to sleep.

The house was buzzing when she woke up the next morning. In the kitchen, Weaver was chattering loudly, her voice filled with excitement. When she caught sight of Stalker, she grabbed hold of her, grinning broadly.

'I had a vision of the Regalia! I know a bit more about them. I found out some new information from the Scroll

Archive! We need to find Lost.'

'Who?'

'Lost! She was a Storm Rider.'

'The Storm Riders are dead,' Stalker said bluntly, heaving a sigh.

'I know, but Lost may have survived. She wasn't really with the pack anymore. As far as I can tell, she sacrificed her entire identity in exchange for some piece of information from a demon. She lost all of who she was; her pack, her sense of self. She wandered off and became a sort of lone wolf. Not many people knew she existed, a lot of people forgot her entirely, others forgot her old name, they just knew vaguely of a shifter in the north. Her pack didn't forget her, but they only knew her as "Lost".' Weaver made air quotes with her fingers. Stalker had rarely seen her so animated.

'How would we even begin looking for her?' Eyes asked, his arms crossed loosely over his chest.

'We might find a demon who knows. Maybe the very one who struck the bargain with her.'

'What did she get in exchange for this massive sacrifice?' Stalker asked, raising an eyebrow.

'No one knows. But it was right before the Storm Riders went all insular and odd, before they devoted themselves so completely to the sea and started preaching about the coming storm. So I think it's a fair guess that it was about that. She must have learned about the threat from the sea and her pack devoted themselves to combating that in order to honour her sacrifice.'

'Were they right? Has anyone learned what happened to them? Was it something from the sea?' Stalker felt the questions bubbling out of her.

'I don't know,' Weaver said, shrugging.

'That would be something to find out,' Eyes said. 'But what does Lost have to do with the Regalia?'

'She wrote about them in the Scroll Archive. She was a Scroll Keeper, she sacrificed that too. Flames knew her.' Weaver looked pointedly at Wind Talker. 'She had visions and she saw the Regalia. She wrote that she had hidden them and that no one else knew where. If she is still alive, then she may be the only person who can help find them.'

'What if she lost her memories too? Or her mind?' Wind Talker asked, his voice not betraying any emotion he may have felt at the mention of Flames-First-Guardian.

'Well, if that is the case, we still have another lead, we can keep searching for Immunsul. I'm certain it will be a location in Hepethia, like the Orchard, hidden away somewhere.'

'I looked at the sketch you gave me and tried to match it up to an area of Hepethia, but it's not possible with just a map. I need a 3D image showing buildings and land contours if I'm going to have any luck with it.'

'I can probably help with that,' Claws said, from his seat at the table. 'Aerial view, and all that.'

The sketches were laid out on the table, where Claws had evidently been studying them. Stalker looked down at them and saw the bizarre concrete jungle, drawn with remarkable detail. She had never had much artistic skill and part of her envied Weaver's abilities. She briefly wondered if all seers were gifted artists, as a means of communicating their visions to their packs. It was possible, she supposed.

'We have possibilities before us, this is great progress. Thank you, Weaver.' Eyes approached her and grasped her shoulder. She gave him a warm smile. Stalker felt as though she were watching from the outside, no longer quite a part of the pack, still not quite trusted. Would Eyes ever give her that brotherly approval again? Did she need him to?

'Stalker, fancy taking a fly around with me? Two pairs of eyes are better than one.' Claws was getting to his feet.

'Sure.'

'Be careful, both of you,' Eyes cautioned. 'Take the opportunity to patrol as well, please.'

'Of course.' Claws nodded. He indicated for Stalker to follow him. Stalker glanced at the others and tried to smile.

'Eyes, Ragged Edge and I talked about restarting the Hunt. I want him to train me to find Spiral Hand. The other Alphas might need convincing. Something to think about.'

Eyes nodded in reply. Stalker hesitated, waiting for something else, but awkward silence hung on the air. She turned and followed Claws down the hall. Before the door, they crossed the veil. Claws' hand was on the door, but Stalker reached out and held him back. 'What do you think of this stuff from Weaver?'

'I think we need to explore every avenue. I don't hold out much hope of finding this landscape though, her visions aren't usually quite so literal.'

Stalker nodded.

They stepped out into the street, closed the door and took flight. The wind rushed against her feathers, lifting her spirits. The jumbled thoughts crowding her mind slipped away, her owl brain too primitive to contain it all. It was her, Claws and the open skies.

In flight, they crossed the veil again, back into the human world and soared high over the city, looking for skylines that resembled Weaver's sketches. Stalker didn't have Claws' eidetic memory, but she tried to recall the details of Weaver's sketch and looked out for buildings that might match the trees. Her imagination wasn't quite up to the task and she quickly grew frustrated. Claws flew ahead of her, and his thoughts reached her through their bond.

This isn't possible.

An image of an upside down tree popped into Stalker's mind, courtesy of Claws' mind. Stalker understood at once that this was what they were really looking for.

Hepethia? Stalker thought in reply. Without any need for further communication, the two of them crossed again into Hepethia and began searching for an upside down tree.

The sky was crystal clear and the air was warm. Stalker's feathers ruffled in the breeze. She was almost able to forget the ticking clock, counting down towards the summer solstice, the deadline that the envoy of the Furies had given them. But they were searching the varied landscape of Hepethia for something that seemed impossible. Stalker felt sure that she would have seen something as distinctive as an upside down tree at some point in her exploration of the area.

The pair of owls flew across the packed terraces of St. Mark's, over to the river and to where the boundary with St. Catherine's was rife with demonic activity. The river served as a moat, keeping the worst of the problems from crossing into the Lightning Lords' territory, but the bridges were weak spots. All seemed quiet on this side of the river, however, and the two shifters flew on.

They swept over the Orchard, which was tucked away behind tall terraces, very easy to miss. But Stalker remembered the evening the pack had spent there. It definitely wasn't home to the tree they were looking for.

Stalker and Claws came full circle. The repair job on the site of the Bone Anchor was holding nicely. All was quiet in St. Mark's. Northgate was chugging loudly, as usual, the living factories churning out smoke. The once demon-infested park in Redfield, which was now the Wrecking Crew's turf, was green and clear. The pair of them flew into Fenwick, now safely theirs, soaring over the clear crystal quartz and tree-like structures of coloured crystals that jutted up from the ground. It was a breathtaking sight. Stalker felt the breeze ruffling her feathers and the sun warming her back and wings. There was no sign anywhere of unruly demons, or intruding Furies. Nor was there any sign of the upside down tree.

The two owls landed, shifting form as their feet met the ground. In their human forms they grinned at each other.

'I am so glad you've got used to that,' Stalker said, beaming at Claws.

'Yeah, well, it's still damn weird and unnatural, but it is what it is and I am what I am.' He shrugged.

'I wish we had found what we were looking for though,' Stalker said with a resigned sigh.

'Yeah, still, we have Weaver's other lead. Shall we?' He held out a hand to indicate crossing the veil in a spot familiar to both of them, a place they had crossed the veil dozens of times.

Stalker grinned again and stepped across, Claws just behind her. The sun was blazing down on the busy street just ahead of the end of the alley that they had crossed into. Stalker squinted against the brightness, still elated from their flight. She turned her head to see Claws shimmer across the veil, smiled broadly at him and took a step towards the bustling street.

A loud crack snapped her head back toward the street. It was a moment before she realised her feet were completely frozen to the spot. She started to sway sideways, her vision blurring.

'No!'

The shout barely registered, it sounded miles away. But she was dimly aware that it was Claws' voice. Stalker's head tilted down slowly to examine the emerging ache in her chest. There was blood down her shirt and her unfocused eyes just about took in the hole that the blood was oozing from before she fell to the ground and everything went black.

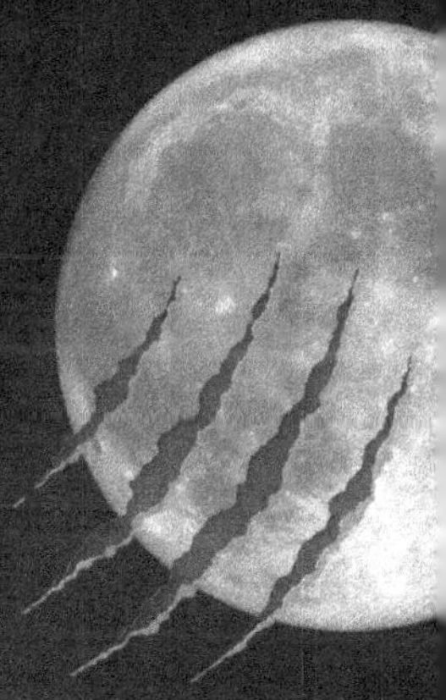

Chapter Seventeen

Fights-Eyes-Open

'Will she be all right?' Eyes ran his hands through his hair for the tenth time in just a few minutes.

'I don't know. Even shifters don't do especially well if they take a shot to the chest,' Wind Talker stated, matter-of-factly, but keeping his voice low.

'But she is still alive, so that's promising.' Weaver placed a reassuring hand on his forearm.

'Who did this?' Eyes asked, fire roaring to life in his belly. He glared down at Claws, who was sitting on a plastic chair, his head in his hands.

'It was a sniper. I had a split second to decide whether to try and pursue the shooter, or get help for Stalker. It was a no-brainer. So I have no idea. But I think we can fairly safely assume Furies are behind it.'

They were all keeping their voices low as the hospital waiting room buzzed around them. She had been shot only a few blocks away from the hospital. It wasn't ideal to have one of their kind in the hands of human doctors, but Claws had done the only thing he could in that instant. Eyes understood that.

'You're Ariana's family?' a doctor asked, approaching the pack. She raised a sceptical eyebrow as she surveyed the odd group. Eyes stepped forward at once.

'Yes. How is she?'

'Out of surgery. She's still sleeping, but we managed to remove the bullet and repair the bleeding. She was very lucky, it just missed her heart.'

'Can we see her?'

'Yes, of course.' The doctor set off along the corridor and the pack hurried after her. Eyes' heart was racing. What if she had changed on the operating table? Her Agrius could have taken over to save her life, she would have slaughtered everyone in the operating room. That still could happen when she began to regain consciousness and realised what had happened.

The hospital stank simultaneously of disinfectant and disease. Eyes wrinkled his nose as they walked quickly along the sterile-feeling corridor.

The doctor led them into a ward and into a private room off the long corridor. Stalker was covered in wires and had a tube under her nose. Her skin was even more pale than usual, almost matching the crisp white sheets on which she lay. 'We don't see many gun-related injuries. But this is the second one today,' the doctor said. 'Even more bizarrely, they were both shot with silver bullets. I believe the police will be along to question you soon.'

Eyes glanced meaningfully at Wind Talker.

'That's odd,' Eyes said, feigning mild interest, rather

than the significant alarm that he felt inside.

'Very,' the doctor replied. 'Well, I'll leave you to it.' She left the room and closed the door.

Eyes took Stalker's hand and squeezed it gently.

'Don't die, Stalker, you tough nut. Come back to us.'

'Shall I see if I can find out who the other victim was?' Claws asked, shifting his feet awkwardly. 'I don't think I can bear to sit in here and look at her like that.'

Eyes glanced at him and nodded. Claws bolted out of the door.

'We need to get her home as soon as possible. She'll be healing far more quickly than a human, it could arouse suspicion.'

'And how do we do that, Wind Talker? Wheel her out under a blanket like orderlies moving a corpse?' Eyes snapped at him, but he quickly regretted it. He looked sheepishly at his pack mate.

'She was shot with silver, that's why she's not already back on her feet. Her body needs time to kick-start the healing process. She is likely to shift form, it could happen at any time now. She can't be here.' Wind Talker's voice was calm and patient. Eyes nodded, still looking at her and holding her hand.

'She's going to heal,' Weaver whispered. 'I promise. But we need to have her in the best place for that. Which isn't here. We could take her across the veil.'

'We can't dodge the police though, they have her name and address.' Eyes closed his eyes for a moment. 'They'll probably be looking at this as a gang incident, and with two victims it could mount a large scale investigation. This is an incredibly dangerous time for our kind.'

The door burst open and Claws flew into the room. He closed the door sharply and stared at Eyes, wide-eyed and breathless. 'What is it? Who is it?' As Eyes spoke, his phone began to ring. Weaver's phone alerted her to a message at almost the same moment, quickly followed by Wind Talker's. 'What on earth is going on?' Eyes asked, tugging his phone from the inside pocket of his suit jacket. It was Theodore Harris. 'Claws?' he asked, holding his phone out and hurrying his pack mate before answering.

'It's everywhere, the whole city,' Claws panted. 'First Strike is here, he's dead. I had a message from Rust too, Herald and Sky Runner are both injured, shot with silver bullets.'

'Oh my goddess!' Weaver cried out, clutching her phone in her hand and shaking. Tears immediately began to fall down her pale cheeks and vocal sobs shook her body.

Eyes could delay no longer, the ringing phone in his hand seemed to grow louder and more insistent. He accepted the call and put it on speaker so they could all hear.

'Theodore, I'm in hospital with Ariana. The rest of my group can hear you.'

'Is she all right?' Theodore asked in a strained voice.

'She's going to be. We need to get her out of here, quickly. Any suggestions?'

'Erm, no, not right now. I can't...' Theodore sounded rattled. Eyes glanced around at his pack mates, who seemed equally unnerved by Theodore's tone.

'Have you been hit too?' Eyes asked. Weaver was still sobbing and clutching her phone. Claws had pulled her into a tight embrace.

'Rachel's been shot too. She's in a critical condition.' Theodore's voice trembled.

'I'm sorry. I hope she pulls through,' Eyes said, looking up at Claws. Rachel was the human name of Vengeance-of-Steel, the police officer who had helped smooth things over when Eyes' family was attacked. He owed her a great debt. 'Has every group been hit? Have you heard from anyone else?'

'It's looking bad, but we should speak in person.'

'Theodore?' Weaver's voice was broken. She pulled out of Claws' arms and moved closer to the phone in Eyes' hand. 'Have you heard about The Hellsclaws? I got the message just as the phone rang.' Her face was red and blotchy, her eyes and nose were streaming.

'What happened to them?' Eyes asked, his voice barely rising above a whisper. He thought he already knew, based on the state Weaver was in and the frenzied thoughts making their way to him through their bond.

'No, what happened?' Theodore asked.

'Scribe is the only one left.' Weaver broke into renewed sobs.

'Oh god,' Wind Talker said, breathlessly.

'Right,' Theodore said with a heavy sigh. 'That's really awful news. Look, I've just had Warden on the phone. They had a major loss too. But I'm not saying on speaker with Ariana in her present state. I gather they were close.'

'Were?' Eyes said, his pulse racing.

'Yes. Look, I've got to go, and best leave you to it. I'm sorry I can't be of any help. I'm sure you'll manage to think of a way to get her out. We will all rally to deal with any repercussions, I promise you, human or other. If they could have done one stupid thing to ensure we were united, it was this.' His voice trailed away into mutters.

'Okay, yes, you're right. I'll speak to you again later.' Eyes hung up the phone and looked at each of his pack mates. The shock and devastation was written on each of their faces. 'How did they manage it?'

'I don't know,' Wind Talker replied, his voice hard and distant, his jaw clenched tight. 'We need to take a good look at our security, all of us, the whole city. How did they get into South Stoke undetected and take out practically an entire pack in broad daylight?'

Weaver was wiping her face on her sleeves. She took a big sniff and shook her head as if to clear it.

'I'm going to go to Scribe now.'

'Don't go alone,' Eyes said at once. 'They could still be in the city taking down anyone they see. Wind Talker, you go with her. Stay safe.' He stood up and pulled Weaver into a hug. They squeezed each other tightly for a moment that drew out. He released her and the two of them left quietly. 'We'll move Stalker to Grove Street.'

Claws nodded, his face still white with shock, and ran around to the other side of the bed.

'Are we taking everything? Or just her?'

'Everything, right now, until her own healing kicks in, she may really need the machines.'

'And what do we do about the police and answering to the doctors about her disappearance?'

'We'll have to figure that out later. Let's do this.' Eyes gripped the rail on the side of the bed, Claws mirrored him. With great focus and straining his imagination, Eyes visualised taking Stalker, the bed and all of the machines around it across the veil.

The hospital shimmered out of focus and he felt a tug at his navel. They appeared in Hepethia. Eyes' breath caught in his throat. They were standing on a mound of rubble in the midst of ruins and the ground was soaked in blood.

'What the fuck?' Claws said, his voice echoing off the partial walls around them.

'The events of today must have had a profound effect on this part of Hepethia. World shattering bloodshed.' He gestured around them at the very literal interpretation of the pack's experience.

'Do you think all of Hepethia is like this?'

'I don't know. I hope not. I think it might just be the hospital. Are First Strike's pack mates here?' Eyes asked, suddenly thinking of The Hand of God. They weren't far from their territory.

'Yes, that was how I found out who it was. I saw Crimson in the hall. She told me.'

'Right. Oh fuck, Stalker used to be close to him, didn't she?'

'Yeah, but not for a while now.'

'How are we going to get her home with all this lot?' Eyes said, staring around.

'The battle van is parked near here. I can fly and get it. Everything should fit in the back.' Claws patted Eyes on the back and leapt into the air, shifting form and wobbling slightly as he took flight. Eyes watched him out of sight, a dark dot against the grey sky.

'Oh, Stalker. What a mess, eh?' He held her hand and brushed her hair out of her face.

Claws arrived in the van, rocking over the bumpy ground, and pulled up with the back close to Stalker's feet. Together, Eyes and Claws managed to get the bed and the equipment into the back of the van. Then they set off for Grove Street.

Once they cleared the hospital, Hepethia looked normal, more or less. They saw fear and anger demons scurrying about. They drove into the St. Mark's area, onto familiar narrow terraces. Claws stopped the van outside the house and they got Stalker across the veil and into the living room, with some difficulty, as the bed wouldn't fit through the narrow front door. They got her settled on the sofa, with the machines around her, and left the bed in the van.

'Is there anything we can do to help her heal more quickly? Anything we can summon to heal her?' Claws asked.

'We tried that, back in the early days of this pack,' Eyes said, with a raw smile. 'It came with a heavy price.' He sat down on the sofa beside Stalker's feet and patted her leg through the blanket.

'Eyes, there is something we should do. But I know you won't like it.'

'What?' Eyes asked wearily.

'We need to let Rhys know.'

'What?'

'She could still die. Do you really want a grieving lover knocking down the door demanding to know why he didn't get to say goodbye? In fact, I'll bet he already knows something has happened. They have a bond, like a pack bond. He'll have felt it. We need to tell him and let him see her.'

'Are you mad?' Eyes strained to keep his voice from rising.

'No, I'm perfectly sane. It's the decent thing to do. No matter what he is, I believe their love is real. Imagine how you would have felt if someone had prevented you going to your family when they were in hospital.'

'Goddammit.' Eyes knew Claws was right, and he had said just the right thing to persuade him. 'Yes, fine. How do we contact him though? I broke her phone. I really shouldn't have done that. She hates me.' He hung his head in his hands and felt the mounting errors and frustrations weighing on him.

'I think I know a way.' Claws bent over Stalker and pressed his palm to her cheek. 'If you're watching over her, please, show yourself.'

Eyes looked up expectantly, nothing had changed. 'Please,' urged Claws. 'I don't know your name, exactly, I know you are her guide.'

There was a soft ripple in the veil and a shimmering light lifted out of Stalker's body. Eyes leapt from the sofa, his heart racing.

'What is that? Is that her soul? Is she dying?' He grabbed hold of Claws and tugged him back.

'I am Fylgia, Stalker's ancestral guide.' The light spoke with a soft voice, it reminded Eyes of gentle rainfall on glass. 'She is not dying, but she is deeply unwell. Her mind is swimming in darkness.'

'She's in love,' Claws said softly.

'Yes, she is, deeply.'

'Can you bring him to her? We have no way to contact

him.'

'Of course.' Fylgia shimmered out of sight again. Eyes heaved a sigh and knelt down beside Stalker. He rested his head on her arm and felt a tear prickle at the corner of his eye.

'What if he can't be trusted, Claws? And we let him into our home? Our headquarters?'

'I don't think there is much he can see here that would cause a problem. I think we need to focus on Stalker right now, and worry about the rest later.'

The minutes seemed to stretch. Eyes could hardly lift his head, the exhaustion was crippling. He wanted to hear from Weaver and Wind Talker, to know they were all right. He wanted Stalker to wake up, or shift, or show some signs of life. But she lay there, still and silent, with just the beeping of the machines to reassure him that she hadn't slipped away.

Finally, after what felt like hours, there was a tentative knock on the door. Eyes lifted his head and looked blearily at Claws. He stood slowly and walked to the door.

'Who is it?' he called through the dull wood.

'Rhys.'

Eyes pressed his hands to the door and took a deep breath, pushing the beast deep down. He knew that having a stranger who he didn't trust here, in the heart of his territory, was going to be a trigger for the Agrius. He stepped back and opened the door slowly, taking in the stranger on the threshold.

Rhys was tall and imposing, built like a warrior. His dark hair hung like curtains either side of his face and his eyes were almost black. Eyes felt the Agrius snarl inside, but he stepped aside and indicated for Rhys to enter. As the newcomer passed him, Eyes felt waves of anguish rolling off him and wasn't quite sure how it was possible. Perhaps Stalker was acting as some sort of conduit.

Claws stood in the doorway to the living room and held out his hand. Rhys took it and shook it firmly. Eyes watched with awe at the ease with which Claws welcomed Rhys.

'Hi,' Claws said softly. 'I'm Claws. I'm glad you came. She's in here.'

'Thank you for reaching out to me. I understand how difficult that must have been.' Rhys brushed past Claws as he spoke and darted to Stalker's side. Eyes watched from the doorway, his arms folded tightly over his chest. He felt as though he were intruding on a private moment, as Rhys stooped to press his head against Stalker's chest and kiss her hand. 'I'm here, I'm right here, you're safe.'

Eyes cleared his throat and Rhys looked anxiously up at him. 'You must be Fights-Eyes-Open. I would say that Stalker told me all about you but she didn't, honestly. I know how much you mean to her, I know how loyal she is to you. But I know almost nothing about you, any of you.'

'That sounded rehearsed,' said Eyes, frowning.

'It was, I suppose. I knew I wanted to say it, just so we're clear, but it's the absolute truth.'

Eyes raised an eyebrow. This was the first shifter he had knowingly met, who didn't give off the shifter aura. Normally shifters could sense one another, smell the supernatural on each other, even in human form. But not this guy, this guy smelled human. That alone was enough to keep Eyes sceptical.

'You're still hiding what you are, even though you've come here knowing that we know.'

'I can't help it, it's not something I can switch on and off. I took steps to hide from your kind when I arrived here ten years ago and it seems to be permanent. I was running for my life, you must understand that. I'd been taught to fear and hate humanity and the Chosen of Artemis, but I was also running from the Furies who slaughtered my entire pack and all my kin. I didn't know if I could trust a single living soul.'

'Yes, Stalker mentioned that.' Eyes shifted his weight and his gaze flickered over Stalker's prone form.

'I understand why you don't trust me. I probably wouldn't either. So I truly appreciate being given the chance to come and see her.' Rhys's gaze settled back on Stalker's pale face. He stroked her hair tenderly and raised her hand to brush against his cheek.

'Don't take your eyes off him,' Eyes ordered Claws, not caring that Rhys could hear. 'I'm going to see our friend in the tower.'

Claws nodded in acknowledgement.

Eyes swept from the house, frustration bristling under his skin. He couldn't bear to watch Stalker being fawned over by a complete stranger. But his duty pulled him away too. He was the Alpha, and he had been calling on the packs to unite for months. He had to respond to the day's events and lead the charge.

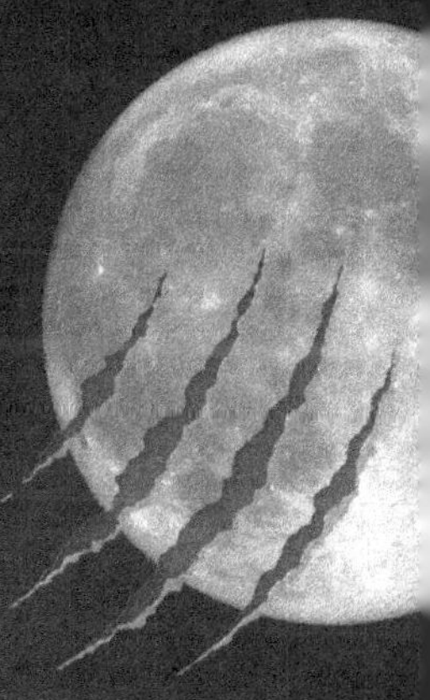

Chapter Eighteen

'This is unprecedented,' Theodore said, his voice shaking slightly. 'This kind of attack. I've never seen anything like it.'

'We need to get all of the Alphas together,' Eyes urged, pacing Theodore's office at the top of Free River Tower.

'I agree. But everyone is a bit busy right now.'

'Have any of the packs apprehended any of the shooters? What do you know?'

'The Watch took out the shooter in Old Town, I know that much. Crimson Dawn's Blood and the Hand of God chased off their attackers. I don't know about the others.'

'What about you? What happened here?'

'Vengeance was working, she was in uniform when it happened and there were dozens of witnesses. Her colleagues were all over the scene by the time I got there. But she had managed to cross the veil, so they couldn't find her. I did. The shooter got away.'

'I take it it was Ragged Edge who was taken down in Old Town?' Theodore nodded and Eyes was sure he saw his eyes tearing up. 'Oh god. Stalker will be devastated.'

'He was one of the oldest dogs I knew. The old bastard had been on the council nearly as long as I've been a shifter. I remember him in his prime. They never would have stood a chance against him then. They could have sent an entire pack and he would have handled them single handed.'

'I wish I could have seen that,' Eyes said, a wry smile playing on his lips. 'Were all of the hits in the human world?'

'As far as I know, yes.'

'That's interesting. Why wouldn't they hit us in Hepethia? Surely shifters are easier to find there. We stick out from the landscape and aren't hidden among millions of humans.'

'The Furies' raison d'être is to dominate humanity. It suits them to have people terrified, so they can present themselves as the protectors of humanity. They refuse to hide from humans, so they want to expose our world.'

'Oh god, did anyone shift form in front of witnesses? How much madness do we have to mop up?'

'I gather there are issues in most territories.' Theodore covered his eyes with a hand and heaved a great sigh. Eyes had never seen him like this, he seemed almost defeated.

'That was what they wanted, wasn't it? They wanted their victims to change and cause outbreaks of the lunacy.'

'Yes, I believe so. They were shooting to kill, also. Silver bullets. They want to thin our numbers so we don't put up a fight when they march into the city.'

'You're not going to bow to them, are you?' Eyes asked, more accusation in his voice than he had intended.

'Of course not,' Theodore snapped, dropping his hand and glowering at Eyes. 'It's been a trying day and I'm worried about my pack mate. But the cowards will know that we won't take this lying down, don't you worry about that.'

Eyes nodded solemnly and stopped pacing. He stood opposite Theodore and ran his hands through his hair.

'You know, you look just like Fortune when you do that.'

Eyes immediately dropped his hands and snorted with derisive laughter.

'Yeah, I hear that. You knew him well, didn't you?'

'Maybe. I'm not sure any more. We were on the council together, but it was never an easy relationship. We certainly weren't friends.'

'Are we?'

Theodore tilted his head and looked at Eyes appraisingly for a moment that seemed to stretch far beyond what was comfortable.

'I think so. Huh.' Theodore shook his head. 'I'm not sure I've ever had a friend outside my pack before.'

'Sorry to hear that.' There was an awkward silence before either of them spoke again. Finally, Eyes cleared his throat. 'So what will happen about South Stoke? Scribe can't hold it on his own.'

'I don't know. I guess that's for him to decide. Have your people spoken to him yet?'

'Weaver's with him now. They've been getting close. Have you heard from the Fyrd at all? Were they hit too?'

'I never hear from the Fyrd,' Theodore replied with a wry smile. 'Or the Savages for that matter. We do need to find out what state the city's southern borders are in. You should coordinate with The Watch on the western border too. With St. Catherine's unclaimed there isn't much in the way of a border in the north-west of the city. You're pretty much it.'

'That occurred to me too. That's probably how they got in undetected actually, straight through St. Catherine's. It would be suicide in Hepethia, but on this side of the veil there are no defences really. We were always so concerned with the Witches to the east, I never really gave much thought to the other side of our territory. A rookie mistake.'

'You're learning. I have to say, Eyes, I was sceptical when I learned that you and your young pack mates had survived and that you were the Alpha. I expected you to be wiped out within the month. Yet here you are, leading the charge against the Furies.'

Eyes didn't quite know what to say in reply. He just stood nodding slightly, his way of thanking Theodore for his frankness, and what was probably meant to be encouragement.

The phone on Theodore's desk rang, shattering the uneasy silence. He picked it up and spoke into the receiver. 'Yes?'

Eyes looked past him and out of the window. The sky was growing dark, a rich purple spreading across the skyline and the first stars just beginning to be visible. 'Show her in, of course,' Theodore snapped into his phone, dragging Eyes' attention back into the office.

The door burst open and Crimson strode in ahead

of a very nervous-looking assistant, who closed the door quickly.

Crimson's face was flushed and her hair was wild.

'What is being done about this?' she demanded, slamming her hands down on the desk and leaning over it so that her nose was inches from Theodore's. Eyes wasn't sure she had even seen him.

'Crimson,' Theodore said softly, standing up and placing his hands on her shoulders. 'Eyes and I are just discussing it now.' He nodded over her shoulder towards Eyes. Crimson turned her head and blushed even more, embarrassment flooding her cheeks.

'I apologise, Eyes, I didn't realise you were here. I heard that Stalker was shot. How is she?'

'Healing, still unconscious. I heard about First Strike. I'm so sorry.'

Crimson nodded her head and stepped away from the desk. She brushed her hair out of her face and straightened her long, red coat.

'Will we strike back?'

'That would be a mistake, I believe,' Theodore said calmly. 'They have the numbers, we are in disarray. We need to pull ourselves together quickly and redouble our efforts to prepare for war. And to summon the King-of-Glass-and-Steel.'

Crimson rolled her eyes at him and shook her head.

'That is a distraction, as I have made clear to you repeatedly. We need to focus on the real world, the Furies.'

'But don't you see? The reason the Furies have been able to make the gains they have, is because the city's guiding spirit is missing. I don't believe we can truly defeat the Furies without getting our fae in order. Eyes, you agree with me, don't you?'

It was a painfully loaded question. Here stood two of the city's elders, two powerful Alphas with dominant packs. Eyes cleared his throat to buy himself time, but he felt two pairs of eyes boring into him.

'Well, I certainly see both sides of the argument.'

'Don't be a lawyer,' Crimson interrupted, crossing her arms over her chest and glaring at him.

'I agree with Theodore on this,' Eyes said, a lump rising in his throat. He was being honest, but he hated to look like Theodore's lackey. 'We can't go on without the King-of-Glass-and-Steel. Once we have him back then we stand a much better chance of defeating the Furies.'

'Thick as thieves, the pair of you, aren't you?' Crimson said, but there was the hint of a smile at the corner of her lips. 'Fine, fine. I'm going home. We'll summon the damn city spirit, then deal with the Furies. Oh, one or both of you might want to talk to Rust. They managed to take a prisoner in the attack.' She gave the two men a knowing wink and swept from the room in as much of a flurry as she had arrived.

Eyes had his phone out before Theodore could react, he just stood watching Crimson leave, an impressed expression on his face.

It seemed to ring forever, but finally Rust answered.

'What? I'm busy.'

'Is it true? I just saw Crimson. Do you have one of them?'

There was a scream in the background, a chilling howl of pain. 'I'll take that as a yes.' Eyes gave Theodore a wary glance.

'We're questioning him now,' Rust snapped. 'I'll let you know what we get out of him.' He hung up. Eyes held his phone out in mild disbelief and looked at Theodore.

'Well, good luck to them,' Theodore said with mild disinterest and utter unconcern for the obvious torture that was happening on the other end of the phone.

'Right. I'll coordinate western defences with Warden and check what the situation is with South Stoke. Are you able to put feelers out to the remaining southern packs and figure out a defence strategy with them?'

'Absolutely. I'll speak to you tomorrow. I hope Stalker pulls through quickly.'

'Thank you, same goes for Vengeance. She helped me out of a very tight spot a few months ago, well, you both did, of course. I haven't forgotten that.'

Theodore simply nodded and began moving papers around on his desk. 'Speak tomorrow.' Eyes strode from the room, satisfied with his standing among the Alphas. Despite the awful events of the day, he had a little spring in his step.

It was only when he got back to Grove Street that he remembered everything that was happening, but as he stood there, not quite ready to open the door, he refused to let himself feel deflated. Progress had been made, nothing was going to take that away.

He opened the door and was met with chatter and bright light. Smells of food cooking in the kitchen greeted him, and someone laughed. This was so at odds with his own reflections on the doorstep that he was somewhat taken aback. But that spring he had felt in his step was a similar manifestation of happiness, so he could at least relate to it.

'I'm back!' he called out. He walked quickly to the back of the house, glancing into the living room as he passed. Stalker was still unconscious on the sofa, hooked up to the machines. But there was distinctly more colour in her cheeks. The rest of the pack was assembled in the kitchen, laughing loudly and preparing a meal together. Rhys was at the stove, stirring what looked like a curry and evidently entertaining the pack with some highly amusing story.

'And that wasn't even the best part!' Rhys blurted out, his face red. He caught sight of Eyes in the doorway and the laugh died on his face.

'Eyes!' Weaver launched herself at him and wrapped her arms around him. He hugged her back, but didn't take his eyes off Rhys. She released him and looked up into his eyes, then back at Rhys. 'Rhys was just telling us about—'

'I can tell you're all having a blast. Have you forgotten about your critical pack mate in the next room? Or our dead friends?'

'No, of course not,' Weaver said, stung.

'We were just getting to know each other,' Claws said, in his frustratingly diplomatic way.

'How's Scribe?' Eyes asked, shooting a severe look at Weaver.

'He's doing terribly,' she replied, turning away from him and moving over to where she had been chopping onions. 'Obviously. I offered him a bed here if he needs it, by the way. But he said he needed to stay on his territory. I told him he can't possibly hold it on his own, but he wants to try. So I said we would support him any way we could.'

'Right. He'll need back up from somewhere. It's not a huge territory, but he can't hold it alone. That whole side of the city is weak. It's now just The Watch on that side of the river. Theodore's going to coordinate with the packs along the southern border and see what can be done to shore up their defences. I cannot believe we are discussing this in front of him.'

Rhys looked down at the curry and stirred it, silently avoiding Eyes' vicious glare.

'Stalker is going to be fine. She's through the worst of it now, her own healing has kicked in already.' Wind Talker placed a hand on Eyes' shoulder and caught his gaze with a firm one of his own. Eyes nodded and moved away from the kitchen, back into the living room to check on her for himself.

'She hasn't woken up yet? Or shifted?' Eyes asked, sensing someone behind him. He turned and saw Claws following him.

'No, nothing. Eyes, you need to lay off Rhys a bit. Don't bite my head off as well. You need to hear this. I know what you and Wind Talker said about my ability, and I get it, I do, but he has done nothing but tell the truth since walking through the door today. And Stalker started to improve right after he sat with her. Bringing him here was the right thing to do, and I believe we can trust him, at least for now.'

Eyes refused to look at his pack mate, but Claws' words sunk in. He had always trusted the judgement and level head of his half-moon pack mate.

Stalker's hand twitched.

'Did you see that?' Eyes asked, keeping his gaze

focused on her.

'No. What?' Claws asked, moving closer.

'She twitched.' Stalker's face twitched now, then her hand again. 'There.'

'I saw. Rhys!'

Rhys came thundering through from the kitchen. Eyes kept looking at Stalker. Her body gave a shudder all over.

'It's getting worse. What's happening? Wind Talker? She's moving!'

Wind Talker and Weaver were already in the room behind him. The little living room had rarely been so full and Eyes felt like it might burst at the seams. Rhys moved closer to Stalker and crouched beside her.

'She's going to shift,' he said. 'Quick! Get ready!'

Eyes braced himself. When the Agrius took over, it could be catastrophic for the house, and any of the shifters present. Stalker's body continued to convulse on the sofa, while the machines she was still hooked up to went haywire. Rhys quickly unplugged everything, pulling wires off her body and the oxygen tube out from under her nose and around her head.

'What are you doing?' Eyes asked, panic rising in his chest.

'I don't want her to get tangled in them. She doesn't need them any more.'

Her body shook violently and fur began to erupt all over her body. Her limbs stretched, cracking and groaning with enormous effort. Eyes hadn't seen anything like it before, though he supposed that first changes might look like this. Practice made shifting into the Agrius a smooth transition, but right now, Stalker's body was changing erratically between human and Agrius, some parts switching between the two, other parts stuck in one form or the other.

'Let's get her across the veil!' Weaver said breathlessly. 'She could get very loud.'

The tight little terrace had reasonably thick walls, but a raging Agrius would still be an alarming sound for the neighbours. Eyes and Rhys grabbed hold of her and lurched across the veil. The pack followed quickly, filling the small living room in the reflection of the house in Hepethia. Stalker roared to life and ripped free of the loose grip that he and Rhys had on her. The full Agrius erupted before them, towering over them, seven feet tall and filled with rage. Stalker's tooth pendant bounced on her chest and Eyes shook his head clear of the reservation holding him back. He shifted form, mirroring her Agrius. It was going to take all of their strength to keep her from tearing limbs off or knocking walls down with that pendant around her neck heightening her strength.

Behind him, Eyes felt his pack mates shifting form too. He glanced at Rhys, who stood looking up at Stalker, stunned disbelief written all over his face.

Stop! Eyes projected directly into Stalker's mind. But her eyes were misted with rage, she wasn't in there. She roared again and lunged at him. He stooped and took her weight against his shoulder, forcing her back against the wall with a crunch. She struggled against him and was more than a match for his strength. But Wind Talker and Weaver were at his side in an instant, helping to pin her against the wall and stop her doing any damage.

Weaver raised a clawed hand and changed just her

hand back into a human one with fingers dexterous enough to grab at the tooth on Stalker's chest. She wrapped her fingers around it and tugged, breaking the cord and pulling the talisman away from Stalker. Weaver tossed it to the ground and brought her now Agrius hand to Stalker's shoulder.

Calm. Her thought radiated through Eyes' mind and he knew they were all hearing it.

Calm, Stalker, breathe. That was Claws. He was back in human form. Eyes looked over his shoulder at him standing with his hands raised, his eyes penetrating Stalker's misty ones.

Stalker stopped struggling quite so hard, her ragged breathing rattling in her chest, which, Eyes saw, now had a large scar that shone almost silver. It was still new and still healing, but it was healing and he knew she was going to be fine.

She went limp and he and Wind Talker caught her weight, and eased her to the floor. She shifted back into her human form and sat slumped against the wall, her gaze unfocused.

Eyes shifted too, as did the others. He turned to Rhys and shot him an angry glare.

'Don't trouble yourself to help.'

'I couldn't shift, I can't... I'm sorry. I haven't shifted in years. I don't even know if I can any more.'

'Really?' Eyes asked, unable to hide the surprise from his voice.

'Really.'

Eyes looked at Claws, who nodded to confirm that Rhys was telling the truth.

'When was the last time you were in Hepethia?'

'I don't know. Eight years ago?'

Claws nodded again.

'Eyes,' Stalker's voice croaked. He rounded on her and crouched down beside her.

'I'm here, I'm right here. How are you feeling?'

'What happened?' Her voice was hoarse.

'You were shot, a silver bullet. But you're going to be all right.'

'Rhys?' Her gaze settled on him and a deep frown creased her brow. 'What are you doing here?'

He was by her other side in a flash.

'They invited me, I had to see you. I've got you.' He wrapped his arm around her and pulled her closer to him. Eyes let her go, a lump in his throat.

'Eyes, stop interrogating my mate, please.' There was a tired smile on her chapped lips.

'Okay, for now, for you.'

She fell asleep right there on the floor, in Rhys's arms. Eyes stood slowly and indicated for the rest of the pack to clear the room. They had Stalker back, that was what mattered most. And maybe, just maybe, Rhys was exactly what he said he was.

Chapter Nineteen

Stalker-of-Night's-Shadow

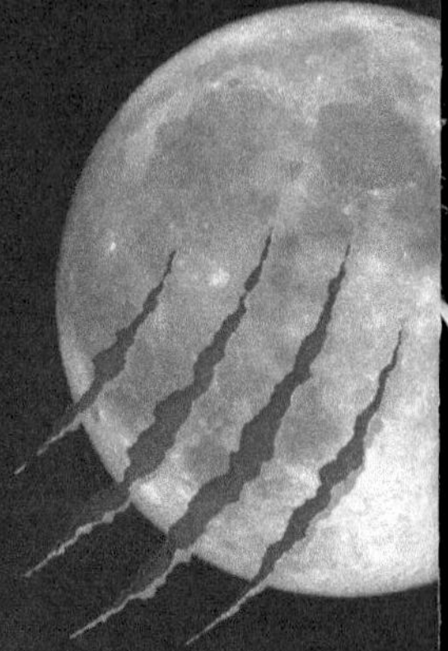

Flecks of red and gold were piercing her dark mind as consciousness tried to return. Little spots of light penetrating her eyelids and murmuring voices swam their way to the surface. Rhys's voice stood out over the rest, he was close, she could feel his deep voice vibrating through her head. She slowly moved her head and felt his chest against her cheek. His hand squeezed her shoulder. Her tongue reflexively moved to moisten her dry, cracked lips.

'Here.' Weaver. Weaver was there. Stalker tried to open her eyes, but the lids were gummed together. She felt a straw against her lips and she parted them to take a sip. 'That's it. It's just water, but you need it. Drink up.' Stalker did as she was told.

A vague memory of regaining consciousness once already began to surface. She had changed, felt Odin's fire raging through her veins. Had she hurt anyone? Panic began to pulse through her blood as she searched her memory, but it was too much of a jumble.

'It's okay,' Rhys said soothingly, squeezing her more tightly and stroking her hair. 'You're okay, everyone is okay. Shhh.'

Calm washed through her and a cough rose in her throat. As she cleared it, her eyes unstuck and the room swirled around her in dizzying circles. Her chest ached and she felt her hand go to her sternum. Pain seared right where her fingers made contact and she felt tough scar tissue. Vomit rose and she was powerless to stop it. She wrenched free of Rhys and spewed on the carpet next to her. She felt his hands capture her hair and hold it out of her face.

'There you go.' Weaver's voice again. 'That's it, get it all up.' She was so calm. Stalker retched again and heaved up more watery fluid. Her stomach must be empty, she thought, as her eyes focused on the sticky puddle. Her abs ached almost as much as her chest.

'You'll feel better soon, I promise. Your body is healing. You nearly died.'

Stalker sat up and craned her neck to look, bleary-eyed at Rhys. His face was serious.

'How?' Her voice croaked, her throat seared.

'You were shot with a silver bullet. Remember?'

They had told her that before, she remembered now. Her fingers went back to her chest. 'Yeah, there's an impressive scar, definitely one to put into a song.' Rhys smiled faintly and glanced at Weaver.

'I'm already working on it,' she said, a smile in her voice. Stalker tried to turn her head, but dizziness took over and she had to close her eyes. It didn't feel like anyone else was there.

'Where?' Her voice failed her.

'Where were you shot?' Rhys asked, stroking her hair. She shook her head.

'My pack?'

'Where are the rest of your pack?' Stalker nodded and swallowed to try and ease the sting in her throat. The straw was at her lips again and she drank deeply.

'They're tidying up,' Weaver replied. 'It was a bad day, lots of mess.'

Stalker managed to force her eyes open and onto Weaver. Her pack sister was pale, dark circles under her eyes. How long had she been out? How long was it since Weaver had slept? Weaver smiled weakly. 'You've been mostly unconscious for just over twenty-four hours. None of us has slept since the morning before you were shot. Stalker, listen, I need you to stay really calm, okay? Can you do that?'

If Weaver could have said anything to ensure that Stalker's pulse began to race, it was this. Rhys held her tightly and kissed the top of her head.

'It's okay, Stalker, we've got you.' Rhys's voice was soothing, but she still felt fear swelling inside her. She grabbed at her throat and felt the cords that held her various talismans. Her fingers ran down them and she searched for the tooth, but it was gone. Her fingers settled on the Vial of Cool Waters, the one Ragged Edge had given her for joining Odin's Warriors. She took a deep breath and felt it settling her nerves.

'Okay, tell me,' she croaked.

'Okay.' Weaver leaned forward and placed a hand on

Stalker's knee. 'You weren't the only one to be hit. Not Claws,' she added hastily, before Stalker could even react. 'The other packs were attacked. All of them. Sky Runner and Herald of the Wrecking Crew were injured but are okay. Vengeance-of-Steel is in a similar state to you. Binds-Iron-Hide of Crimson Dawn's Blood and Walker-in-Rain's-Embrace of the Factory Boys are both dead.'

Stalker felt very little for these losses, she barely knew of the shifters. Though the injuries were bad news. She started to sigh with relief, but Weaver's timid expression gave her pause.

'Go on, who else?'

'First Strike was killed.'

Stalker took a sharp breath but quickly looked up at Rhys. He didn't meet her eye and she knew that he must have been told what First Strike meant to her already. She swallowed hard and nodded. 'There's more,' Weaver went on. 'Scribe is all that's left of the Hellsclaws.'

'Oh god.' Stalker's voice caught in her throat and a cough burst up out of it. As the cough subsided she met Weaver's eyes, there was still something she hadn't said and Stalker knew she didn't want to. All the packs had been hit. Who hadn't Weaver already mentioned? The Watch. Weaver was crying. 'I'm so sorry, Stalker.'

Stalker's hand tightened on the vial. A sob rose and she felt tears prickle at the corners of her eyes. Rhys tightened his grip on her.

'Ragged Edge?' Her voice broke and tears fell. She didn't need the nod that Weaver supplied. A desperate cry tore from her throat and her body began to shake. 'No!' She buried her face against Rhys's chest.

It felt like hours that she sat slumped against Rhys, crying continuously. Weaver came and went, cleaning up Stalker's vomit and bringing her fresh water and dry toast. But Stalker couldn't eat. Rhys was a rock for her, he didn't move or complain; he simply held her. At some point, she became aware that they had moved to the sofa, though she had no memory of getting there, so she must have fallen asleep.

Eventually, her body began to complain about hunger and she felt gross from the sweat and vomit. Rhys took her upstairs and helped her to shower, while Weaver made her a bacon sandwich. Stalker knew once she had some food in her that her body would be able to finish off the healing that it needed to do. So she ate the food, even though it burned her throat to swallow anything solid.

It was dark outside when Claws and Wind Talker arrived. She heard their hushed voices in the hall as she sat, curled up against Rhys. The shock and pain she felt had little to do with the bullet she had taken. The Furies had taken another mentor from her and she felt sure that the thirst for vengeance would soon make itself known.

'Hey, you're back with us.' Claws came over and sat beside her. He hugged her gingerly.

'Thank you,' she croaked. 'Thank you for getting me to safety.'

'Don't be daft, you don't need to thank me.'

'I do.'

'Okay then,' he said with a smile.

'Where's Eyes?' she asked, looking up at Wind Talker.

'He's with Warden. We've been securing the city. Every pack has contributed people for patrols, even on areas outside their own territories that are vulnerable. We've summoned about a hundred fae to help. Spark is... incredible.' Wind Talker's face softened in a way that Stalker had never seen. A smile crept onto her lips. 'Anyway,' he said, returning to his usual manner. 'Eyes and Warden are setting up some defences in St. Catherine's now, traps and the like.'

'Has anyone seen Scribe?' Stalker asked, looking around.

'He's busy,' Weaver said softly. 'He's trying to maintain his territory alone. I think the Factory Boys are trying to help, but he's being stubborn.'

'I'm sure the Factory Boys have considered making a grab for that territory in all of this,' Wind Talker said, his expression grim. 'Like the Wrecking Crew did when the Blue Moon were taken out. Scribe probably doesn't trust them.'

'We need to make sure everyone is united. We can't let this attack divide us further.' Claws rubbed his temples. 'I wonder if I can help smooth things over.'

'It's worth a try,' Weaver said. 'But look, we can't ignore my vision. I know it's crazy and everyone has a million things to do, but the clock is ticking, now more than ever, and we need to crack on with our preparations.'

'What can we do? How do we find Immunsul? Stalker and I had no luck when we searched.'

'Immunsul?' Rhys asked. All eyes darted in his direction. It was as if the pack had forgotten he was sitting right there amongst them. All mistrust forgotten until that second. Stalker squeezed his hand and smiled at him. 'I've heard of it. There was a song, when I was a kid.'

Weaver bounced on the spot.

'Yes! I know it too, or rather, I've forgotten it, but I remember hearing it as a kid.'

'Shine the light,

You shall see,

The Regalia in the willow tree.

Immunsul,

Feast for crows,

He's the one who knows.'

Rhys half spoke, half sang the verse, with every eye in the room trained on him.

'Do you know what or where it is?' Wind Talker asked.

'Not really, I mean, it was just a lullaby. I never knew it was real. You're looking for it?'

'We are. Is that going to be a problem?' Wind Talker asked, his arms crossed.

'I haven't been a Fury for a very long time. They just tried to kill my mate, so I'm pretty pissed off with them, to be honest. Anything I can do to help, I will.'

'Do any of them know you're in the city?' Claws asked, his voice steady as a rock.

'Not that I'm aware of. Even if they did, they'd probably want to kill me as much as any of you. They wiped out all of my kin for some, unknown reason. I'm sure they would assume that by now I'd become one of you folk.'

'Why haven't you?' Wind Talker challenged, his cheeks blazing.

'Wind Talker, cut it out,' Stalker warned.

'You're hardly in a position to stop me,' he said with a wry smile down at her. 'We have a right to know.'

'You do, absolutely.' Stalker tried to interject, but

Rhys squeezed her hand and continued. 'You invited me onto your territory, right into your home, and I absolutely acknowledge the risk you took in doing that. It's only fair that I answer your questions in return. When I first came here, I was newly changed, running for my life. I had no idea who I could trust. I had been raised to hate the Chosen of Artemis, but I thought that hiding in Caerton was the best way to evade the Furies who killed my family. So I hid from your kind too. After a while it was habit, it felt like the only way to protect myself. Then I went and met Stalker.' He smiled. He pulled his arm out from around Stalker's shoulders and bounced forwards, enthusiasm surging through his body. 'Weaver, do you have a pen and paper I could borrow, please?'

Weaver nodded and rushed from the room. She was back seconds later with a sketch pad and pen. She passed them to him and he began scribbling. 'I'm sure between us we can remember all of the words. There must be a clue in them.'

Stalker watched the pair of them as they bounced off each other, recalling verses and odd lines, shuffling them about on the page and making the pieces fit together. Not once did Rhys ask how Weaver had heard a lullaby sung to Fury children, nor was there any hesitation on either of their parts to work together. She looked Wind Talker in the eye and gave him an "I told you so" glare. He chuckled and left for the kitchen to prepare a meal.

Claws ate with the group, then went out to see Scribe. Wind Talker set off to patrol, while Weaver and Rhys kept working on the song and any clues it might contain. Stalker slept a little. Dreams of fallen comrades troubled her and the memory of feeling the impact of a bullet to her own chest ripped her from sleep. She woke with a cry.

'Stalker, it's okay, it was a dream.' Rhys was at her side, holding her tightly.

'No, it wasn't. It happened.' She burst into tears and sobbed onto his shoulder. She had never felt so vulnerable. All that she had been through before and since her first change paled in comparison to this. 'I was shot! I nearly died! My friends died!' Her body shook with sobs and she felt shame flood her body.

'I know, I'm sorry. I know it was real. I know you're not okay. I'm sorry. I'm here.'

'Stalker,' Weaver spoke softly beside her and she felt her pack mate's hand on her back. 'You'll be back to full strength in no time and we'll get revenge for this. I swear it. Everything they have done to us; the Blue Moon, all the losses we've suffered, it'll all come to a head really soon.'

Stalker turned and looked at Weaver, surprised to hear such words coming from her. Weaver had killed her own sister in the last major confrontation they had had with the Witches, still just weeks ago. Weaver knew loss too and Stalker could feel her own anguish through their bond. She took Weaver's hand and nodded solemnly.

'We need the Regalia.'

'Yes, we do, and Rhys and I think we know where to find it.'

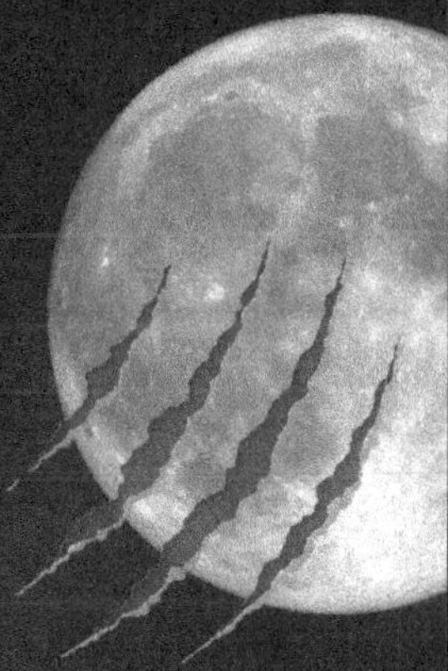

Chapter Twenty

It was the next morning when the Lightning Lords were finally all together again, with the addition of Rhys, who was rapidly becoming one of the pack. Eyes still met him with coolness, however, and Stalker suspected that part of Eyes keeping so busy away from the house was in order to avoid Rhys. But they ate a hurried breakfast together. Once they had finished, the six of them crossed the veil into Hepethia and went out into the street.

Stalker had regained most of her strength, she no longer shook when she tried to stand. But in the street, seeing the battle van parked carelessly in front of the house, a hospital bed still in the back, Stalker flinched and fought a flashback that seemed to shout angrily inside her skull. Her body may be mostly healed, she thought, but her mind still had a long way to go.

Eyes and Wind Talker pulled the bed out of the van and discarded it on the kerb.

'We're going to avoid your flat for a while,' Claws said softly, as he helped Stalker up into the back of the van. 'I gave your address to the hospital when I took you in and I expect the police will be looking for you. Best we don't let them see you up on your feet so soon. Awkward questions and all that.'

Stalker simply nodded and took a seat next to Rhys, who gripped her hand. Claws drove the van quickly across the rough terrain of Hepethia. Each bump, each sharp turn, caused Stalker to grip Rhys's hand even tighter. She closed her eyes and took steadying breaths, trying to keep at bay the images of blood on her chest, of the world swaying dangerously as she collapsed. The more she fought it, the worse it became. Rhys seemed to know exactly what was going on and he pulled her close to him.

'It's okay. We'll be there soon. I've got you,' he murmured softly against her hair.

When the van came to a halt, Stalker was the first out of the back door. She jumped down onto the cracked tarmac and turned her face up to the bright sun and let the warmth soothe her.

'About time,' a lazy voice drawled. Stalker opened her eyes and looked around for the source, as the others climbed out of the van to join her. Tar Peter was leaning against a concrete pillar a few feet away. His sallow skin shining in the sunlight, his slick, black hair reflecting it like a pool of oil.

They were in a part of Hepethia Stalker didn't recognise. There were crumbling buildings all around them, rough, broken tarmac underfoot. Weeds were bursting up through the cracks and plants were climbing all over the ruins around them. In the centre of the courtyard in which they stood was a broken bench and a dead tree. It was about fifteen feet tall and its brittle branches hung limp. Once it must have been a magnificent weeping willow.

Tar Peter moved forward to greet them, a grim expression set on his greasy face. 'Bad business, the sneak attack. Cowardly thing to do.'

'Get a good look at the destruction, did you?' Wind Talker asked, snidely.

'You're never going to let that go, are you?' Tar Peter asked, his head on one side, a smile playing on his dark lips.

'No.' Wind Talker turned his back and reached back into the cab of the van to retrieve his satchel.

'Fair enough. Anyway, what am I doing here?'

'What is he doing here?' Stalker asked, looking confused. 'And where are we?'

'Near the coast, Storm Riders' old territory.' Eyes patted her firmly on the shoulder.

'Oh.' A seagull cawed overhead, as if on cue, and Stalker watched it cross the sky, flying north towards the sea.

'We need a demon who knows things. That's you.' Eyes looked pointedly at Tar Peter. 'You travel around the city, you see things, you know where things, and people, are.'

'Yeah, I have my ways.' The demon gave Eyes a wary glance, but wouldn't meet his eyes.

'You were extremely helpful when we fought the Witches.'

'Yes, and it was my understanding we were square for that.'

'We can compensate you for any assistance you might be able to offer today,' Eyes said, crossing his arms and giving the demon a wry smile.

'Appreciated. What do you need to know?'

'Do you have any idea what's special about this place?' Weaver asked.

Tar Peter looked around and heaved a sigh.

'No.'

'Do you know the word Immunsul?'

'No.'

'Do you remember Lost?'

'N—' The word stalled on his slick tongue and he seemed frozen for a moment.

'You do, don't you?' Weaver challenged.

'As much as anyone can recall a person who never existed.' He glanced around cautiously. Stalker watched him carefully, sure he was about to disappear on them. 'Why?'

'Is she alive?' Claws pressed.

'Maybe. I don't know. Why are you asking about her?'

'Because she hid something, a very long time ago, and we're looking for it. She is likely to be the only person who ever knew where it ended up,' Wind Talker explained in clipped tones.

'I don't know anything about that.' Tar Peter shifted his weight. Stalker readied herself to grab him if he tried to shift into his slippery self. Though how she would hold onto him if he did she did not know.

'Can you find her?' Weaver asked patiently.

'What you're asking is not a small favour, it's a fucking huge undertaking. How is anyone supposed to find someone who may or may not be alive, who has no identity, is forgotten by all who meet her as soon as she's out of their sight? Even if I do find her, I might not even remember doing so. It's not possible.'

'Ah, but you do know who she is, you do remember things about her. And the fact is, you have eyes and ears everywhere. It's possible you can find the demon who made the bargain with her in the first place. Isn't it?' Eyes said, a glint of triumph in his eye. 'And I'm willing to bet my right hand that that demon knows where she is at all times. Am I right?'

Tar Peter winced. He shrugged and cleared his throat.

'Possibly. I don't know the nature of the deal they made, obviously. But, if it had been me, I would have absorbed her identity, yes, creating a connection that only death could sever. But it's been years. Whoever it was is probably long gone.'

'I doubt it. It must have been a very powerful demon, who had extremely potent information. No pack would make a trade like that with some underling who would be easily killed in a skirmish.' Wind Talker's voice rose a little. Stalker glanced at him and saw his cheeks flushed with the memory of sacrificing his childhood memories to the Uplink, one of the most powerful supernatural creatures they had ever encountered.

'That sounds very logical,' Tar Peter said slowly, nodding his head. 'I won't promise anything, except to try. Okay?'

'Fine,' Eyes replied.

The demon sighed and sank down into the ground, leaving behind a small puddle of thick, black oil.

'What was all that about?' Stalker asked, looking at Eyes with a sceptical eyebrow cocked. 'Isn't this the willow tree? Immunsul?'

'Yep,' Weaver said, picking up a bag from by her feet and striding over to the bench. 'We just wanted him out of the way, not lurking about watching us.'

'Right,' Stalker said slowly, following Weaver to the bench.

'Besides, if the Regalia aren't here, we're back to square one and finding Lost really will be a priority.'

As Stalker approached the tree, she sensed the thinness of the veil; she could feel it fluttering gently, like a fine, silk drape in a breeze. Eyes slid a shovel out of the back of the van and strode over.

'You won't need that here,' Stalker said softly, staring at the tree. 'This isn't it, not quite.'

'No, it's not,' Weaver said, looking up at the branches. 'It's the right way up. But we think this is the doorway to Immunsul. It's in another plane.'

Stalker nodded and watched as Weaver took out a few thick, black candles from the bag. She placed one on the soil and pressed it down a little to root it to the spot. Wind Talker took a few of the candles from Weaver and moved around the tree, placing them at even intervals. Weaver continued around the other way, until they met on the far side.

'Why do we need a ritual? Can't we just cross the veil?' Rhys asked, walking slowly around the circle of candles as Weaver went around lighting them.

'We can only cross easily between Midgard and Hepethia,' Stalker explained. 'It takes extra effort to cross into the other worlds. Isn't that true for Furies?'

'They don't go to other realms, they don't believe in them.'

'What do you mean, they don't believe in them?' Wind Talker asked.

'Well they don't believe in Odin and all of that. They're all about Nyx.'

'But we saw Angela Carter go somewhere else,' Eyes said, his brow furrowed. 'She must have believed she was going somewhere.'

'I don't know who that is, but I'm sure there are some Furies who have got the world a bit more figured out. But most subscribe to the dogma we're taught by the Rutherford Estate.'

'Now, there's a term I haven't heard in a while,' Wind Talker said. He stood still and gazed towards Rhys.

'Aren't they a pack of Furies?' Stalker asked, an early conversation with Wind Talker about the Spiral Hand coming to mind.

'Not quite,' Rhys said, stooping to scoop up a small handful of loose soil. 'They're *the* pack, the top of the food chain. The Family.'

'Like the mob?' Stalker scoffed.

'Pretty much,' Rhys said, nodding and letting the soil fall between his fingers. 'The heir's closest followers. They're horribly inbred. Most are related to each other.'

Stalker glanced at Weaver, who was keeping her head down, dutifully marking out a circle that connected the candles.

'What do you know about the heir?' Stalker asked, her curiosity roused. She had spoken to Rhys about the

Furies before and he had always been forthcoming, but it occurred to her now that she had never asked some rather crucial questions. Rhys straightened up and brushed the soil from his hands.

'Gleaming Blade, a ruthless and single minded shifter. I know my family was terrified of the Rutherford Estate, but they dutifully passed on the doctrine that they were sworn to spread. I never met any of them, I just knew the name and the fear it induced.'

'But Gleaming Blade was the heir back then and still is?' Eyes asked.

'As far as I know, but as it's been ten years since I had any contact with anyone who would know, I suppose Gleaming Blade could be dead by now.'

'Eyes,' Stalker said sternly, fixing her gaze on him. 'We know Gleaming Blade is still the heir, that envoy said so after the fight with the Witches. You're trying to trick Rhys. Cut it out.'

The Alpha turned away. Rhys placed a gentle hand on her forearm and shook his head.

'It's okay, I understand his mistrust. I wouldn't trust me either.' He gave her a small smile and she rolled her eyes in resignation.

'Let's just get on with this.' Weaver stood up and brushed the dirt from her long skirt. She roughly pushed her glasses up her nose and strode to the bench. It was missing one leg and sat at an awkward angle. Weaver shook out her long hair and sat down on it, embracing the way it rocked with her weight. She placed her palms on her knees and closed her eyes.

Stalker watched and waited. She became aware of a

large, black bird sitting on a broken bit of wall nearby. It was a crow. Another joined it a moment later. Stalker glanced around and saw more crows flying in and perching around the square of derelict buildings. Silence hung like a heavy blanket over the eerie square. Stalker looked anxiously around, but aside from them and the birds, there seemed to be nothing else in the vicinity. But the buildings could be hiding any number of threats.

'You wish to cross,' a voice croaked. Stalker looked at Weaver, who still sat with her eyes closed. A crow had landed on her shoulder.

'We do,' Weaver replied.

'You must pay the price,' the bird said, in its coarse croak.

'What is the price?' Weaver asked, opening her eyes and tilting her head to look at the large crow.

'You must be willing to pay.'

'I can't know that if I don't know the price.'

'You must pay.'

'I don't think it understands,' Wind Talker said softly. 'Either you're willing to pay anything, or you can't cross. It's likely to be a significant sacrifice, I think, given the highly secret nature of the place. If Lost put any protections on it, then I think we can assume she will have given it a hefty value, given what she sacrificed.'

'I'll pay it, whatever it is,' Weaver said, nodding firmly. 'We need to cross, don't we?' She glanced at the others. Eyes nodded solemnly.

The crow gave a squawk and shook its wings. Without warning, it lunged forward and plucked Weaver's eye from its socket.

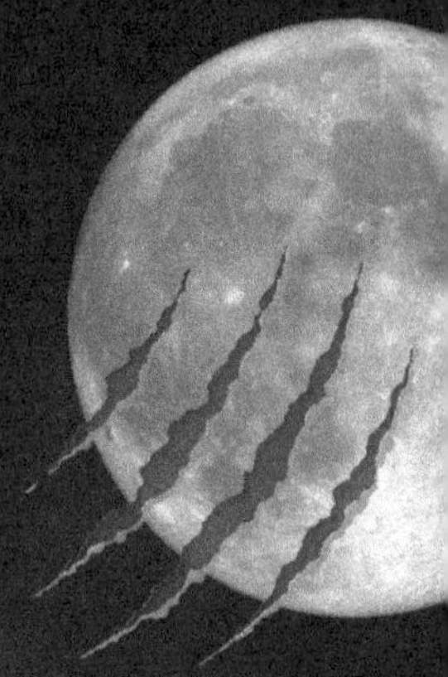

Chapter Twenty One

Weaver-of-Sky's-Loom

Pain seared through her eye socket and blood poured down her face, but Weaver remained perfectly still and silent. Her glasses had been knocked from her face and she felt them in her lap, but she couldn't move, the pain was too severe. She breathed hard through the unbelievable agony. She could hear her pack mates screaming and scrabbling around, desperate for a way to help. She raised a hand to calm them and let them know she was all right.

'Next?' croaked the crow, still perched on her shoulder, Weaver's eye still hanging from its beak. It hopped onto the back of the bench and looked around at the other shifters expectantly.

'It's okay,' Weaver said. Her voice trembled. Ever so slowly, she took a handkerchief from her jacket pocket and held it to her face, mopping up the blood. 'No one else is sacrificing anything.'

'Have to, to cross,' the bird squawked.

'No,' Weaver said firmly, dimly aware of protests around her. She couldn't look at any of them, she knew the panic she would see in their faces. There was one calm presence, not any of her pack mates, not the bird. She turned her head towards Rhys. He stood a few feet away, firmly holding Stalker back from attacking the crow. His cheeks were flushed and his muscles were straining against Stalker's remarkable strength, but he was utterly calm. Weaver clasped her glasses tightly in one hand as she stood up, though her legs shook. Her face was throbbing and she knew she must look frightful. 'I can go on my own.'

'No, you can't,' Eyes said firmly. 'We have no idea what you'll find.'

Weaver kept her one remaining eye fixed on Rhys. Her thoughts were a jumble and it was hard to focus in on anything, but Rhys's calmness was soothing. He looked right back at her, no hint of shock or disgust on his face. Did he know what she was thinking?

'I'll go,' he said, perfectly at ease.

'What?' Stalker snapped.

The crow flew to Rhys's shoulder and landed there. Stalker reached up for it and tried to shoo it away but Rhys stepped back, releasing her, his gaze still fixed on Weaver.

'Even if we were prepared to let you sacrifice an eye for us,' Eyes said, his voice resolute, 'if you won't shift in an emergency then how can you protect Weaver?'

'I don't need protection,' Weaver said. She felt mildly offended, but her voice remained steady.

'You're injured,' Eyes said gently, placing a hand on her shoulder. 'I have no idea if you'll be able to regrow your eye, but even so, right now your vision is impaired. You can't expect to be at full strength. You're also still losing blood. Wind Talker? Can anything be done about this?'

Wind Talker was at Weaver's side in an instant, fishing around in his bag.

'I'm going through the door now, and Rhys is coming with me.'

'No!' Stalker protested again.

The crow bobbed its head and gazed into Rhys's eyes. Weaver watched, waiting for it to strike. It let out a rough caw and flew back to the bench.

'What? What's the problem?' Rhys asked, looking anxiously at the crow.

'You already paid the price.'

'What?' Rhys asked, his cheeks filling with even more colour. 'When?'

'Big sacrifice. In the past, in the present. So much loss.'

Weaver understood. She nodded her head and brushed off Wind Talker's fussy attempts to address her wound.

'I'm fine.'

'You're still bleeding.'

'It'll stop in a minute. Rhys? You coming?' She moved towards the dead tree, staggering slightly as she turned, her balance was all wrong. Rhys rushed forwards and supported her.

'I don't understand,' he said softly. 'Why can I cross?'

'The crow said, you've already sacrificed so much. In living apart from shifters, in hiding for so long, you have given up a huge part of yourself. More than a small body part.'

He smiled softly, pity in his eyes.

'We'll be back soon,' he said, addressing the others.

'Weaver, are you sure about this?' Eyes asked, casting Rhys an obviously wary glance.

'I am. I trust him.'

Stalker rushed forward and kissed Rhys, Weaver averted her gaze, fixing her sights on the tree. A stone archway shimmered into existence. The crow flew up and perched on the keystone of the arch, bobbing its head softly. 'Let's go,' Weaver said, stepping towards the arch. Rhys took her elbow and helped her across the rough ground.

'That's going to hurt like a bitch while it heals, you know.'

'I know,' she replied, sighing heavily. They walked together through the archway. She felt a tug at her middle, like she did whenever she crossed the veil. 'Maybe I can get a patch and get everyone to call me Captain. What do you think?' She smiled up at him and was met with his dazzling laugh, his eyes twinkled. For a second she forgot that he wasn't part of the pack.

Her breath caught in her throat as she caught sight of what lay before them. They had stepped into a dark, cavernous place. High cliffs surrounded them and she could hear the unmistakable sounds of mining; hammers and pick axes clunking on stone far away in the distance. Right where the dead willow tree had stood in Hepethia, was the upside down tree from her vision. The roots were a tangled mess above her and Rhys.

'Are we in Nidavellir?' Weaver asked softly, her one eye fixed on Immunsul.

'I have no idea.'

'This is it though, isn't it? Immunsul?'

'Looks that way. Do we need to do anything?'

'I don't know,' Weaver whispered. 'But I think we should be quick.' She stepped towards the tree and ducked under the hanging branches of roots, Rhys was close behind her. She reached out and placed her ringed hand on the trunk. The bark was dry and flaking off in places. She walked slowly around it, keeping her fingers against the calming warmth of the trunk.

'Could it be buried? I mean, we were never going to find it just lying here.'

'I think we need to do something to get the tree to reveal it.' She squatted down and felt the earth, where the trunk disappeared into it, hiding the branches. A drop of blood from her eye socket dripped down off her face and landed on the soft earth. Weaver tried to blink her eyelid, but pain shot through her face and she winced. The lid wouldn't work, it remained resolutely folded up over the hole.

'Are you okay?' Rhys asked softly, placing a hand on her shoulder. Weaver nodded, unable to speak through the pain. Where the blood had dripped onto the ground, the soil was shifting slightly of its own accord.

'We need more blood.' The blood on her face had mostly dried and crusted, but she used a fingernail to scrape some of it off and dusted it onto the ground. It seemed to do the trick. The ground began to almost bubble, like boiling liquid. She lurched backwards, falling onto her backside. Rhys helped her up and kept hold of her, as they watched the ground moving.

A space opened up next to the trunk, exposing the first branch. The wood was knotted and gnarled, ancient and long-undisturbed. The smell of fresh earth filled the air. The ground stopped moving, leaving a hole the size of a bicycle wheel. Weaver moved closer again and peered into the hole. It was all dirt and mangled branches. She sent energy to her hands, shifting them into bear-like Agrius claws, and began to dig.

Panic began to swell inside. Surely they should have found the Regalia by now? Why hadn't the tree revealed it?

Rhys knelt beside her and started digging too. Dirt went flying out behind them. Weaver's pulse was racing.

'There!' Rhys gasped. He dug more furiously and Weaver looked at the spot he was working on. There was a glint of metal. The faster they dug, the faster the loose soil fell back into the hole. Weaver reached in, and dug her huge claws into the earth next to the fraction of metal they could see. She drove her claws deeper, feeling the shape of the item. Her haired and padded hands were ideal for digging, but no good for feeling around the edges of this thing. It was smooth and curved. She shifted them back into human hands and grasped with her fingers. Metal gave way to something else, glass.

'It's the Orb, I think.' She wriggled her fingers through the soil and got hold of it on both sides. With a great tug, she pulled it free of the soil and tangled branches and fell back. The Orb was covered in dirt, but was unmistakably the one from her vision. It was crystal, with a fine band of gold around its middle. 'Oh my goddess, this really is it!' She began brushing off the dirt. 'Keep looking, maybe the Sceptre is here too.'

Rhys went back to digging as Weaver gazed at the

Orb. She had been wrong, it wasn't simpler in real life compared to her vision.

The roots overhead rustled in a sudden breeze, showering fine dirt down on her and Rhys. He stopped digging and looked up. Sunlight was breaking through the mangled tree roots. The distant sounds of mining had stopped.

Weaver thought she heard a sigh on the wind.

'Hello?' she whispered. The shafts of light shining down through the tree were flecked with slowly falling specks of dust that caught the light.

'Weaver-of-Sky's-Loom,' the voice sighed. It seemed to be coming from the light itself.

'Yes?'

'You will not find the other that you seek here. I only guard the Orb.'

'Oh. I see. Do you know where I might find the Sceptre?'

'No.' The sigh lingered on the air and sent a shiver through Weaver's skin. 'You seek to raise the King-of-Glass-and-Steel.'

'That's right. Will the Regalia help us?'

'Perhaps. But you must be warned, if you succeed, there is a chance he will not be whole when he returns. He has been imprisoned in the darkest place and may be corrupted.'

'I see. Who did this to him?'

'The Spiral Hand.'

'Well, yes, I think we had surmised as much. But who, which shifter? Do you know their name?'

'No, I do not.'

'Who are you?'

'Hope-For-A-New-Day.'

Weaver smiled and caught Rhys's eye. He smiled back.

'That's lovely. Will we meet again?'

'Perhaps. Go, now. You are not alone.' The light faded, as though a cloud had passed overhead. Weaver heard thundering feet rushing towards them from all sides.

'Let's get out of here.' She got to her feet, wrapping the Orb under her jacket. She stumbled towards the stone arch, Rhys right behind her. They ran through it, and were projected back to Hepethia, where the others stood waiting anxiously. The moment their feet were back in Hepethia, the arch crumbed and fell to the ground, closing the door. Something told Weaver this was permanent, there was no way back to Immunsul.

'What happened?' Eyes asked, rushing over to them. Stalker was wrapped in Rhys's arms before Weaver even had chance to draw breath.

'We found the Orb.' She pulled it out from inside her jacket and held it up to the light. The sun glinted off it, dazzling her.

'Weaver! Your eye!' Claws pulled her around to face him fully. The fingers of her free hand went reflexively to her face. The blood was gone and the pain had stopped, but she still had sight in only one eye. Her fingers inched gingerly towards the socket, nervous about what she would find. The lid was knitted closed, hiding the empty socket, fresh scar tissue had formed, closing it neatly. 'It's healed already,' Claws finished.

The warmth spreading from her hand holding the Orb, all the way down her arm and up through her shoulder, neck and face, told her that the Orb had sped the process.

'I'll be most put out if the eye grows back and I don't get to milk the pirate jokes.' She grinned at Claws, who burst out laughing and pulled her into a hug.

'What about the Sceptre?' Wind Talker asked. He gently took the Orb from her to examine it.

'It wasn't there. I don't know where on earth we'll find it. I don't even know where to start.'

'We'll talk to Warden,' Eyes said, gazing at the Orb. His thoughts betrayed him, as he looked resolutely away from Rhys, he could think of nothing else. Weaver tugged free of Claws and looked firmly at the Alpha.

'Rhys helped me. He dug through the ground and was the first to find it. Eyes, we can trust him. Listen, we met a fae who told us the city spirit might come back wrong.' He still wasn't really listening to her, his thoughts focused on Rhys. Weaver snapped, losing patience. 'Eyes, we have to warn Theodore.'

'We will,' Wind Talker replied, stowing the Orb in his satchel. 'And we have another job to do, another fae to summon.'

'Oh?' Weaver raised an eyebrow.

'We need to find Caeruleum Lunulam.'

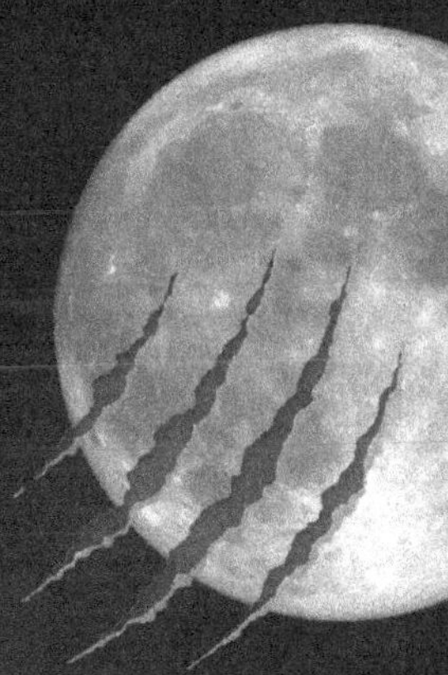

Chapter Twenty Two

Stalker-of-Night's-Shadow

'Why?' Weaver asked, staring at Wind Talker.

'What does that mean?' Rhys whispered.

'Blue Moon in Latin,' Stalker replied. 'Our old pack was the Blue Moon. The others were killed by The Witches. Caeruleum Lunulam was their guide, but she's been missing for years.'

'I think it's important that we find her,' Wind Talker said. 'I think she might have serious answers about all of this; the Witches, the Furies, the Spiral Hand and the Blue Moon's role in it all. I think we need to know what happened.'

'Actually, I agree,' Weaver said, brushing dirt off her hands and clothes. 'The warning we just got about the King-of-Glass-and-Steel got me thinking. We could use some more allies really, and we need to be prepared if we can't get him back, or if he comes back wrong. The city will need a new Patron.'

'Let's go to the ruins of the betting shop,' Wind Talker said, a slight crack in his voice. 'I think that will be a more potent place to try summoning her.'

The group piled back into the van and set off across Hepethia. Stalker stroked Rhys's hand.

'Are you okay?' she asked.

'I'm fine. How about you?'

'Getting there.'

'You seem steadier on your feet now.'

'Yeah. You and Weaver seem to have connected.'

'Yeah, I think so.' He glanced across the van to Weaver, who was sitting with Wind Talker on the other side, muttering together about the ritual. 'That thing she can do with her hands is cool.'

'Heh, yeah. She can change whatever bits of herself she wants, without shifting her whole body. It's her Artemis-given gift.'

'See, Furies don't get those shiny benefits.' He smiled down at her.

'It almost feels like you're one of us now. If that was an option, would you want to join us?'

'Aren't there rules about that?' He leaned closer and kissed her lips softly.

'Oh, yeah,' she murmured, barely conscious of her surroundings, lost in the warmth of his lips.

'I don't know if pack life is really for me, to be honest. I've been on my own for a long time. But I want to help. So however I can best do that, I guess.'

They sat in easy silence for the rest of the drive, bumping over uneven terrain. Stalker's mind drifted to the last time she had seen Ragged Edge. They had talked about resuming the Hunt for the Spiral Hand, he was going to train her. Who would mentor her in Odin's Warriors now? She had lost Shadow's Step, and now Ragged Edge. Was she meant to find her course on her own with her young pack mates?

The van juddered to a halt.

'We're here,' Claws called from the front. Stalker took a deep breath. She had avoided this place for months, ever since they patched it up. Her patrol route had skirted the end of the street, on both sides of the veil. It was like a mental block, a place she simply couldn't go. The doors of the van swung open, Claws stood holding one side open, his face smooth and impassive. He had never been part of the Blue Moon, this place had no hold on him. Rhys was the first out of the van, the same was true of him. Stalker glanced across at Wind Talker and Weaver.

'Have you guys been back here since?'

They both shook their heads.

'Come on, guys,' Eyes said from the front. 'Time to do this.' He slid out of the front seat and Stalker heard his feet land on the tarmac. If he could do this, then so could she. Eyes had been here when the attack happened. Stalker had been kissing Rhys. The memory stung.

She shuffled to the edge of the van and looked out onto the street. It was one of Hepethia's narrow terraces, but where once stood their home and business, was a gap, filled with rubble. It looked just the same as they had left it. Gingerly, she slid to the ground and stepped towards the hole in the terrace.

Weaver grasped her hand and squeezed it tight. They walked together towards where the betting shop had once stood. This was where they had first met Tar Peter. Stalker looked around, half expecting him to stick his head out from somewhere, but there was no sign of him.

A wave of sadness rushed up inside her and tears fell silently down her cheeks.

'I'd almost forgotten,' Weaver whispered.

'Forgotten what?' Stalker asked, glancing sideways at her one-eyed pack sister.

'Them. I mean, not really, but you know, I can go days and days without thinking about them.'

'I know what you mean.' Stalker wiped the tears from her face.

'So much loss,' Eyes muttered. He kicked a chunk of broken red brick and it skittered across the road.

'I'm sick of it,' Stalker said, bitterness spitting over her tongue.

'Me too,' Wind Talker said flatly. He passed her a silver candle and lit it, then did the same with Weaver and Eyes. 'Claws, Rhys, could you keep watch, please? Keep anything from getting too close? I think this will be more effective if it's just the four of us.' He indicated the four old Blue Moon members. Claws nodded and took a few steps away. Rhys gave Stalker a searching look, seeking her approval. She nodded and he moved away in the opposite direction, covering the other side of the little circle of shifters. 'We should have waited until nightfall, and preferably on the full moon, actually.'

'Well, if it doesn't work, we can come back.' Weaver gave him a reassuring smile.

'If the Spiral Hand was behind her disappearance as well, she might be able to tell us who it is.' Stalker looked hopefully at Wind Talker. He merely nodded and she saw sadness swimming in his eyes. This was as hard for him as any of them.

'Here, Stalker, wear this.' Wind Talker passed her the mask from his satchel. She took it and lifted it to her face. There was a moment of strong suction as it sealed itself to her skin and she drew a sharp breath. The world came into sharper focus at once. The mask gave her a clarity that was both reassuring, and stimulating. She could see far more detail than with her eyes normally, every flicker of light, every twitch of movement. There was no gap between worlds to peer through, but she felt sure that with a little focus, she could see right across the veil if she wanted to. But she kept her focus on Hepethia. 'Picture the shop as it was,' Wind Talker instructed. Stalker did as she was told and looked hard at the gap, imagining it filled with the neat little house that had once been there. They were in the front street, where the shop front had been. It had a glass front, which was painted dark blue, and a sign above that, that read The Blue Moon. Above the shop had been two floors, plus a converted attic. It was deceptively large inside. Up the back of the building had snaked a black fire escape.

She could see it as clearly as if it were real, imposed over the hole and the pile of rubble, both existing at once in this weird pocket of the world where time had no meaning.

Wind Talker and Weaver were chanting, but Stalker was barely aware of what they were saying. She was lost in the memory of her old home. She imagined Fortune and Shadow's Step walking down the street, Fortune laughing his big dog bark of a laugh and Shadow smiling. She saw them open the door and step inside. Flames-First-Guardian was in there, scribbling notes at the kitchen table. Speaks-With-Stone was working in the shop, her kid sister, Lily, at her side. Lily would have changed if she had lived, she would have become part of the pack too.

Life with the Blue Moon seemed to play out in her mind, meals around the kitchen table; the warmth and laughter seeping into her pores. Training with Shadow in the basement, learning to master her different forms. Flames teaching her how to read runes. Fortune putting her to the test against various fae and demons, smiling at her with pride as she accomplished all that he laid out for her. Stone, forever calm and reasonable, trying to bridge the gap between the Blue Moon and the Wrecking Crew. Muddling through her complicated parentage with her shifter family, discovering the truth about her father from Fortune, instead of being left in the dark to guess.

She saw Grins-Too-Widely, sitting outside the shop, his head on one side with his grim, cartoon-like grin slapped across his face, watching her, studying her.

She saw the shop in Hepethia, with the paper money lining the walls and fluttering in the breeze; the too-big safe concealing the mask and the Orb, which they would have found together.

Then she saw Her, the patron she never knew, Caeruleum Lunulam. She was pure silver and had no form other than undulating energy, like thin clouds moving across the full moon. She would watch over them and guide them through life, like a mother.

Weaver gasped and Stalker's attention was yanked

back to the ritual circle. Night had fallen. The sky was velvet black and dotted with bright stars. They must have been stood there for hours. The street was bathed in moonlight. Stalker yanked the mask from her face to get a fuller view. Hovering over them, crystal clear, was the fae she had just been visualising. Stalker gasped too, drenched in her beautiful light.

'Oh my goddess,' Weaver said, breathless and awed.

'Caeruleum Lunulam.' Wind Talker dropped to one knee and dipped his chin to his chest in an old-fashioned bow. Eyes glanced sideways at him, then did likewise. Weaver and Stalker followed suit.

'I do not know you. Why do you summon me?' Her voice was soft, it jingled slightly.

'We were the Blue Moon,' Wind Talker said, glancing up at the beautiful fae.

'Liar.'

'No, it's true,' Weaver said, looking up. Her face was white, the scar where her eye had been taken shone almost as silver as the fae herself. 'We joined the Blue Moon after you were gone. But the others, they all died, and we formed a new pack. We are the Lightning Lords.'

As if on cue, Unchained Lightning hurtled towards them out of the black night and landed with a heavy thud, causing the ground to shake. He was enormous, having grown fat on the power from the substation, and he dwarfed the goddess hovering over the shifters. He crackled, his own light shimmering from between the scales all over his long body.

'I see,' she replied, twinkling lightly, seemingly not remotely intimidated by any of this. 'I feel as though I was in a dark place. It was cold and I was alone for a very long time. How long have I been gone?'

'We're not sure exactly,' Wind Talker replied. 'We think perhaps ten years or so. I don't know if that means anything to you.'

'How many lunar cycles?'

'About one hundred and thirty.'

Something that might have been anger flared up. Stalker thought she saw a face in the glow, an angry, ugly face at odds with the beauty around it. She glanced at Weaver, who looked shocked too.

'Fortune? The others? They are all gone?'

'They are.' Eyes looked uncomfortable on his knee, Stalker noticed, he was shifting his weight about and fidgeting. He seemed to decide it was acceptable to get to his feet, but Wind Talker stayed down. Stalker couldn't decide what to do. She looked for Claws and Rhys, but couldn't see them. The light from the two fae was so bight that it cast the distance into utter blackness.

'Merde,' the fae swore in French, her voice filled with bitterness. 'We were so close.'

'I'm sure you were. We all lost them, it was awful,' Wind Talker said softly.

Stalker frowned, sure she had meant something else and that Wind Talker had misunderstood.

'Who took you?' Weaver asked.

'Witches.' Caeruleum Lunulam spat the word with venom.

'Somehow, I'm not surprised,' Stalker said, and she got to her feet.

'Hmm, me neither. It was the Witches who killed the

others,' Wind Talker said, addressing the fae loudly.

'We destroyed them,' Eyes added. 'In retribution.'

'That is how I am free. I felt the Blue Moon calling to me over and over again, but could not free myself. Now that the Witches are no more, I am free of my bonds.'

'Why did they take you? Why did they have such animosity towards the Blue Moon?' Eyes asked.

'Because we were so close to defeating the Spiral Hand.' Her voice cut through the night like icicles.

'You were what?' Wind Talker asked, his mouth hanging open.

'You!' The fae rounded on Stalker and moved closer to her. She flinched, dazzled by the brightness of her. 'You have the Crown of the Regalia!'

'Yes.' Stalker held up the mask.

'And the Orb?' She spun towards Weaver, who was empty handed. 'You found it?'

'Yes,' Weaver said, her voice cracking slightly. 'At great cost.'

'Hmm, so I see. The Regalia must be united to defeat them. This was the last task remaining for my pack; hunt down the Regalia and use them to destroy the Spiral Hand forever. There is a shard inside the King-of-Glass-and-Steel, a piece of glass that reflects all chaos and evil. It will uncover and repel the Spiral Hand. It can be taken from him with the Regalia.'

'Ah,' Wind Talker said, looking down at the ground. The fae rounded on him next, moving right up to him.

'What was that?'

'Well, he's missing too.'

'The Spiral Hand must be on to us.' Her voice had

hardened, Stalker noticed, it was no longer soft and bell-like. It was crisp.

'We're working with the other shifters in the city to summon him. We should be ready to perform the ritual soon.' Wind Talker was almost bouncing on the balls of his feet, like an eager schoolboy.

'Good. Once he returns, we must be ready with all three pieces of the Regalia. Where is the Sceptre?'

'We haven't found it yet, but we will.' Eyes stood with his hands on his hips, his brow was moist with sweat and it glistened in the silvery light.

'One of you must unite the Regalia and weaponise the shard. Then the Spiral Hand will be exposed and weak enough to be destroyed.'

'Did the Witches know what you were up to? Are they Spiral Hand?' Wind Talker asked, still filled with energy and enthusiasm.

'I believe so. It is like a sickness. You never know who is infected or how far the infection has spread. But it is my belief that the only way to be rid of it is to cut out all of the infected tissue.'

'It makes sense,' Eyes said.

'The Witches were in with the Hunger, who was using the mask. It's all connected. I feel like everything is becoming clear now.' Wind Talker looked almost giddy.

Stalker crossed her arms over her chest. Something didn't feel right.

'You will help me, won't you? We have to make their deaths mean something and finish what they started.' Caeruleum Lunulam circled them all slowly, bathing each of them in her light.

'Of course,' Eyes and Wind Talker said together.

Weaver and Stalker exchanged nervous glances. Weaver was unsure too. Stalker nodded at her pack sister, a silent agreement between them to remain sceptical.

'Excellent.' The fae seemed to nod with satisfaction, then shimmered, faded and soared up into the black night.

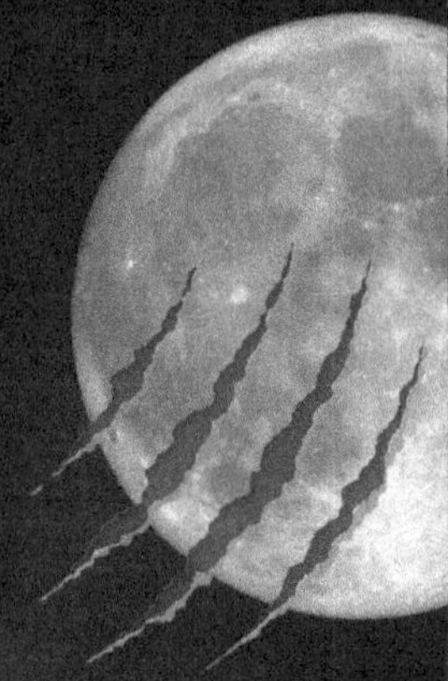

Chapter Twenty Three

'Listen!' Eyes had to raise his voice to be heard over the din. Every Alpha in the city was gathered, even from the Fyrd and the Savages. Most had brought someone with them. Stalker sat beside Eyes at the huge board table in the office at the top of Free River Tower, suitably impressed and intimidated by the place. The sky outside was black and glowing with the light pollution of the city. The great window all along the wall behind Stalker felt like it was pressing in against her back. She could almost feel eyes peering in at the collection of shifters, but she hoped that it was her imagination.

The tower below was virtually empty, but for perhaps the cleaning staff and the odd eager employee working serious overtime. The city's most powerful shifters would never have all assembled here in the day, to be seen by hundreds, or thousands of workers.

Theodore had, of course, seated himself at the head of

the table, but Eyes was sitting directly to his right. Stalker cared little for shifter politics, but it was interesting to see where everyone had sat, it suggested the general pecking order. She felt utterly out of place among these powerful shifters, especially so close to the top dog.

Warden sat to Theodore's left, her fingers pressed together in front of her face. She looked exhausted and drained. Her once immaculate and tight bun was now a dishevelled mess of hair that looked like it hadn't been washed or brushed in days. The Watch wasn't a big pack, but now they had lost one of their finest, and Warden had come to the meeting alone.

Scribe was there, sitting down the end, next to the Alpha of the Fyrd, Rending Claws, looking more uncomfortable than Stalker had ever seen him. Scribe barely looked up from his lap and sat chewing his fingernails, which were coated in chipped, black nail polish.

Crimson was opposite Stalker and wouldn't meet her eye. She kept her counsel and her lips tightly pursed. She looked from speaker to speaker, her brow furrowed.

Stalker just sat there longing for it to be over. Eyes had not mentioned the summoning of Caeruleum Lunulam and had instructed her not to mention it either. Stalker didn't like what had been agreed with the fae, yet she couldn't place her finger on why. It was the way her tone had changed and the talk of cutting out infected flesh. A shudder ran through her at the memory.

'Quiet, please,' Theodore said, standing and commanding the attention of the shifters at the table.

'Thank you,' Eyes said, nodding appreciatively at him. 'As I was saying, we now have two pieces of the Regalia and are beginning to understand them better. They will be essential in summoning the King-of-Glass-and-Steel. We need to find that last piece, not only to keep the set from the Furies, but in order to defend the city properly.'

Renewed jeers rang out around the table. Warden had fixed her gaze on Stalker, her grey eyes piercing across the huge board table. Several of the Alphas had leapt to their feet and Eyes shook his head, unable to make out any one voice clearly. Stalker sat silently, watching everything. Warden would not look away and after a while, Stalker glared straight back at her.

'Warden, if you have something to say to me, would you please spit it out?' Her voice carried across the table and those around them fell quiet, the hush spreading down the table. Every eye seemed to fall on Stalker and Warden.

'Fine,' Warden said stiffly. She cleared her throat. 'Fine. Yes, I do. I am stunned, frankly, that you have found the two items. This is something that our kind has failed to do for over half a century. I'm not sure what that tells me. Either your pack is extraordinarily skilled, or freakishly lucky.'

'Maybe we're both. We had help, anyway.'

Eyes gave her a frustrated glance, which Stalker ignored.

'What sort of help?' Theodore asked.

'From a few fae, and a vision from Artemis,' Stalker replied.

'I see,' Warden said, raising a sceptical eyebrow.

'Once we have the third, we can proceed with the ritual,' Theodore said, pressing the advantage of the tense silence. 'The underground network is on schedule, so the essential lines will be in place in a matter of days. I'll be meeting again with all of the city's ritualists to go over the plans. We really need to be prepared for combat, when the Furies come. I believe we will be able to dictate the battleground.'

'The castle,' Warden interrupted, her voice ringing clearly around the room.

'I agree,' Theodore said, tension in his chiselled jaw. Stalker never thought she would see the day that these two Alphas would agree on something so significant.

'Why there?' Stalker asked, looking from one to the other.

'History, heritage,' Warden said, shrugging, as if it were obvious.

'And it's central, defensible, there's open ground and it's close to Crescent Park, which makes it easy to dispose of the bodies.' Theodore's pragmatism was slightly chilling.

'We'll need to create signals,' Stalker said, leaning forwards on her forearms. 'So that we can coordinate. We'll need fae or demon messengers, lookouts, patrols.'

'Much of that is now in place,' Warden said, mirroring Stalker's posture and leaning on the table. 'We have various defences set up around the claimed limits of the city. We have the advantage of knowing the day they intend to enter the city. So we can assemble at the castle, in Hepethia, and direct their forces there for the confrontation.'

'There's no way they'll leave without a fight, is there?' Scribe's voice was broken and barely made it up the long table.

'No, none.' Warden didn't look at him as she answered, she gazed fixedly at Stalker.

The shifters around the table began to break up into smaller conversations, many getting up from the table, apparently satisfied that formal business was concluded. Eyes and Theodore began muttering feverishly to each other. Stalker got to her feet and strode quickly around the table. Warden was on her feet and moving for the door by the time Stalker caught up with her. The elder Alpha stopped and heaved a sigh, before turning to face Stalker.

'I'm glad you're okay. I heard you were badly injured.'

'Thank you.' Stalker blinked in surprise. She hadn't expected such concern from Warden. 'I'm so sorry about Ragged Edge. I can only imagine what it must be like to lose someone you've been close to for so long.'

'It's hard, of course. You were close to him too.'

Stalker nodded, no words managing to overcome the lump in her throat. 'Look.' Warden took hold of her arm and pulled her firmly towards the door, away from the other shifters. 'I need to show you something. Get Weaver and meet me at the museum in an hour. Don't tell anyone, not even your other pack mates.'

'What? Why?' Stalker couldn't keep the alarm from her voice.

'Just do as I ask, please. You know how critical it is to make sure nothing falls into the wrong hands.' Warden glanced past Stalker, towards Theodore.

'Yes, of course.' Stalker nodded and Warden released her arm, turned, and slipped out through the door. Stalker made her way over to Eyes and tapped his arm. 'Sorry to interrupt, but I need to get out of here.' She indicated the boardroom, without looking at Theodore. She knew Eyes would assume she was uncomfortable in the tower block, among Caerton's elite. He nodded in acknowledgement and she left without another word to anyone. She wished there was something she could say to Scribe, but she had no words of comfort for him, or for Crimson.

An hour later, Stalker and Weaver approached the back door of the museum. The back street was dark, no street lights reached the secluded back entrance to the museum from the main road. The city was still and quiet, as the thick of night wrapped itself like a heavy cloak over the streets.

The door opened just as the two shifters reached it and Warden stood there in the dark. She looked them up and down before stepping aside to admit them. Once Stalker and Weaver were in the dark passage, Warden closed the door and locked it.

'Come, quickly.' Warden set off along the passage, in the opposite direction to the way down to the secret council chamber. Stalker could barely see in the dark, but her eyes started to adjust. Weaver trailed behind her. Warden led them into a back room of the museum, in the dark it looked like an office. It was crammed with cluttered desks and chairs, shelves lined the walls and there were boxes stacked up all over the place. They marched straight through the room and into another like it. Beyond that, Warden took them through a small hall that housed a few exhibits, then into a corridor and up a narrow flight of stairs that was marked "Staff only".

'Warden?' Stalker hissed. 'What's going on?'

They got to the top of the stairs and Warden came to an abrupt halt. She turned to face Stalker and Weaver and placed her hands on her hips. There were tall windows all along the corridor, which spilled orange light onto the floor from the lit main street outside. Warden blanched when she looked at Weaver in the dim light.

'What happened?' she asked, indicating Weaver's missing eye.

'There was a price for retrieving the Orb. I paid it.'

'I see, sorry.' Warden flushed slightly.

'No problem. I'm owning it, going to get a patch.'

'Right.' Warden raised an eyebrow. 'Look, the reason I asked you here is that I have something to show you. No one else knows it's here. It's been here for years, but how many of our kind do you think have ever come to look at the exhibits here?' She waved a hand around them at the wood panelled corridor with its polished wooden floor. When neither Stalker nor Weaver answered, Warden went on. 'And even if they had, how many would have recognised it for what it is?'

Without waiting for an answer, Warden turned and swept away down the corridor. Stalker and Weaver exchanged curious glances and then hurried after her. They were taken through a large set of double doors into a vast hall of exhibits. There were all manner of weapons and armour in polished glass cases, and along one wall was a huge tapestry. 'This way,' Warden said softly. She set off again towards one end of the hall.

Warden came to a halt next to a small display. One item was displayed inside the case, an ornate Sceptre, about a foot and a half long. It was encrusted with jewels and had a small crown at one end. It was held up on a prop so that it sat at an angle in the case.

'Oh my god. Is that...?' Stalker said, her words failing

her.

'Yes.' Warden unlocked the case and reached inside. As her fingers closed around the Sceptre, there was a loud bang from the other end of the hall. The three shifters immediately froze and their heads whipped in the direction of the sound.

Stalker took a few steps, but her feet stuck to the floor, like she was walking in thick treacle. Weaver stumbled and bumped into her. Stalker's head was pounding. Her hands darted reflexively to her throbbing temples. Dizziness swept over her and she felt the room spinning. Pressure intensified around her head, squeezing it on all sides and she slowly collapsed to the floor. She managed to focus her gaze on Weaver, who was similarly crumpled on the floor. Warden was a few feet away, also incapacitated.

The whole floor of the museum hall was twisting, like something from a macabre funfair. The walls began to twist and rotate slowly around them.

'What's going on?' Stalker shouted. Her voice sounded like it belonged to someone else, someone on the other side of thick glass. Weaver was up on all fours and was trying to shift, but it looked like she was struggling. Stalker watched, unsure what to do, as Weaver's body slowly took the form of a small, black cat. One of its eyes was missing and bore a silver scar across the knitted flesh.

Stalker fought against the overwhelming dizziness and made her body change. One limb, then another, one bone at a time, every one an effort. Eventually she was in her fox form. The room was still spinning and her feet slid on the shiny floor. She tumbled towards the centre of the twisting point, bumping into warped display cases. It was like a huge drain and she was caught in the rotating flow towards the centre. But she kept panic at bay and allowed herself to be dragged. There was a scent on the air, so faint, but definitely a shifter. It wasn't Weaver or Warden, it was someone else. She relaxed and took small sniffs. A figure stood at the far end of the hall, a tall staff in hand with a spiral pattern running down it. The figure was hidden in darkness, but Stalker felt something familiar in the scent. Frustration began to take over as she tried to place it, but it was too faint to identify.

She began to fight the tugging sensation that was dragging her across the floor. Weaver was close by, also being pulled towards the centre. Stalker didn't know what would happen when they reached it, she couldn't see a hole or any threat, it was just a point in space that turned and turned, pulling everything around it closer. The display cases seemed to fold and bend, then spring out again, winding their way back outward.

Weaver started running hard against the drag and made progress away from the middle. Stalker set her sights on the mysterious figure at the end of the hall and leaped up, shifting in mid-air, albeit a little more slowly than normal, into an owl. The spinning floor no longer pulled at her, but the crushing sensation in the room was still pressing in on her and she struggled to flap her wings. She tried to fly towards the shifter, but just jerked about hopelessly on the spot. She fell to the floor and landed with a bump, shifting immediately into her human form.

The room stopped spinning and the figure at the end made a run for it. Stalker tried to stand, but she felt sick and was shaking all over. She felt someone grab hold of her, it was Warden, her hair was wild, her eyes even wilder.

'Take this! Get it to safety!' She pressed the Sceptre, hidden inside a thick cloth, into Stalker's hands. 'Get out of here now!' Stalker stood frozen. She couldn't leave. She had to pursue the Spiral Hand.

'Stalker! Let's go!' Weaver grabbed her by the elbow and dragged her back towards the door they had entered through.

'But, Warden? She can't fight on her own!'

'She's perfectly capable,' Weaver snapped, still dragging Stalker. 'It's far more important that we get this to safety. We can't let the Spiral Hand get it, we can't. You know that.'

They ran down the corridor, down the narrow stairs and into the offices below. Stalker's heart was pounding, her breathing was ragged and the wrapped up Sceptre in her hands felt hot. Weaver led the way and Stalker ran along behind in blind panic. Weaver leapt at the locked back door of the museum and smashed through it, shattering the lock and splintering the wooden frame.

The two of them didn't look back, they sprinted all the way from Old Town to St. Mark's without stopping and all Stalker could think about was that scent and the fact that she was sure it was one she knew.

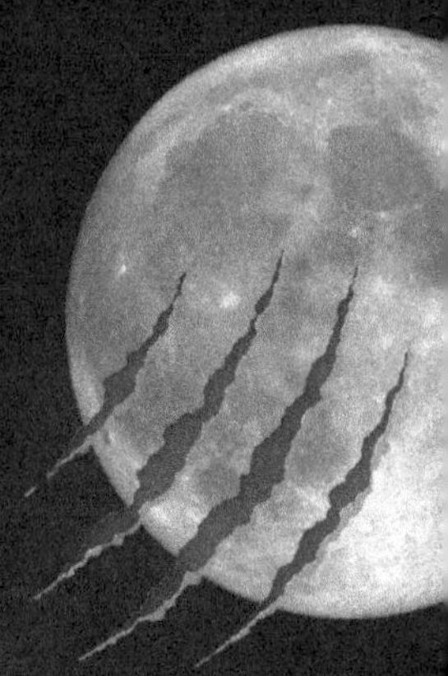

Chapter Twenty Four

THE LIGHTNING LORDS sat around the kitchen table in silence. The Regalia laid out on the table, looking at odds with the dated little room in the back of a narrow terrace. The wooden mask, the glittering Orb, and the bejewelled Sceptre.

'Any word from Warden yet?' Eyes asked, breaking the heavy silence. No one answered.

'What do we do with them?' Weaver asked, staring transfixed at the precious items. 'How do we keep them safe?'

'I don't think we should keep them here,' Wind Talker said, his voice too loud in the quiet kitchen. 'Too many people know about this place. If the Spiral Hand you encountered at the museum recognised your scents they will know who has the Sceptre, at least. I think it's a safe bet they're after the Regalia.'

'Why?' Stalker asked, her brow furrowing as her

thoughts raced to keep up.

'Well, if we really can use them to summon the King-of-Glass-and-Steel, and if the Spiral Hand is behind his disappearance, then they probably want to stop us,' Wind Talker replied, his finger stroking his unshaven jaw. Stalker nodded in understanding.

'What happens when we unite them?' Claws asked, leaning forward to inspect the Sceptre.

'I don't know.' Stalker shrugged. Curiosity gnawed at her, but at the same time she felt apprehensive about the idea. 'I feel like we shouldn't try it. Something epic could happen.'

'I agree,' Eyes said softly. 'But I also don't want to leave it until the ritual to find out.'

'We'll try a controlled test in Hepethia,' Wind Talker said, his voice unwaveringly confident. In a way, Stalker envied that, she was forever second guessing herself. It would be nice to be so self-assured and to exude confidence, no matter what.

'When?' Claws asked.

'We should all sleep, and we should check in with Warden. Do we want to let anyone else know that we have all three? It might be helpful to have some more back up when we test it, just in case anything happens that is too big for us to handle.' Eyes leaned back in his chair and surveyed the rest of the pack.

'What about Rhys?' Stalker asked, her voice tentative.

'No,' Eyes said flatly. 'I'm sorry, Stalker. I'm trying, I really am, but there are still limits.'

Stalker opened her mouth to object, but the look on the Alpha's face told her it was pointless.

'I think we should keep this to ourselves for now. We really don't know who we can trust,' Claws said, his voice steady and low.

'Okay,' Eyes replied, nodding his head. 'And where do we hide the items until we need them?'

'How about in our vault at the market?' Weaver asked, looking up at last.

'That's not a bad idea,' Eyes said, glancing at Weaver. 'But I don't like the idea of moving them so far off our territory. How about a human bank? Would any shifter think to look for these in the human world? There's a reason the Sceptre stayed safe for so many years, hidden in plain sight.'

'But what do we do if we need to get them out outside of bank opening hours?' Claws asked, raising an eyebrow.

'We could bury them with Spirals-of-Bright-Agony.' The words tumbled out of Stalker's mouth before she could stop them. It was a grim prospect. 'As far as we know, the only people in the whole world that know about that are dead. We didn't even tell Father Ash where we dug up that skull.'

The others stared at her, Wind Talker blinked in mild surprise.

'That's actually brilliant,' he said.

'No need to act so surprised.' Stalker bristled with resentment. She had been known to have bright ideas in the past.

'Sorry,' Wind Talker said, dipping his head slightly. 'It is a really good idea.'

'Wind Talker, can you set up some sort of barrier around the garden so that no demons or fae can see what we're doing?' Eyes got to his feet as he spoke and everyone seemed to be stirred into action.

'Yes, I believe so.'

'Good. Let's do this now and then get some rest. I don't want to leave these lying around. We'll sleep in shifts too, I want someone on watch at all times.'

The pack crossed the veil and trooped out into the dark back yard. Dawn was rapidly approaching and the sky had turned from velvet black to deep purple. With a few muttered words of protection, and by scrawling runes in blood on the high walls around the garden, Wind Talker was able to conjure a misty dome over the garden. The Lightning Lords couldn't see out, and nothing could see in.

Weaver and Stalker began digging through the dirt in the centre of the garden. The only light came from the kitchen light spilling out through the open door. Wind Talker kept watch, with his talisman active he could see both sides of the veil for any intruders. Eyes and Claws helped to shift the dirt away as Weaver and Stalker dug it out. Soon, they struck hard wood. They swept back the last centimetre of soil and uncovered the coffin.

Bracing herself against the smell, Stalker prised open the wooden box. The decomposed body inside just smelled old and musty, all rotten flesh was gone, leaving nothing behind but bones. Eyes jumped down into the hole and carefully placed the three pieces of the Regalia under the bones, then sprinkled a little dirt over them to conceal them. He climbed back out, Stalker dropped the lid closed and together they quickly filled the hole.

'It looks freshly disturbed,' Stalker said once they were finished. 'It's obvious.'

'It'll have to do. Maybe tomorrow we can plant something there, so it looks like we've just been gardening,' Weaver suggested. Stalker wasn't convinced, but it seemed pointless to argue. They brushed the dirt off their hands and clothes, Wind Talker dropped the dome, and the pack went inside to clean up and sleep.

Stalker's dreams were plagued with images of demons and Furies, of blood and war. She saw Hands-and-Face, her ancestor spirit who had berated her on the beach, pointing an accusing finger at her. She woke in a cold sweat and couldn't get back to sleep.

It was early morning. The sun was blazing through the windows already and the city clunked and churned around the house. Stalker trudged to the kitchen and found Claws reading one of his journals, casting frequent glances towards the garden.

'Morning,' he said, his voice gruff. 'Can't sleep?'

'No, not really. Have you slept yet?'

'No, I took first watch. Wind Talker is out patrolling.'

'Are you okay?'

'Shattered. You?' He looked up and fixed his gaze on her pointedly. He wasn't just asking about the lack of sleep.

'Mending. Thanks.' She poured coffee from the pot and sat down with him.

'I've been through everything I have on the mask, from when it was my case. Nothing at all pointed towards any of this. I remember thinking at the time that the Carlsons must be in with a demon. The level of fear around them, and the power they hold over people, it just seemed, well, odd. But I dropped it. I couldn't prove anything, I couldn't do anything about it, so I let it go.'

'You know what Weaver would tell you, don't you?'

'What?'

'That you were thinking like a human. You should have used us, used your abilities, turned to supernatural resources, to solve the case.'

Claws chuckled.

'Yeah, she would have told me that, you're right. But back then I wouldn't have listened.'

'Now?'

'Now? Yeah, sure. Because we know the mask is a powerful supernatural object and is of importance to our survival.'

'But would you take her advice on your PI cases? The seemingly straightforward ones?'

'If I had any, yeah, maybe I would.'

'Things have changed for all of us, haven't they?'

'Just a bit.' He smiled and went back to his journal. Stalker gazed out of the window at the little, sunlit garden. It looked so different in daylight. There was no hint of the dead body buried there, or the secret treasures buried with him.

'Do you have any hunches about who the Spiral Hand might be?'

Claws put the book down and leaned back in his chair. He crossed his arms over his chest and stared at her.

'I wish. Do you?'

'No. I don't know. I knew that scent though. I just can't place it.'

'That must be really frustrating. Was it male or female?'

'I couldn't even tell that much, it was too faint. They were masking it.'

'Like you can?'

'Yeah.' Stalker closed her eyes and groaned. It was maddening.

'So does that mean they had to be a new moon?'

'Maybe. I don't really know how it all works. Sure, we each have our blessings from Artemis depending on our birth moon, but we pick up so many abilities from different patrons and talismans. I don't think we can assume anything.'

'Fair enough. It would be nice to have something to go on, anything really.'

There was no hint of accusation in his voice, but Stalker couldn't help feeling frustrated and like she was somehow letting everyone down.

'I'm going for a run.' She stood up abruptly and downed the rest of her lukewarm coffee. Claws simply nodded and raised no objections.

Stalker left the house and set off, without giving much thought to where she was going. She ran through their territory, towards the river, and ran the length of the border there. It was different running through Caerton in daylight. At night it was like her special time with the city, even though there were cars and lights and noise in many places at all hours, there were still silent streets and dark alleys. In daylight there wasn't a corner of the city untouched by humanity. Traffic chugged along every road, pedestrians filled the pavements, planes flew overhead. She could smell the sweat of the people, the smog clung to the air she breathed and every inch of the city seemed to be exposed by the glaring sun.

She was definitely a creature of the night. It went

beyond her being a shifter, it was the moon she was born under, and the path she had chosen. The night called to her, the shadows soothed her, the quiet enabled her to think. But as she ran, she could begin to tune out some of the life of the city and tune in to her breathing and the feel of her feet pounding on the tarmac. She vaulted fences, ran along walls and scaled buildings as she ran, pushing her body, letting the adrenaline flood her senses. It helped. It helped her to not think about being shot, about the threat of imminent death.

Without even realising where she was going, Stalker ended up, as she had so many times before, running to Rhys. She was knocking on his door before she even recognised the street of neat houses in the city centre.

The door swung open and she darted inside and into his waiting arms.

'Are you okay?' His breath was soft on her hair and she looked up into his dark eyes.

'Yes.'

'I felt something, late last night, I couldn't sleep for worrying. You were petrified.'

'I was. Something happened.' She breathed deeply, taking in his scent. She realised at once what she was doing and pulled away from him. Frustration with her pack for sowing suspicion in her thoughts. It wasn't him. She was certain; it wasn't his scent that she had picked up at the museum, it couldn't be. 'I had an encounter with the Spiral Hand.'

'You what?' Rhys blurted out. The shock was written all over his pale face.

'I'm okay. I was with Weaver. We got away. So did he,

or she. I don't really know. Oh god, Warden! I need to find out if she's okay. She was there too.'

'What do you need?'

'We need to go to the museum.'

'Okay.' Rhys grabbed his shoes from behind the door and wedged his feet into them, he was out the front door before Stalker had even taken in what was happening.

He took her hand and they walked briskly towards the river. They crossed the bridge by the castle, and Stalker's gaze fixed onto it, knowing this was where it would happen. In the human world, the castle was not much more than a few old, crumbled walls. There was a little shop and cafe there and a map on a board showing what the castle would have looked like a thousand years ago. She had never been here in Hepethia, the city centre was strictly off limits to shifters due to being utterly overrun by demons.

The two of them marched into Old Town, with no thought for territorial etiquette. Stalker began to feel nervous as they approached the museum. She didn't know what they would find. The broad and bustling street that led to it seemed normal, no sign of police presence or any disruption. The huge front doors of the museum stood open and the sandwich board outside declared the day's special events.

Rhys led her inside, still holding her hand, and walked quickly through the grand foyer. 'Where?' he whispered. Stalker pointed to the wide, stone staircase ahead that led up to the upper galleries. Rhys led her again, confidently striding through the vast hall towards the stairs. Stalker looked around anxiously for signs of disruption.

They found their way into the hall that she had been

in the previous night. It looked completely normal. The floor and walls were in their right places, the displays were undisturbed. Stalker's gaze went to the far end of the hall, there was a roped off section and she caught sight of a high visibility strip on a jacket. She pointed and Rhys set off, pulling her along. She stumbled slightly on her feet as they moved too quickly beneath her. Her thoughts were stuck hours previously when this hall was a nightmare.

As they approached, Stalker saw a police officer standing by the rope and saw the empty display case behind him. And there, talking to another officer, was Warden. Her voice carried down the hall towards Stalker. She was dressed in a smart suit, her hair neatly pulled back. She was in curator mode. But she did glance over as Stalker approached, clearly aware of a shifter intruder. The flash in Warden's eyes told Stalker to hang back and she pulled hard on Rhys's hand to lead him away to look at the tapestry on the wall.

'That's her,' she hissed. 'Talking to the police. That's Warden. She's fine. She's alive and doing her job. She must have had to declare it stolen.'

'What was stolen?' Rhys whispered, bending his head closer to Stalker's own.

'Nothing, she gave it to me, I didn't steal it. But obviously it's gone now and she had to say something.'

'What was it? Where is it now?'

'The Sceptre, the last piece of the Regalia. It's...safe.' She stumbled over the last word, knowing she would be in trouble with Eyes if he knew she had said anything.

'Oh god. And the Spiral Hand was here?'

'Yes. This was all—' she gestured around at the hall '—

wrong. They did some funky mojo and made everything twist. It was awful. I've never felt so powerless.'

Rhys pulled her into a tight embrace. 'We ran, Weaver and I ran away. We left Warden behind.'

'But she's okay. Do you want to talk to her?'

'Yes, I have to know what happened.'

'We'll wait.'

'What happened with Father Ash? Did you go to him? I haven't had a chance to ask before now.' Stalker looked up into Rhys's dark eyes.

'I went, he took me in. I was there until I got the message about you.'

'What did you make of him?'

'I don't know. He's, interesting.'

'Did he give you any advice or anything?'

'Not really. I told him you'd sent me and that I was suspected of being Spiral Hand. He didn't even ask if I was or not, he just let me in. We talked a little, he asked about Caerton and I told him what I felt I could, which wasn't much. He's a pretty intimidating guy.'

'Is that why you came home, rather than going back there? Are you still being followed?' She looked around, half expecting to see someone in the museum, covertly watching them.

'I wanted to be closer to you, in case you needed me. And I don't think so, but I hadn't gone anywhere until now.'

'Did you get the feeling Father Ash would welcome you back?'

'Yes, he said as much when I rushed out. I was trying to work out if he's just incredibly trusting, or totally fearless.'

'The latter. He has nothing to fear from any shifters. I'm sure he's the most powerful shifter I've ever encountered.'

'Do you think he's Spiral Hand?'

'I really have no idea.'

'But you sent me to him?' They had kept their voices low, but Rhys's rose a little at this. Stalker squared up to him and held his gaze.

'Yes. I didn't feel like we had a choice. I was worried that some of the city's shifters might come after you with pitchforks. But they haven't, yet. Now we just have to convince enough of them to trust you.'

'That's easier said than done.'

'I know.' Stalker sighed and rested her head against his broad chest. The sound of clicking shoes on the wooden floor, marching straight towards them dragged Stalker's head up. Warden was approaching, fury in her face.

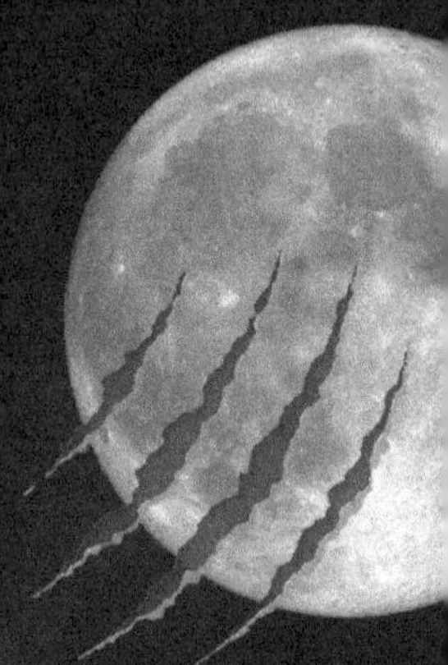

Chapter Twenty Five

'You shouldn't be here,' Warden snapped in a threatening and low voice as she tugged Stalker roughly by the elbow towards the back corridor.

'I had to know what happened and that you were all right.' Stalker pulled her arm free of Warden's vice-like grip. She lifted her chin defiantly, stung by Warden's harsh tone.

They stepped out of the hall into the deserted corridor that they had entered through the night before. Warden stopped and glared at Rhys, as if seeing him for the first time.

'Who the fuck are you?'

'He's with me. He's fine.' Stalker positioned herself slightly in front of Rhys and fixed Warden with her firmest stare.

'He smells human.'

'Yeah, I get that a lot,' Rhys said with a smirk.

'He's one of us. We can trust him. He helped find the Orb.'

'Where's the Sceptre now?' Warden asked, her hawk-like eyes switching back to Stalker as if deciding she had too much on her plate to worry about Rhys as well.

'Safe, hidden. But what happened last night?' Stalker's voice skipped away from her, her words spilling out rapidly in a rush to get to her burning question.

'I pursued whoever it was but they got away, I didn't even get a glimpse of their face.'

'Did you recognise anything about them?'

'I'm pretty sure it was a male. That's it.'

'Okay. What was that freaky magic?'

'Demonic, no shifter could do that. It was an illusion though. As you can see, everything's normal here now.'

Stalker nodded in agreement.

'You weren't hurt or anything? What will happen with the police?'

'No, I wasn't hurt. It'll get buried soon enough. Report filed, nothing will come of it.'

'Okay, good.'

'But you really should leave.' Warden's voice was softer now, but Stalker could still tell there was no sense arguing.

'Sure.'

'Be really careful with the items.' There was a firm warning in Warden's voice.

'We will.' Stalker tried to give Warden a reassuring smile, but feared it came across more like a nervous tick. She and Rhys left the museum quickly.

'Eyes will be livid when he finds out I saw you today and that I told you as much as I did. He says he's trying to trust you, but there's a way to go yet.'

'I understand.' Rhys nodded gravely. 'As long as you stay safe.'

'You know me.'

'Yes, I do, that's the problem.' He took her by the shoulders and kissed her intensely, lifting her onto the balls of her feet. Someone passing by wolf whistled at them, but Stalker didn't care. When Rhys finally broke the kiss and set her back on her feet, he fixed his eyes on hers and stared right into her soul. 'Stay safe, I mean it.'

'I will,' Stalker said, a lump rising in her throat. 'I'll see you soon.'

They parted ways and Stalker got on a bus back to St. Mark's.

'Warden's okay,' she declared as she entered the house. 'So is the museum. But the Spiral Hand got away.' She walked into the kitchen to find Scribe sitting at the table with Weaver. His eyes were red. 'Hi,' she said sheepishly. Neither of them answered. Weaver was rubbing Scribe's back.

'Have you slept at all?' Weaver asked softly. Scribe shook his head.

'I can't. Too much to do.'

'You have to rest,' Weaver urged. 'You can't keep on like this. Rest here if you like, there's a bed upstairs. We can take turns patrolling your territory.' She glanced up at Stalker, who nodded reassuringly. She felt her cheeks sagging and a prickle at the corner of her eye. She knew some of what Scribe was feeling. She knew the loss and the overwhelming feeling of having to rebuild. But when the Blue Moon was destroyed, there were four of them left.

She had never been left alone, as Scribe had. Her heart ached for him.

'It's my responsibility.' Scribe's voice cracked and he started sobbing.

'No, it isn't.' Stalker sat down opposite him and grabbed hold of his hands. He looked up at her in alarm, tears streaking down his face. 'We aren't meant to be alone. We're meant to be in packs. Being alone will get you killed. You cannot hold that territory alone, you just can't. It is not your responsibility to do so. Please accept the help that is being offered.'

'Stalker's right,' Weaver said. 'We have to work together. It's the only way we'll win this fight. They want us divided, but we must stand strong together.'

Stalker's partial lie hung in the air. She and Weaver both knew that it was possible to survive alone. Rhys had done it for a decade. But he hadn't staked a claim to territory. He hadn't been doing his job as a shifter: controlling the demon population, protecting humanity. He had shunned everything to do with shifter life and pretended to be human. That was how he had survived. Scribe would never choose that life.

Scribe seemed to accept their words. He nodded and got control of his tears. Weaver led him upstairs to settle down to rest. Before she came back down, Eyes arrived. He strode into the kitchen and presented Stalker with a smile and a small box.

'What's this?' she asked, taking it from him.

'An apology.'

She opened it and found a new phone inside.

'Oh. Thank you.' She tried to smile, but the memory

of him smashing her phone resurfaced, along with a little guilt over going to Rhys earlier that day.

'You've earned my trust, Stalker. I'm sorry for doubting you.'

'Okay, thanks. Erm, Scribe's upstairs. Weaver's looking after him. He's not doing so great.'

Eyes heaved a sigh and leaned against the door frame.

'Sure, that's understandable. What can we do to help?'

'Weaver offered to do patrols for him.'

Eyes shook his head and looked at the floor.

'We're stretched enough as it is.'

'I know, but we have to do something.'

'I'll talk to the other Alphas and see what we can do together. Maybe we can each contribute a little time.'

'That's a good idea.'

Eyes' phone started ringing and he made to answer it, but paused on seeing the display. 'Who is it?' Stalker asked.

'I think it's the House of Cards. Hello?'

Stalker waited, watching his face carefully. She couldn't hear the speaker at the other end. Eyes nodded and his mouth twitched towards a smile. 'I see. Sorry to hear that.... Well, that is welcome news. Thank you. Is there anything you need?'

Stalker gaped at him, impatiently bouncing on the balls of her feet.

'What?' she mouthed at him. He raised a hand to indicate for her to wait and she rolled her eyes at him.

'Okay. Yes, we can definitely arrange new boundaries. Well, I'll be in touch then.' He ended the call and stared at his phone for a moment.

'Well?'

'It was Mrs Feng. They're going to fight with us. One of her sons was injured in the attack. She didn't know the Furies knew about them. It has caused them to rethink their position in the city.'

'Well that's good news.' Stalker smiled.

'They want more territory in exchange, which, frankly, is a very welcome demand, seeing as I wanted to offer some to them anyway in order to ease our burden.'

Stalker nodded in agreement. It seemed that everything was coming together. She only gave Eyes the vaguest details about seeing Warden, deciding not to mention Rhys or what he knew. She was thankful for the trust Eyes was showing in her, but equally bitter about needing to earn it. The conflict raged in her almost every moment, but she fought it, burying it deep enough to hide from her pack mates.

Eyes left again to go and negotiate with the House of Cards, and to fill them in on the details of the plans.

Stalker sat down to set up her new phone, it was with some discomfort that she realised how few contacts she had to include now. She had lost touch with all of her human friends, and half of her shifter friends were now gone.

Her pack mates came and went through the revolving door of patrols and tasks and preparations. Scribe slept upstairs right through the day, finally able to catch up on the nights he had lost. The afternoon stretched into evening and as the setting sun turned the sky crimson, Stalker felt the weight of what was to come pressing on her.

Scribe left to return home, refusing the food that Weaver offered him. Stalker saw the pain in Weaver's eyes and knew that her heart was invested in Scribe. Stalker could relate to that.

After dark, the Lightning Lords assembled in Hepethia. Wind Talker had dug up the Regalia again in secret and was carrying a box with the items in. They walked quietly through the dark streets towards the unspoilt landscape of China Town. They stopped short of the boundary, out on the open crystal plain, which reflected the silver moon overhead.

Wind Talker began casting a ritual circle, creating a silvery dome over their heads to protect them. Stalker's pulse raced under her skin and her palms were sweaty, which was nothing to do with the balmy summer evening. If precedent was anything to go by, it would be her wearing the mask and uniting the Regalia. She knew that something would happen, it would be almost a disappointment if nothing did, after all they had been through. But not knowing what it would be was causing her stomach to do uncomfortable somersaults.

Once they were sure that the defences were in place, Wind Talker opened the box.

'We should each try the mask again,' Wind Talker said, not meeting Stalker's eye.

'Fair enough,' Eyes said. He picked up the mask first and lifted it to his face. Stalker waited, nothing happened. He lowered it with a shrug and passed it to Weaver. Again, nothing happened. The mask made its way around the pack. Each time, Stalker grew more certain that it was going to fall to her, for whatever reason.

All eyes were on her, as she was the last to take the mask. She raised it to her face. As the smooth wood closed on her skin she felt the familiar suction kick in, pulling the mask against her face. She let go and it stayed in place. She hated how little she could see in this thing, the narrow eye slits were extremely limiting. And yet, the power of the mask opened up a whole world of detail that she could never see with her own eyes.

It was unveiling itself now, that extra sight that she had experienced before. Hepethia seemed to come to life, colours brightened and intensified. She could see out through the dome to what lay beyond. She knew there were fae in the distance, doing their own thing, oblivious to what was going on under the dome. The moon was smiling down on her.

Someone pressed the Orb into her hand. It was cool and smooth and large enough that she had to spread her fingers wide to keep a good grasp of it in one hand. A moment later the Sceptre was in her other hand. Her feet lifted off the floor and she gasped. There was a collective ripple of surprise around the shifters in the circle. Stalker rose up a short way, then stopped, suspended in mid-air as if her levitation talisman had been activated. Perhaps that was exactly what had happened? She ought to be in a blind panic, yet she felt calm. Was that her Vial of Cool Waters protecting her? She was glad she had not yet put back on her Savaging Fury tooth.

'Stalker? Are you okay?' Eyes asked from just below her.

'Yes, I'm fine.'

'What's happening?' Wind Talker asked, pressing

closer.

'Nothing. I can see things.'

'What things?' Warden pressed.

'The world, clearly, like when I wore the mask before. Hang on.' She peered into the distance and saw four figures walking towards them. 'Someone's coming.'

But there was something unreal about what she was seeing. The figures were far away, but looked too big. She closed her eyes and could still see them, even though everything else had faded to black. 'No, wait, it's not real. I think it's a vision.' She felt Weaver's fingers close on her wrist, her rings warm against her skin. Their bond increased and she felt Weaver in her mind.

'Yes, I think you're right,' Weaver said softly.

The four figures came closer, emerging from thick fog. They were all wearing masks identical to the Regalia, but Stalker could make out their clothes and body shapes; three men and a woman. She frowned and waited, unsure of what she was being shown. They were standing right before her now, close enough to reach out and touch. The Sceptre and Orb grew heavy in her hands and she longed to put them down.

The air was pressing in on her, like it had in the museum, but not as severe. The world beyond the four figures twisted and spirals of stars spun slowly behind them. Stalker felt a wave of nausea rising up her throat.

The four figures reached up and slowly removed the masks. Stalker wanted to not see, she wished that her eyes were not already closed. She tried to turn away, but the vision moved with her.

'No, no. It's not true.' Tears began to fall as the faces

became clear.

Speaks-With-Stone, Flames-First-Guardian, Shadow's Step and Fortune stood before her, clutching the masks in their hands, smiling serenely, each with a bold spiral tattoo emblazoned upon their brow.

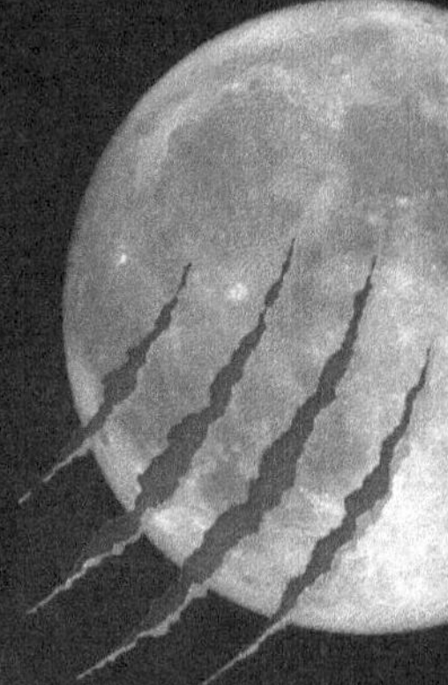

Chapter Twenty Six

Stalker dropped the Sceptre with a clunk and her feet sank to the floor. Weaver took the Orb from her and she tore the mask from her face. Tears were pouring down her cheeks.

'What did you see? What is it?' Eyes was by her side, clutching her shoulder.

Weaver looked at Stalker warily. Stalker couldn't share this devastating blow with her pack mates.

Before she could share anything, however, a silver glow filled the dome.

'You found them!' A ringing voice cried out and a column of shimmering light appeared in the centre.

'Wind Talker!' Eyes yelled. 'I thought this would keep everything out!'

'So did I!' Wind Talker shouted back.

Caeruleum Lunulam hovered just above the ground, bathing all of the shifters in her silver light.

'The Regalia called me.'

'How is that even possible?' Weaver asked, her voice strained. Stalker glanced sideways at her and saw a tear track on her cheek. The other cheek was unstained, having no eye to cry from. Stalker reached out and grasped her pack sister's hand and squeezed it.

'I do not know. But here I am. You found them all! Well done. Now we can really begin.'

'You lied to us!' Stalker shouted, stepping closer to the fae. 'You told us that you and the Blue Moon were working to defeat the Spiral Hand. But I know the truth, I was just shown in a vision.' She rounded on Eyes and Wind Talker, tears still streaking down her face. 'They were Spiral Hand.'

'What?' Eyes snapped.

'That's not possible.' Wind Talker shook his head resolutely.

'I saw it. I saw them in masks, they took them off and had spiral tattoos on their foreheads.'

'No, no my dear,' Caeruleum Lunulam said softly, her voice tinkling like tiny bells. 'No, they were pretending.'

'What? What do you mean?' Stalker turned back to her and wiped her cheeks on her sleeve.

'I told them, we must fight fire with fire. We can defeat the Spiral Hand from within. The Blue Moon sacrificed much for this cause. They became Spiral Hand in order to uncover the true agents in the city and expose them. The best way to fight such an insidious force is to understand it and use their own weapons against them. The Blue Moon were so close when they were killed.'

'There's never been a whole pack before,' Wind Talker

said, his voice low. 'It never happens. The Spiral Hand work alone. It makes no sense that the Blue Moon could all be Spiral Hand. She must be telling the truth.'

'Just because it's never happened before, doesn't mean it never could.' Weaver didn't look at Wind Talker as she spoke. She still held Stalker's hand.

'Do you have any suspicions as to who the true Spiral Hand could be?' Wind Talker asked, pressing closer to the shining fae.

'There are two. The Blue Moon discovered one just before I was taken but I do not know if they captured him.' Her voice was still soft and bell-like, but Stalker refused to be fooled by its softness. She felt the hardness in the fae's tone.

'Oh?' Eyes raised an eyebrow. 'Do you have any details?'

'He was a Fury working as a spy in the city, hidden among the humans.'

'Hidden Voice?' Wind Talker asked, his voice cracking slightly. Stalker's eyes flickered in his direction but she didn't meet his eye.

'Yes!' Caeruleum Lunulam seemed to spin in excitement. 'That was it. How do you know?'

'We found him,' Stalker said, her voice hard. 'They kept him alive and imprisoned. Like you.'

'I see.' The fae fell still and soft again. Tension prickled in the air. 'What happened to him?'

'He died,' Claws said quickly, before anyone else could speak. 'You said there were two. Who is the other?'

'I had my suspicions, but I could never prove it.'

'Who?' Eyes asked, a deep frown on his brow. Stalker

groaned in frustration. How could her pack mates believe this?

'Theodore Harris.'

The Lightning Lords stood in silence at her words. Somehow, Stalker had been expecting this name.

'We wondered about him. Remember?' Wind Talker rounded on Stalker and Weaver. 'Way back.'

'Yes, I remember,' Weaver replied.

'Could it have been him at the museum?' Eyes asked Stalker, not looking directly at her.

'I suppose, yes.'

'Because whatever the Blue Moon were up to, they're dead. And there is definitely someone alive and well messing with the world.' Stalker couldn't argue with Eyes' logic. He was right.

'You can use the Regalia in the ritual to summon the King-of-Glass-and-Steel,' the fae said, her voice filled with excitement. 'Then destroy Theodore Harris when he is revealed as Spiral Hand!'

'If!' Weaver called.

'If, yes, of course, if he is revealed as such.' Caeruleum Lunulam seemed flustered for just a moment.

'All right,' Wind Talker said, puffing up his chest. 'I agree to that.'

'So do I.' Eyes squared his shoulders to the fae.

Stalker looked at Weaver, who simply squeezed her hand more tightly. Claws put his hand softly on Stalker's shoulder and she felt his calm resolve easing her anguish.

It's okay, go with it.

Stalker nodded slightly in acknowledgement of Claws' projected thought.

'Very well, that is good enough for me. I will see you at the ritual.' She shimmered and disappeared.

'Eyes,' Stalker snapped, tugging free of Weaver and Claws. 'What did you agree to that for?'

'Because I believe her,' he said, blinking in surprise at her tone.

'But you've been working with Theodore for months.'

'Yes, and I never said I trusted him.'

'If he is Spiral Hand, and if he is responsible for banishing the King-of-Glass-and-Steel, why would he be working so hard to bring him back?' Weaver asked calmly.

'Perhaps because he wants to weaponise the shard for himself,' Wind Talker replied. 'He's a very accomplished ritualist. I'm certain he could have done the banishment ritual.'

'But bringing him back requires help?' Stalker asked, folding her arms defensively.

'Maybe, yes,' Wind Talker said. 'Or maybe it's a trap, a way to get all of the ritualists in one place to kill us all?'

'That would not surprise me,' Eyes said. He ran his hands through his hair and Stalker felt anger threatening to erupt. 'We should have a few other shifters there to guard the ritualists. Stalker, could you get a few Berserkers to be up there? You'll have to be, obviously, as the Regalia seem to only respond to you.'

Stalker simply blinked at him.

'I won't help that crazy fae. I don't believe you two are doing this.'

'Look, however this unfolds, I need you on that rooftop, Stalker. If it comes to it, and Theodore is innocent, then great, I will be relieved to be honest. And you can defend him if necessary. Or take on the real agent if they are up there too. Okay?'

'I suppose,' Stalker mumbled, not entirely satisfied.

'Let's get out of here, and get these buried again.' Eyes indicated the Regalia. The pack put them back in the box and Wind Talker dropped the protective shield around them.

'Do you suppose it worked and kept everything else out?' Weaver asked as they stepped away from where the dome had stood.

'We have to hope so,' Wind Talker replied.

The Lightning Lords got back to the house and reburied the Regalia. Stalker was exhausted, every muscle ached and she was the first to collapse onto her sleeping spot. Sleep swept over her almost instantly and wrapped her in a safe, warm blanket, free from nightmares.

She couldn't remember the last time she had slept right through the night, but when she woke up the next morning it was already light and the rest of the pack was already up. The heavy weight of all she had learned still kept her tired and somewhat hunched as she showered, dressed and ate breakfast. The pack seemed to buzz around her like flies, filled with plans and motivation. She hadn't seen Wind Talker looking so animated in months.

But Stalker felt as though she were in slow motion. Perhaps it was the effect of having been shot and nearly killed, or maybe it was the loss of her midnight runs in solitude finally affecting her. Something kept her from being fully herself.

She was dragged from her stupor by a clicking sound at the window.

'Stalker, I think it's a message for you.' Weaver opened the back door and Stalker looked up to see a raven perched on the windowsill. It croaked and hopped off the sill and flew into the kitchen, landing with a skittering of talons on the table right in front of her. There was a tiny scroll tied to its foot. She carefully untied it and nodded to the bird in thanks. It waited, bobbing its head as she unfurled the scroll. The small, scruffy writing of Red Scythe was scrawled on the slip of paper.

Meet us at the Old Fire Station at sunset - R.S.

She nodded her head and found no words able to come out of her mouth. The raven cawed and took flight, apparently understanding. Eyes read the note over her shoulder and gave her arm a squeeze.

'Good,' he said softly. 'Go to them, honour them.'

'I want to meet with Rhys today. He can help in the battle. He's a good fighter but he needs some help with his ability to shift.'

Eyes heaved a sigh and pinched between his eyes.

'Okay. Yes. Bring him onto our turf to train though. I don't want you too far from us.'

'Fair enough.' She cracked a smile and dashed from the room, clutching her new phone.

An hour later, Stalker was in Rhys's arms and the tears fell as he held her. She shook but he kept hold of her and stroked her hair.

'In here,' she managed to croak out and led him to the door of St. Mark's Dojo, her old workplace. The shabby sign over the old, abandoned electronics shop was freshly painted, as was the yellow brickwork. The door was unlocked and the stairwell was free of the faded posters and notices that had once lined the walls.

'Why are we here?'

'I need to put some demons to rest.'

'I really hope you're speaking figuratively.'

'Sort of.' She set off up the stairs and Rhys followed her. The dojo was quiet but for the sound of a fan whirring in the room opposite the top of the stairs. 'Ron?' she called out.

'Yes?' The voice lacked its old exuberance, but it was undoubtedly his. Stalker pushed the door to his office open and saw him sitting behind the desk. The once cluttered office was virtually empty and Ron had lost a lot of weight. His balding head shone in the sunlight pouring in through the large window behind him. 'Ariana!' His mouth erupted into a huge smile and he moved quickly around the desk to greet her. She smiled back and allowed him to pull her into an awkward hug.

'How are you? How's business?' She patted him on the back and he released her. He rocked backwards and forwards on his feet and tugged his trousers up at the waistband.

'Oh you know, ticking along. Still rebuilding after the fire.'

'Sure.'

'Do you want your job back?' he asked, a little too eagerly.

'Possibly. I'm not available for work right now, but maybe in a couple of weeks?'

'Grand, grand. Who's this?' Ron looked over her shoulder towards Rhys, who stood stiffly in the doorway.

'You remember Rhys? From Central? He helped bring

in the new equipment last year.'

'Of course, yes. Yes. How can I help you?'

'I was hoping to use a bit of space to train. I'm a bit rusty.'

'Sure, yes. No classes today.' There was a sad awkwardness in his smile.

'Thanks,' Stalker replied, trying to raise a smile in return. She led Rhys out of the office and into her old studio. It had a new floor, but was completely empty.

'What was that about?' Rhys asked in a whisper as he closed the door.

'I need to make amends. I destroyed his business. I lost it in here, shifted into the Agrius and ripped the place to shreds. Wind Talker had to burn it down to hide the damage.'

'Ah, right. But he doesn't know it was you?'

'Of course not.'

'And you want to try training in here now?'

'Not exactly. I'm training you.'

'Excuse me?'

'And in Hepethia, not here. Just in case.' She looked into his indignant face. 'I know you can kick arse like this, but if you're going to be of any help in the battle, you need to be able to shift.'

'Oh, right.' He looked down at the floor and hugged his arms across his chest.

'I want you there,' she said softly. She stepped forwards and gently took hold of his hands. 'I trust you and I want everyone to know that. I want us to be able to be seen together. I want you to come out of hiding.'

'What about what I want?'

'What do you want?'

He sighed and closed his eyes. Shaking his head, a smile creeping onto his lips, he looked back at her.

'I want those things too. I want to be out in the open. But I've been on my own for a long time and I don't want to rush anything. I don't see how we're going to get everyone to trust me in time to fight alongside you all though.'

'You helped find the Orb. Your life's sacrifices were acknowledged by the crows. But if that's not enough, you'll have the backing of all of Odin's Warriors.'

'I will?' He raised an eyebrow.

'You will. But right now we need to get you comfortable in your shifter skin and see what you can do.'

Stalker led Rhys across the veil. The dojo was reflected in Hepethia, but it was the charred remains of the old studio, with a gaping hole in the wall where Stalker had ripped the fire door right off its hinges. The destruction that her actions had wrought had been picked up across the veil and shaped the appearance of the place.

'Oh wow.' Rhys stepped away from her and looked around.

'Have you ever seen what your house looks like over here?' Stalker asked, looking at him shrewdly.

'No, I haven't.'

'You should,' she said with a wry smile. He nodded meekly and gazed around at the blackened rubble. Stalker surveyed him, eyeing him the way she would an enemy in a fight, searching for a tell or weakness. She circled him, as he stood there taking in the oddness of Hepethia, apparently unaware of what she was doing. She remembered standing in the basement of the betting shop with Shadow's Step when she was freshly changed. He had coaxed her into shifting by shifting himself and attacking. She wasn't convinced his method was fair, but it was effective. Would it work now on Rhys? He was hardly a new shifter, but for his lack of shifting over the last decade he may as well be.

Stalker leapt towards him, shifting into the Agrius mid-leap. Rhys stumbled backwards in alarm, his face pale with shock and a cry bursting from his open mouth. But he didn't reflexively shift; he lay sprawled on his back looking up at her in horror. She skidded to a halt in front of him and shifted back into her human form.

'I'm sorry,' she said, quickly scrambling to her knees and reaching out for him. 'You really can't do it, can you? The reflexes aren't there. I thought they would kick in under pressure.'

'Apparently n-not.' He wiped a hand across his sweating brow. Stalker held out a hand and helped him to his feet.

'Okay, slowly. Let's do this together. Focus, breathe. You have the Agrius inside you, you've taken that form before.'

Rhys took a deep breath and closed his eyes. 'Imagine yourself changing: imagine your limbs growing, fur growing quickly up out of your pores.' Stalker watched as Rhys stood there, hopefully doing as she asked. One of his hands twitched. A shudder rippled through his body and his eyes popped open. He looked down his body and examined his hands. He was still resolutely human.

'I thought something happened.' He looked disappointed.

'Nearly, I think you were close. Try again.'

He closed his eyes again and Stalker watched as he slowly flexed each group of muscles, testing them, it seemed. He took slow breaths. 'You need to let go. You've been hiding who you are for so long it's obviously hard to shed that. But you need to get back in touch with what you are.'

It struck Stalker as odd to be on the other end of this advice, having been lectured on this by Weaver not so long ago.

'I'm a shifter,' he said softly, barely above a whisper. 'Not human. Chosen.'

It was like a switch. Saying the words out loud made something change in the air. In a flurry of movement, Rhys transformed. It wasn't smooth like Stalker was accustomed to seeing, it was a jumble of limbs flickering between states and Rhys seemed to roll into a ball and spin uncontrollably. She took a few steps back and readied herself, in case when he solidified he wasn't himself.

The air was filled with the crunching of bones taking on new shapes, joints clicking and his breathing growing harsh and ragged. A snarl ripped from his throat and he spun one last time before skidding to a halt on all fours, his snout jutting out towards Stalker, saliva dripping from his bared teeth.

Stalker tensed up and fixed her gaze on his wild eyes. He was afraid, but he was still there, the Beast hadn't taken control.

'Good, well done Rhys.' She smiled and stepped closer. 'Can you shift back?'

He shook his head, not in the negative, but like a

dog trying to shake a fly away. Stalker stifled a laugh and stepped back again, giving him room. The transition back to human was a little smoother and quicker, but Stalker's smile froze as she saw his skin returning in place of the thick, grey fur that had covered his body. His clothing was shredded on the ground around him and his bare skin was pale and clear. His tattoos were gone. She clapped a hand to her mouth and stared at him. He got to his feet slowly, his legs shaking slightly and he looked up from the ground, his eyes darting rapidly from side to side. He looked down at his arms and chest and then looked up at her in alarm.

'They're gone.'

Stalker nodded and moved over to him. She reached out and ran her fingers over his chest and shoulders where the ink had been covering his top half almost completely.

'Well, they were magical, weren't they? They were designed to hide you. You're not hiding any more.'

'I think my cloak is gone too.'

Stalker nodded again. She hadn't thought of it until this moment, but in Hepethia he had always had a demon cloaking him before, but it hadn't been there at all since they crossed the veil.

'I'm sorry about your clothes.' She looked down at his naked body and couldn't help smiling. She had seen him like this before, but it wouldn't be appropriate to cross back into the human world and walk through the city in this state and they both laughed at the thought. 'It's okay; we'll go back on this side. Ron will just think we slipped out quietly. But not yet. Shift again for me.' She stepped back and grinned at him. He grinned back and instantly transformed into the Agrius again, new-found confidence in his eyes.

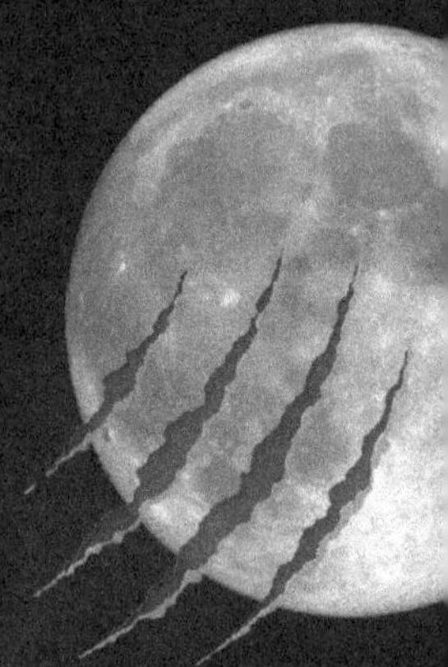

Chapter Twenty Seven

'You'll be fine,' Stalker said softly. She kept walking briskly through the city centre, leading the way, Rhys a step behind her.

'Why do I have to come?'

'Because I want them to endorse you. It'll help with the rest.'

'But I feel like I'm intruding.' Stalker came to an abrupt halt and Rhys almost bumped into her. The people walking quickly along the pavement parted around them like water around rocks, barely aware of the shifters in their midst.

'I know, but it's important. There isn't much time. Be honourable, pay your respects to the fallen and try to mention Odin. If we can get you in good standing with them, then the rest will accept you more easily. You never know, you might decide to join us.' She gave him a wink and set off walking again, this time clutching his hand tightly. He took an extra quick step to fall into step with her and smiled down at her.

'Thank you.'

'What for?'

'You know what for. For helping me get back to who I should be. I feel like I have a lot of lost time to make up for, but I know that with you by my side I can do it.'

Stalker glanced up at him and smiled. There was such warmth in his eyes, they sparkled.

The two of them had spent hours that afternoon, just shifting forms over and over again until it became as easy as breaking into a run for Rhys. He didn't have an Artemis-given form, so it was just his human and Agrius forms that he had to perfect switching between. Stalker felt confident that he would be capable in battle, with his martial arts training. She had taken to combat very quickly and had every reason to hope he would be the same.

She had taken him to Grove Street afterwards and got him some of Wind Talker's clothes. But now, having been back to his house quickly to change into his own, they were running late for the meeting at the fire station. The sun had already set and the sky blazed red and purple with the last rays of dusk.

When they arrived, the doors were closed and the street was empty. She pulled on the large handle and the door swung open. Inside was dark and still, but Stalker could hear voices deep in the belly of the building. She led Rhys inside and pulled the door closed again, making sure it *clunked* shut properly. She took his hand and walked quickly along the dark and dusty corridor.

The corridor opened up into a large open area, lit

with several old strip lights hanging from the ceiling. Odin's Warriors were assembled, still in small clusters talking amongst themselves. Their number was somewhat depleted, Stalker noted with a sad lurch to her stomach. Red Scythe sat on a tall stool, clutching his weapon beside him. He looked weary as he rubbed his head with his free hand.

A few heads turned in Stalker and Rhys's direction as they entered and one of her brothers made a move towards them, a scowl on his face.

'This is meant to be a private gathering,' Crimson said, holding back her pack mate.

'I know, I'm sorry,' Stalker said, her voice echoing in the cavernous room. 'This is Rhys. He would like to pay his respects.'

'I know how important Ragged Edge was to Stalker,' Rhys said, his voice calm and confident.

'That's not enough to attend our rituals,' Red Scythe said, standing and striding across the concrete floor towards them, the end of his scythe thudding against the ground on alternate steps. 'Else we would all bring pack mates.'

'I understand, but please, I'm still healing and he's sworn to protect me.' Stalker reached for her chest and gave her shoulder a roll as if to emphasise the stiffness still in it. She wasn't completely lying to her brothers and sisters, but a little guilt at the mistruth did intrude upon her thoughts. She only hoped no one would sense it.

'I see.' Red Scythe frowned at her. 'He may observe, but I want him sworn to secrecy and he won't be permitted to attend again unless he petitions to join.'

'Fine, yes, agreed.' Stalker nodded ardently and Rhys did likewise. She saw him to the edge of the room and got him seated. 'You have to swear out loud, all solemn-like.'

'Okay,' he said, smiling softly at her. 'I swear I will tell no one what happens here tonight. I honour the sacred rituals of Odin's Warriors.'

'That should do nicely.' Stalker grinned at him and kissed him swiftly on the lips before turning and jogging to join the circle that had formed.

'We will proceed to Crescent Park shortly,' Red Scythe said, commanding the attention of the small circle of Berserkers present. 'It is with great sorrow that we assemble tonight. We have lost three more of our own: Binds-Iron's-Hide, First Strike, and of course, Ragged Edge. Many of us here counted these men our brothers. We also acknowledge the heavy losses throughout the city. We are the chosen few who are sworn to defend the city as a whole and we failed in that duty. The city is weaker now, we are weaker now. This war has claimed enough casualties. We must be united and stand tall in this moment. When the Furies come, we will not succumb, we will fight and we will triumph!'

Stalker was not the only one to pump her fist in the air and shout. The roar echoed off the walls and ceiling.

Red Scythe strode to a large whiteboard on wheels just outside the circle, and pulled it into view. It had a rough map of Caerton on it in red ink. Stalker grinned as she saw the small lines and markings on it that showed the battle plans that he had drawn up. It was exactly what she would have done, if this were her army to command. She beckoned Rhys forward out of the shadows and he came to stand beside her as Red Scythe went over the plans.

The shifters around them cast wary glances at him, but no one spoke out.

Everyone had a role, no gaps had been left in the defences of the city. The primary objective was to funnel the Furies towards the castle ruins and force them across the veil. There was every chance that the human population would know something was happening. They had to be protected. Red Scythe had accounted for all of Odin's Warriors and had included the packs in the plans.

'I had an interesting day with your Alpha,' he said, looking pointedly at Stalker.

'Oh?' Stalker was taken aback. 'I didn't know that.'

'Yes, some of this was his idea.' Red Scythe gestured towards the board.

'I'm glad,' she said with a wry smile. 'He'd be most put out if he hadn't been involved.'

'Shaping up to be quite the leader, that young man.'

Stalker smiled and nodded in approval. Although it saddened her to have drifted far enough from Eyes to not have known he was meeting the leader of Odin's Warriors without her.

'Rhys needs a job,' Stalker said. All eyes turned to look at the outsider amongst them.

'Do I?' Rhys asked, his voice barely above a whisper.

'He doesn't have a pack,' Stalker went on. 'He's not automatically included in any of these plans.'

'What do you mean, he doesn't have a pack?' Crimson asked, a deep frown furrowing her pale brow. 'Where did he change?'

'He's not newly changed,' Stalker said, feeling her

cheeks burning.

'New to the city then?' Crimson asked, her eyes narrowed.

'No,' Rhys said, lifting his chin. 'I've been here ten years. I changed on my own and have been living in the city centre.'

'That's impossible,' Red Scythe shook his head.

'It's the truth,' Rhys said, calm as Stalker had ever seen him, full of the charm that had attracted her to him when they first met.

'But the city centre is unclaimed, it's an infested mess.' Crimson scowled at Rhys.

'I haven't attempted to control it. I had no idea how to do that. I had no one to guide me when I changed. I just did what I had to in order to survive.'

'He was blending in with the humans,' Stalker explained, taking his hand firmly in hers. There were mutterings and gasps among the shifters. 'He could help protect them during the fight. Couldn't you?' She looked up into his eyes and gave him a searching look. He nodded firmly.

'Absolutely. I can keep them away from the battlefield and make sure no Furies take human hostages or lives.'

'On your own?' Red Scythe raised an eyebrow.

'No, with others, of course. But I know the area like the back of my hand and people tend to trust me.' He shrugged, as if this were something out of his control, his natural charm only, and nothing to do with the demon who had been hiding him so effectively for so long. Stalker squeezed his hand and looked expectantly at Red Scythe.

Fury was standing beside the leader and she rolled her

eyes.

'People just trust you?' she asked, clucking her tongue.

'I'm very adept at mixing with humans without them realising I'm not like them.' Rhys looked Fury right in the eye, unflinching.

Stalker glared at Fury, willing her to back down.

'You definitely have less of the aura about you,' Red Scythe said, looking Rhys up and down. 'I can barely tell you're one of us.'

Stalker gave Fury a sanctimonious smirk and Fury turned away, flicking her long braids over her shoulder. 'Very well,' Red Scythe continued. 'You can help with crowd control.'

Stalker squeezed Rhys's hand again before releasing it. He smiled down at her, and gave her an appreciative nod. She was relieved to have him included. Whether any of her fellows suspected Rhys or not, no one said anything now that Red Scythe had given his approval.

Once the plans had been covered in enough detail, Red Scythe led Odin's Warriors from the meeting place out into the city. It was a warm night, a clear sky was dotted with stars. Stalker held Rhys's hand tightly as the group walked quickly to Crescent Park. The streets were quiet and there was nothing to prevent Stalker's mind from diving into memories of those who had been lost.

Funerals were normally a pack affair, but Odin's Warriors always found a way to honour their fallen brothers. They passed through the deserted plaza where the war memorial stood. Red Scythe strode up the steps to the tall column and touched his scythe to the smooth sandstone. The stone blazed with golden runes in neat rows all around the column. It was the list of fallen Berserkers, hidden from human sight and only revealed to those who knew of it. Stalker gazed up as new runes appeared there among the honoured dead. First Strike, Binds-Iron's-Hide and Ragged Edge were memorialised there now for generations of Odin's Warriors to see.

'I never knew this was here,' Rhys whispered as the group began to move away. 'All these years in Caerton, and I never knew such a thing existed.'

'You've missed a lot, I think.'

'Yeah.' Rhys looked back over his shoulder at the cenotaph as they walked away. Stalker saw sadness in his eyes, a layer of regret. She squeezed his hand and caught his gaze.

They followed Red Scythe and the others to Crescent Park, down the winding path from the road to the little lawn at the bottom that gave the park its name. It was almost midnight and utterly still and quiet. A faint breeze rustled the leaves of the trees that sheltered the park. The group clustered around Red Scythe and he passed a black candle to each of them. He paused for a moment when he came to Rhys and with a reluctant grunt, passed the outsider a candle. 'Thank you,' Rhys said earnestly. Red Scythe nodded and moved on.

The candles were lit and the group formed a circle in the centre of the lawn. The air fell still, the breeze dropped and every flame stood tall on its wick. Stalker shuddered, the losses of the last year piled on top of one another. She had said goodbye to too many fellows on this spot. There seemed to be no need for words. Stalker glanced around at her brothers and sisters and saw their solemn faces.

Crimson was crying silently and Stalker's chest gave a painful twang. She had cared deeply for First Strike at one time, but she had let him go when she realised that he was filling Rhys's space. She looked up into Rhys's dark eyes as he gazed into the flame of his candle. She cast aside any guilt she was still holding on to and decided to hope that First Strike had forgiven her.

'They are feasting in Valhalla,' said Mjolnir. Someone chuckled and Crimson cracked a smile.

'Imagine the women and beer that will be flowing.' Howl-of-Flames, pack mate of Red Scythe and Binds-Iron's-Hide was grinning as he spoke and Stalker knew it must have been him that had laughed. She smiled too, trying not to imagine Ragged Edge, whom she had only ever known as an old man, having sex with young wine-bearing maidens. A ripple of subdued laughter ran around the circle.

'In times of peace, we would feast now,' Red Scythe said, a smile on his lips. 'We would celebrate their lives and honour their achievements. It is a disgrace that they were not afforded the opportunity to die in glorious battle. The cowardly Furies picked off the best warriors from afar. We won't allow them to get away with such dishonour. We will avenge our fallen brothers and bring honour to their deaths through our deeds on the battlefield. We will face the Furies when they come and we will cull them.' He twisted his scythe in his hand and his knuckles turned white. The smile was gone from his crinkled lips and his eyes shone with bitter tears. 'The reaping is coming.'

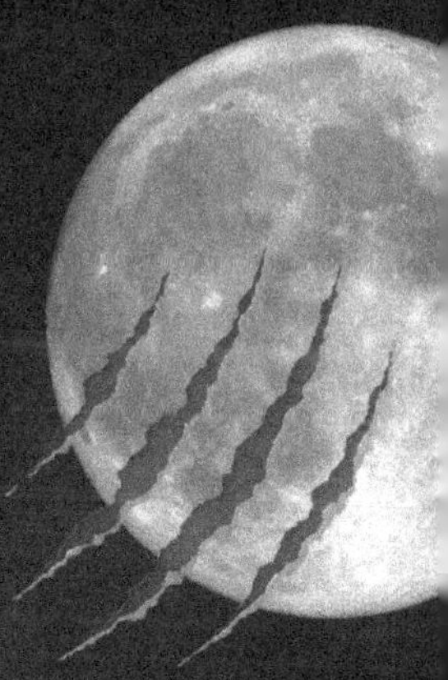

Chapter Twenty Eight

Fights-Eyes-Open

'We're ready,' Theodore said, his voice cracked with eagerness. 'We can proceed with the ritual tonight. The ley lines are prepared, everything is in place.'

'We're cutting it fine,' Eyes said, checking his watch. 'The Furies are due tomorrow.'

'I know. I wish it could have happened sooner, but it was a huge undertaking and it took until now to get everything in place.'

'I know,' Eyes said with a sigh. He rubbed the spot between his eyes. He leaned forward and rolled up the large spread of papers in front of him that included the underground railway plans, city plans and battle plans that he had drawn up with Red Scythe. 'I feel like something's been forgotten, though.'

'I know what you mean. I think we're all anxious. So much is riding on this.' Theodore got to his feet and drained his coffee cup. He turned and gazed out of the huge window of his office. Eyes finished gathering up the papers and looked out past Theodore. The city lay at their feet, bathed in glorious sunshine. Cars and people scurried like ants far below. This was why Theodore was the way he was, so detached. He looked down at humanity from this great height and didn't relate to the world.

'Well,' Eyes said, drawing Theodore's attention back to the room. 'I'll see you tonight. Good luck.'

'And to you, Eyes. We'll raise a glass when it's all done.'

Eyes nodded and left the room. The ride down Free River Tower in the lift seemed to take longer than ever. A thousand thoughts tumbled over in his mind, none lingering long enough for him to focus on them.

Outside, it was a hot June day and the city was bursting with life. Eyes bought a newspaper from a street vendor and took the time to sit in the bustling central plaza to read it. Though he didn't take in much. He hadn't followed the human news in some months and barely understood what was happening. He was becoming more and more like Theodore: detached and superior. He hated it. He flipped the paper closed in frustration and stared at the people rushing past him. The newly opened underground station nearby hummed with activity, people dashing in and out of the archway that led to the stairs down to the station. Only one section of the route was open, it took people between the plaza and the bus station. Eyes shook his head. It was only a ten-minute walk, yet dozens of people passed through the arch while he sat there.

He took his phone from his inside jacket pocket and stared at the screen. He had an important call to make that he had been putting off. He could delay no longer. The phone rang for an agonisingly long thirty seconds. Just as he was sure it was about to go to voicemail, a cool voice answered.

'Hello Martin.'

'Hi Chloe. How are you?'

'Fine. What do you want?'

'I was hoping to talk to Amy.'

'She's at ballet.'

'Oh, right. How is London? Are you settled? Do you need anything?'

'We don't need anything from you.'

'Right. As long as you're both safe and happy, that's all that matters.'

'What does that mean?' Her tone changed. He heard a note of concern in her voice. A tear came to his eye and he brushed it away. 'Martin? What's going on?'

'Nothing.'

'Why did you call?'

'Just to check in, make sure you're both okay. I miss you so much.' The ache in his chest became almost too much to bear. Another tear fell.

'Amy's right here, I'm sorry. Here she is.' Chloe's voice cracked and there was a rustle.

'Daddy?'

'Hey munchkin!' Eyes felt his face lift, a smile erupted on his lips and he leaned forward, clutching the phone more tightly.

'Daddy! Miss you so much! Nana doesn't do the voices when she reads.' Eyes let a laugh escape his dry lips.

'Oh no, that's no good at all.'

'She said there were no monsters under the bed.'

'Oh? Were you frightened?'

'No! I wanted there to be. I was looking for monsters. They don't scare me.'

Eyes grinned and let the tears fall down his cheeks.

'That's my girl. Never be scared of the monsters. Promise?'

'I promise. Daddy? When will you come visit?'

'I don't know, sweetie.'

There was another rustle and it was Chloe's voice that greeted him.

'We'll sort something out. We will. It's been too long.'

'Okay, thank you.' He wiped his face and cleared his throat. 'I'm trying to prevent a merger at the moment. When it dies down I'll have some time. I can come to you, or you can come here.'

'We'll talk when you don't have work to do.' Her tone was a little cooler again.

'It's not *work,* work. It's... you know, hard stuff. Big stuff. End of the world stuff.'

'Oh, right. Be careful, then.' There was tension in her voice, the weight of everything she didn't want to know or be part of loaded into her short words.

'I will. Speak soon.'

'Yeah, bye.' Chloe rung off and Eyes slowly lowered the phone. It was wet with his tears. He wiped it on his trousers and put it away. A shaking breath left his lips. He looked into the azure sky and heaved a sigh. He had been so consumed with plans and preparation that he had forgotten what he was fighting for. He needed to make Caerton safer for his family, bring them home and put it back together. It was no longer about revenge, not really.

He thought of Caeruleum Lunulam and the promise he had made. Stalker had been right to be sceptical. They didn't really know anything about the fae, or how being imprisoned might have affected her. They had been warned about the King-of-Glass-and-Steel and how he might be when he returned. It was worth considering, wasn't it, that the lunar fae might be messed up too? The vision Stalker had had of the Blue Moon unsettled him, he didn't want to believe they had really been Spiral Hand. Caeruleum Lunulam offered them an explanation that fit what he wanted to hear.

Well, they would soon find out who among them was the Spiral Hand who had been interfering in the city. It would soon be over, one way or another.

He got to his feet and set off for the car park. It was a short drive into China Town, where he parked in a side street, amid the usual hustle and bustle of the place. The street market was in full swing, with vendors lined up behind their stalls and the air was thick with smoke and steam. The heat was stifling as he weaved his way up the busy street towards the restaurant that belonged to the House of Cards. A closed sign hung in the glass of the door, but Eyes could see a light on in the kitchen at the back and glimpsed movement. He knocked sharply on the glass and waited.

A moment later a figure moved in the dark to the door, navigating the tables and chairs with ease. There was a click and the door opened.

'Mr Eyes, sir, come on in.' Eyes pressed his lips together to keep from smiling. It was the host who had greeted the Lightning Lords when they first came here to meet their neighbours. He was human, but Eyes got the strong impression that he knew of shifters and the nature of his employers. He led Eyes up the narrow staircase to the room above the restaurant, where Mrs Feng and the twins, Harry and Jack, were sitting, poring over papers. None of them stood, or even acknowledged Eyes' arrival.

Mrs Feng seemed to gaze down the table, her eyes like milk.

'Welcome, please sit,' she said at last. The human waiter hurried away and Eyes took a seat at the long table. 'Is everything ready?'

'Yes. We're conducting the ritual tonight. If all goes according to plan, we will have the city's patron back by midnight. With any luck, he can rally the disordered demons and fae and we will have a vast army at our command for when the Furies attack. Are your plans in place?'

'Yes. We have tightened our security here. My boys will be ready.' She waved a wrinkled hand at the twins, who didn't react. Eyes got that feeling again that the old woman might not really be blind, or that she had some other way of seeing or sensing accurately what was around her. He held his composure and drew a breath.

'How many of your people are you keeping back for defence? And how many will be joining the battle at the castle?'

'Half and half,' Mrs Feng said, her voice resolute.

'We'll send word when we begin to assemble.'

'We will know.'

'Okay, well I'll send word anyway.'

'If you wish.' Mrs Feng shrugged and turned her face

towards the invoices laid before her. Eyes knew that their meeting was concluded. He left feeling as though relations with the House of Cards would never be friendly. But as long as they could cooperate like this, then he had some hope of a victory when it really counted. They had agreed to take control of the section of St. Mark's that sat south of Red Bridge, and some of Crossway, his old neighbourhood, in exchange for their help against the Furies. It would give the Lightning Lords less territory to protect. It had been an easy agreement to come to with the House of Cards.

As night approached, and the pack assembled at Grove Street to grab food, Eyes felt butterflies in his stomach, a sensation he hadn't felt since his first appearance in a courtroom. Rhys joined them and Weaver had managed to extend the kitchen table using a large piece of wood that she had salvaged, so that all six of them could sit around it to eat the chilli they had made.

There was a prickle of anticipation in the air, and conversation was low and infrequent. Eyes watched the others as he ate.

'You know, I was thinking about when this is done and everything settles down, we could find premises for a business. Something we can do to bring in some money and keep us going.' Weaver smiled as she spoke and Eyes felt optimism rolling off her.

'Like the Blue Moon?' Stalker asked, an edge to her voice.

'Well, yes, and the Wrecking Crew, and Glass Wolves and pretty much every pack. It's common sense. We've been cramped into this little house for too long. It was great in the emergency that we found ourselves in last winter, but I really do think we need to have bigger plans.'

'Are you going to go back to teaching?' Rhys asked Stalker, pausing with his fork halfway to his mouth as he spoke.

'I don't think so. It's too dangerous.' Stalker didn't look up as she spoke, she gazed down into her food.

'I thought a hardware store might be good,' Wind Talker said, his mouth full of food.

'Yeah, that's a pretty good idea,' Weaver replied, nodding fervently.

Eyes kept quiet, eating slowly. He had very little appetite. His stomach kept doing uncomfortable flips. The casual meal felt so at odds with what was coming. At six o' clock he patted his mouth with a napkin and took his plate to the sink. Everyone recognised the signal and followed suit with no need to talk. Eyes felt a hard lump in his throat, which he cleared with a firm cough and everyone stood still and looked at him expectantly. They wanted a speech, some words of encouragement.

'If tonight goes well, we'll soon have the King-of-Glass-and-Steel back. He'll have full command of all of the demons, fae and constructs in the city. When the Furies arrive tomorrow, we'll be able to face them with the entire city behind us.'

'And if tonight doesn't go well?' Stalker asked, an eyebrow cocked.

'It will.' He saw her sceptical frown and nodded. 'We all know the contingency plans. We all know our own responsibilities. We know fallback positions. We know emergency procedures. We've drilled this down. You all know where you need to be and what to do. We'll meet up again after the ritual and raise a toast to our success, then get a good night's sleep to be ready for tomorrow. Good luck to you all.'

He hated it; the words didn't do the situation justice. He wished he had something better to say. Wind Talker and Stalker exchanged glances and she picked up a bag that contained the Regalia, and slung it onto her back. Rhys pulled her into a tight hug and Wind Talker said his goodbyes to Claws and Weaver. He came to Eyes last and embraced him like a brother.

'I'm proud of the leader you've become, Eyes. Artemis be with you tonight.'

'You too,' Eyes said. He patted Wind Talker on the back and watched him out of the door. He caught Stalker's arm as she tried to pass him and pulled her into a hug too. 'Take care. Kick butt if you need to.'

'I will,' she said with a slight chuckle then followed Wind Talker out into the night.

'Okay, folks. Let's go.' He led the others out of the house, which Weaver locked up after them. Rhys placed a hand on the door and closed his eyes. Eyes watched as the walls either side of the door squeezed together. The old door with its peeling paint was gone and Rhys's hand touched only red brick. It was as if number thirty-two Grove Street had disappeared. Eyes had left his car at his mother's house and the four of them set off on foot for the city centre.

It was a quiet journey. There was nothing left to plan or say. Rhys and Claws peeled off at the plaza to go their own way, and Eyes and Weaver walked on alone to the cathedral that stood in the heart of the city. 'Ready?' he asked Weaver as they stood gazing up at the vast windows. She grasped his hand and they stepped, together, across the veil. Their mission: Stay alive to greet the King-of-Glass-and-Steel upon his return.

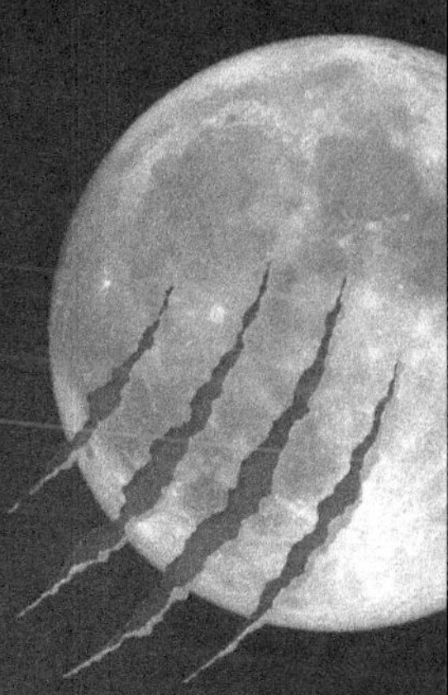

CHAPTER TWENTY NINE

LIGHTNING CRACKLED IN THE BLACK SKY and thick purple clouds rolled across it, obscuring the distant stars. Unchained Lightning swooped low over the city, a ripple of static following his swishing tail. Stalker watched him from her rooftop perch.

Her sharp eyes focused on the distant buildings that leaned treacherously, like massive struts of crystal bursting up from a cave floor. Between her and them was the enormous wall that the Glass Wolves had erected to protect their territory from the monstrous demons that claimed the city centre. Their territory was meticulous and she felt a stab of envy. Box-like buildings in neat rows stretched as far as the eye could see. Here at the heart of Theodore's domain, Stalker stood on the highest of skyscrapers, Free River Tower. An exact replica of the human world tower, and at the top she could see almost the entire city.

All of Hepethia lay around her, its varied landscape a testament to generations of shifter packs who had sculpted it to suit their own purposes. The Blue Moon's legacy remained all over her own territory. *We should really change that*, she thought.

Lightning flashed overhead again and the chanting behind Stalker grew louder. She turned back to watch the ritualists gathered on the rooftop. A pentagram was painted in white on the floor and at each point stood one of the shifters who had been assembled to conduct the ritual: Wind Talker, Crimson, Spark, Mjolnir and Red Scythe; and at the centre was Theodore Harris.

Caerton's most accomplished ritualists made a formidable sight, with their arms raised to the sky, palms bleeding, and smoky haze surrounding them from the burning incense. On the raised edges of the tower's flat roof stood the Guard: those, like Stalker, who had been asked to watch over the ritual and protect those conducting it from any interference. The rest of the Glass Wolves were there: Vengeance-of-Steel and Word Spider; Sentinel-on-the-Steps of the Hand of God; and Howl-of-Flames of Crimson Dawn's Blood and fellow Berserker. The rest of Odin's Warriors, along with almost all of Caerton's shifters, were patrolling Hepethia on the ground, ready and waiting for the beast that they were trying to summon, and any enemies that might be attracted to the ritual.

Theodore had told them that it was likely that The-King-of-Glass-and-Steel would appear somewhere in the heart of the city, rather than on the top of the tower, where the ritual was being performed. So Stalker turned her attention back to scanning the distant city centre for signs of something stirring. Unchained Lightning soared above, scouting the city from the sky. Claws was up there somewhere too, and many other flying shifters and their fae allies.

Stalker watched Wind Talker, wondering what he was going to do about Caeruleum Lunulam's request. His thoughts were jumbled and she couldn't pick out anything clear. He slowly reached into his pocket and drew out a small phial filled with dark liquid. Stalker frowned and squinted to see what it was. It looked like blood. With his thumb, Wind Talker swiftly uncorked the tiny phial and sprinkled the contents into the pentagram, just in front of his feet. A faint ripple flowed out from them, barely visible in the dark. The two pack mates caught each other's gaze and Stalker glared at him. He looked back solemnly.

The chanting grew louder, its haunting rhythm sending a pulse through Stalker as she stood there on the edge of a seven-hundred foot drop. Lightning flashed behind the clouds and a clap of thunder ripped across the city. Forks darted down from the pendulous clouds at five points around the city, striking Hepethia in unison. Stalker startled, her heart leaping into her throat, and looked around at the other shifters gathered on the rooftop.

The Glass Wolves didn't seem surprised, those involved in the ritual remained sharply focused, but Sentinel and Howl-of-Flames were looking mildly alarmed and clutching their weapons.

Stalker spun around, quickly trying to assess where each fork of lightning had struck. Smoke was rising in three places: one in South Stoke, another in Old Town and one in Redfield, on her own turf. It seemed the strikes had formed a circle with the tower it the centre. Howl-of-Flames was staring across to his pack's territory where another strike had been.

'Stalker, it's time.' Theodore's voice was soft, yet she heard it perfectly over the tumult of the storm. She moved into the centre of the circle to stand beside Theodore. He handed her the mask and she slipped it onto her face, once again feeling it stick to her skin. She took up the Orb and Sceptre too and looked up at the sky, unsure what to expect.

Thoughts of Caeruleum Lunulam popped into her mind and she swept them aside. She wasn't doing this for the crazy fae, she was trying to help bring the King-of-Glass-and-Steel back from whatever hell he was being held in. Everyone seemed to agree that the Regalia would help with this. Would it also reveal any Spiral Hand in their midst?

She looked into Theodore's face. He was gazing up at the sky; the flickering of lightning lit his skin and shone in his eyes. He was smiling, almost radiant. There was no sign of anything untoward. Stalker looked around at everyone else. The other ritualists were still standing with their arms raised, their eyes closed, focusing their will on the summoning of the city's spirit. The shifters guarding the ritual looked on anxiously, glancing around for signs of trouble. Aside from the wind whipping Crimson's long, red hair and the long coats of several of the shifters, all was still on the rooftop.

The extra depths of reality that the mask revealed showed Stalker nothing, no clues, no hidden truths. She looked to Wind Talker, who had opened his eyes and was watching her, an anxious frown on his face. She shook her head.

Nothing, there's no Spiral Hand here. Theodore's innocent.

A huge sonic boom broke the silence. There was a cry from below and the tower trembled. Stalker dropped to her knees and the Regalia clattered to the floor.

The ritual circle broke as shifters ran to the edge of the tower. Stalker leapt up and ran with them. She leaned out over the concrete rim of the tower. At the base a party of shifters scurried like ants, sprinting away from the building and towards the vast wall that separated Glass Wolf territory from the perilous city centre. Stalker could hear her pulse pounding in her ears and felt a powerful tug at her chest. *Rhys.* She stood up and looked towards the city centre.

'What's happening?' Sentinel was at her side, looking out across the city.

'I don't know.' Stalker spun around and ran to Vengeance-of-Steel, grabbed her arm and glared into her face. 'Has it worked?'

'I don't know,' Steel snapped and yanked her arm free of Stalker's tight grip. The pair of them turned to look at Theodore, who stood perfectly still in the centre of the rooftop. Above him, swirling in the thick clouds was something alive. A silver glimmer. Theodore looked up at it, his face gently lit by the shimmering light.

'What the...?' his voice croaked.

A sudden wind whipped around the top of the tower and the silver glint in the cloud expanded, reached down and scooped Theodore up as if he weighed no more than a small child. A shout rang out from several shifters and bodies lurched forwards. The Alpha of the Glass Wolves was tossed across the roof and released into the air. He flew straight out for a second, before plummeting towards the ground, seven hundred feet below.

'No!' shrieked the Glass Wolves and everyone tore to the edge of the rooftop to watch him drop. Stalker watched for an agonisingly long three seconds before sense kicked in and without thinking, she leapt off the roof and shifted into a huge Andean Condor, the biggest, strongest bird she could think of. Her vast wings rippled behind her as she dove. All thought vanished from her mind. She fixed her gaze on Theodore's falling body and aimed straight for it. She was gaining on him, letting gravity do most of the work. She reached out for him with her talons. Closer. Closer. She stretched a little further and grabbed hold of one arm and one leg, then beat her wings hard to slow their descent.

Theodore's eyes latched onto hers as she strained to keep hold of him and defy gravity. They approached the ground, slowing down just enough that when her strength gave in and she dropped him he only fell a few feet and rolled awkwardly along the ground as his momentum slowed. Stalker shifted form and landed at a run on human feet just behind where he lay sprawled on the ground. She looked up, her heart beating so hard she could practically hear it. She searched for the fae, but she was gone.

Rhys. She had to find him, she had to know if he was okay. She had felt his fear the moment before Theodore was attacked. She spun on the spot at the sound of feet pounding towards her. Red Scythe and Sentinel ran towards them, the fastest to reach the ground from the top of the tower due to their own gift of flight as half-moon owl shifters.

'What the hell was that?' Sentinel snapped, glaring at Stalker.

Stalker glanced warily at Red Scythe. He looked stern but unsurprised. Had Ragged Edge told him her secret before he died? She looked past him towards the tower and saw Theodore emerging from the revolving glass door. Her breath caught in her throat and she spun, confused, to where she had last seen him lying on the ground. He was there, getting slowly to his feet.

'What?' Her head swivelled between the two identical figures, dressed in the same suit, the same square glasses perched on their beefy faces. The one she had rescued from his deadly fall was brushing dirt from his suit. She charged forwards and grabbed hold of him, shaking him.

'It's okay,' the other Theodore called out. He jogged over, straightening his tie as he approached. A cluster of shifters appeared behind him, everyone else from the rooftop. Confused expressions filled many faces. Steel broke free from the group and sprinted forward, catching up with her Alpha and getting quickly between him and Red Scythe, who had turned deep vermilion and was gripping his namesake tightly in both hands.

Stalker's hand was still latched onto Theodore's arm, but suddenly her fingers gave way and her gaze snapped back to where he had stood. A puff of smoke swirled in his place and when it cleared Stalker saw a strange wolf-like figure with a dark mask over his face. Stalker looked at the large wolf and back at Theodore. The others had caught up now and gathered around them.

'This is Wolf-In-Sheep's-Clothing,' Theodore said calmly, approaching the wolf and laying a hand on his back. 'He is our ally and tonight he was my decoy.'

'Oh,' Wind Talker blurted.

'Thank you for saving him, Stalker. He would undoubtedly have been killed by that fall. I'm curious though. How did you take that form?'

'It's her Odin-given form,' Red Scythe answered quickly. He caught her eye and gave her the subtlest of nods. She returned it, relief washing over her. She may never be ready to have her secret exposed, but in the middle of such an important night was definitely not the right time.

'I see. How odd,' Theodore replied, looking at each of them in turn. Wary eyes were on her from several shifters present. She cast her gaze down to the ground and a dark thought crept into her mind. How could they be sure they had ever met the real Theodore before? What if it had always been the mysterious demon? What if the Regalia had failed to identify him because it wasn't really him?

'More importantly, what on earth happened up there?' Steel said, her voice urgent and impatient. Stalker glanced at Wind Talker, knowing he could almost certainly name the silver mist that had thrown Theodore's decoy from the roof. He avoided eye contact and offered no information.

Do you have the Regalia? Stalker asked silently. Wind Talker gave a small nod and patted his satchel, which was bulging more than usual.

'It was something called Caer-u-le-um Lu-nu-lam,' Spark said, tripping awkwardly over each syllable. Stalker let out an awkward half-gulp, half-splutter and instantly regretted it. Theodore glared first at her, then at Wind Talker. He knew something.

'Care to explain?' he snapped. Every eye was trained on them.

Wind Talker cleared his throat but didn't speak. Theodore rounded on him. 'That's Latin for Blue Moon. No coincidence, I think. Explain!'

'She was the Blue Moon's old patron. She was captured by The Witches and held by them for years. When they were destroyed she was released and she found us. She wanted me to disrupt the ritual.'

'What?' Steel said, fixing her narrowed eyes on him.

'I didn't do it!' he said, hastily holding up his hands. 'You know I didn't. She tried to do it herself when she realised I wasn't going to. But she was too late.'

The ground shuddered and Stalker wasn't the only one to stagger. Something big was on the move.

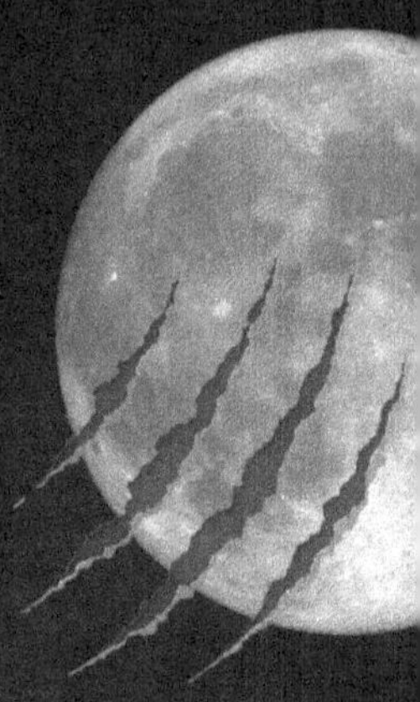

Chapter Thirty

The roar that erupted from between the crooked towers made the ground tremble as Stalker's feet pounded on it. She had sprinted flat out, along with a handful of the quickest shifters, from Free River Tower. Those who could take flight did so in their owl forms and they swooped silently overhead. The vast wall stood between those on the ground and the city centre, where the vibrations were coming from.

'Is there a way through?' Stalker asked as she skidded to a halt before it. Her head snapped towards Steel, who nodded. Theodore padded up behind them in the form of a sleek black panther. He walked up to the wall and raised his front paws, pressing them against the cold, grey stone. The stone rippled out from his paws, like water. Steel charged against the ripples and disappeared through the wall.

'It's one way,' Word Spider said, slightly breathlessly.

'And only Theodore can open it. Go on through.' He held up his hand and one by one, the gathered shifters stepped through. Stalker watched them disappear into the shimmering surface. She glanced at the panther, still standing with his paws against the wall. He cocked his head and looked at her quizzically. They were both a surprise to one another, it seemed. Stalker nodded and stepped through.

It was like stepping into a flowing waterfall. She took a sharp breath and every inch of skin ached in an instant. Pressure cascaded down on her that threatened to overwhelm her. She fought for breath and forced her reluctant feet to step forward. All she could see was grey mist and she reached out to feel her way, her eyes squinting against the extreme force pressing in on her.

Stalker stumbled forward and felt air once more. She gulped for breath and dropped her hands to her knees to quell the dizziness that swamped her brain. A firm hand patted her on the back and she looked up into Wind Talker's face.

'You okay?' he asked softly. She nodded and stood up straight. The nine of them were packed close together in the dark. They had the narrowest of passages to stand in, between the wall and the first row of dark and twisted buildings. Stalker craned her neck and took a shuddering breath. This was it, the city centre they had been warned again and again not to enter. Here it was, so close she could touch it. The building before her was dark purple, reminiscent of the crunchy shell of a beetle. It leaned over the gap, almost touching the huge wall that the Glass Wolves had built, obscuring the dark sky above. Either side of it were similar buildings, each slanted at their own angle, a discordant mess of architecture.

'Have you been here before?' Word Spider whispered softly at Stalker's ear. She shook her head slowly, still transfixed by the buildings pressing in on them. 'We need to move. Come on,' he urged her softly. She felt a hand on her arm gently tugging. She took a breath and shook her head, clearing the fog that remained from passing through the wall. Red Scythe and Sentinel were nowhere to be seen, but were presumably in flight somewhere. The rest of them moved quickly and quietly along the tight passage. Every few seconds the ground shook.

Theodore had shifted form and was leading them. Stalker had been the last to shake off the effects of crossing through the wall and had ended up at the back of the group. Word Spider scurried ahead of her, looking at the buildings on their left every few seconds.

Stalker could hear it too, the scuttling noise of many small feet. She thought of Jorogumo, the spider demon to whom she had nearly sacrificed her pack mate, who was now running briskly just ahead of Word Spider. The sound was similar. She suppressed a shudder and increased her pace.

The group ahead began to peel off to the left one by one and Stalker followed through a narrow gap in the row of misshapen buildings. Rough cobblestones lined the ground and the path was littered with broken glass and other debris. The pace slowed as the shifters carefully traversed the narrow path. Stalker looked up at the buildings on either side of her. None of them were terribly tall, the glass in most of the windows was long since gone and every one of them was pitch black inside, with little on the outsides to distinguish them. Along one blank wall they passed were huge letters in red spray paint declaring this the territory of "Mr Shatter".

Something moved in one of the glassless windows, catching Stalker's eye as she dashed past. She ignored it, but became even more alert as she quickly followed the others.

Another roar ripped through the night and an almighty crash shook the ground so hard that Stalker staggered sideways and bumped into the building to her right.

'What was that?' someone ahead shouted. There was another rumble and the terrible sound of crunching and smashing that echoed all around them and made the ground tremble. Undoubtedly a large building was collapsing somewhere nearby. The group had slowed to a halt, shaken. Various people clutched the walls and every eye was wide. Stalker heard fluttering wings and looked up to see a large owl descending. As it neared it shifted and Red Scythe landed gracefully right next to her.

'It took me an age to find you in this mess. You're close. Just around that next corner. He's back. He's not happy.' He panted and leaned heavily on his scythe as he rushed to get the words out.

'We could tell that much,' Stalker said softly. 'Where is everyone?'

'The Factory Boys and the rest of The Watch are already there. I'll go back up and scout for more people. Come and help me,' he said pointedly to Stalker. She nodded, then looked along to Wind Talker. He gave her a firm nod and the group set off again as fast as they could.

Stalker watched them out of sight then turned to Red Scythe.

'Thank you,' she said softly, catching his arm before he could shift and take flight. 'For keeping my secret.'

'I think our old friends were right to protect it, Stalker. You're a very special young woman. If every shifter and demon out there knew that, well, those with targets on their back never tend to live long, do they?' He gave her a wry smile. She jerked her head awkwardly in agreement, her mind suddenly filled with thoughts of Shadow's Step and Ragged Edge, her former mentors within Odin's Warriors, the friends to whom Red Scythe was undoubtedly referring.

Once the others were out of sight, both Stalker and Red Scythe took owl form and flew up between the clustered buildings.

As the two of them broke the surface of the tangled mess of buildings, Stalker breathed in the open space. She looked down and saw the group they had just left running down the path she had left behind. It was hard to see the ground, as the buildings leaned towards each other, almost as if they were deliberately trying to hide it. But through narrow gaps, Stalker could see other figures moving towards the source of the commotion. She looked ahead and swooped forwards. The buildings grew taller the closer to the heart of the city she flew.

The purple storm clouds overhead rolled over one another and lightning continued to flicker inside them. There was a rush of wind and Stalker glanced sideways to see Unchained Lightning swooping towards her. He rippled with energy and crackled, static charge making the air around him hum. She was glad he was there. They flew along together with Red Scythe, searching for others in flight and for the action on the ground.

Where the building had collapsed there was billowing dust and they turned in that direction. The skyscrapers leaned treacherously out from the gap in the cityscape, almost as if they were trying to get away from something. Stalker glimpsed movement amidst the dust cloud. Something large was twisting around. It bumped into another building, which wobbled for a moment, but didn't fall. More glass shattered and rained down the side of the building into the dust below.

Where the flickering light from the lightning overhead caught the glass in the city, it shimmered, and Stalker saw that the thing that was moving caught the light too where bits of it protruded from the dust. She swooped lower and searched for signs of shifters. There was scurrying movement everywhere, but she couldn't tell what was causing it, it was too dark and there was too much dust billowing through the small passages between clustered buildings.

Something inside told her that Rhys was not in Hepethia. He was meant to be in the human world, checking for signs of anything crossing the veil and guarding against attack. He had a little help from other shifters, but most of them were here, on this side. She hoped he was safe and tried to trust that she would know if he weren't.

Her pack mates, however, their feelings were a mad jumble inside her head. Eyes, Claws and Weaver were on the ground somewhere in the thick of it, she felt their adrenaline flowing. Wind Talker was somewhere below, still making his way with the other ritualists to where the action was. Relief that he hadn't gone ahead with what the crazy fae had asked washed through Stalker as she flew towards the ground. Red Scythe dipped down alongside her, but Unchained Lightning flew on towards a bigger gap in which he might land.

She shifted a few feet from the ground and dropped gracefully onto her feet with the aid of her talisman. The dust was beginning to settle, but it clung to the air and made it hard to breathe.

'We need to clear this,' she said, wary of raising her voice. Red Scythe stood beside her and nodded, but before he could do anything, a sudden breeze rushed towards them, blowing the thick dust down the passage they had landed in, away from where they were trying to get to. Stalker closed her eyes and shielded her face. She coughed and spluttered against the dust that clawed at her throat. The wind died down and she looked up to see Wind Talker standing at the end of the passage, his hands stretched out, his face flushed. It had been him.

Just beyond him was an open space, and movement. The noise hit her then; the shouts and cries, the roars and rumbles.

Hurry! Wind Talker's voice inside her head shouted. She broke into a run and sprinted towards him, Red Scythe's heavy feet pounding just behind her. She burst out from the narrow passage and skidded to a halt. The King-of-Glass-and-Steel stomped across in front of her, his towering, powerful body a jumble of metal and molten glass. His whole body shimmered and rippled.

Little rivulets of water trickled between chunks of stone and brick like veins. He had four thick legs and a long tail that undulated behind him, swishing back and forth and coming perilously close to the buildings on either side of his great bulk. His head was huge and his eyes were white glass. He was reminiscent of a great dinosaur, but ten times more intimidating. He roared and the ground shook again.

Stalker's pulse raced as she took in the scene. Beneath the lumbering construct were a dozen shifters, running, trying to steer clear of his house-sized feet. No one seemed to know what to do. They didn't want to hurt him, but the destruction he was causing was problematic, to say the least. He was a beast, evidently afraid or angry, with no awareness of the ant-like shifters beneath him.

Pounding footsteps coming towards her drew Stalker's wide-eyed gaze away from the construct. Eyes came thundering towards them, his face blazing. He came to a halt and gripped his side, taking big gulps of air.

'He's mad. He doesn't know where he is. Theodore and Warden are trying to reach him,' Eyes panted. Stalker looked past him towards the head end of the King-of-Glass-and-Steel. He was the length of a large warehouse, almost as vast as one of the huge dry docks just north of where they stood. She could just make out Theodore in his suit, standing underneath the head, his arms up.

'What are we going to do?' Stalker asked, still staring towards Theodore.

'I have no idea.' She looked at Eyes. He was never lost for a plan.

'Something has corrupted him,' Red Scythe said, his

voice completely calm, almost curious.

'If he was being held in the Underworld, then he may have been tortured for months on end.' Wind Talker had joined them. He looked windswept and his face glowed. He was loving this.

'What happened at the ritual?' Eyes asked pointedly.

'Caeruleum Lunulam tried to kill Theodore,' Stalker said, anger swelling in her chest.

'But your young marvel here saved the day.'

'Yes but it wasn't really him,' Stalker said, swivelling to look up at the wizened old face of Red Scythe. 'Eyes, he has a decoy, a demon that can take his form. When I wore the Regalia...' She paused and glanced back at Red Scythe, who was watching her with puzzled interest. 'It didn't show me anything, but it wasn't really Theodore on the roof. When he caught up with us I didn't have the Regalia any more.'

'Where is it now?' Eyes asked. Wind Talker pulled his satchel around his body and tugged the mask free. He passed it to Stalker and she put it to her face.

'What are you doing?' Red Scythe asked. Stalker didn't look at him, she could feel a painful lump in her throat and didn't want to explain anything. She trusted him as much as any of her fellow Berserkers, and he had shown up clean at the ritual, but what if the Regalia never had the power to reveal the Spiral Hand? What if that had been a lie? Wind Talker passed her the Orb and Sceptre and she stood clear of the little group of shifters to see everything else.

The mask sharpened her vision; she felt the tear in the veil flapping as if caught in a harsh gust of wind.

'The veil is torn,' she reported.

'I think we can all feel that,' Wind Talker scoffed. Stalker clucked her tongue and continued looking around. She could see right through the veil into the human world. They were at the plaza. It was night and the space was lit by orange street lamps. There were a few people around, but no sign of anything wrong. 'It doesn't look like anything has crossed over, but a hole that big could result in a significant breach, including him.' She pointed up at the King-of-Glass-and-Steel.

'I'll start fixing it,' Wind Talker said at once.

'I'll assist,' Red Scythe said, and the two of them moved away to get to work.

Stalker could see every inch of the vast construct in Technicolor detail. The city around him came to life too. Each building was unique, not just in the angles that they stood, but their original architecture too. The history of the two-thousand-year-old city was etched into the landscape.

She searched the ground for the shifters that were scurrying around, frantic for a way to get control of him. She saw Theodore, still with his arms raised, as if trying to get the construct's attention. The mask allowed her to zoom in on him, like a telescopic lens. She could see no sign of him being anything other than a shifter trying to communicate with a being that barely knew he existed.

'I think Theodore's okay. I mean, if this even works. I don't even know what I'm looking for.'

'Focus on finding the shard inside the King-of-Glass-and-Steel,' a soft voice said. Stalker spun around and bright light filled her field of vision. Caeruleum Lunulam was shimmering just above the ground. 'Find the shard, draw it out and it will reflect the Spiral Hand.'

'You tried to kill Theodore!' Stalker yelled, fury rising.

'Yes, because he is the Spiral Hand! It was exactly the sort of trick they play, that decoy. Use the shard and see for yourself.'

Stalker turned and found Eyes. He nodded encouragingly and she turned back toward the construct as he stomped about in a huge circle. His head turned towards Stalker and he roared, blasting hot air over her and causing her to stumble backwards. Deep in his throat she saw it, a slither of shining silver. She focused on it and pointed the Sceptre towards it.

As the huge beast roared again, the shard trembled and tugged its way free. It flew out of his throat and soared through the air towards Stalker. It was like a bullet, but sharp as a knife and sped through the air in a blur. But the mask allowed her to see it clearly and time her move precisely. She raised the Orb into the path of the shard and it hit with a splintering *crack*. The shard lodged itself into the glass Orb and bright white light burst out of it.

It was dazzling and Stalker turned her face away, still holding the Orb high. The light narrowed into a single beam and she was able to look back up at it. Like a powerful torch, the Orb shone straight out away from Stalker towards the top of a huge skyscraper. She followed the beam of light and there, invisible to all but her with the telescopic vision of the mask, was a dark figure. The light illuminated him briefly, before he ducked out of sight. Stalker had just caught sight of the black and white staff in his hand before he vanished.

The King-of-Glass-and-Steel roared again and lifted up on his hind legs. He came back down with a massive thud and the ground cracked and shook. Stalker fell backwards and the Orb fell from her hand. She reached, feeling it knock against her fingers but unable to grasp it. She saw it fall as if in slow motion, unable to move fast enough. It hit the ground and shattered into a million pieces, the light blinking out, the shard shattered along with it.

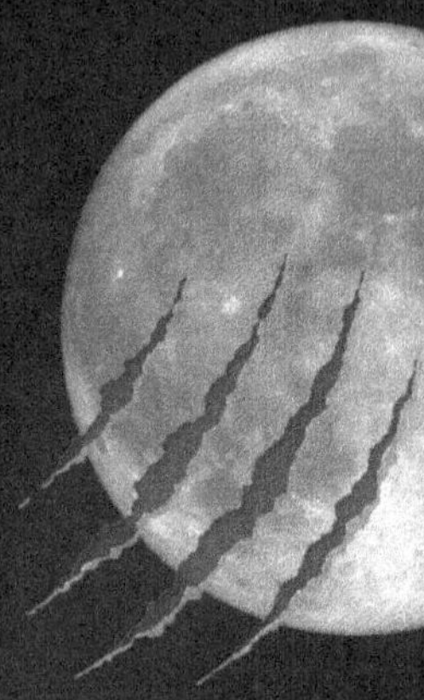

CHAPTER THIRTY ONE

'No!' Caeruleum Lunulam shrieked. All softness gone from her voice.

The Sceptre clattered to the ground and Stalker searched the rooftop for a sign of the figure.

Claws! she appealed, hoping he would hear her inside his head. She projected the image of the figure on the roof and hoped he would understand. He was here somewhere, maybe on the ground, maybe in the air. Either way, she was on the ground with a huge construct in her path.

The King-of-Glass-and-Steel thundered forward towards Stalker and Eyes. Eyes grabbed her roughly and dragged her to her feet. She scooped up the Sceptre and tore the mask from her face. They ran out of the path of the lumbering beast and it hurtled past them, straight for the shimmering fae.

Theodore and Warden came sprinting past Stalker and Eyes. They hurtled out in front of the construct.

'Hey! Hey there! Stop! Stop!' Warden shouted, her arms raised.

But it was deaf to her. Their old connection was gone, Stalker saw it in her face. The separation that she had felt when Grins-Too-Widely perished was written all over Warden's hard face. The desperation there, the grief-stricken eyes, it was a look Stalker knew well.

'Take him down,' Theodore called, dropping his hands in defeat. 'He's lost to us. Take him down.'

Eyes immediately shifted form and leapt towards the construct. Stalker gawked in disbelief. She had no idea how they were supposed to take down anything that vast.

Caeruleum Lunulam flew into the air, out of the beast's reach. She hovered there, casting her silver light down on the scene. Other shifters appeared now, running to the heart of the action. Weaver crashed into Stalker and held her tightly.

'Thank Artemis you're all right,' Weaver breathed.

'I'm fine. We need to get these to safety.' She pressed the remaining Regalia towards Weaver. 'The Orb is gone. Destroyed.'

'Right. What was that light?'

'Did you see? On the roof?' Stalker looked up to where the light had shone. 'The Spiral Hand was up there. He could be anywhere now.'

Weaver passed Stalker the mask and she put it back on, frustration mounting and helplessness threatening to swamp her. She wanted to fight, or track. But this was the only hope they had. She searched the rooftops and windows as a battle erupted beside her. The ground shook every time the construct stumbled. She scanned quickly, desperately. Movement, on the next building along from where she had seen the figure before. She narrowed in on it. With no torchlight, all she could make out was a dark figure wielding a staff. He was waving it back and forth. She looked back at the construct and saw his head weaving. Back on the rooftop, the figure pulled the staff back and the construct took a step back away from the shifters now attacking it. The figure swung the staff forward and the construct charged.

'He's controlling it!' Stalker shouted. 'The Spiral Hand is controlling the King-of-Glass-and-Steel!'

'What?' Theodore roared and broke away from the fight.

'If we stop him, the construct might be all right!' Weaver said, glee in her face.

'Well?' Theodore said, glaring at Stalker. 'Get up there!'

Stalker tore the mask from her face and thrust it at Weaver. She ran forward, her heart thumping so hard that she truly believed it might burst from her chest. The figure on the roof was conducting the scene like a macabre orchestra, and what was left of the King-of-Glass-and-Steel lumbered blindly between the towering skyscrapers at the conductor's command. He crashed into one of them, shattering a hundred windows and raining down shards of glass on the street below. The ground shook and sent Stalker stumbling sideways. The splinters of broken glass rained down on her and bounced off her head and skin, some of them slicing into her and drawing blood.

Caeruleum Lunulam landed in her path, shimmering brightly.

'I can't let you do that.' Her voice was soft and tender.

'You wanted us to find the Spiral Hand. It wasn't Theodore. Get out of my way.'

'No.'

'What's wrong with you? We did what you asked, we used the shard to find the Spiral Hand and I have to get up there.'

'Not that one. That one is with me.'

'What does that mean?' Stalker gaped at the fae.

'Stalker?' Weaver shouted, running up behind her. 'Stalker? Get away! Something is wrong.' Stalker took a step back and looked over her shoulder towards Weaver sprinting towards her.

There was a *whoosh* and a sudden, searing pain in her chest. Stalker turned her head slowly and looked up at the fae who had grabbed hold of her and was pinning her tightly. A thin blade of silver light emerged from the folds of light and Caeruleum Lunulam placed it against Stalker's throat. Weaver stood still, her eyes fixed on the fae.

'Leave him alone, or I kill this one,' the fae said, her voice low and hard.

'Why?' Weaver asked.

'He is with me. He is doing what I asked him to do.'

'But he's the real Spiral Hand. I don't understand.' Weaver frowned, but kept her composure.

'Yes.' That was all the fae needed to say for Stalker and Weaver to see everything click into place.

'We were the backup plan,' Stalker said, moving ever so slightly. For a pillar of light, the fae was mysteriously strong and corporeal. She was being held so tightly she couldn't move her arms or legs at all, she was suspended just above the ground, wrapped in light. The blade at her throat cut into her skin and Stalker winced with pain.

'Looks that way, yes. You manipulate people, don't you?' Weaver asked the fae.

'I get my own way,' the fae replied.

'Stalker? Do you trust Artemis?'

'What?'

'Do you trust that Artemis put you here for a reason and that your job isn't done yet?'

'Yes, absolutely,' Stalker croaked.

Caeruleum Lunulam drew the knife across Stalker's throat with a snarl of frustration, but Stalker felt nothing but mild warmth. She dropped to the floor and crawled away from the fae, one hand going to her throat. A tiny trickle of blood wiped off on her fingers where the knife had slightly cut her, but she was fine. The fae roared in anger and blazed more brightly.

'How did you survive that?'

'I am an instrument of Artemis,' Stalker said, getting to her feet and squaring up to the fae. 'She protects me.'

The thick clouds above parted and a full moon shone brightly down on them. Caeruleum Lunulam looked up and screamed.

'Looks like you're being called home,' Stalker said with a smirk. A beam of light appeared from the moon and caught the fae in its glow. She writhed as if in torment and was lifted up into the night sky as if pulled by an invisible rope. The moon shone more brightly for a moment and the clouds dispersed, revealing a black sky dotted with stars.

There was a crash behind them and Stalker and Weaver both staggered. The King-of-Glass-and-Steel had staggered sideways into a building and was righting himself. Stalker placed a hand on Savaging Fury, resting lightly at her collarbone. If there was ever a time to draw on its full power, it was now.

She charged forwards and leapt into the air, her fists raised as she shifted into her Agrius form. She came hurtling down on top of the lumbering beast and drove her fists down hard onto the middle of his back. He lurched with an almighty roar, his back breaking with a series of angry crunches as the shock wave rippled through his body.

Stalker leapt down next to a shocked Weaver. The massive construct collapsed to his knees and moaned.

'Go!' Weaver said. 'Go find the Spiral Hand. We'll take it from here.'

Stalker sprinted across the street and leapt into the air, transforming into a huge eagle and soaring up to the tops of the surrounding buildings. He was still there, apparently unaware or unconcerned with what was happening below. She was drawn to the mysterious figure. Familiarity clawed at her consciousness, something deep and primal. The fight raged below her, though she was barely conscious of it. She had eyes only for the shadowy figure.

He raised his staff in her direction and lightning flew out from its tip straight towards her. She swooped sideways to avoid it. Another came hot on the heels of the first, but she dodged that one too. Her sharp eyes fixed on him, and she made sweeping circles in the air, avoiding the streaks of lightning that issued from the staff in the hands of the familiar stranger. She didn't think they were aimed at her, they were too easy to dodge. Was she being warded off rather than attacked?

The shadows seemed to fold around the figure, making it impossible to make out any features. She couldn't tell species, or gender. It could be a demon, shifter or human, or something else entirely. All she knew was that she had to get closer. She had to know who it was.

She swooped down and around the back of the building. The King-of-Glass-and-Steel roared and continued to smash his way slowly up the street, while the army of shifters below tried desperately to hold him back and do some damage. But the conductor on the roof was too fast, too strong and too clever. The city's soul personified was fuelled with rage and madness.

Stalker gained on the puppet master, flying up the side of the building and coming to land silently on the flat roof behind him, shifting smoothly into her fox form.

It was a him, though he was enveloped in darkness, Stalker could sense him for certain now. She took a cautious step forward and sniffed the air. There was a mighty explosion in the street below, and the building shook ominously as The-King-of-Glass-and-Steel crashed into it. Then there was silence. Everything went black and Stalker swayed on the spot, caught up in the darkest of nightmares as recognition filtered through her fox senses. It was the same scent as the shifter at the museum, the one she had struggled so hard to place. It was still faint, supernaturally subdued, but she knew it now, without doubt. It was a scent she knew well.

The world seemed to spin silently in blackness for an eternity. She felt fog all around her, confusing and disorienting her. She dropped to her knees and a small whimper escaped her snout.

He whipped around and stared at her. The sounds and smells of battle crept back into the back of her mind, still a hundred miles away. He was distracted, the others could finish off the insane construct now.

How could this be? How could he be standing there, looking at her like that? Was it pity on his face? Sadness?

'Stalker,' he whispered. She shouldn't have heard him, with the din of battle so close.

She stared into his hypnotic, amber eyes, stunned disbelief paralysing her. She shook her head and sent every shred of energy into her limbs, forcing them to shift form. She rocked back to sit on her feet and covered her face with her hands. Maybe when she managed to summon the courage to drop them again he would be someone else. He wouldn't be a man she believed dead. He wouldn't be Shadow's Step.

There was a crack in the air, and Stalker's hands fell to her sides instantly.

His face was frozen in shock. A small, dark circle appeared in the centre of his forehead and a small trickle of dark blood oozed from the wound. She looked at his face, his almost black skin had a fine sheen of sweat on it and he looked confused.

He didn't fall down. It wasn't like in the movies. He just stood there, frozen in that moment right before the light goes out. Then his knees crumpled and he fell to the floor in a pool of shadow.

'No!' Stalker croaked. She scrambled across the floor to him and grabbed his face in both of her hands. A hysterical scream tore her throat and ripped through the night air.

Tears stung her eyes as they poured out.

She cradled his head and curled up around him, shielding him. Her whole body shook with uncontrollable sobs.

The sound of beating wings drew her gaze up. Claws landed clumsily on the rooftop and shifted form. His sniper rifle in his hand.

She gazed at him with blurry eyes, her shoulders heaving erratically as she struggled to breathe. He had shot Shadow's Step. She lurched forwards, dropping her old mentor's head with a sickening thud. She wanted to tear Claws' eyes out, and she scrambled over Shadow's body to get to him.

Claws tossed aside his gun and dropped to his knees. He grabbed hold of her, pinning her arms to her sides. She screamed and lashed out, but he was too strong. He held her against his chest and whispered in her ear. She couldn't hear his words, the sound of her own blood pumping and her screams drowned out everything else.

Somewhere in her subconscious she was aware of other people arriving on the rooftop, movement and voices echoed dully in the background.

'There must be a mistake,' someone said and the words punctured Stalker's fog.

'Yes,' she hissed. 'Exactly! There must be a mistake.' Shadow's Step couldn't have been there, it must be someone disguised as him. There was no conceivable way that he was the Spiral Hand responsible for all of this. *But the Blue Moon were Spiral Hand*, a small voice inside her head whispered. 'He could have explained himself,' she whimpered, going limp in Claws' arms. 'You killed him, and he could have explained all of this.'

'And persuaded you of his innocence,' Claws said softly, stroking her hair with his cheek. 'He could have got inside your head and turned you away from your real family.'

She was incapacitated with renewed sobs, the tears pouring over her dirty and bloody cheeks.

Through her grief-stricken haze, she was aware of Eyes kneeling over the body, a look of confusion on his pale face. Weaver and Wind Talker stood behind him, holding each other tightly and crying.

Warden-of-Stones bustled through the middle of their torment, her hair wild, her eyes fierce.

'I'm sorry to break this up, but we don't have time for grieving now. The Furies are coming.'

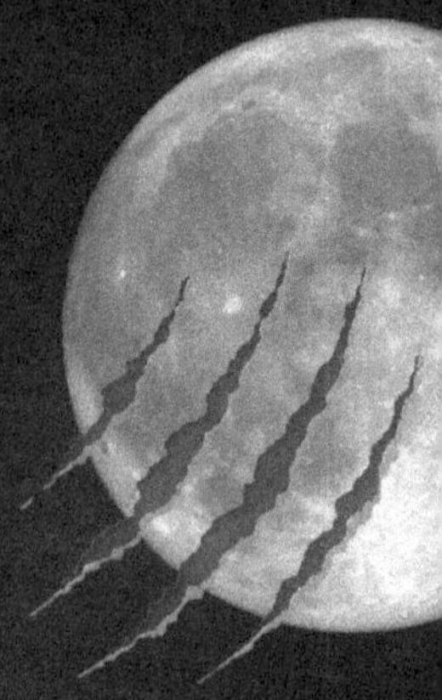

Chapter Thirty Two

Stalker and the others had no time to stop and mourn or ask questions. Warden was hurrying them on. Stalker looked over her shoulder as she was bustled from the rooftop. A strange construct of security was squatting over Shadow's body to protect it until the shifters could return to collect it for burial.

They raced down a concrete staircase, around and around in a dizzying spiral. Stalker could barely make her feet move and several times she stumbled, but steady hands caught her and set her right again. She was dimly aware of them belonging to Claws. The Lightning Lords and Warden burst out onto the moon-bathed street. The King-of-Glass-and-Steel lay there, a vast heap of building materials, no longer resembling a dinosaur.

'Quickly, we don't have much time,' Warden said and led them over to the rubble, where Theodore was standing, kicking feebly at the loose stones. 'Theodore, come on. We have to get to the castle.'

'What?' He looked up. His eyes were blank.

'The Furies are coming early.' Warden started to turn away but stopped. She looked down into the rubble and bent closer.

'What is it?' Eyes asked, stepping over to look. 'Oh.'

Stalker and the others joined them, but Stalker could barely raise a glimmer of curiosity. She kept seeing Shadow's Step's face suspended in shock, a hole through his brain. She focused her eyes on the rubble and saw a hint of golden light shining from between chunks of stone and steel.

'What are we looking at?' she asked, her voice sounding a mile away, like it wasn't hers.

'Hope-for-a-New-Day,' Wind Talker said softly.

'Oh!' Weaver exclaimed and dropped to her knees. She began gently brushing away the dirt and broken glass. 'I met her at Immunsul, she showed me the Orb.'

The light shone more brightly and a small bird-like head appeared, moving slightly, like it was looking around. It was gold and red and seemed to be glowing like fire embers.

'Is it a phoenix?' Eyes asked, his voice full of wonder.

'I think so.' Weaver grinned. The numbness Stalker had been feeling drained away and anger leapt into her chest. How could Weaver smile? How could they all crouch around a fucking bird like that when they had just found out that Shadow's Step had been alive all this time and plotting against them?

'I think we should leave it,' Warden said, straightening up and stepping away. 'I think it may be a new start, a new soul for the city. We have to let it grow and emerge when it's ready. We have to go and face the Furies. Now.' She set off, her long hair rippling behind her. Theodore strode after her and Stalker fell into step beside him, leaving the rest of her pack to trail behind.

As the group walked quickly from the open area they had been occupying and into the cover of the disjointed tower blocks, the moon's soft light dulled, obscured by the tall buildings. It was quieter now, with no giant construct stomping around. It seemed that the ruckus had kept the area clear of dangerous demons and Stalker now felt the hairs on the back of her neck standing on end. Scuttling noises surrounded them, identical to those that she had heard when they first entered the heart of the city after the ritual.

'Quickly,' Warden urged from up ahead and she picked up the pace. Theodore broke into a run and Stalker followed his lead. Their feet pounded on the rough terrain and Stalker tried to keep listening for approaching threats, but the sound of her own heavy breathing filled her ears. A flicker above drew her attention and she glanced up to see Unchained Lightning soaring along overhead. Movement in one of the empty windows to her right caused her to pick up the pace even more, running ahead of Theodore and catching up with Warden. The rest of the Lightning Lords were just behind, along with Red Scythe and a handful of other shifters.

The scuttling grew louder and there was more movement up ahead.

'How far?' Stalker called in a hushed voice.

'Not far,' Warden replied quietly.

A dark shape burst out of an empty window just ahead of them, filling the alleyway. It was spider-like and huge, with long legs that glimmered in what little light reached into the space. Pincers clicked and the demon towered over them. Stalker and Warden stopped dead and everyone behind them caught up, almost piling on top of them. Stalker began drawing one of her dha, when a whistling sound from above halted her. Unchained Lightning crashed to the ground, crushing the demon flat with a series of sickening crunches. A ripple of static charge rushed out from where he had landed, causing Stalker's hair to lift. She dropped her dha back into its sheath and shrugged her shoulders.

'That takes care of that.'

'He's handy,' Warden said, a smile creeping onto her lips.

'Very.' Stalker nodded and strode forwards. Unchained Lightning gave a small crackle, then took off, flying straight up between the buildings. Stalker climbed gingerly over the remains of the demon and the others followed. They emerged from the tangled buildings onto a grassy bank down to the river. Stalker could hear the water rushing past. Just ahead was a wooden drawbridge over the river, quite unlike its equivalent in the human world, which was broad, stone and had a major road crossing it. On the opposite bank, bathed in the moonlight, was a huge castle.

The wall stood right up against the river, windowless and towering above, an impenetrable fortress. The stone was smooth and looked new, quite in contrast to the ruin in the human world. The bridge over the river led up to a grand portcullis, flanked by massive stone statues of knights.

'So this is what the Furies are coming to claim?' Eyes asked. Warden didn't even glance his way. She set off across the bridge. The moment she stepped onto it, the stone statues came to life, moving swiftly to block the bridge with their stone spears. Stalker walked along behind Warden, looking warily up at the guards. As Warden approached, the guards stood down again, raising their spears for her to pass.

'They're all with me. But no one else gets through.'

One of the statues gave a rumbling nod, the stone grinding as it moved its head. The great wooden door ahead opened and the iron portcullis went clattering up. A member of the Watch that Stalker barely knew even by sight greeted Warden. He was short and wiry with wild black hair that stuck out at odd angles.

Warden strode through the grand entrance, Stalker scurrying in her wake. 'Is everything prepared?' Warden asked, her voice echoing off the high stone walls that surrounded the courtyard. Stalker gazed around. It was like stepping back in time. Torches burned on the walls, casting their flickering light over the cobbled ground.

'Yes, we're ready for anything.'

'Famous last words,' Theodore said coldly. As the last shifter crossed the threshold, the portcullis rattled back down and the drawbridge began to lift on its heavy chains. The thick doors slammed shut and the wiry shifter slid a bar as thick as a tree trunk across it.

The veil rippled and Mjolnir stepped across it, slightly out of breath.

'They're not crossing over. They were able to ignore

our funnel.'

'Impossible,' Warden snapped.

'Like the one we had for the Danegeld?' Stalker asked, remembering how Odin's Warriors had set it up so that shifters entering the cave would be funnelled across the veil.

'Precisely. How can they just ignore it?' Warden demanded of Mjolnir.

'I don't know. Everyone else is here, on the other side.'

'Black Rat,' Warden said, and the wiry shifter was at her side in an instant. 'Stay here. Any sign of trouble, come and let me know.' He nodded and scurried away. Warden glanced at Theodore and Eyes, who both looked uncharacteristically submissive here on Warden's territory. She turned and crossed the veil and they all followed.

They appeared in the centre of the ruined castle. The most significant remaining wall at their backs, and beyond that, the river babbling past. All around were rows of shifters. Stalker did a double take and gazed around. They had crossed the veil right in the heart of the assembled army of Caerton.

'Where's Rhys?' Stalker asked no one in particular. Theodore ran off with the rest of his pack to find their place. Red Scythe patted Stalker on the shoulder before stomping off to find his pack.

'The sirens went off,' Mjolnir was saying in a rushed voice to Warden. 'As soon as their forces crossed the boundary. They're coming up through South Stoke. The Savages and Factory Boys got here first. They must be nearly here by now.'

There was no traffic on the road that ran alongside the castle ruins. It was a major route through the city and even in the dead of night there was often a car passing. But it was utterly still. Stalker looked at the time on her new phone. It was 2 a.m. The vast majority of humans would be in bed. On the other side of the river were apartment blocks and hundreds of shops with residential flats above them. Beyond the road were rows and rows of houses and at the foot of the gentle hill that led away from the castle was a vast housing estate.

'If we fight them here, people will see. They'll wake and see everything.' Stalker glanced anxiously around.

'I know. But with the funnel not working, what choice do we have?' Warden sighed and strode away from the Lightning Lords with Mjolnir.

Lights from a car swept across the park from the road that a moment ago had been so deserted. It was a large van that crossed the bridge and came to a halt close by. The doors slid open and The Wrecking Crew poured out. They had come from the far side of the city.

'Don't start the party without us,' Rust called out. A ripple of laughter spread among the gathered shifters.

'How's the eastern border looking?' Eyes asked, greeting Rust with an outstretched hand, which Rust gladly shook.

'Dead. We have allies patrolling, but I can tell you now they're not coming that way.'

'No, they're coming up through the hole they made in the south.' Eyes spoke with venom and Stalker's thoughts leapt immediately to Scribe. She searched the crowd for him but there were so many faces and it was still so dark, she couldn't see him.

'Vengeance-of-Steel has set up a roadblock up there, by the way,' Rust said, indicating where they had come from. 'It's cordoned off, but she let us through. She'll be here in a minute. There was someone new with her. Big bloke. Didn't smell all that shifter-ish.'

'Rhys!' Stalker pushed past Eyes and Rust and sprinted for the road. She hurtled right and over the bridge. She could see the barrier across the road ahead, yellow lights blinking and a police car with its blue lights flashing. Steel was there, talking to a tall man. The lights flashed and lit up his face. It was him. Stalker charged for him and he turned to see her just in time to catch her.

'Hey there!' he said with a laugh as he hugged her tight.

'You're all right.'

'So are you. What's been happening? Steel was filling me in some.' He indicated the woman beside him and Stalker glanced awkwardly at Steel, who stood with her shotgun slung over her arm and a frosty expression.

'Too much to report right now. How about with you?'

'It was a bit alarming when he came back. We all felt it on this side of the veil. Humans too. There was a bit of panic, but I got the area cleared. Then Steel here showed up with this lot.' He waved a hand towards the cordon.

An explosion rent the air and sent Stalker staggering into Rhys. A great plume of smoke erupted in the distance, in the heart of South Stoke.

'What was that?' Rhys asked, panic rising in his voice. The three of them looked out towards the rising smoke.

'With any luck, a diversion,' Steel said, her voice calm and distant, her gaze fixed on the smoke. Her attention snapped back to the present and the radio inside her car bleeped. She leaned in through the open door and responded. Stalker and Rhys heard the voice broadcast into the car, an appeal for first responders to an explosion in South Stoke. Nothing they didn't already know.

Steel waited and sighed with relief when someone else said they were nearer. 'I'll probably be able to cover this with a riot story,' she said, climbing back out of the car. 'But I don't really want humans anywhere near this, not police or anyone.'

'Okay, let's get back over there.' Stalker grasped Rhys's hand and tugged. He resisted, not falling into step with her. 'What? You are coming, right?'

'Yeah. Yeah I'm coming.' He squeezed her hand and they set off with Steel back towards the waiting army.

Stalker led Rhys into the heart of the army, past the Fyrd, who were wearing heavy armour and over to where the Lightning Lords were assembled.

'Is everyone ready?' Eyes asked. They nodded and muttered their replies. 'We're ready for this. We've trained hard and prepared well. We can beat them.'

Stalker wasn't convinced. So far, the night had been full of nightmarish twists and turns, nothing seemed to have gone according to plan. The King-of-Glass-and-Steel was dead, the Spiral Hand had turned out to be her own mentor, who was now, actually dead, and the Furies were turning up ahead of schedule. Nothing seemed to have gone their way and she couldn't see that changing.

The soft thudding of feet on the grass could be heard from the shadows at the bottom of the park.

'They're coming!' A shout came out of the darkness.

'They're coming!'

'It's Scribe,' Weaver said. She pushed past Stalker and weaved quickly through the crowd. She burst out onto the open field and leapt into Scribe's arms, kissing him passionately. Stalker laughed and clapped a hand to her mouth.

'The explosion?' Warden called, an edge of impatience in her voice. Weaver and Scribe broke apart, shock written all over Scribe's face. He grasped Weaver's hand however, and cracked a smile before turning back to Warden.

'It was me. I blew up the club. When I saw they weren't crossing the veil I thought we might need a distraction. There are fire engines and everything streaking that way now, should give us a bit of time.'

Weaver dragged Scribe over to the Lightning Lords and Stalker gave her a knowing smile, which Weaver returned. Rhys and Scribe stood alongside the Lightning Lords and Stalker allowed herself a moment to appreciate her pack's willingness to take in strays.

From the bottom of the park, where a line of trees stood to mark the boundary, Stalker heard marching. The smile dropped from her face as the tree line rippled with movement. From out of the darkness, an army emerged. Row upon row of Furies, each brandishing weapons. They marched in unison, one seamless organism, well trained and disciplined. It was hard to make out exact numbers in the dark, but it looked as though they outnumbered the Chosen of Artemis three to one. Stalker swallowed a hard lump in her throat and slowly drew her dha.

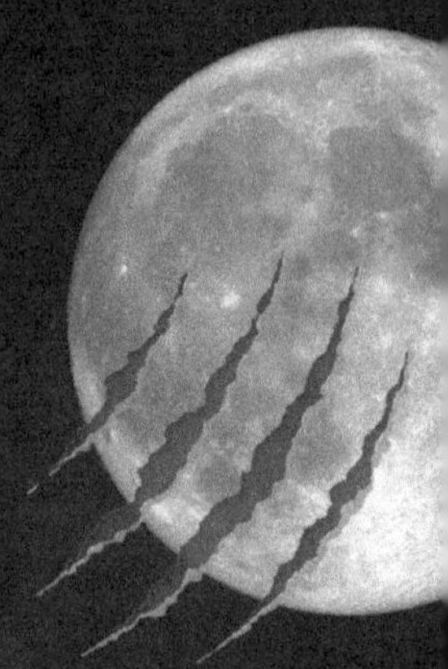

Chapter Thirty Three

In the centre of the front row was a tall figure in shining armour. Tall and proud, the hilt of a broadsword glinting in the moonlight over the shoulder. Walking just a step ahead of the shifters on either side, and nearly a foot taller, this had to be the Heir. A small noise of surprise escaped Stalker's open lips when she saw that Gleaming Blade was female.

Her long, blond hair rippled in the breeze and she wore a helm of shining steel. She was so tall and broad that she would be mistaken for a man at a distance, but as she drew closer, Stalker could make out her features. Her armour was sculpted to her body, a combination of leather and metal, giving her freedom of movement, while clearly protecting key areas of her body. Gleaming Blade's army was an impressive sight, and Stalker saw the anxious faces around her having second thoughts about this fight.

It wasn't too late; they could kneel.

Eyes stepped forwards, brushing past Theodore and Warden who were standing front and centre.

'We have come to claim our territory.' Gleaming Blade's voice echoed across the park. 'Kneel.'

'We will not kneel. We claim this place and have no intention of bowing to a false monarch. You don't even have the Regalia!' Eyes jeered and there was a ripple of whispered voices on both sides. Stalker remained silent, watching carefully.

'What do you know of the Regalia?!' another voice shouted from across the park, not Gleaming Blade, but a man standing just behind her.

'Enough to know that without them, there is no legitimacy to Gleaming Blade's claim!' Eyes called out.

'How do you know we don't have them?' cried the man's voice.

'Because we do!' shouted Warden.

Stalker shifted her feet uncomfortably. The Orb was gone, destroyed. The mask and Sceptre had ended up god-knows-where.

I've got them, they're safe. Wind Talker patted his satchel and gave her a reassuring nod.

'So are you claiming the throne?' Gleaming Blade asked, her commanding voice carrying easily up the hill. Eyes shook his head and smiled.

'No, Caerton needs no king, nor queen.'

Gleaming Blade drew her sword. It was a huge broadsword, razor sharp and the hilt was encrusted with shining stones. 'Nice sword,' Eyes called out, still smiling.

'Come and claim it,' Gleaming Blade replied, a smile on her full lips.

Oh, I will. Stalker just caught the thought from Eyes before the Furies set off sprinting up the hill and Eyes rushed forward to meet them, his huge hammer raised over his shoulder. The front line of Caerton's shifters charged forwards with a roar and Stalker was swept along with them.

Stalker caught a glimpse of Red Scythe, leading Crimson Dawn's Blood. He was striding down the slope, his weapon raised and a glint in his eye. Other shifters ran past him, but he remained steady and calm, a seasoned warrior in no rush to prove himself. She stopped to watch him as he shifted form mid-stride. His long coat vanished and his body erupted in thick, grey fur. His scythe was still in his hand, but now he was as tall as it was long and when he swung it, it glided through the air with ease, slicing through three Furies that had chosen him to run at first. They were all cut neatly in two and toppled to the ground, their blood spilling, thick and dark on the grass.

Stalker felt a rush of adrenaline and roared into her Agrius form. Rhys was at her side and shifted too. Together they bounded towards the enemy and clashed with bestial soldiers, their armour and weapons having shifted with them. Stalker plunged both of her dha into one Fury, who dropped beside her. Another came at her, and she cut him down swiftly too.

More came, and her two swords were drenched in blood in mere minutes. Rhys fought fiercely nearby, ripping chunks out of oncoming Furies without hesitation.

Among the Furies, Stalker could make out some small differences, now that she was in the thick of them. Their armour bore markings; some of them had shields covered in flames, the Phoenix Guard. Others wore silver jewellery, which burned and scarred their skin and left bald patches in their fur; the mark of Megairia, like The Witches.

Rage surged through Stalker's chest at the sight of these symbols. Those who had been responsible for the deaths of her old pack mates, evil though they may have been, and Eyes' human family, were here among the fighters. Stalker felt a thirst for vengeance rushing through her veins and she waded deep into the swarm of Furies and swung her dha indiscriminately, slicing off limbs, thrusting through chests and taking off heads.

Somewhere in there was Gleaming Blade, and an Eyes intent upon taking her sword, as well as her head. Stalker had lost track of everyone. She was surrounded by Furies and the air was thick with roars and the clang of weapons.

Regroup! Fall back! roared Eyes in Stalker's head. She spun around in confusion, trying to locate her pack mates. She could see nothing but the enemy all around her. She sheathed her dha and bounded back up the hill, shoving past other shifters, barely aware of which side any of them were on. She leapt over countless dead bodies and pools of blood. Swords, hammers and clubs swung at her, but she ducked and swerved around every one until she skidded to a halt right next to the castle wall, where a handful of Caerton's shifters were assembled. There were some wounded, being attended to by their pack mates. She shifted form and gasped for breath. She looked around and located Weaver and Claws, standing behind the wall looking worried. Stalker ran to them and looked them over. They both seemed unharmed. Claws lifted his sniper rifle and looked down the scope.

'I see him!' He lowered the gun for a moment and pointed. 'There, engaged with three Furies.'

'Has he taken out Gleaming Blade yet?' Weaver asked, chewing her nails.

'No, she's fighting – someone – I can't quite...' He squinted down the scope and Stalker followed the line of the gun, trying to pick out individuals in the seething mass of fighting shifters, most of whom were unidentifiable in their Agrius forms. 'I think it's Fury!'

'Really?' Stalker snapped. Claws passed her the gun. She took it gingerly and looked down the scope. It was painfully unfamiliar in her hands, a weapon far outside her own remit. Claws helped direct the rifle into the battle and she found what she was looking for. Gleaming Blade had not shifted form, she was swinging her sword with immense grace for someone so large. There was an Agrius ducking and weaving around her, almost black fur and long braids all down her back. It was Fury alright. Stalker watched, a tightness in her chest that hadn't been there a moment ago.

Gleaming Blade's sword cut through the air and sliced into Fury's forearm. Stalker winced but kept watching, unable to tear her gaze away.

'Where is he?' panted Wind Talker, now joining them.

'He's coming,' Weaver said. A moment later Eyes was with them.

'What are you watching?' he asked, his breath short.

'Fury is fighting Gleaming Blade.' Stalker's voice felt strangely detached from herself. She passed the rifle back to Claws. Without a second thought, Stalker vaulted over the wall and sprinted into the fray, knocking other shifters aside. She made a direct line for Gleaming Blade.

Gleaming Blade was out-manoeuvring Fury at every turn. The fierce warrior who had nearly bested Stalker on two occasions was on her back. Stalker's old rival, the one who had humiliated her and nearly broken her arm, the one she had beaten in her initiation trials for Odin's Warriors, was prone. The silver blade glinted as it hurtled down towards Fury's chest.

Stalker launched herself at the Heir and knocked her to the ground, rolling away from Fury. Stalker's immense strength had saved Fury just in time. She released Gleaming Blade and jumped to her feet, ready to take on the Heir herself.

'Friend of yours, I take it?' Gleaming Blade said as she got to her feet.

'Not remotely. But she is my sister.'

The Heir cocked her head and gazed at Stalker quizzically. She spun her sword in her hand and smiled.

'Shall we dance?'

'With pleasure,' Stalker said with a smirk. She drew both of her dha and spun them the way Gleaming Blade had done, grinning with confidence.

The blades clashed and the battle seemed to fall still just around them. Stalker pulled back and went in again for another strike, but the Heir blocked. They danced around each other, an equal match.

A rumble made the ground shake as it grew louder. Bright, white lights swept over the corpses littering the ground and dazzled Stalker. She leapt back from Gleaming Blade and saw the Wrecking Crew's white van hurtling towards her, Rust at the wheel. The van skidded to a halt on the wet grass and Rust leapt out of the cab.

'Stalker! Help me!' He was at Fury's side, lifting her by the shoulders. Stalker snarled in the direction of the Heir and sheathed her swords. She dashed to Rust and helped him hoist his injured pack mate onto his shoulder. They turned towards the van but had been cut off from it by a dozen or more Agrius-form Furies. 'Run!' Rust yelled and turned away from the van. They sprinted up the hill towards the castle, leaving the van behind.

They got to the relative safety of the castle walls and Rust placed Fury on the ground. She was unconscious, but breathing.

'You saved her life,' Rust said, looking straight into Stalker's eyes.

'Of course. We're rivals, not enemies. We're on the same side here.'

'Well, thank you.'

'What's happening?' Wind Talker asked, suddenly at Stalker's side. The rest of the Lightning Lords gathered around them. 'Why did you call us back?' Wind Talker asked Eyes.

'Because we're losing, horribly,' Eyes said, frustration in his voice. 'We need to fight together, like we trained to. Rolling Thunder style. Okay?' The others murmured their ascent.

Calm seemed to settle over everything. The sounds of battle washed away by the rushing in Stalker's ears, like waves upon a beach.

'Word Spider's dead,' came a croak of a voice just behind them. 'And a couple of the Factory Boys.' Stalker turned and looked into Scribe's ashen face.

'What do we do, Eyes?' Weaver asked.

'Start a fire, quickly,' he replied. 'We need more light and a barrier between here and the battle. This wall won't do.' It was only three feet tall, so while the wounded could slump behind it, it wasn't much of a cover for anyone on their feet. Weaver and Scribe ran into the dark. Stalker searched for Rhys, she could feel him in her heart, still fighting.

'I haven't seen the House of Cards,' Claws said. He had raised his rifle to his eye again and was scanning the fight.

'Me neither,' Eyes said, a deep frown on his brow.

Claws adjusted his gun quickly, then pulled the trigger. Stalker flinched.

'That's not terribly honourable,' she said, giving him a sideways glare. 'Firing into a melee.'

'I wasn't,' Claws said, his eye still glued to the scope and scanning the distance. 'They've got snipers in the trees. I just took one out.'

'What?' Eyes snapped.

'Yep. The cowardly bastards.'

'Okay, you stay here and keep firing. Stalker, Wind Talker, you're with me.' Eyes led them back into the battle. There was a blinding flash over to the right and Stalker reflexively raised a hand to shield her eyes from the blaze that had flared up to the side of the battlefield, between the park and the road. A figure was silhouetted, running towards them from the fire. Weaver joined them and the four of them strode towards the Furies.

A panther streaked past them and leapt through the air, onto the back of an enemy shifter.

'What the—?' Eyes staggered sideways.

'Theodore,' Stalker and Wind Talker said together.

'No way!' Weaver's face was aghast, as they watched Theodore ripping into the flesh of the Agrius upon whom he had pounced.

'Let's do this,' Eyes said, directing them back on track. He shifted into his Agrius form and the other three fell in behind him. They all broke into a run and charged towards a group of about ten Furies trying to break away and come up the side of the battlefield. The Lightning Lords bowled straight into the middle of the cluster, Eyes at the head, and his hammer struck the first of the Furies. The armoured soldier went flying backwards, knocking over three of his comrades, toppling them like skittles. Wind Talker was the next to shift form, joining the Alpha in increased size and strength. Together they ripped apart another Fury. Weaver shifted next and pounced on the three that had fallen to the ground, her teeth and claws tearing through flesh. Eyes and Wind Talker joined the feast and when they raised their blood-covered snouts, there were only a few Furies left. Stalker shifted and drew her dha at the same time. She charged forwards, the others making a path for her, and she swept her swords through four Furies, spilling their guts out onto the bloodstained grass.

The groans and whimpers all around them became deafening. So many bodies littered the ground that Stalker found it hard to place her feet without stepping on someone.

Again, Eyes said, his voice clear inside Stalker's head. The four of them formed a loose square again and charged into a fresh group of Furies. They took out a dozen more

Furies this way, before finding themselves once more isolated from the rest of their peers. They retreated back up the hill and took shelter behind the wall to lick their own, minor wounds.

Rhys came rushing over to Stalker and scooped her up into a tight embrace.

'I'm okay, I'm good. Are you?' She drank in his scent as he gripped her tightly. She could feel his heart racing in his chest.

'Yeah, I'm okay. I fought one who, I don't know, smelled familiar, I think. I think they might have been there when my family were killed. It was a Phoenix Guard.'

'Oh Rhys.'

'I killed him. Ripped his throat out.' She squeezed him even tighter and felt a rib crack. She released him at once and they stood staring at each other.

'Your name has changed,' Eyes said stiffly, looking Rhys up and down.

'I felt something strange happen out there,' Rhys said, shaking his head. 'Like a light shining on me. It was weird.'

'Welcome to the fold, Spartan-of-Artemis,' Eyes said, extending his hand. Rhys smiled and took it, shaking it firmly. Stalker gazed up into his shining eyes and a tear formed in the corner of her eye. The full moon shone brightly overhead and instinct told her that Rhys's new Artemis-given form would be the wolf.

'All those dead, and they just keep coming,' Weaver said, her voice faint. The fire that she had started had spread towards the ruins, forming a barrier between them and the road. But the battlefield before them was strewn with the dead and yet the Furies still seemed to outnumber them. More of Caerton's shifters were falling back to the castle ruins, pursued by a horde of Furies.

'Cover me,' snarled Warden. She charged down the battlefield, a great sword in her hand. She strode into battle, cutting down all who tried to come near. Red Scythe was quick to follow, covering her from behind. Claws put down his sniper rifle and took out his handgun. Stalker watched out of the corner of her eye, not wanting to take her eyes off Warden, as Claws took a paper bag from his inside pocket, and loaded a single bullet into the barrel. He saw her watching him and quickly finished the task.

'Just in case,' he muttered under his breath, so only she could hear. She pleaded with her eyes for him not to fire it. He simply shook his head once and Stalker's gaze was wrenched back to the battle. There was nothing she could do if he decided to fire it: his special bullet that was guaranteed to kill its mark, but the price was the shooter's own life too.

Warden had disappeared. Red Scythe had cut a path through the Furies and was using his huge scythe to cut them down like wheat. He was just about the most impressive thing Stalker had seen and she understood how he came to be the leader of Odin's Warriors.

Stalker searched for Warden, and finally caught sight of her crawling under the van.

'What is she doing?' Stalker cried. It seemed all eyes had fallen on the white van, with blood smears all over the front of it, Furies swarming all around it.

There was a moment's silence, followed by a huge explosion. The front of the van burst into flames, the lid of the bonnet blown clean off. It soared up and then plummeted back down, impaling a fleeing Fury and pinning her to the ground by her legs. The Furies that had been closest to the van had gone flying and their bodies smouldered on the ground. The whole van was engulfed in flames. 'Where is she?' Stalker cried. 'Did Warden get out?'

'No,' Claws said softly. 'No she didn't.'

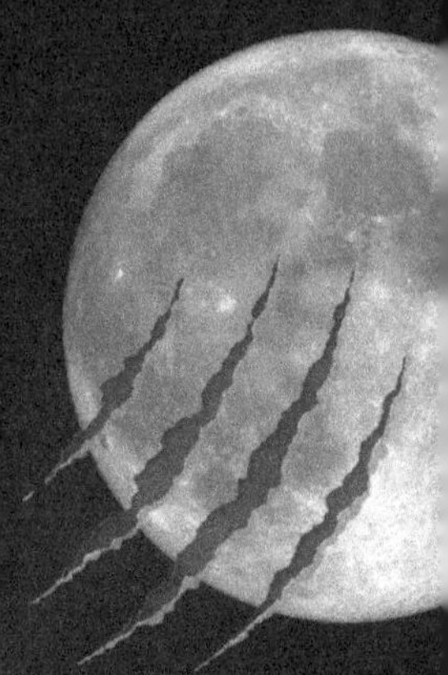

Chapter Thirty Four

Mjolnir roared and started to lurch forward, but Theodore caught his arm and yanked him back. Crimson was at his side and pressed her hand firmly against his chest. The last of Caerton's fighting shifters scurried for cover and the Furies retreated down the hill to surround Gleaming Blade.

The burning van sat between what was left of the two armies, while the fire by the road still raged. Stalker became aware of lights in windows overlooking the park and knew they were being watched. Countless humans had been woken by the terrifying sounds and a good number of them had undoubtedly gone insane by now, having seen these monsters at war. But she was paralysed and helpless, unable to do anything except stare over at the Furies as they scrambled to reform their line.

Stalker tore her gaze away from the enemy to look at the shifters by her side. Their number was uncomfortably reduced, even with the House of Cards, who stood nearby, sweat and blood shining on their faces in the firelight. She nudged Eyes and nodded her head in their direction.

'I'm glad they came, but it isn't enough,' he said softly.

'No, it isn't.' Stalker tried to quickly count heads, but it wasn't looking good. Her ears were ringing from the explosion and she couldn't focus properly to count. It looked like there were still twice as many Furies as them. Near the fire, Stalker saw the dark outline of Tar Peter, standing watching. She shook her head in disgust. He was back to watch again, just like he had when the Blue Moon were killed. Well, when she had thought they had all been killed. Bitterness left a foul taste in her mouth. She was about to look away when she saw a slight figure by his side, a woman with a dazed and confused expression on her face.

'Wind Talker? Do you have the Orb and Sceptre?' Stalker asked, not taking her eyes off the stranger.

'Yes, here.' Wind Talker slung his bag from his back and passed it to Stalker. She took it and ran quickly, keeping low behind the wall, to where Tar Peter stood. She reached them and he turned to look at her in alarm.

'They came early,' he said, a crack in his voice.

'They did.' Stalker looked between him and the woman, who was ghostly pale in the orange firelight.

'Oh, sorry,' the oily demon said. 'This is Lost.'

'I'm sorry?' Stalker blinked at him in surprise.

'You asked me to find her. Well, I did. She's... she's difficult to communicate with.'

Lost was staring at the battlefield, frowning and shaking her head.

'You're Lost?' Stalker asked, her voice soft but urgency creeping into it. Lost turned to gaze at her, her eyes wide. She looked old, but lean and wiry. Her grey hair was wild and unkempt and the lines on her face showed a traumatic past. 'Please take these and hide them. Hide them where no one will ever find them again.'

The bag exchanged hands and Lost looked down into it. The frown vanished and she looked back up at Stalker, her eyes piercing and alert. She zipped up the bag, turned and walked away through the flames.

'How did you find her?'

'Find who?' Tar Peter replied, a vacant expression on his face. He sank into the ground and vanished. Stalker looked into the flames and saw a figure walking quickly away from the fight, but couldn't for the life of her remember who she was.

The sound of the army marching up the hill towards the ruins drew Stalker's attention back to the battle. Gleaming Blade at the centre of the front line. Stalker ran back to her pack and their puzzled expressions.

'What?' she asked, unaware of the cause of their confusion.

'Nothing,' Eyes said, shaking his head.

'I have Gleaming Blade in my sights,' Claws said, his voice hard, his handgun raised.

Eyes reached across him without taking his eyes off the approaching Furies. He placed a hand on Claws' gun and gently lowered it. He pulled a white handkerchief out from the inside pocket of his jacket and waved it in the air. Eyes vaulted over the low wall and stepped out alone.

'What are you doing?' Weaver hissed.

'Gleaming Blade!' Eyes' shout rang out across the field of death and the Furies halted.

'Fights-Eyes-Open,' came the Heir's reply.

'We should settle this in single combat. You and me. No one else has to die.'

'No,' Stalker whimpered. She felt Rhys's hand grasp hold of hers and squeeze.

'Single combat?' Gleaming Blade sneered.

'Yes. For the fate of Caerton. If I win, you and your forces leave forever. If you win, you claim the throne.'

'What do you think you're doing?' Theodore snapped furiously. 'You can't strike a deal like that on behalf of all of us. You aren't in charge.'

'Yes, he is,' Red Scythe said, his voice low and dangerous.

'Agreed,' Crimson said firmly. 'Two Elders to one, Theodore.'

'You intrigue me,' Gleaming Blade said, a curious smile creeping over her face.

No, Eyes! It shouldn't be you. Let me fight her, Stalker pleaded. It seemed at once that all her life had been leading to this moment. If she was ever going to get to Valhalla, it would be here and now. Surely there was no bigger battle, no greater threat and no more glorious way to go? Wasn't this what Artemis had in mind for her all along?

This is my fight, Stalker. Trust me. He glanced over his shoulder and gave her a wink. She had never seen him oozing so much confidence. He tossed his hammer up and grasped it again more firmly by the handle then took a few steps down the hill towards Gleaming Blade, who had stepped out from the line of her soldiers. An image of

Fortune striding out into the path of an oncoming chaos demon on Red Bridge sprang to mind as Stalker watched Eyes. They walked slowly towards each other, their weapons readied.

Claws had raised his gun again and had it trained on Gleaming Blade, his breathing slow and steady, though Stalker could feel his mind racing.

'What if he loses?' Theodore whispered nearby.

'Then we kneel,' Vengeance-of-Steel said coldly. She was glaring at the back of Eyes' head, bitterness in her twisted snarl.

'He won't lose,' Weaver said. Stalker looked at her and saw that she was smiling.

Eyes and Gleaming Blade began to circle each other slowly, the firelight flickering over them and throwing out long shadows over the dark grass.

Stalker couldn't breathe; she waited, her heart thumping madly in her chest. The two shifters with the fates of hundreds on their shoulders circled one another in the firelight, neither making the first move. But Stalker knew it had to come soon.

'Is this to the death?' Gleaming Blade asked, her voice carrying on the quiet air.

'It doesn't have to be. You could yield. I'm capable of mercy.'

'And you believe I am too?'

'Yes. But it's irrelevant. I'm going to win.'

Without warning, Gleaming Blade's sword slashed Eyes' shoulder. He swung his hammer and it clattered against her blade. He was no longer smiling; a fierce determination had set into his jaw. She thrust again but he dodged easily. They began this twisted dance, swiping at each other, dodging and circling, their weapons clanging against each other periodically. Stalker winced each time Gleaming Blade came close to landing a blow.

The onlookers began to gasp, shout and clap, spurring on their respective leaders.

Eyes drew his hammer back and ducked behind Gleaming Blade, striking her hard on the back and sending her stumbling forwards.

'Yes! Get in, Eyes!' Wind Talker shouted. A ripple of laughter went through the crowd.

Gleaming Blade quickly recovered and went in for an attack, but Eyes dodged. He landed another blow to her off shoulder, that sent her spinning, but she ran a few paces and came back around at him as if she hadn't been hit. She thrust her sword towards him and he wasn't quite quick enough. She landed a blow to his right thigh and a slash appeared in his trousers, scarlet blood trickling from the wound. He barely reacted, keeping his cool as he went back in for another attack at her. And so the dance continued, strangely hypnotic in the light of the dancing flames.

The noises among the onlookers grew louder and more frantic each time one of the fighting shifters landed a blow. Stalker remained silent, rigid. She managed to drag her eyes around to Claws, to see him drag the back of his hand across his sweating brow and return it quickly to his raised gun, gripping it in both hands. His finger was poised, ready to pull back the trigger the moment he had a clear shot. He was going to do it, Stalker felt it and her mouth made a silent "O" as she saw his finger begin to squeeze the trigger. But at the last possible second, he relaxed his grip and dropped the gun, panting hard.

'I can't,' he whispered. 'The price.'

Stalker reached out and put a hand on the back of his neck.

'It's too high. I know.'

There was a whooshing sound and Stalker's attention whipped back to Eyes. He was spinning his hammer quickly in his hand by its strap and thick clouds rolled across the moon.

'What's that supposed to be?' Gleaming Blade sneered. She was limping as she slowly circled him. Her armour was damaged and she had blood on her face. 'Some sort of party trick?'

The Furies behind her began to laugh.

Lightning flickered overhead and a few large drops of rain began to fall. Eyes' hammer started to glow, silvery blue light emanating from it. Gleaming Blade stepped back, her face contorted in confusion. Eyes raised the spinning hammer over his head and lightning streaked down from the sky, striking the large head of the hammer.

Eyes launched himself at Gleaming Blade and struck her hard in the chest. She went flying into the air and landed on her back with a crunch. Stalker winced and held her breath once more as a collective gasp went up from the Furies.

The Heir wasn't dead; she hoisted herself up on her elbow as Eyes strode over to her, towering over her.

'Do you yield?' he demanded.

'Never,' she spat and clambered quickly to her feet. How her back wasn't broken, Stalker didn't know. The fight resumed, more rough and bitter than before. The dance was over, this was the real deal. It was messy and scrappy. Two tough-as-hell shifters determined to kill each other. Eyes shifted into his Agrius in an effort to gain an advantage, but she shifted form too. She towered over him by a foot and her armour, what was left of it, shifted with her. Eyes managed to get a few more blows in, but so did she. His blood spattered the grass and bodies that lay beneath his feet.

The shouting of the crowd reached a fever pitch and the night was punctured by distant screams. Humans, humans seeing the monsters in the park. Stalker was dimly aware of sirens. Dawn just touched the horizon, spilling purple light into the sky.

Gleaming Blade had the edge over Eyes, Stalker could see it.

Go for her weakened leg, she urged, silently.

Through the fog of the fight and his Agrius brain, he seemed not to hear her, but then he went for it, lunging swiftly under her arm as she brought her blade down. He smashed her knee with his hammer and tiny fragments of bone went flying, as her knee smashed to pieces. She buckled and went down. Eyes leapt up and brought his hammer down hard, a roar ripping from his throat.

Stalker took a deep breath and her body lifted as she went up onto her toes to see him land the killing blow. His hammer hit its mark, coming down right on her head with a crunch.

A cheer rang out from Caerton's shifters and several of them began to rush forwards. But Stalker stood suspended on her toes, as if the wind had been knocked out of her with the blow of Eyes' hammer. Weaver, Claws and Wind

Talker were equally frozen, their eyes wide and shock written all over their faces.

Eyes staggered backwards, his hammer falling to the ground. The hilt of Gleaming Blade's sword was sticking out of his chest and as he turned, the firelight reflected off the blood-soaked blade sticking out of his back.

The cheers died, along with the momentary look of triumph on his face. He stumbled and then fell and Stalker felt her bond to him shatter.

Chapter Thirty Five

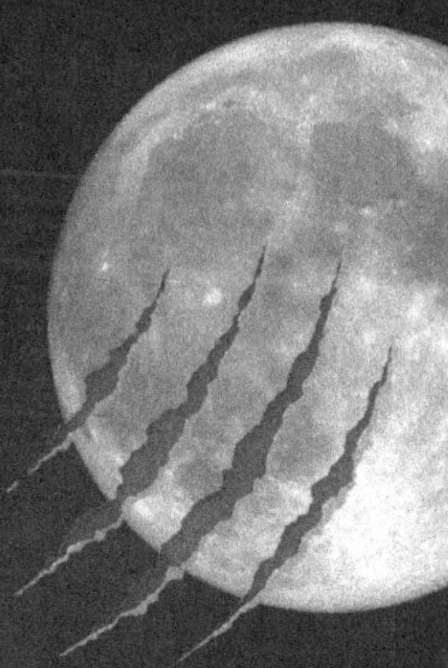

 Then an eruption of roars.

Who had won if both champions were dead? It seemed both sides disagreed as they rushed towards each other again. A streak of silver and blue flew through the air, rippling through the veil violently. Unchained Lightning soared down from above and landed with an almighty crash on top of the Fury army, sending a current of electricity through each and every one of them. Many of them fell, charred, dead in an instant, but those who had been further from the blast scurried for the trees, clutching their injuries and weapons and in utter disarray.

Unchained Lighting was smoking and his light had gone out. The Lightning Lords ran out into the battlefield to find Eyes' body. Stalker felt tears soaking her cheeks, though she did not remember shedding them. She dropped to her knees at Eyes' body and vocal sobs tore from her throat. The others were crying too. Claws was still clutching his gun and he grabbed at his head with both hands, beside himself.

What remained of Odin's Warriors chased off the surviving Furies, and Stalker was dimly aware of Vengeance-of-Steel issuing orders to handle the humans.

A hiss came from Unchained Lightning and he keeled over, hitting the ground with a heavy thud that shook the ground. The bond shattered, ripping Stalker from Weaver, Wind Talker and Claws.

'No!' Weaver cried.

'Oh god!' Wind Talker whimpered.

Claws dropped to his knees, still hugging his head in his hands, his gun waving dangerously around. Stalker leaned over and snatched it from him. She opened the chamber and tipped the deadly bullet out.

'It's my fault!' Claws shouted. 'I could have ended it. I had the shot and didn't take it.'

'You would have died!' Stalker snapped.

'Yes, but they wouldn't.' He waved a hand over Eyes and Unchained Lightning.

'I think it may have been inevitable,' Weaver said. 'Given Eyes' nature and everything he went through. He was always going to die a hero's death.'

A blur of red and gold flashed past them and Stalker looked around. A huge, Chinese dragon swooped across the sky, raining a shower of golden sparks over everything. The sea of corpses melted away, the sirens went quiet, there were no more screams, just stillness. Stalker looked over her shoulder and saw blind Mrs Feng picking her way carefully across the grass, conducting the dragon with a walking stick.

'What is that?' Weaver croaked.

'She will make them all forget,' said one of the Feng twins. 'She cleans.' He held out a hand and helped Stalker to her feet. 'You want to forget too?'

'No,' she said sharply, glaring at him. 'No, none of us do.'

He nodded and walked away. The dragon soared away over the city, showering it with gold.

The pain in Stalker's chest was crushing, she felt empty and alone, without her pack mates' feelings rushing through her. Their bond was destroyed with Unchained Lightning's death, just as it had been when Grins-Too-Widely died.

'That's how Shadow's Step got away,' she said, her voice quiet and distant.

'Huh?' Weaver said, her face red and puffy.

'When Grins-Too-Widely was killed the telepathy broke, so we all assumed the others were all gone. We never knew he survived because we weren't connected to him any more.'

'Do you think any of the others survived?' Weaver asked.

'No,' Wind Talker said, a croak in his voice. He wiped his sleeve across his face. 'No, they died. Shadow's Step was alone. I saw Flames go. Eyes saw Stone and Fortune. They're gone all right.'

A blue light shimmered from across the veil and a beautiful, glowing woman stepped across.

'I recognise you,' Weaver said softly, staring at her. 'You were at our hearing at the Hundred Court.'

'Nicaea?' Wind Talker said, his voice husky.

'That's right,' she replied, her voice tinkling softly. 'I wanted to thank you, on behalf of Artemis, for halting Caeruleum Lunulam.'

'Oh,' Stalker said, a rasp in her tight throat.

'She will be dealt with now. She had gone horribly astray, mad, even.'

'We gathered.' Bitterness soaked Stalker's aching throat. 'Can Artemis bring anyone back? As payment for our service?'

'Sadly, no, that is not within her power.' Nicaea dropped her head and silver droplets fell from her fingers to the ground. The blood in the grass drained away. 'But she can answer your question, Stalker-of-Night's-Shadow, Ariana Yates.'

'Which question?' Stalker asked.

'Where you come from.'

'Oh.' Stalker blinked in confusion. It couldn't be so easy, could it? After all this?

Nicaea shimmered and the blue glow dimmed, then disappeared and in its place was a ghostly pale young woman. Her face looked familiar and Stalker took a step towards her.

'Oh!' Wind Talker raised a finger and pointed at the ghost. 'Symphony!'

'Sorry?' Stalker stopped and glanced his way.

'It's Symphony!'

'My mother?' Stalker took a step back and was relieved to feel Rhys's firm hands on her shoulders, holding her steady. She relaxed against his chest and breathed a sigh of relief. 'My mother?' she asked again, gazing at the grey figure.

'Hello Ariana.' The ghost smiled. 'I had a vision, while I was pregnant, of a moment not long past. You, bearing the Regalia and revealing the Spiral Hand.'

'Oh.'

'You saved the city, Ariana.' The ghost beamed at her. Stalker didn't feel very heroic. It must have shown in her expression. 'Without you, the truth might never have been known.'

'But he was my mentor, my brother. He took me in, guided me. And he... he died before I could speak to him.'

'He was a trickster and a liar. He would have twisted your mind. You needed to drag him from the shadows. That was your gift to this world.'

'Why am I different, then?'

'Because a piece of Artemis lives inside you. You are truly her daughter, her chosen one. Chosen to shine a light into the darkness.'

Rhys squeezed her shoulders gently and kissed her cheek.

'Like with me,' he said softly.

The ghost smiled again and nodded her head slowly.

'What happened to you?' Stalker asked, tears trickling down her cheeks.

'The Blue Moon. Your father was never truly one of them; he learned their plans to shatter the Bone Anchors and banish the King-of-Glass-and-Steel and was plotting to stop them. They discovered his true allegiance and killed him. They captured me, tortured me to find out what I knew. I knew too much and they killed me. I had already hidden you from them, though, and knew you would be safe.'

Stalker's shoulders shook and sobs took over. Hearing the truth was heartbreaking. Rhys held her, Weaver came closer and held her too. When she had calmed down, she pulled loose of their grasp and looked up at the ghost of her mother, a woman she had never known.

'Am I free now? Free of my destiny?'

'Absolutely,' the ghost replied, smiling.

Several days passed in an exhausting blur of sadness and clean-up. The House of Cards swept through the city with their ancient magic, erasing the evidence of what had happened. The shifters took to Hepethia to begin the arduous clean up of the mess left in the city centre, shaping it and destroying the demons that had infested it. Scribe was invited to join The Watch, their numbers having taken a serious blow. Rhys, now Spartan-of-Artemis, was accepted and offered a place in Crimson Dawn's Blood. He reluctantly accepted.

Funerals were held for all who had fallen and wave after wave of grief filled the city, causing an influx of demons in all corners. It felt like there would never be a chance to just stop, even for a moment.

It was after saying their final goodbyes to Fights-Eyes-Open that Wind Talker approached Stalker, Weaver and Claws. He cleared his throat and glanced at each of them anxiously.

'I'm leaving Caerton,' he said solemnly.

'What?' Weaver gasped.

'I'm going to London to keep watch over Eyes' family. Amy may change one day and want to know who her father was. I owe him a great debt, one that I never managed to fully repay before he died. This is part of my atonement.'

'I see.' Claws nodded.

Stalker couldn't meet his eyes.

'The three of you will be fine. I know it. You're a great team.' Wind Talker nodded and a small smile touched his lips. He gave each of them a brief parting hug, coming to Stalker last. 'You'll be fine,' he whispered. 'You're amazing.'

She let out a small laugh and hugged him back.

'Be careful. You'll be welcome back any time.'

'Thanks.'

With very little fuss or fanfare, Wind Talker packed a bag and left.

In the quiet that followed, Claws and Weaver muttered between themselves just out of earshot of Stalker and frustration mounted over what they could be discussing. Stalker resented no longer being attached to their thoughts and called them out on it eventually.

'What are you two wittering about?'

'Well,' Claws said, smiling anxiously as he approached her. 'We were just discussing the pack situation. Obviously we need to reform and get organised.'

'We think you should be Alpha,' Weaver finished, grinning. Stalker rolled her eyes.

'Seriously? Me?'

'Yes,' they said together.

'I can't.'

'You don't have to fill his shoes. No one can do that. You'll do things your own way, we know that. But it's just the three of us now and one of us has to step up.'

'Neither of you want to do it. Short lifespan comes

with the job.'

'Not at all!' Weaver looked aghast. 'We think you'll be the best at it!'

There was a knock at the door and Stalker went to answer it, mainly to get away from their eager faces. They all knew she would accept in the end. She opened the door and was greeted by Theodore Harris, bouncing on the balls of his feet, yet ever the gorilla stuffed into a suit.

'Stalker! Great, just who I wanted to see. I have a plan!'

Please Leave a Review

I hope you enjoyed *Rise of the Furies*. I would really appreciate it if you could take a few minutes now to review the book on your favourite retailer. Independent authors rely heavily on reader reviews, they really are like oxygen. Reviews help other readers decide whether a book is a good fit for them or not. Much as I want everyone to love my books, I also know that it's important to find the right readers, so just a few words from you could help me to do that and reach other readers who will enjoy my dark and twisted tales!

Thank you!

About the Author

H.B. Lyne is an urban fantasy author, podcaster and bullet journal enthusiast with a knack for organisation and getting stuff done.

She lives in Yorkshire with her husbeast, two children and midwife cat. When not juggling family commitments, she writes dark urban fantasy novels, purging her imagination of its demons. Inspired by the King of Horror himself, Holly aspires to be at least half as prolific and successful and promises to limit herself to only one tome of The Stand-like proportions in her career.

Check out my website for all the latest updates and offers
hblyne.com

Follow me on Instagram
@hblyne

And on Facebook
facebook.com/authorhblyne

Coming Soon

Redemption: A Shifters of Caerton Companion Story

Wind Talker has a cause: protect his Alpha's human family. He sets out for London with this mission in mind… but he is woefully unprepared for what he finds there.

Join my Tribe of Rabid Readers to be notified when the book is available

Sign up today and also get more of Last-Breath-Echoes in the prequel novella *From Ashes to Echoes*. It's free when you sign up for email updates via my website

landing.hblyne.com/fate

ALSO BY H.B. LYNE

In the Shifters of Caerton series:

Fate of the Blue Moon

Ghosts of Winter

Demons of the Past

Rise of the Furies

Dark Echoes: Tales from the Shadows

From Ashes to Echoes

Lies the Dead Tell series:

In The Blood

www.ingramcontent.com/pod-product-compliance
Lightning Source LLC
Chambersburg PA
CBHW051002180726
48291CB00006B/1940